P9-DZY-341

NUREMBERG
THE RECKONING

ALSO BY WILLIAM F. BUCKLEY JR.

God and Man at Yale

McCarthy and His Enemies (With L. Brent Bozell)

Up From Liberalism

Rumbles Left and Right

The Unmaking of a Mayor

The Jeweler's Eye

The Governor Listeth

Cruising Speed

Inveighing We Will Go

Four Reforms

United Nations Journal: A Delegate's Odyssey

Execution Eve

Saving the Queen

Airborne

Stained Glass

A Hymnal: The Controversial Arts

Who's On First

Marco Polo, If You Can

Atlantic High: A Celebration

Overdrive: A Personal Documentary

The Story of Henri Tod

See You Later Alligator

Right Reason

The Temptation of Wilfred Malachey

High Jinx

Mongoose, R.I.P.

Racing Through Paradise

On the Firing Line: The Public Life of Our Public Figures

Gratitude: Reflections on What We Owe to Our Country

Tucker's Last Stand

In Search of Anti-Semitism

WindFall

Happy Days Were Here Again: Reflections of a Libertarian Journalist

A Very Private Plot

Brothers No More

The Blackford Oakes Reader

The Right Word

Nearer, My God

The Redhunter

Spytime: The Undoing of James Jesus Angleton

Elvis in the Morning

NUREMBERG
THE RECKONING

William F. Buckley Jr.

Harcourt, Inc.
New York San Diego London

www.HarcourtBooks.com

Library of Congress Cataloging-in-Publication Data
Buckley, William F. (William Frank), 1925–
Nuremberg: the reckoning/William F. Buckley Jr.—1st ed.
p. cm.
ISBN 0-15-100679-2
1. Nuremberg Trial of Major German War Criminals, Nuremberg, Germany, 1945–1946—Fiction. 2. Americans—Germany—Fiction. 3. Nuremberg (Germany)—Fiction. 4. German Americans—Fiction. 5. Translators—Fiction.
I. Title.
PS3552.U344 N87 2002
813'.54—dc21 2002000465

Text set in Electra
Display set in Compacta
Designed by Cathy Riggs

Printed in the United States of America

First edition
K J I H G F E D C B A

For my fellow author,

sister, and godchild—

Carol Buckley

ACKNOWLEDGMENTS

The libraries teem with books about Germany under Hitler, about the Nazis' concentration camps, and about the Nuremberg trials. This is, to be sure, a novel, but it tells the story of the trials at Nuremberg. I have been informed (and here and there engrossed) by several of these books, including *Death Dealer: The Memoirs of the SS Kommandant at Auschwitz* by Rudolph Hoess, edited by Steven Paskuly; *The Rise and Fall of the Third Reich: A History of Nazi Germany* by William L. Shirer; *Nuremberg: Infamy on Trial* by Joseph E. Persico; *Justice at Nuremberg* by Robert E. Conot; *The Third Reich: A New History* by Michael Burleigh; *Into That Darkness: An Examination of Conscience* by Gitta Sereny; *By the Neck Until Dead: The Gallows of Nuremberg* by Stanley Tilles; *Inside the Nuremberg Trial: A Prosecutor's Comprehensive Account* (Vols. I and II), edited by Drexel A. Sprecher; *The Anatomy of the Nuremberg Trials: A Personal Memoir* by Telford Taylor; *Eichmann in Jerusalem: A Report on the Banality of Evil* by Hannah Arendt; *Adolph Hitler* by John Toland; *Prelude to Nuremberg: Allied War Crimes Policy and the Question of Punishment* by Arieh J. Kochavi; *The New Meaning of Treason* by Rebecca West; *Cracow*, published by Krakowska Oficyna Wydawnicza; *The Nuremberg Trials* by Earle Rice Jr.; *Auschwitz, Nazi Death Camp*, published by the Auschwitz-Birkenau State Museum in Oswiecim; *The Holocaust Encyclopedia*, edited by Walter Lacqueur and Judith Tydor Baumel. I tender my thanks to the authors and their publishers.

I am very lucky to have attentive and keen-eyed friends who have been kind enough to read the manuscript and make suggestions. I am grateful to editor and translator Sophie Wilkins; to professors Thomas Wendel, Jeffrey Hart, and Chester Wolford; to Christa and Heinz Hary; to my siblings (themselves authors) Priscilla Buckley, Patricia Bozell, Reid Buckley and Carol Buckley; to my wife Pat and son Christopher; to colleagues-in-trade Lance Morrow and David Pryce-Jones; to my oldest friend, the historian Alistair Horne, and the youngest, Erik Gordon; to Ambassador Evan Galbraith, my companion at sea and on land. Wesley Tooke was with me in Switzerland for day by day work on the first draft, during which he tended also to his own novel, *Ballpark Blues*, soon to be published by Doubleday. I must acknowledge Dr. Harry Fiss, who heard mention of this book and wrote asking to see the manuscript, advising me that his own biography was startlingly similar to that of my protagonist, Sebastian Reinhard. He read the manuscript with reassuring approval: "That," he said, "is exactly how it was at Nuremberg."

My agent Lois Wallace read the book, as did André Bernard, my publisher, making suggestions. Kathi George did a splendid job of copyediting.

In my own shop, I am grateful as always to Tony Savage, whose patience bore him through my seven drafts; to Julie Crane, who read searchingly; to Frances Bronson, who, happily, continues to govern my lit-life.

And finally, as always, there is Samuel S. Vaughan, my editor. He is, for me, first, last, and always, friend and guide.

NUREMBERG
THE RECKONING

BOOK ONE

CHAPTER ONE

Hamburg, August 30, 1939

His eyes lingered longer than usual on the headlines as he walked by the corner newsstand, the summer leaves of the overhanging oak trees brushing down over the canvas awning that protected the papers and magazines and cigarettes of the little kiosk from summer rains. Today, no headline especially arrested his attention. There was nothing beyond the run of diplomatic crises he was now numb to—*England denounces German threats to Poland... Poland asserts its independence... Great Britain and France pledge aid to Poland if attacked... Moscow signs nonaggression pact with Berlin.* Nothing new; nothing brand new—this last, the Ribbentrop-Molotov pact was already a week old. Axel tried to close it all out of his mind.

Past the stand, turning right on Abelstrasse, Axel Reinhard was only three blocks from his apartment. He gripped hard the handle of his briefcase and looked fleetingly at his watch.

Back at the office there had been a bon voyage party. Franz Heidl, the senior partner of the engineering firm, had invited a half-dozen colleagues of Heidl & Sons, and also Debra—always—the office manager, to the tenth floor partners' meeting room. They had come to the boardroom at 1900, as bidden ("Please to be prompt!") to have a brandy and wish Axel a happy holiday in America (*As you know,* the invitation read, *Axel is taking a month's leave to accompany Annabelle and their son Sebastian to New York. Young Sebastian will be going to school in America.*).

"Heinrich and Fritz Hassler—" Herr Heidl called for silence, tapping lightly on the cognac bottle with the back of his fountain pen. "—phoned in their regrets. I don't need to tell you, Axel, about the press of work at Heidl & Sons. Fritz sends his compliments and Debra, who couldn't be with us, sends her..." he raised his brandy glass and paused for emphasis, "her love!" There was a murmur of appreciation (Debra, Hassler's secretary, was seventy years old; Axel was not yet thirty-six). "Be sure and tell that to Annabelle when you get home tonight. She may refuse to sail with you!"

Axel, looking down on his short, bald boss, accepted the toast with a smile and a little bow of his head, his abundant dark hair insufficiently tended. "I'm surprised Debra didn't send her love to my son. After all, Sebastian is almost fourteen."

"Is he also a lady-killer?" Heidl's leer was theatrically contrived, and the company laughed.

"What school in America are you sending him to?" Heinz Jutzeler, the youngest of the engineers in the room, wanted to know. Jutzeler had spent three years in Washington when his father served as cultural attaché for Chancellor Hindenburg, in the last days of the Weimar Republic. Though he had returned to Hamburg at age thirteen, Jutzeler fancied himself something of an expert on America.

"He will go to school in Phoenix. Phoenix—" Axel assumed a professorial air and began with a word or two in an exaggerated British accent "—iss the capital of *Ahr-isohn-a.*" He ended the imitation and, in his native, idiomatic German, told his colleagues and well-wishers (more properly, he *reminded* them: Like almost every German in the professional class, the engineers at Heidl & Sons were well-grounded in geography and history) that the state of Arizona had been incorporated into the United States in 1912, that Phoenix was the state's capital, that to the south of it lay Mexico, to the east, New Mexico, to the west, California.

"Why did you and Annabelle choose Arizona?"

"My mother-in-law—my generous mother-in-law—has property there and will superintend Sebastian's education after Annabelle comes back here to us."

The silence was considered, though nobody gave voice to the reason for it. Why would a thirteen-year-old with a U.S. passport hurry to return to Hamburg, Germany, in 1939?

Jutzeler broke the silence, harking back to the subject of Arizona. He liked to frame his remarks in the practical coin of his trade. "For the benefit of my colleagues, Phoenix, Arizona, would be, traveling west from New York, about the same distance as Moscow, traveling east, is from us here in Hamburg. Now that Herr von Ribbentrop has made a pact with Comrade Stalin, we must all expect, one day, to visit, as tourists, the Communist land we were taught so diligently to scorn—"

"Heinz!" Axel's face contorted with derisive pain. "*No no no!* Moscow is *much* closer. From here to Moscow by train—two days, one night. To Phoenix from New York, three days, two nights."

"You may be right. Just my impression..."

"You get back when, Axel?" Germaine, the heavyset archivist, her eyeglasses hanging below her neck, wanted to know.

"In one month," Axel said. "Don't let them muck up the Rohrplaz Tower while I'm gone." There was laughter. Herr Heidl beamed with pride, taking a folder from a shelf alongside and opening it to exhibit an artist's sketch of the Rohrplaz Center in Hamburg's industrial zone, scheduled for completion in three months; perhaps, with the hectic construction schedule in Germany, in time for Christmas.

A quarter of an hour later, after downing a second brandy, Herr Heidl said that he couldn't speak for everyone in the room but he, as senior partner in Heidl & Sons, had more to do, before finally going home, than merely drink brandy with his colleagues. "We all know that engineers are not exactly busy in America, never mind the vigorous economic policies of Mr. Roosevelt's New Deal," he jibed. "But unemployment certainly isn't a problem in the Third Reich. Lieber Axel, may God be with you."

Axel shook Herr Heidl's hand, and then the hands of the others, who had got the signal that the party was over. He kissed Germaine lightly on her ample forehead and returned to his office at the other end of the floor to pick up his meticulously packed briefcase. A raincoat over one arm, he stepped into the freshly painted hallway and rang for the elevator. At the desk in the entrance hall he initialed the register and wrote down the hour. The one-legged clerk nodded at him. "Heil Hitler."

"Heil Hitler," Axel responded.

CHAPTER TWO

August 30, 1939

He passed through the wrought iron gate at 38 Hempelstrasse into the compound of the twin apartment buildings. In the stretch of carefully tended lawn, used as a children's playground, he spotted Sebastian. The tall, determined boy was dressed in navy blue playing shorts and the red-and-white-striped soccer shirt of the Bismarck Gymnasium. His trim brown hair askew, he was manipulating with gangly yet deft legs the soccer ball, shunting it into the sturdy wooden standing board with the painted white markers that framed the prime target area. Spotting his father, Sebastian stooped to pick up the ball as it bounded back. "Papa, can I take this with me to America? It is a very special ball, not just like any other ball."

"You are to speak to me in English," Axel reminded his son. That was the household rule: At home, Annabelle would join in the convention, speaking in English, her native tongue. Axel, emigrating to America, would soon have continuing practice in English, the language he had learned during his four years at the Massachusetts Institute of Technology. And Sebastian, though speaking in German all day long at school in Hamburg, would maintain the English spoken to him by both his parents, since his birth in Hamburg just after New Year's Day in 1926.

But that little correction was beside the point for Sebastian, the point being: Would he be permitted to take his beloved soccer ball with him on the SS *Europa*, on which, at midnight tomorrow, they'd set sail for New York?

"You can take it if it will deflate to absolutely flat."

"I thought you said the *Europa* was a luxury liner?"

"It is. It and its sister ship, the *Bremen*. They are the transatlantic pride of the . . . Fatherland."

"Are they better than the *Queen Mary* and the *Normandie*?"

"The British make good ships and have a long tradition. And the French crossing with the *Normandie* last year—or was it the year before?—set a world record—"

"So ours are only the *second* best?"

Axel put his arm around the shoulder of his son as they walked together to the elevator.

"When you get to school in Arizona and you speak of 'our' ships, you will need to remember that you will be thought to be speaking of the *America* and the *Manhattan*."

"But I am German."

"Perhaps. That decision you'll need to make—we'll need to make—on January 3rd, 1944, when you become eighteen. At that point you can declare yourself an American or a German, as you will. Right now you share your mother's U.S. passport, dating back to when you were born. One day, before long, you will have your own passport, and you can choose to be an American or a German."

"Which would you prefer me to be, Papa?"

The elevator drew to a stop at the ninth floor. Without answering the question, Axel weighed his shoulder against the apartment door, swinging it open into a room with heavy wooden furniture, three standing lamps, a comfortable couch, two armchairs covered in blue corduroy, and a substantial library of books. There were sprightly prints at either end, and in the little dining area an oil painting of Cambridge, Massachusetts, after a snowfall.

Annabelle kissed her husband and got down to business. She addressed her son, already as tall as she. "They will be picking up our trunk at 1400 tomorrow, Sebastian, and you are to put the sports equipment we agreed on into it."

"And my soccer ball?"

Axel nodded. "I told him yes, provided he got all the air out of it."

Annabelle was flustered. She looked up covetously at the oil painting.

"You don't think, maybe, Axel— "

"Annabelle!" In practiced tones, for the benefit of Sebastian, he said, "We are hardly going to empty an apartment I'll be living in again in thirty days."

"Yes yes. Yes." To Sebastian: "We'll be taking the suitcases later. They'll come with us when we're ready to board."

"Yippee!" Sebastian had become reconciled, in the last fortnight, to the prospect of leaving Hamburg and going to school in Arizona. What he mostly relished was the idea of crossing the Atlantic Ocean. "What time exactly will we be boarding, Mama? I have a lot of friends I have to call on to say good-bye."

"A car will pick us up here at eight."

"I don't think that gives me enough time."

"Then you'd better shorten your list of friends." Annabelle smiled to one side at Axel.

"I'm going to miss my friends," Sebastian said gravely. "Especially Frederica and Bearthe. And Wilhelm and Gorky. And Pauline. Especially Pauline. I have promised to write to Pauline every day. Will they take the mail from us every day on the *Europa*?"

"What are they supposed to do?" Axel said, thinking to deflate more than just the soccer ball. "Give your daily letters to a pigeon to deliver to Pauline?"

Sebastian, his expression serious, turned playful. "Maybe they can give my letters every day to a submarine, Papa? You know, we have a *lot* of submarines. The Fuehrer is *crazy* about submarines."

Annabelle turned on her son. "Sebastian. Do not use that kind of language about the Fuehrer."

"I was just joking."

"Don't joke about the Fuehrer."

"In Arizona can we joke about President Roosevelt?"

Annabelle thought quickly of her imperious mother and almost smiled. "In America, in the presence of your grandmother, you can say anything you like about President Roosevelt, provided it's unpleasant. She voted for Governor Landon. He was the Republican."

"Why did grandmother go to live in America?"

"Because she fell in love with your grandfather, grandma's first husband, and he was American. Just like me, your mother, Kitten"—Annabelle sometimes called him that, *Kitten,* ever since at age three Sebastian announced that he would not go to bed without his kitten—"I'm an American and I fell in love with your father, a German."

"Maybe it would be easier if Hitler just conquered America."

His father turned sharply in surprise. Sebastian moved quickly: "—Or if President Roosevelt just conquered Germany."

They had supper. Sebastian, in high excitement over the great voyage in prospect, was in no mood to go to bed. Annabelle had anticipated his high spirits. But she and Axel had business to look after. Leaving Sebastian at home, they set out for the Olden.

They reached the restaurant-bar on Glacischausee, convenient to the park. Strollers headed for the great Pflanzen und Blumen, or coming from it, passed by. Patrons could sit outdoors during the season, drinking their beer or coffee, until the October cold led them indoors. A dozen soldiers were there tonight, evidently in from maneuvers because their regimental language and manners were boisterous, self-satisfied, and declamatory. Zoti spotted Axel and Annabelle coming in from the sidewalk and motioned them to the table where they often sat. Zoti had lost an arm in the Great War, but managed adroitly to bring in the tray, putting it down on the table, and then off-loading the pilsner beer he was most often asked for.

He knew that the Reinhards were leaving the next day on their exciting visit to America. He addressed Axel. "Since you will be only one month away, would you bring me a souvenir from New York?"

"Anything in particular?"

Zoti asked them to wait. He returned with an envelope. Putting it down on the table, he held it in place with one elbow and withdrew a clipping with his good hand. The story, datelined Milwaukee, described the photograph of a postcard displayed at the bottom of the page. It was a photograph of the United States flag, a minipicture of Adolf Hitler occupying the space in the upper left-hand corner where the forty-eight stars conventionally appeared.

"If you find a postcard like this, would you buy it for me, Herr Reinhard? Buy me . . . two? It shows we have true friends in America, even if they aren't running the government."

Annabelle said hastily, "Of course, Zoti. We will look out for it."

They sat back after Zoti went off to look after other customers.

"So this is it for Hamburg, Axel. We've had happy years here. I wonder if we will see it again."

Nobody, by any measurement, sat within earshot, and it was inconceivable that the table they sat at was being bugged. Even so, Axel winced at what his wife said. He began to speak in slight tones. Teeth slightly gritted, he spoke matter-of-factly, as if addressing a partner in the firm. He recited their carefully framed lines.

"*I* will of course see it again in one month. You will stay a month or two with Sebastian and your mother Henrietta and then rejoin me in Hamburg, and Sebastian will come to us for the summer vacation. Perhaps even we can bring him over for Christmas..."

"*Have we forgotten anything?*" Her tone jolted him from the rehearsed lines.

"I can't think what," he said softly, too weary to keep up the charade. "I'll wait in America about two weeks. Then I'll write to Heidl, explain that they've offered me a good job in Phoenix and that we have regretfully decided to settle there, with your mother and Sebastian. You have an exact inventory of everything we're leaving at Hempelstrasse. We can have what we want shipped to us, no problem there. What we don't want to ship we can give away. The St. Lucas church is always glad to have *anything* anybody gives them."

"There's no problem about turning in the return passages we've paid for?"

"We have open tickets for you and Sebastian. Nothing suspicious in that. My own return booking is for September 28th. I'll just... cancel it after I arrive. Maybe wait a few days."

"What have you done about our Heidelberg account?"

"I didn't check all the money out, not that we have that much in savings. But they watch that kind of thing. I withdrew 1,800 marks. A plausible amount—a month's vacation, initial schooling bills for Sebastian. The Gestapo is thorough, but I can't imagine they know that we have other resources. They wouldn't know that Henrietta Chapin inherited a few stocks and bonds."

Annabelle sipped her drink and extended her hand under the table. "Darling, I hope you don't have regrets. Mother *was* right: A general war is a real possibility. The Chamberlain government's guarantee to Poland, that really did it— "

"Actually, Annabelle, the diplomatic scene has for a few weeks been pretty quiet— "

"*Pretty quiet?* I mean, His Majesty's government promised in March to—what? *Go to war,* is the only way I can read it, and that's how Mom's State Department buddy reads it—if there's a Nazi attack against Poland."

"Yes yes. But there's no sign of any military strike by Hitler. The British declaration was five months ago. Hitler seems to have spent most of the summer going to operas in Augsburg and Bayreuth." Axel tried to look hopeful.

"Darling, I'm not, I promise you, I'm *not* going to analyze Hitler. And—you know—I was in favor of staying on here, hoping for the best, even after the seventeenth letter from Mother urging us to go to America, to go to her. But I was really scared after the birthday celebration. So Hitler was fifty years old on April 20th. *The whole country* goes crazy celebrating... and that military parade in Berlin! That made it look like he was preparing for a *world* war, never mind just Poland."

"*Don't even say things like that,* Annabelle."

She moved her head sharply to one side to avoid the cigar smoke snaking in from the table in front. She reached simultaneously for her purse. "Sebastian brought me this. He went this morning to Bismarck to say good-byes—the semester there is about to begin. Pauline showed him a poem being taught to first graders. Pauline has a sister in first grade. Listen— "

"Keep your voice down."

"Listen." She spoke in a quiet tone, moving closer to the candle housed in the red-tinted glass. "This is a—I guess they'd call it...what? A poem? An ode? The first graders will be committing this to memory:

Adolf Hitler is our savior, our hero
He is the noblest being in the whole wide world.
For Hitler we live,
For Hitler we die.
Our Hitler is our Lord,
Who rules a brave new world.

Axel bit his lip. "Awful. Terrible, terrible stuff. My own guess is that Hitler himself knows nothing about the lengths some of his worshipers go to. But on the big questions, the strategic questions, Hitler is a tough realist."

"Tough realists can make mistakes."

"But not on the scale you're talking about, I'd judge. Invade Poland? With Great Britain pledged to defend it?"

"Look, he's got his eastern flank protected by the nonaggression pact with Russia. So what's Britain really going to do to impede a Polish invasion?" Annabelle asked. "Introduce a censure resolution at the League of Nations?"

"Let's not talk about it, Annie. We've made our plans. Twenty-four hours—" he looked down at his watch and smiled—"twenty-*six* hours from now we'll be on the high seas, headed for New York City. It's been fifteen years since we left—"

"On that terrible freighter."

"It was slow. But it was cheap. Fifty-five dollars. Which was about half the money I had in all the world."

"But you had a German-speaking wife—"

"Yes, darling, your German is as good as mine—"

"And a degree from MIT—"

"Yes. All that got me was the job in the casino here." He smiled bitterly at the memory. "Between the time the gamblers put down a chip and the time they cashed it in, half their profit was inflated away."

"Weimar time."

"Yes, Weimar. *The great Weimar Republic.* The great postwar democratic fiasco, ten years of it. And I know—*I know*—it was Adolf Hitler who brought Germany together. And I voted for him." He paused. "And it wasn't until just a while ago I had the answer to the question, *Would I do it again?*"

"Not until Crystal Night."

"Not until Kristallnacht. And Kristallnacht was as recent as only ten months ago."

"But you knew, back in 1933, what his attitude was on the Jews."

"Yes, we all knew. So he was anti-Semitic. So was dear old Mom. So . . . who isn't?

"Axel, that's silly, saying that."

"You know what I mean. I mean that we—the people who voted for him—didn't think he'd go in for looting Jewish stores, that kind of thing."

"*That kind of thing?* Looting Jewish stores? You mean, burning down a hundred and ninety synagogues. Levying billion-mark fines on wealthy Jews. Declaring them an infidel race."

"Annie, let's drop it. I'm German, your mother was Austrian. I love Germany, I have to hope that the . . . Fuehrer is—"

"Here today, gone tomorrow?"

He had had enough. He changed his voice, changed the subject. "Yes . . . Annie, who will be meeting us in New York?"

"I'm not sure. But Henrietta Chapin isn't going to let us land with nobody at the dock to meet us. She may be there herself, though it's a long trip from Phoenix. We'll stay together a week in New York, show Sebastian the sights."

"You know what?"

"*Bitte wiederhole.* Say that again."

Axel paused, and then, "I think it would be nice if we took a day and went to Cambridge. I'd like to see the old haunts, and maybe see whether Professor Schlosser is still around—I had a couple of letters from him in the early days. Nothing from him after you-know-who was elected."

"You-know-who wouldn't like that, your friendship with him. I remember Henry Schlosser. I read his book."

"The first one? On the Versailles Conference?"

"Yes. *Illusory Peace.* He was certainly prophetic. We've walked into that shaky postwar world he predicted."

"John Maynard Keynes said the same thing—"

"—differently. Keynes is always different. But he hasn't taught Roosevelt how to bring us—us Americans, Axel, me and Sebastian—" she winked at him affectionately, "out of the Depression."

"Maybe he should look into some of the economic policies of you-know-who."

Annabelle rapped him on his knuckles. "Cut it out, Axel. Anyway, we ought to be going. It'll be exciting tomorrow, but also long."

"Yes." He signaled to Zoti.

"I'll get the umbrella," she said.

She came back and found Axel standing with Zoti, talking. She caught the little nod of his head. . . . Yes, she could hear him saying, he would come by the Olden just as soon as he returned from New York. Their hands were clasped. She extended her own hand, and Zoti lowered his head for a little farewell kiss, which she gave him, brushing back her full head of hair.

Axel was silent on the walk home. Back in the apartment, Annabelle walked to the side room to check on Sebastian. *Good night, Kitten,* she thought.

Axel went into his little study, turned on the desk lamp, and closed the door.

He opened the envelope Zoti had slid into his hand. He held the letter under the light.

The stationery was that of the Wassen SS on 34 Ilsenstrasse.

The letter was addressed to Herr Axel Reinhard, giving no street address. It read: "Herr Reinhard: You will meet me at 1000 exactly at the Rialto Hotel lobby on Frankfurtstrasse. I will identify myself. You will be unaccompanied. No one need know about our appointment. Heil Hitler."

It was signed, "Ernst Gradler."

Under the signature appeared the words, "Kapitan, Geheime Staatspolizeiamt."

CHAPTER THREE

August 31, 1939

Axel tossed in his bed.

What indiscretion might he have been guilty of? If any? Boarding the *Europa* for a trip to America with his—American—family was not itself an indiscretion. He was permitted, by German law and custom, to leave Germany, provided he didn't take more than the allowed sum of German marks with him.

Why would the Gestapo call him in? His cash withdrawal was legal and reasonable.

He had confided to no one his plans to leave Germany permanently.

What about his political sentiments? Had there been any public expression of those of them that were negative? There was no—

The night in Vienna reached his memory, pounding on it.

Not long after voting in 1933 for the National Socialist Party and endorsing its early economic policies, Axel Reinhard had begun diverting any talk away from the question of whether he approved or disapproved of Hitler's various policies. He didn't discuss

Hitler's demand that Germany be permitted to rearm, or analyze out loud the hectic rearmament program. Nothing about Hitler's initiative in forming the Axis alliance with Italy and Japan, or Hitler's apocalyptic confrontation with the British and French followed by the cannibalization of Czechoslovakia, or Hitler's denunciation of the Polish government and assertion of Germany's right to the Danzig corridor. Nothing about Hitler's progressive impositions on the Jews, and the near-genocidal outbreak against German Jewry on Kristallnacht. He did not comment on Hitler's covert approach to Stalin, or the sensational disclosure—just last week—of the nonaggression pact. On all these questions Axel could not be enticed into comment. There was only the one exception, Vienna, 1938.

He looked over at Annabelle, soundly asleep at his side. He touched on the pocket flashlight he kept by his bed and looked at the alarm clock on the bed table. It was slightly after four in the morning.

Yes, there was that one evening in Vienna, Sunday, the 25th of February, eighteen months ago.

Axel Reinhard was in Vienna on business for Heidl & Sons. Franz Heidl had dispatched him to conclude arrangements with Donneheim, AG. Heidl would turn over, for an appropriate fee, the innovative designs drawn up by the Heidl firm for their much-admired Untergrin bridge, crossing the Danube from the old town to the new, bustling factory district. Axel was to dine that final night with Eric Eisenstadt, the Donneheim partner in charge of their bridge construction in Vienna. The two engineers had spent a pleasant week together in Germany exploring the bridge plans and sketching out the necessary modifications for the Austrian model.

But it wasn't Eisenstadt who met Axel at Vienna's sprawling railway station. It was, instead, a junior associate of the Donneheim firm. He introduced himself and conveyed the apologies of his superior. "Herr Eisenstadt has canceled all his appointments. He will be leaving Vienna for London in a few days. Arthur Seyss-Inquart is arriving tomorrow from Berlin to take charge of *their* country. He will be our Minister Interior, and he is not—you are probably acquainted with his record—exactly friendly to Jews." Axel knew that. Everyone knew that in the three preceding days, Hitler had contrived the virtual annexation of Austria, his great Anschluss.

Taken to the Innsbruck Hotel, Axel checked in and deposited his bag and briefcase in his room. He proceeded down to the bar-restaurant for the highly seasoned Paprikasuppe he much enjoyed. He would listen to the widely anticipated speech by Adolf Hitler proclaiming the "union" between Germany and Hitler's native Austria.

His voice came in over the radio. He was speaking in the Kroll Opera House. Ever since the great fire of 1934, the Opera House had served as the Reichstag.

This afternoon, Hitler spoke what seemed endlessly, but with the hypnotic eloquence that overpowered so many listeners, near and far. Axel was yet again stunned by the force of the Fuehrer's rhetoric and drawn by the magnetism that radiated from the large radio unit that sat on the elevated shelf adjacent to the bar. The customers were silent. Beer and brandy and coffee were untouched until after the uproarious climax. Then the shouts rang in, "*Sieg Heil! Heil Hitler!*" They began then to talk; everyone at once, it seemed.

That was on Sunday afternoon. At 2000, Axel met for dinner at the hotel with Donneheim's substitute host, the Austrian engineer deputized to take over Eisenstadt's commission. Ludwig Heller was in his thirties, tall and athletic in appearance. He wore glasses that reached back over his ears but gave good clearance to his clipped brown hair.

"Well, it's been quite a day," Heller said, calling the steward over to order wine. Axel agreed that it had certainly been a momentous day.

Axel drank heavily, and when time came for dessert, the diners had finished a bottle of Riesling and a robust Burgundy. Axel put in for brandy with his strudel. He was left tired from the journey and itching with exasperation over the twin experiences of his day, the Anschluss speech and the elimination of his partner. Eisenstadt would have to flee his native country for the sin of being Jewish. And Austria had lost her nationhood, degraded—however willingly—to provincial status by the hypnotizing ambition of a single.... He abandoned his caution and, fueled by drink, set his thoughts free.

"What's the matter with you Austrians? You feel *anything* Hitler wants he can have because he was born here and absorbed his racist ideas here in Vienna?" Axel did not stop there. He confided to his fellow engineer with some passion other Nazi policies he resented or feared the consequences of. His dinner companion hinted at his own misgivings about the Third Reich.

It was later that night that Axel renewed his solemn pledge never, ever, to comment again on Reich policies.

Might Ludwig Heller have reported on his conversation? Would word of the indiscretion have seeped in through Austrian National Security to the Schutzstaffel? The SS had ears everywhere. When, two weeks later, Adolf Hitler drove triumphantly into Vienna, consummating resoundingly his plans, long laid and well prepared for him by indigenous agents, the SS gained access to everything in Austria of conceivable use to the state security apparatus.

Was Vienna the reason the Gestapo wanted to see him? That morning? He had been awake for hours, and there was light enough already to let him view the hands of his wristwatch. It was six and he could hear Sebastian stirring. As usual, the boy, treading lightly in the kitchen to avoid waking mother and father, was making a great racket with the refrigerator and the toaster.

Or could it be—conceivably?—a mark of preference? Was the Gestapo, apprised of Axel Reinhard's forthcoming visit to America, perhaps seeking something from him? Something he, Axel, could do? A mission?

But who on earth did Axel know in America who could be of any use to the Nazis? Nobody! It had been years since he was there and when he left in 1924 it was as an impoverished, freshly anointed young civil engineer. What could Axel Reinhard conceivably do for the Reichsfuehrer?

"You didn't sleep well, Axel. You tossed and turned." Annabelle was back from the kitchen.

Axel turned his head, as if to ward it all off. "Must have been the excitement over our—little vacation."

"Sebastian has already left. He's started off on his social rounds—"

"He's off early."

"Your son—"

"Our son."

"—our son likes to stay in touch with all his friends."

"Especially Pauline. Have you met Pauline?"

"Yes. Very attractive, blue-eyed fourteen-year-old, daughter of Brigadefuehrer Hauswirth. The local head of the SS."

"Well. I'm sure *he* keeps busy. Which reminds me, I have to drop back to the office. I told Heidl I'd be in about ten. Forgot to brief Jutzeler on a Rohrplaz Tower detail."

"But you will be back when they come for the trunk?"

"I wouldn't let the trunk go off without my blessing, Annie. And without Sebastian's soccer ball."

CHAPTER FOUR

August 31, 1939

Axel thought to make a little show of life.

He would not arrive at the stipulated place at exactly the stipulated time. To do so would suggest an apprehensive punctuality. He would arrive late. Not very late, perhaps seven or eight minutes late.

When he approached the corner of Abel and Frankfurtstrasse he slowed his pace, stopping, even, to peer into the windows of the Weinhandlung, which advertised an early harvest of 1939 French Bordeaux wines. It was six minutes past the appointed hour when finally he walked into the faded Victorian lobby of the Rialto Hotel, where Hitler had spent the night after the Niedersachsen celebration of his 1933 appointment as Chancellor. Carrying in his pocket a folded copy of the morning issue of the *Hamburger Nachrichten,* he looked about the formal, wood-paneled lobby, designed for commerce in the days of the Kaiser, for an empty chair. With an offhandedness perhaps studied, he sat down and pulled out the newspaper. The voice directly behind him said, "Please follow me, Herr Reinhard."

He turned and looked up at a stout man with graying hair.

The SS representative wore a cotton-knit gray suit, a dark blue shirt, and a thin black tie. A small swastika, on a lacquered background, adorned his tie clasp. Captain Gradler, who introduced himself as having issued the summons, was blue-eyed and clean shaven. His hair had probably been blond. A thin scar stretched from close to his right eye diagonally toward his ear. His features were regular, his nose and lips full. The smile of greeting was genial. He spoke with a pronounced Prussian accent, rolling his r's almost lasciviously. "We are going to a little room upstairs. You will be so good as to accompany me?"

Axel nodded and, wordlessly, followed him to the elevator. The operator was directed to take them to the fourth floor. Axel followed the officer down the shopworn, faded blue hallway to Number 430. Captain Gradler took a key from his pocket and opened the door. The room was stripped of its bed and bureau. There was only the desk, facing the door. Behind it, the window, one of its shades drawn. Three straight-backed chairs faced the desk. Gradler proceeded to the chair behind the desk and, with a courtly tilt of his hand, motioned Axel to one of the other chairs.

Axel thought it wise to make mention of the voyage ahead. "Captain Gradler, my family and I are sailing to New York tonight, so my schedule is a little crowded. What can I do for you?"

"The end of summer is a fine time to sail. I sailed on a destroyer twenty—twenty-two—years ago. We held the Royal Navy to a draw, but then of course the United States came in with their formidable production machine, destroyer after destroyer." His eyes sharpened. "When were you planning to return to Hamburg?"

"I have reservations to sail from New York on September 28th."

"We know you have the reservation. But you have no intention of actually using it, do you, Herr Reinhard?"

"What do you mean?"

"Do you know, Herr Reinhard, dissimulation only heightens suspicions."

Axel's heart pounded. He strained to organize his thoughts, to say the least provocative thing. "I don't understand you. My partners expect me back at the end of the month. I am taking some drafting material with me to work on a continuing project. My apartment is—my lease is—"

"Uncanceled."

"Yes. We rent by the month, with a deposit of two months."

"And you have not been in touch with the landlord, Herr Ausnitz?"

"No. There are no changes in our arrangements with Herr Ausnitz. My wife will be delayed in returning, but we will keep our present quarters indefinitely."

Captain Gradler stood up and turned to the window looking out over the Frankfurtstrasse. He said nothing.

Axel thought to expand on the matter of the lease and of work committed to Heidl, but a sixth sense stopped him. It would only make matters worse if, inexplicably, the Gestapo knew about his private plans. He took another tack.

"You may know it, perhaps not. Six years ago I voted the National Socialist ticket."

"Yes. But you came to regret that, did you not, Herr Reinhard?"

"What do you mean?" Axel spoke sharply.

"We have in mind your outburst in Vienna on the day the Fuehrer announced the glorious annexation."

So the rat Heller had reported Axel's diatribe to the new security officials in Austria. Axel hesitated a brief moment.

"What I said in Vienna was only to register a personal disappointment over a single partner who felt he had to leave the country—"

"You are opposed to the Fuehrer's policies on Jewish criminals?"

He would have to back away, by whatever means. "No, I understand those policies, but I confine myself, confine myself exclusively, to my work. In Vienna I was simply expressing disappointment at a very personal level, over the effects of the German-Austrian union on a friend, a civil engineer."

"Was that when you decided to abandon the Fatherland?"

Gradler turned from the window, a smile on his face. He returned to his rotating desk chair, pivoting it first to the right, then to the left. He lit a cigarette. After an initial puff, feigning absentmindedness, he proffered one to Axel, who shook his head.

Now Axel stood up and walked over to the abandoned fireplace. He said, wearily, resting his left elbow on the mantelpiece, "Captain Gradler, your suspicions are unfounded. Besides, my German passport permits me foreign travel. My wife and son have American passports— "

"Not quite accurate. Your wife and son have a *single* U.S. passport. And your son is under German protection. Because he is underage and a German-at-birth."

"I am not a lawyer. I am the boy's father, and he has a U.S. passport."

"But your son is thirteen and subject to German protection."

Gradler drew a pen from his pocket, opened the desk drawer, and removed a sheet of paper.

"Let me put it this way. You will not be leaving Germany tonight. You will not be sailing to America."

Axel moved back to his chair. "On what grounds would you detain me from leaving?"

"It is as simple as that the Fatherland is taken up with great diplomatic events. The Fuehrer has decreed that all the resources of the nation are needed for the purpose of creating an impregnable defense. A civil engineer is a valuable national resource. Now—sit down, Herr Reinhard. There is, after all, no place for you to go, until after we have concluded our conversation."

"I will of course consult with an attorney. We have strong affiliates at Heidl—"

"I know that. And I don't mind acknowledging that the Gestapo wishes to avoid... messy problems involving foreigners, involving your wife."

"My wife and son."

"Under German law your son has the right to renounce citizenship in this country when he is eighteen. In the case of young Sebastian, that would be... in 1944. But you must believe me," Gradler ground out his cigarette, "we at the Gestapo are perfectly willing to cooperate with you in avoiding a diplomatic imbroglio. To avoid this, we are willing for you to *board* the *Europa* with Frau Reinhard and the boy. But immediately before the ship sails out, you will come down the gangway—"

"My wife would never stand for that—"

"Your wife need not know you are not aboard."

"How inconceivable that we would not be... arm in arm at the moment of sailing!"

"At the critical moment you will simply slip into the crowd. She will assume you have pulled away for a few moments. Perhaps," Gradler chortled, his hands on his waist, his head tilted back, "perhaps to visit the bathroom!"

Axel desperately needed to talk to someone. Not Heidl. Perhaps not even a junior associate—he would be compromising his carefully concealed plans. The American consul? Axel had not met him. An emergency meeting would have to be contrived by his wife, a U.S. citizen. But how could he give her the least intimation of the problem? He would need to think. But not now, not in the presence of this porcine Nazi.

"You must realize, Herr Reinhard, you have no alternative than to cooperate. Perhaps it is passing through your mind that you might succeed in concealing yourself aboard the *Europa* until it left port. Ah, but Herr Reinhard, it pays to remind yourself that the *Europa* is a part of the national German merchant fleet. If you were absent from our rendezvous point when the *Europa* is ready to pull away, we would simply advise the captain to delay sailing until he got a clearance from us.

"And—" Gradler himself rose, looking directly at Axel—"if you put us to that trouble, we would bring not only you on shore, but also your son Sebastian."

"Sebastian! How could you lay hands on him?"

"Because he is a German ward. And because he is an enemy of the Fatherland."

"*What are you saying, Gradler?* How do you make a thirteen-year-old boy an enemy of the Fatherland?"

Axel listened to what Gradler then said.

It didn't take long to hear the words. But they were enough to end the meeting. His face pale, Axel walked toward the hotel room door.

"Wait for one moment, Herr Reinhard. Just two points. At 2358, two minutes before sailing time, I will look for you at Embarcation Station B, dispatcher's office. The second point: If there is any indication of diplomatic interference, then the boy Sebastian will be brought away from the ship."

Axel opened the door and walked down the fire escape stairs to the lobby, and out into the blazing, hellish sun over Frankfurtstrasse.

BOOK TWO

CHAPTER FIVE

Munich, Summer 1899

At nineteen, Henrietta Leddihn had finished her schooling and did what most girls of her age and her father's standing did, which was to help out at home and wait until something happened that led to marriage and a family of her own. Life at home was not idle. She practiced her piano and spent much time with her twenty-year-old brother Walther, dearly beloved, who aspired to a post as a regular violinist with the Munich Symphony Orchestra.

That was the family dream in the Leddihn household: Walther to play the violin with the Munich Symphony. Walther played occasionally with lesser ensembles and regularly at the Lutheran church, where his mother sang and also served as assistant choral conductor. His father, Erik, had played with the orchestra for twenty years, serving as one of the orchestra's twenty-two violinists. Seven years ago, in 1892, he had been tapped by the Musikdirektor to be first violinist.

It was a big job. The orchestra had a large string section—first violins, second violins, violas, cellos, and two basses—making up forty-three of the seventy-eight instruments of the proud institution that had given the world premieres of Wagner's *Tannhauser* and *Lohengrin* at the great Risenztheater, opened in 1864. Erik Leddihn's responsibility as concertmaster was to hire and fire players for the entire string section and, as first violinist, to lead the orchestra.

Henrietta had been born in Innsbruck, 100 miles south, in Austria's Tyrolean countryside. She was tall and blond, pretty, and exuberant, a full-blown Austrian, vivacious and decisive in manner. She routinely instructed her submissive older brother on what to practice, what to play, and what not to play, accompanying him on the piano at some of his practice sessions. The musical excitement, in their Munich circle in the summer of 1899, was the Generalmusikdirektor's resolve to inaugurate a Mozart festival and to launch it as a part of the general cultural festivities celebrating the turn of the century. A guest conductor had been retained, Alois William Steiner from New York, a thirty-year-old who had made a mark as a performing violinist and was now conductor of the Rochester Symphony Orchestra.

Herr Leddihn, back home from a rehearsal for next Friday's concert, sat with his family drinking tea in the comfortable living room with the mullioned, oval windows. He opened his briefcase, took out a folder, and passed about a publicity picture of Alois William Steiner and a curriculum vitae.

"Notice," he said to his wife, Christa, "the fine reviews he has received. Our music director didn't tell us, when he visited New York, that he had young Steiner in mind for the Mozart festival. But he has sent around two critical testimonials to Steiner from important New York critics who especially praised his Mozart. He did the Thirty-ninth, the Fortieth, and the Forty-first, in a single concert."

"I think he looks mysterious and haughty," Henrietta said, studying the photograph. "And anyway, why didn't the director hire somebody from Germany? Or—from Austria? There is talent enough in our part of the world."

"Henrietta, you always make judgments impetuously," her mother said, putting down the oratorio score she had been studying.

"I bet he's not as good a violinist as Walther," Henrietta, undeterred, continued.

"*Schwesterlein,* how can you *say* that?" Walther, embarrassed, looked down at the biographical material. "Herr Steiner began performing *publicly* when he was twelve!"

"Well, I heard *you* perform when you were *eight.*" Henrietta looked over slyly at her father. It was strictly forbidden, in the household of the Konzertmeister, to make any mention of Walther's career that could be interpreted as an appeal for special consideration by the august Munich Symphony. Shortly after Erik Leddihn had attained his high office, he came home one afternoon and expressed his exasperation with the constant politicking he was now exposed to by family, however distant. "Christa, is *anybody* related to you or to me *un*musical? I would like to collect such a person, or persons. All I get now is suggestions from the Leddihn family and the Kuehnelt family—you have more relatives than King David!—who want to compose music for us or write musical notes for our programs or perform as soloists with the symphony or play in the symphony. We have, applying for positions, violinists, drummers, piccolo players—"

"Erik, don't exaggerate."

"Well I intend to draw up a form letter to be sent to all members of the Leddihn family and the Kuehnelt family: *Do not address any musical requests to the Konzertmeister. He is too busy rehearsing to consider them!*"

Henrietta's reference to the skills of her brother was a risky violation of that taboo. But her father Erik, and her mother Christa, and her brother Walther, let it pass. And anyway, Herr Leddihn had more to say that afternoon on the subject of Alois Steiner.

"Yes, he is American, and yes, we have great talent here. But the Generaldirektor has committed the Munich Symphony to encouraging visiting artists ever since he took office, and this policy has had reciprocal benefits. You will remember, Henrietta, that our own Fritz Hesse was in New York and Boston as guest conductor just a year ago.

"Now," he turned to his daughter. "A practical matter. Henrietta, I have arranged for you to interpret for Maestro Steiner when he is here. You have time on your hands and he knows—to quote him exactly—'only about ten words of German.'"

"Well, I only know... *eleven* words of English."

Her brother intervened. "Come on, Henri. I've heard you speak in English and you do very well. Fraulein Jaspar taught me English before she taught you." He turned to his father. "Papa, Henrietta speaks quite... adequately."

"Quite well enough to get Herr Steiner through his six concerts, I can assure you," Christa said. "Fraulein Jaspar," she reassured her husband, "was very pleased with Henrietta."

"When does he get here?" Henrietta wanted to know. "And how much are you going to pay me?"

The Konzertmeister smiled, leaned over, and patted his daughter on the back of her head. "*Me,* pay *you*? For this great experience?"

"When exactly is he coming?" Christa asked. "Will he be staying at the Buergerhof?"

"Yes. He arrives on November 15th. The first of the six concerts will be November 20th. And the *Requiem*—the farewell to the nineteenth century—will be on Century Eve. December 31st, 1899."

"I am free on that date." Henrietta smiled, kissed her father's cheek, and patted the back of his head.

CHAPTER SIX

December 30, 1899

New Year's Eve was on Sunday. On Saturday, her parents were having afternoon tea. Henrietta came into the room, her cheeks flushed. She informed her mother, in a voice edged with defiance, that she would be dining that night with Alois, as she by now referred to the visiting American conductor.

"You've already had dinner with him twice this week," her mother commented, looking up from the newspaper account of German warships standing by to protect German ships against British interruption in the pursuit of the Boer War.

"I *know,* mother." Henrietta braced herself. She turned her head not to her mother, nor to her father, but to Walther. He sat on the bench by the fireplace with his tiny little screwdriver, tightening a nut on the peg box of his violin. "But . . . I will be dining with Alois *every* night very soon."

Mother, father, and brother turned to her.

"Yes, he asked for my hand in marriage yesterday and I accepted." Now, the words having been spoken, she beamed out her pleasure and walked over to embrace her father.

"Oh, my little girl," was all he could say.

"Oh, Henrietta," Christa began to sob. "I cannot stand to think of you living in another world."

Henrietta turned to her father. "Papa, why don't you use your influence to get Alois appointed permanent conductor of the Munich Symphony?"

Walther, who relished her audacity, smiled appreciatively.

"You admit he has conducted brilliantly, don't you? And our old Termi, he's going to *die of old age* while he's conducting, if he isn't replaced!"

"Herr Doktor Termi is a very distinguished musician, Henrietta, and I do not believe that the Generaldirektor has any plans to replace him immediately. And your Herr Steiner, I agree, is very accomplished, scholarly, methodical— "

"And sexually appealing."

The shock filled the room. The conversation stopped. Then Christa began to chuckle. "Henrietta, you are *impossible.* You have always been impossible. If you mean he is good looking, yes, I agree. But you shouldn't mention that—other thing."

Henrietta laughed, and now she embraced Walther. She had lost all modesty. "And Walther, if Papa doesn't make you a violinist with the Munich orchestra, I shall see to it that you are offered a post with the Rochester Symphony."

Every member of the family now spoke at once. The sheer joy Henrietta radiated overcame them all. A half hour later she got up. "I have to get ready for dinner. He is sending a coach for me at 1930."

She walked coquettishly to the staircase and bounded up to the second floor. Walther, violin in hand, said he would go off to the practice room. He called up to her. "Henri, I love you!"

Erik and Christa sat opposite each other. The newspaper, abandoned, rested on her lap. Erik rose and tinkered with the embers. He hesitated, then reached for a fresh log and placed it on the faltering fire.

Christa blew her nose into her handkerchief.

Herr Leddihn sat back down in his chair. "We must try to stop it, Christa."

"Why?"

"Alois Steiner is a Jew."

CHAPTER SEVEN

At sea, September 1939

Every morning on the *Europa* when the message center opened, Annabelle Reinhard was there waiting for the passenger telegrams to be sorted out. On the midnight of the departure, as the great ship began to pull away from the dock, she had been vexed that Axel wasn't at her side, with Sebastian, to hear the orchestra playing, view the crowds waving, and join with what seemed a thousand people leaning over the ship rails, some laughing with excitement, some teary, some ending a vacation in Europe, some—like the Reinhards—off to a vacation in America. When the champagne tray passed by she took one glass and handed it to Sebastian ("He'll hold it for my husband," she reassured the steward; "he'll be right along") and took another for herself. Minutes after the ship was released from land, impatience overcame her. Sebastian, taken by the excitement, was waving to the slowly receding crowd on shore, adopting one after another from the hundred-odd who crowded the balcony above the wharf as target of his exuberant leave-taking.

"I'll go look for your father. I'll be back. Remember, we're in C-228, you're in LL-101."

"I *know* where we are—" Sebastian's quarters were a bunk in an inside cabin. "Tell Papa hello!"

Annabelle frowned on his insolence. Then smiled and, mock solemnly, "I know Papa will be glad to hear from you."

That was her last lighthearted moment of the night. When she opened the cabin and read the letter she cried out loud. *Don't under any circumstances attempt to protest the ship's sailing—that would place me in very great danger.* Those were the lines, written on top of the page, and then underlined.

"Darling, believe me, there was no other way to do it. I am not permitted to leave. I am not detained or restrained. I will write in care of Henrietta. Remember how much I love you and just tell Sebastian I am delayed—and that I love him, too. Axel."

Why, why hadn't he explained? Why hadn't he said that there had been a snarl and he would be there on the next passage? All he had given her were those spindly but alarming lines, committed already to memory, lines she would repeat to herself for weeks and months.

Her impulse was to call.

Call whom?

Was Axel truly unrestrained? Might she . . . ring their own apartment number at Hempelstrasse?

The wild thought crossed her mind and she grabbed up the telephone, clicking desperately to get the ship's operator. "*Koennen Sie mich mit Hamburg verbinden?*"

Yes, the operator said, she could place a call through to Hamburg, but the caller would have to wait a few minutes.

Annabelle froze. Then, "*Lassen Sie das bitte.*" *Cancel the call.* She would put it in . . . tomorrow.

What the letter hadn't said was there for her to read: *I am helpless so don't try anything*. That would include an attempted telephone call.

Her priority now was to avoid immediate contact with Sebastian. She could not trust her emotions. She reached for a sheet of paper and scrawled on it: "Kitten, Papa had to suddenly stay home on business for a week or two. I am going to sleep. I will bang on your door for breakfast."

Her bang on Sebastian's door that Friday morning in September, on the scale of bangs heard round the world, was all but inaudible, drowned out by the roar from the Nazi artillery shells raining down on Poland, and triggering a great world war.

CHAPTER EIGHT

Phoenix, Fall 1939

The plans to spend time in New York and to make an excursion to Cambridge were set aside. Henrietta Chapin, reached by telephone in Phoenix, was not told anything more than that Axel had had to "postpone" his trip. Annabelle would not risk saying into a telephone from midocean words that might routinely be sent to German security. She told her mother, simply, that she and Sebastian would be going directly to Phoenix. She would telephone on landing and get details on Pullman reservations—for two, not three Reinhards.

They were still on board when the news came that Great Britain and France had declared war on Germany, demanding a withdrawal of Nazi armed forces from Poland. Annabelle found herself staring at her passport with the listing of her son Sebastian and the citation of his birthplace in Hamburg, Germany. Naziland. She told him at lunch not to discuss the war. "We'll leave all that until we reach Oma's." *Oma* was German for grandmother, the only word that Sebastian would ever use for Henrietta Steiner Chapin, who greeted them at the station in Phoenix, on one of those bright Arizona days, and packaged them into her Ford, driving to her desert house, La Quintana.

Ten days went by before a letter from Axel was delivered. Annabelle tore it open, read it, then, her voice strained, handed it over to her mother, saying: "It's written in English. Axel does not like to write in English. This letter is written for the Gestapo. Not for us." Sebastian waited his turn. His face was solemn as he read his father's words.

What did he say? . . . He hoped the trip was smooth . . . He hoped the "events" in Europe had not caused any disturbance on the boat . . . He hoped the trip to Arizona had been pleasant . . . He hoped that his "beloved mother-in-law" was well. Henrietta had commented on that line. "Axel hasn't laid eyes on me since your wedding. He's trying to suggest a family intimacy to the Nazi who is reading his mail. Make it sound more natural that he should be sending Sebastian here to school."

"And more probable that I'd be planning to return." Annabelle read out loud the succeeding paragraph in Axel's letter. "'I think, dear, it makes sense under the circumstances to postpone for a period your scheduled return to Hamburg.' There, that tells it all, since we never intended to return to Hamburg." She continued with the text. "'Of course,'" she read out loud from the letter, "'with the declarations of war, British and German passenger liners will have stopped operating, but the Dutch and American liners continue, so there will be plenty of opportunity as soon as things straighten out a little here. . . .'"

She folded the letter and put it in her purse. "We will have to hope that his next letter tells us more."

A second letter came three months later, when Sebastian's Christmas vacation time had begun. It described informally various projects at the Heidl company and a symphony concert he had attended. That letter and others that came after, at intervals of several months, told nothing more, though they were scanned intently for hidden meaning.

"I wish he was here," Sebastian said, looking over at his Oma after one letter had been read out loud. He addressed his mother. "You know, Mama, I pray for him every night. And for Sunday school I wrote a special prayer. Pastor Neuhaus liked it a lot."

Henrietta reached over and put her hands on either side of her grandson's face, so sad at just that moment, in that pose.

"I know you do. And those prayers can't be lost."

Moments later Annabelle had come back into the living room, briefcase in hand. Sebastian had slipped out of the room. "Sebastian? *Sebastian!*"

Answering the summons he walked back in.

"Thank goodness you continue to call him by his proper name," Henrietta said. "This 'Sebby' business I hear him referred to—"

Sebastian interposed himself resentfully. "So what am I supposed to do, Oma? Tell the guys they can't call me what they call me by?" He turned to his mother. "When you decided to name me Sebastian, what nickname did you and Papa think people would use? Shall I tell them to call me *Kitten*?"

"There's nothing wrong with just plain *Sebastian.*" Henrietta Leddihn Steiner Chapin was sticking to her guns.

"Did everybody in Munich call you Henrietta? I bet some people called you—Hetta? Henri?"

Grandmother and mother laughed. Henrietta thought back on her brother Walther, to whom she was always "Henri."

What did it matter? So the boys and—they were discovering—some of the teachers called him *Sebby.* So mother and grandmother would live with it, though, at La Quintana, they would stick to the full Christian name, most of the time.

"Hurry, Sebastian. That's why I called you. The bus will be here in"—she looked at her watch—"eight minutes. Don't make it wait for you. And I can't be late for my work, either."

CHAPTER NINE

Phoenix, May 1942

Henrietta Chapin had lived in America for some forty-two years, mostly in Rochester and New York. It was there that her only child, Annabelle, had been born—"just a year, Sebastian, after Queen Victoria died. I assume you did not know about that. I have no reason to believe that Central High School pays any attention to European history."

Sebastian didn't raise his head from his model airplane but in a voice only recently changed said, "I think I knew about her. But I'm not sure. And anyway, we haven't celebrated Mama's birthday since—Hamburg." He was bent over the work desk in the corner of the living room, only the back of his head visible, the brown hair inching down under his collar. He had given the whole of what was left of his Saturday afternoon, after release from homework and soccer practice, to the job of gluing together his model of the new B-29 bomber.

"She will not celebrate her birthday until she is reunited with your father."

Sebastian began to comment on the long period, now almost two years, since hearing from his father. He bit his lips to keep silent. What had begun as sadness and anxiety for the thirteen-year-old had passed through despondency to a resigned fatalism in the sixteen-year-old. Pearl Harbor was five months ago, the German invasion of Russia almost a year ago. Japan was laying waste to British and U.S. assets in the Pacific. Hitler had sent Rommel to North Africa where, Cairo-bound, he was steamrolling east. That morning's paper had spoken of a thousand RAF bombers attacking Cologne. His head still bent over his work, he asked, "Have you ever been to Cologne, Oma?"

"Yes. Your great-grandfather's orchestra did a concert at the great cathedral there, Beethoven's Ninth Symphony. My mama took my brother Walther and me along."

"I've been there, too! That was when Papa met with Albert Speer. Herr Speer is maybe the closest person to Hitler—did you know that?—ever since Herr Hess dropped down by parachute in England, isn't that right, Oma?"

"They are said to be very close, Herr Speer and Herr Hitler."

Henrietta Chapin liked to chat, especially in German. In English, she was always consciously working in a foreign language. She had been exposed to English as a schoolgirl but her study had been merely dutiful. When she married, the custom was: only-in-English. Alois Steiner wasn't much of a talker, and she hardly had time, in the short time they had together, to egg him on to an alien social mode. When Alois Steiner felt expressive, he would pick up his violin and play for her. Sometimes she would accompany him on the piano. In those moments, she wrote lyrically to her mother in Munich, they were speaking to each other in a universal tongue.

But the pneumonia killed him after only eighteen months of marriage, five months before Annabelle was born. She was comforted by Roderick Chapin, a colleague of Alois and a trustee of the symphony. A bachelor in his thirties, a Harvard graduate, and churchgoing Episcopalian, Chapin induced her to abandon any thought of traveling, pregnant, back to Germany to live. He pressed his case ardently, wooed and won her. They were married two months after her daughter was born.

Roderick Chapin liked people and loved parties. After the First World War, Henrietta and Annabelle moved into the new house on Fifth Avenue in New York City where Roderick entertained prodigiously. Henrietta more than carried her weight, however crabbed she judged her thoughts to be when transcribed into English.

Roderick's health declined, soon after the inauguration of the new Democratic President, Mr. Roosevelt, and he lived, progressively, an invalid's life. The Depression had meant an end to the domestic servants they had been accustomed to for almost three decades, and there hadn't been much conversation in the sickroom where Henrietta spent so many hours.

Henrietta's main pleasure in these years had come from her closeness to her beloved Annabelle. It had been bad enough when her daughter went off to college in Cambridge, but then came the decisive interruption: Annabelle met, loved, and married the engaging young German engineer, Axel Reinhard.

Henrietta was poorly placed to object to the union, having herself, at the turn of the century, left Germany to live in America. So she would call overseas to Hamburg once every month and talk joyfully to her daughter in the allotted ten minutes on the telephone—talk to her in the German language she had used when they were at home alone.

After Hitler's reoccupation of the Rhineland, Henrietta Chapin began to urge Annabelle to return with her son to the safety of America. She was horrified—and affronted—by reports of the Austrians' public acquiescence in the loss of national sovereignty in 1938. She shuddered, in private, at the very thought that residents of her native city in the Tyrol should be sympathizers of Hitler. She did not touch on the subject in the letters, now infrequent, to her aged parents, writing only that, Hitler having annexed Austria, she was sure he would go no farther. "Among other things, Mama, there are other countries out there. I mean, Great Britain and France, which will surely step in and say, *No farther, Herr Hitler!*"

But six months later Hitler had given his ultimatum to Czechoslovakia and proceeded with the absorption of the Sudetenland. Henrietta wrote again to urge Annabelle to come home. Shrewdly, she put her emphasis on the need to protect her son—"Hitler has had his universal military draft since March of 1935 and it will be only a few years—time moves quickly!—before Sebastian is old enough to be drafted. The clouds of war are over Europe and Sebastian will soon enter his teens." When six months later, on March 15, 1939, after pledging to the British and the French that he would move no farther in Czechoslovakia, Hitler entered Prague, another, more urgent, letter from Henrietta went out.

But this time the letter went to Axel.

This time Annabelle listened. Quietly, she resolved to comply.

Her objective became to persuade Axel to uproot the Reinhard household: to leave his job, leave Germany, resettle in America, find a new job. She broached the idea. He resisted it, as expected.

Then came the cry of alarm from London, on March 31, 1939. Hitler's menacing gestures against Poland triggered the electric British announcement: *Great Britain would resist any aggression against Poland.* Axel listened on his shortwave radio to the solemn voices of the BBC.

The next day, dispirited, he came around: Yes, he would leave Germany. But his departure had to be planned with great care. He must not let on that he would be leaving permanently. That would arouse disappointment, distrust, and perhaps even reprisals of some form or another.

In Phoenix, Henrietta clenched her teeth as she thought back, yet again, on the terror her daughter must have felt that night of the departure of the *Europa*. She could visualize the scene: Annabelle looking about the festive ship with increasing concern. Then the desperation on reading Axel's letter.

Had she slept at all? Henrietta wondered. She had never probed the day-to-day details of her daughter's six days at sea. On arrival in Phoenix, Annabelle, pale and exhausted, had merely remarked on how stunned the whole ship had been on hearing the shipboard radio's toneless announcements, first that the Nazi army had invaded Poland and then, two days later, that Britain and France had declared war against Germany.

The next two years, at the remove of Phoenix, Arizona, were tranquil, but Henrietta and Annabelle could not blot away the terrible sorrow abroad, let alone the benumbing question of Axel: Where was he? Living at La Quintana, Henrietta acknowledged that she had personal reasons to be grateful. She was reunited with her daughter, had been introduced to her German-speaking grandson—who in a matter of days, had captivated her—and, for the first time in many years, was living where her beloved German was the household language.

Henrietta had bought La Quintana, the house in the desert country outside Phoenix, with the proceeds of the sale of the

Fifth Avenue house. She had been lured to Arizona by its relative remoteness. She didn't want to linger in New York after her dear Roderick's death. She had thought before to take her ailing husband to Arizona. For a dozen years, its benefits had been expounded in a string of letters from Alois's asthmatic sister, who lived in Phoenix and wrote of the benefits of the dry climate, the low cost of living, and the fine public schools. La Quintana, constructed only three years earlier, was up for sale after the death of its owner. She viewed the photographs and closed the deal by telephone.

The elongated, one-floor, western-style stucco house was large enough for grandmother, daughter, and grandson, permitting privacy to all three generations, as desired, or required. Henrietta, sixty-two years old and spry, took the west wing. Annabelle and Sebastian each had a bedroom in the east wing, sharing a bathroom. The central section had the kitchen, living room/dining room, and a sequestered little study, bit by bit requisitioned by Sebastian as he pursued his studies and his hobbies, but regularly used also by Annabelle. It was there that she prepared to teach the daily classes in German and graded the papers of the U.S. military—lieutenants, sergeants, and corporals—she coached in German at the army intelligence unit.

Sebastian rose from the table, exhibited the model to his grandmother, and said, "Oma, at church on Sunday, do you pray for the victory of the Allies?"

There was a slight hesitation. "Well, yes."

Sebastian held aloft his model airplane. "The RAF had a massive bombing of Lubeck last week, did you read? This"—he dangled his creation before her—"is a B-29. It is the new, great airplane of the United States Army. It will be sent on bombing missions very soon. Is it right to pray that the bombing missions will be successful?"

"Yes. But those bombing missions will be directed only against—you know. Munitions factories, that kind of thing."

"The bombs would not fall on civilians?"

"Inevitably, Sebastian, bombs directed at military targets go astray and kill some civilians."

"But they also kill civilians who are working in military factories."

"Yes. The modern bomb doesn't, well, make many distinctions."

"But bombing missions aren't always restricted to things like munitions factories, are they? The bombing by General Doolittle of Tokyo in April, those bombs fell over civilians."

"Not intentionally. They were—victims of general warfare."

"Would it be wrong to drop bombs intending to kill—just people? Civilians?"

"Very wrong. That is forbidden by the Hague Convention."

"What's that?"

"Don't pin me down, dear. There are a lot of conventions governing what you can and can't do in war. For instance, the use of gas was outlawed after the last war. And other things."

"Like what?"

"Well, we just spoke about bombing civilian populations."

"Is that outlawed?"

"I could not give you chapter and verse, but I certainly assume so."

"If you pray for an Allied victory, then you pray for successful bombing raids by the RAF and by us. You're praying, at least, that bombers will find their legal targets. That means that a bomb aimed at a—whatever, a bridge, a building that is a part of the military—would be hit. That could be a building where Papa is working. So God would be saying it was all right to kill my father?"

Henrietta stood up. "We don't know that your father is working in a military operation. Let us hope not."

"And pray not?"

Henrietta walked away toward the kitchen, and hid tears of sorrow and of impotent rage.

CHAPTER TEN

Phoenix, July 1943

Dressed in a loose, floral-printed skirt and blouse, Henrietta sat on La Quintana's terrace under the awning. The sun was well past its zenith and soon, she knew from long experience, she could reasonably expect the comfort of the breeze generated by the Santa Quinta mountain fork on hot summer afternoons. She brought the radio in from the living room. With its long extension cord she could prop it on the glass table next to where she sat, her book in hand, and her iced tea. She would bring in the midnight news from the BBC—1700, Phoenix time.

The day before, they had got word of the British–U.S. landing in Sicily. "We are, finally, fighting in Axis territory," Henrietta had exulted. She was eager to hear now how it was going, twenty-four hours later, for the Allied troops. She still had eight minutes to wait for the BBC when the postman arrived. Spotting Mrs. Chapin outdoors, he took the mail to her directly, tipping his postman's hat.

"Evenin', Mrs. Chapin."

"Good evening, Sam. How's your boy enjoying basic training?"

"Not much. They work you pretty hard at Fort Sill where he is. Oklahoma. An' it's hotter than here, he tells us, Minnie and me. His mother and me. How's *your* boy enjoying the Grand Canyon? He must feel pretty good, at his age, being made an official guide."

"He likes it fine, Sam. But not my *boy*. My *grandson*. Yes, Sebastian is glad to be doing something. You know, there's a great shortage of people everywhere to do anything. Ten, fifteen million people in the army, factories working day and night. No wonder they'll allow a seventeen-year-old to be an official tourist guide. Now Sam, go away." Henrietta talked that way, her native German accent pronounced, her manner hortatory, and that was just fine with everyone in Phoenix she dealt with, the tradesmen, the workers at the gas station from which she eked out mobility, drawing only the licensed three gallons per week of rationed gas. "I've got to listen to the war news."

"On my way, Mrs. Chapin." Sam smiled, waved his long arm, and left, adjusting his cap to the sun.

Henrietta looked down at the little assortment he had left. A newspaper, *Life* magazine, a bulletin from the local movie theater, a couple of bills, and a letter addressed in heavy script to Mrs. Axel Reinhard.

Henrietta stared at it.

The BBC news broadcaster came on, but she didn't focus on what he said. A half hour later, Annabelle returned from work. Her mother was in the kitchen preparing a salad.

"There's a letter for you," Henrietta said, and nodded at the coffee table in the living room.

The letter was in German, from the War Ministry in Berlin. There was no salutation. The text read simply WE REGRET TO INFORM YOU THAT HERR AXEL REINHARD IS A CASUALTY OF THE WAR FOR THE DEFENSE OF THE FATHERLAND. HIS NAME WILL BE HONORED AFTER OUR VICTORY. The signature was indecipherable. The signing officer's rank was Technical Sergeant, Oberscharfuehrer. The date, affixed by stamp, was May 17, 1943.

Henrietta stayed in the kitchen, shredding carrots mechanically.

A few minutes later, Annabelle joined her.

Henrietta tried to say something, but failed. Henrietta's arms were close around her daughter, and together they wept, mother and child, both of them now widows.

Not much was spoken during their dinner.

Turning on the water tap to wash the dishes, Annabelle said, "I haven't decided how to tell Sebastian."

"When is he coming home?"

"He has Mondays off. This is Wednesday."

"Sebby wasn't here last Monday, was he? I can't remember." Even Henrietta had given up. Now, often, Sebastian was "Sebby" to her.

"No." Annabelle ducked into the living room and brought out the penny postcard. She squinted her eyes to read the tight script. "*Mama, I won't be home Monday. Will be shooting rapids with Cherokee Bill. Getting real good at it. He might take me again next Monday. I hope so. Please get me some more sun oil, I'm running out, and also a paperback Agatha Christie, ditto. Oh, and please buy a frame for my diploma. When they draft me in January I'll tack it on the wall behind my bunk to impress whatever general gets assigned to look after me. I hope basic training camp will be close by to a FAST river rapid. I will go SWOOSH down the river and the fastest helicopter won't be fast enough to catch me! Tell Oma hello. No, give her a big kiss—*"

Annabelle had to stop reading. "I don't see much . . . much point in going up there just to. . . ." The tears began again.

Henrietta nodded. She thought to say something but it was all banal, mechanical. "You'd have to travel to Flagstaff by bus, you couldn't make it with the gas coupons we have."

Annabelle looked yet again at the letter.

"What I wonder is, Mutter, what I wonder is... was he dead a long time ago? Months ago? Last year? *I think so.* I think he would have found a way to get a letter to us, if he was alive until—May 17th, the date on this. But if so, I can't think why the War Ministry delayed so long. Waited...." Her voice trailed off.

She went to the bureau and stared at the picture taken at the Hamburg Fair, July 1939. Four years ago. Sebastian, a broad smile on his face, his hair loose over his forehead, was holding tight to his airplane model. Annabelle, with faint signs of matronliness on her cheeks and torso, wore glasses and only a forced-for-the-camera smile. Axel had on his beloved lederhosen, and a green hunting cap with a feather. His eyes were alight with intelligence and enjoyment, she thought, reaching for her handkerchief.

Just four years ago. How many millions since then had died from war's violence? How did Axel's life end? Could he have been a victim of an Allied raid? Of Soviet tanks? Yes, yes, he must have been dead long ago. She taped the picture back on the wall.

CHAPTER ELEVEN

January 1944

The telegram, six months later, was hand delivered at La Quintana soon after breakfast. DARLING SEBASTIAN. THINKING OF YOU TODAY. I HAVE BOOKED A CALL FOR EXACTLY ELEVEN PM GMT SO BE SURE TO STAND BY AT LA QUINTANA AT FOUR PM. AND PRAY THEY'RE NOT BOMBING US WHEN I MAKE CALL. THEY DID THAT YESTERDAY. FUEHRER'S NEW YEAR'S DAY PRESENT. LOVE TO OMA. --MAMA

Sebastian adjusted his crutch, reached over, and poured himself more coffee. When he spotted Sam through the window he called out to him to bring the mail into the house. Sam opened the door and walked in.

"Thanks." Sebastian took in his outstretched hand the little mail packet. "I could have got to you and opened the door myself but..." Sebastian smiled up at him, "I can't move very fast, not for a while."

"Your leg knitting up all right?" Sam asked.

"Yeah. Sam—want to know something? Today's my birthday. I'm eighteen." Sebastian's tanned face, with traces of freshly shaved blond hair on his chin, lit up with a smile.

"Well, if you could stand up, you could dance a jig! Congratulations, Sebby. Selective Service is going to have to wait a bit before they get their hands on you, the shape you're in. They nabbed my Lester when he was eighteen years and thirty days!"

"Les doing okay? Still in the Pacific somewhere?"

"Yep. We don't know exactly where, of course, but he writes every couple of weeks. He wants Minnie and me to send him, guess what, some comic books. Got to go on my rounds. Stay away from the rapids, Sebastian Reinhard."

His mother—the telegram had said—asked Sebastian to pray that that night in London should be without bombs. They had last prayed together in July, widow, grandmother, and son, at the little church service in memory of his father. Nobody in Phoenix had ever met Axel Reinhard. Anybody in America who ever knew him, Sebastian reminded himself, would have to have been with him at MIT. Sebastian didn't remember his father's making any mention of his classmates. His mother Annabelle, on the other hand, regularly responded to alumnae notices from Radcliffe. ("Here's a picture of my former roommate," he remembered her saying one day. "Lillian Booth." His mother had pointed to a picture of a statuesque woman who had been appointed professor at the School of Music at Indiana University.) So there were none of his father's schoolmates at the service in the Lutheran church, only a dozen friends of Annabelle, paying their respects. It was nice that Sam and Minnie were there.

The outsiders had been kind to come, Sebastian thought. Like just about every human being in America, all of them there at St. Mark's Church had been directly affected by the war's reach. Killed or wounded father, husband, son, sweetheart, best friend. The minister's words were (had to be) carefully chosen. Nobody at the service knew what Axel Reinhard had been doing when he died. They knew only that he was—a German; in

Germany. Doing what, nobody asked; and if anyone had done so, Annabelle wouldn't have been able to say. In 1943, Axel Reinhard was thirty-nine years old. Everybody who knew anything knew that anyone of that age living in Germany was doing service, directly or indirectly, for—the Fuehrer? The Fatherland? Or just plain Germany? "*Take your choice,*" Sebastian had said a year ago to the new young teacher at Central High School who asked whom his father served.

The minister talked about the solace of the next world. He spoke of Axel as a fine husband and father. He went on to say that the dead man had been "distinguished in his profession." Sebastian had never really thought about that! Was his father, at age thirty-five when last they were together, a successful civil engineer? A *very* successful civil engineer? A rising star in his profession? A risen star in his profession?

He thought to ask his mother about it after the service, but it was safer not to talk about his father anymore. Letters from Axel had stopped so very long ago. Sebastian could come up with the exact day after which Mama didn't seem to want to talk about his father. It was last year, May of 1942. The letter in the post office box, stamped in Germany, had been addressed by hand to her. She had torn it open.

It was a black-bordered death notice from their former landlord's wife at 38 Hempelstrasse. Annabelle's address had got into one of those Prussianlike files, renowned for their comprehensive exactitude; the widow had evidently sent the news of her husband's death to all of Herr Ausnitz's former tenants.

Ausnitz. Sebastian wondered. *Was Herr Ausnitz Jewish?* Without his mother's noticing, he scrutinized carefully the gothic German text in the notice. It gave Herr Ausnitz's date of birth, the names of his mother and father, of his wife and son and daughters. There were several lines of poignant, solemn thoughts and memories. There was no indication of a Christian burial service, or of burial in a Christian cemetery.

If Herr Ausnitz was Jewish, would the Nazis have taken away his apartment house? In the wanton spirit of Kristallnacht? Sebastian felt a fury in his stomach.

It was after opening that letter that his mother had said: "I don't think we are going to hear anything more—" she corrected herself "—anything much more—about Papa. We just have to do what we can. Without him." Annabelle had hastily arrested the melancholy in the room. She congratulated Sebastian on the home run which, that afternoon, had tipped the score against Valley High, making him Central's hero of the day. "Maybe you will be a professional baseball player."

"Yep," Sebastian said. "I'll practice baseball in the army. Or in the navy."

"I don't think the navy has boats that negotiate Sebastian's rapids," Henrietta intervened. "Can you practice batting on one of your canoes?"

"Not *canoes*, Oma. They're rafts." And he grinned.

A week after the memorial service, Annabelle had come back from her work at the army intelligence unit and broken the news to her mother and son. She had been recruited for special work. "It has to do with decryption."

"Will it change your work schedule?" her mother asked.

"Mama, they want me to work in London."

It had been an awful wrench, but then—as Henrietta remarked to her grandson a fortnight later, lips tight, after the tearful goodbyes and the departure of Annabelle on the DC-3—the whole war was a terrible wrench. "Your father is dead. You and your Mama had to leave your home. And now your mother has gone off to get nearer to the front lines. It is a wrench for everybody."

That wrench would now affect Henrietta, though it was less than a wrench. She had spoken with "Major Henry" at the army unit, agreeing to take on the German-language course Annabelle had had to abandon when called to duty abroad. Henrietta Chapin, grandmother, would no longer be at La Quintana all day. Never mind. "You're seventeen now, Sebby, very bright and resourceful, and when you graduate from Central High in June, I know you will be going up to Flagstaff to your beloved Grand Canyon until the army picks you up."

Indeed he would; but Sebastian, that summer, continued to come home to La Quintana on the bus every other week, on his days off, to mow the lawn and place records on the record player and play Russian Bank with Oma and talk voraciously about the news of the day on the war fronts. After studious inspection of news of the battlefronts in Europe he fancied himself something of an expert on army divisions, brigades, regiments, and their commanders, studying also the nomenclature, both of the regular German army and the SS, and the corresponding ranks in the U.S. Army. The older woman and the boy wondered what exactly had gone on at conferences of the heads of state. In Cairo, Chiang Kai-shek had met with Prime Minister Churchill and President Roosevelt. Allied leaders had met in Teheran the following week. Imagine! Prime Minister Churchill, President Roosevelt, and General Secretary Stalin! The RAF had bombed Berlin. The Allies entered Italy and quickly occupied Naples; the Soviet army had retaken Smolensk.

Sebastian was gleefully happy with his work at the Grand Canyon resort. It was that primarily, of course—a resort. The naturalists there—the botanists, geologists, speleologists, vulcanologists—were everywhere, focusing hungrily on their separate disciplines and ignoring the tourists who came to see, stare at, and experience the vast source of their endless fascination.

But it was the tourists who were indispensable. Their income was critical to the maintenance of Grand Canyon, Inc. Sebastian, age sixteen when he first started, was given to do only work maintaining the trails—keeping them open and even trimmed for the tourists who climbed down them, or rode down on horses and donkeys. But his enthusiasm for the entire scene caught the attention of Dennis Howard, the personnel supervisor. He was a tall, angular figure in his range hat with his obtrusive mustache. He told Sebastian that he would have to spend more time on the tourist end of the enterprise.

"What does that entail, Mr. Howard?"

"Well you ought to know by now. There are tourists here every day, and they come in heavy, nine, ten months every year. Some want to think of themselves as explorers. But they aren't, most of 'em. They need guidance. I want you to be able to act as a guide for them. Show them how to get down the trails, try to keep them from falling a thousand feet into the canyon; help them climb back up. If they're lame and numb from their workouts, get them hot dogs or whatever they want, bring it to them from the cafeteria. The whole bit. Oh. We'd lift your pay to $1.25 per hour."

"I'd like to think about that, Mr. Howard."

"You'd what?"

"I'd like to think about it. What I like most is the wildlife. And, especially, the rapids. I want to learn how to handle those. I mean, that's what I really want to do."

Dennis Howard waited. He assumed that Sebastian would quickly capitulate and simply take on whatever work he was assigned. But he studied the muscular young man with the tanned face and the guarded smile and the bright eyes: he had a mind of his own. Dennis Howard didn't resent those who came to the Grand Canyon enthused by nature or adventure, but he had his own priorities. So he settled for, "Let's talk about it tomorrow."

"Yes sir, that would be fine."

A compromise was struck. On even weeks Sebastian would act exclusively as a tourist guide and aide. On odd weeks he would continue to work on maintenance, but he would serve also as assistant to Cherokee Bill, if Bill approved of him.

The wiry American Indian had worked in the Grand Canyon since he was a boy, thirty years ago. He maintained the little fleet of rafts for adventurous and demanding tourist explorers. Cherokee Bill kept a private kayak and exultantly set out in it once or twice a week, after hours. He surveilled Sebastian carefully, observed him at work on the trails and in the workshop, and agreed to take him on. Carefully, he introduced him to the lore of boat maintenance and rapid river work, and helped him to acquire carpentry skills which Sebastian practiced at the lodge's workshop on the long nights, after supper.

By the summer of Sebastian's seventeenth year, Bill was giving Sebastian more time for the river work; and, a few weeks later, he entrusted Sebastian to guide river-bound tourists down to rapids territory. Bill kept a close eye on Sebastian but there was no way to do that around the clock, and Sebastian was now, after work hours, going downriver in the auxiliary kayak he had persuaded Bill to let him experiment with, an experiment that led, one bright day when the gorge and the resplendent cliffs that served it as gigantic color guards seemed to ache for young adventurers to test its resources, to a high-speed collision with the jagged rock lying just below the swirling surface. The kayak was gone. Sebastian lay, crippled, on the narrow, rocky embankment when—it was after ten that night—Cherokee Bill's searchlight discerned Sebastian's white, shivering frame. There was no way to take the crippled boy upstream. Bill massaged him, wrapped him in a blanket, and gave him to drink from a flask Sebastian's first taste of whiskey. The next morning, Cherokee Bill was back with a rescue party.

"How're your students doing, Oma? I mean, do they get to talk German like—like us?"

"No. These young men—and there are two women—aren't going to be taken for native-speaking Germans."

"What are they being trained to do—after you teach them *Ein Zwei Drei*?"

"Sebastian. If I knew, I would not tell you."

"Are you training them to be spies?"

"Their German would not equip them to pass as Germans. They couldn't do clandestine work posing as natives. But, Sebastian, we are not to speculate on the matter of what my students will be doing in the field. All you need to know is that I teach German, as your Mama did, to young military candidates. I think, from the headlines on how the war is going, we can safely suppose that my students will not be interpreting orders from German-speaking Nazis who have occupied London and Washington."

"You're very optimistic, Oma. I hope there will be something left for *me* to do."

"The war is hardly won. Herr Hitler commands all of Europe and the Japanese most of the Pacific. There will be plenty for you to do when you go off to the army."

"I'll be ready to go. Now that I know that Papa is dead, I know

I won't have to, you know—run any risk of firing bullets at some place where he might be, or dropping bombs on his office."

Henrietta Chapin was furtively glad, after she was assured that Sebastian would completely recuperate, that he had had the accident on the rapids. It kept him away from the war for at least a few more months.

Exactly five months, it turned out. In June 1944, his broken leg completely repaired, he kissed his beloved Oma good-bye and got into the troop train that would take him to Camp Wheeler in Georgia for something called basic training in the infantry.

CHAPTER TWELVE

Fort Benning, Georgia, April 12, 1945

Platoon A of Officers' Candidate School Class #364 was engaged in maneuvers in the pine forest of Columbus, Georgia. Sixteen weeks earlier, when the candidates drawn in from basic training graduating classes and other army echelons numbered sixty, making up a full platoon, they had begun the stiff, competitive eighteen-week program. By April, they were reduced to thirty-four in number, twenty-six of them cashiered.

Most of the failing aspirants, for any one or more reasons, were simply judged less than officer material and were being sent back to the field. Others, deemed potentially qualified but doing less well than acceptable, were sent back to try, from Week #1, one more time. The surviving candidates assembled now in the opening in the pine forest around the lieutenant. He had called them in from the exercise. They had been fanning the forest for "snipers," and responded to his whistle. They followed the whistle sound, and wearing full field packs, carrying M-1 rifles, and sweating even in the Georgia cool spring, met up with their platoon leader. They eased into the pine beds, tilting their helmets up and off, many of them lighting cigarettes. It was getting warm and the maneuver had begun at dawn. The lieutenant blew his whistle again, this time calling for attention.

He had very bad news to give them, he said. "The president of the United States is dead."

He waited a minute or two for the buzz of soldier-to-soldier reaction. There were murmurs that could be taken as expressions of grief and sorrow and shock. But their focus, quickly, was on the single question, *Might this mean an earlier end to the war?*

Sebastian leaned over to Ed Coady. "Could be good news. FDR was the unconditional surrender man, right?"

"Right." Coady had been drafted in July, after finishing freshman year at Princeton, where he had matriculated at age seventeen. He and Sebastian had been trying diligently, in the few minutes not spoken for by the Infantry School, to keep abreast of the news. They sequestered the shortwave radio in the Rec Room at nine every night to take in the BBC broadcast, subsequently amusing themselves, while undressing for sleep in their barracks before lights-out, by mimicking what George Orwell had spoken of as the "genteel and throaty" voices of BBC newscasters. *Private Edward Cooodee was repohted seen at Fort Benning in Georgia, which is an . . . administrative centah of the United States . . . Infantry.* And Sebastian would improvise a reply built on the day's news. *And so we say good night to Private Reinhard, inasmuch as it is two hours pahst midnight. Sleep well, Private Reinhard. You will probably be dedd in a month.*

"Yes," Coady said now. "It was FDR at Casablanca who came up with 'unconditional surrender.' That'll keep the German fuckers—I mean, Sebby, the Nazi—well yes, the Nazi fuckers—fighting to the last—" The whistle blew.

OCS candidates were instantly compliant with any order from

their platoon leader. To be less than attentive was to run the risk of a quiet, invisible demerit in the platoon leader's ledger. Enough of these and a candidate got called before the OCS Review Board and given the news: 1) He was out. Or, 2) he had to begin the whole nerve-shattering, bone-breaking eighteen-week business all over again.

The first lieutenant elaborated. "The president died this morning at Warm Springs. We are the closest army base. Colonel Hayes has instructed us by radio to stand by for the selection of an honor guard for the president's removal tomorrow morning to the presidential train that will take him to Washington. The last two hours of the maneuvers today are canceled. After chow we will go back to Checkpoint Baker where the trucks will be. At 1800 the honor guard will be chosen. Report to the assembly point and stand at parade rest at 1755."

They were there promptly, the platoon reduced, after the "death sentences" of the Review Board, to two files of seventeen soldiers. They were neatly aligned at parade rest position, their khaki shirts open at the collar, their name tags on their breast pockets. A few minutes later the major stepped down from the jeep, accompanied by a Technical Sergeant. The men were called to attention and he filed by the first row, then the second. A nod of his head signaled to the T/Sergeant, who would look up, then write the candidate's name on his pad.

Sebastian was amused by the exercise. It had happened two or three times during basic training. The criteria of the reviewing officer were never explicit, but those who had eyes to see understood what they were. At basic training in Macon, privates were selected for public viewing on the basis of whose appearance would be most appealing at the designated local function — a Veterans Day parade, a bond-selling rally, the funeral of the senator from the Armed Services Committee. Today's men would be lined up, Sebastian supposed, to escort the coffin departing from the president's little retreat, or perhaps alongside the presidential train. There would be lots of news cameramen, and the commanding general, back at Camp Wheeler, wanted the most photogenic young men to represent the infantry.

Sebastian had an eye for objective reality; he knew he would be picked; he always was—handsome, muscular, brown-eyed, appearing even younger than the nineteen years he had celebrated, or rather passed by, in the early weeks of the officer training course. He was certain that Ed Coady would also be picked—a pleasing-faced, freckled redhead from New Bedford, Massachusetts. As the major walked by, Sebastian let himself reflect, with a smile deeply buried, on how Resplendent Young American Reinhard and Resplendent Young American Coady would have looked if a cameraman had been there to film their writhings the Saturday night before in Phenix City, the sin city just over the river in Alabama. The camera would have caught the two All-Americans in the arms of Rosita and Sally on twin beds, abandoning, after much thought and discreet planning and beer consumed, their virginity. Well, he thought, the dead, worldly president would know all about boys being boys—he had served as Assistant Secretary of the Navy during the other war, and that was before the docs had invented penicillin, which made nights-out-on-the-town, back then, a lot riskier.

"Paaa-*rade REST!*"

The candidates moved to separate their feet and allow arms to rest behind their backs. The major read out loud a very long tribute written by the general in honor of the departed Commander-in-Chief. Then Lieutenant Bryant called out ten names. The ten Resplendent Young Americans were told to report to company headquarters at 2000. They were told by their platoon leaders, who read from a regimental order sheet, what their duties would be. The late president's departure on the train from Warm Springs was set for 0830.

At taps, the flag was at half-mast. On their return from the mess hall the candidates busied themselves as always. The scattering of empty beds on the thirty-bed barracks floor were stern reminders of the consequences of negligence or of flagged concern for perfection. They labored now to clean and reclean and hunt out specs of lint from their rifles. At any given moment, in the morning before reveille and at night before lights-out, up to a dozen candidates would be working on their pull-ups, using the iron pipes that served as beams across the ceiling. Most had by now achieved the required eleven pull-ups (and forty-four push-ups), but Andy and Henry, who were in their late twenties, past athletic prime, hadn't quite gotten there, and now their brothers-in-arms, sitting on their beds or working on their rifles, egged them on and cheered when Andy, straining and breathless, reached ten. The final test would be the following Thursday—eleven pull-ups or back to the ranks. There was little conversation about the death of the president, and Sebastian knew nothing, after five days on maneuvers, about other developments on the war fronts.

By the time Sebastian and others in the special funeral detachment reported the next morning and dismounted their buses at Warm Springs the crowds were already gathering. By 0800 two thousand paratroopers from Fort Benning and three thousand from the great infantry base were massively there. The OCS detachment—in battle dress, at stiff attention, guns at their side—stood on both sides as the flag-draped green hearse inched past them, followed by the honor guard on foot, led by Mrs. Roosevelt. The file stopped only after reaching the railroad car. The coffin was taken up the ramp, the great covering flag in black crepe. From the corner of his eye Sebastian could see the coffin slide up into the cavity of the railroad car. The crowd was silent except for the weeping, which seemed uncontrolled. There was Jim Crow in Georgia, but not early that morning, on April 13, at the Warm Springs station, where the tears were copious on black faces.

On the ride back to Fort Benning not much was spoken. Ed Coady said he would try to get through on the telephone to his mother in New Bedford. "She'll be very torn up. What about your people in Arizona?" Sebastian said there was just his grandmother there. "My Oma—my grandmother, Henrietta—will take it stoically, she's that way." After supper, Ed went off to the message center to try his long distance call, and Sebastian went to the radio for the BBC news. A half hour later, Ed joined Sebastian. "How's your mother?" Sebastian asked.

"Okay. She said, well, Mr. Roosevelt was only sixty-three. But what I want to know, Eddie, is, will you be alive at twenty-three?" Ed laughed. "Either Hitler or I will be dead by then."

CHAPTER THIRTEEN

Hamburg, February 1942

Three years before Sebastian had played his small role at Warm Springs, his father, Axel Reinhard, was hard at work in Hamburg for his firm, Heidl & Sons. It had been a very long time since the *Europa* pulled away from the dock, transporting to safety his wife and son, most of what Axel lived for. His own world was nothing more now than the world of his professional life.

The Gestapo official had told Axel, that night, as they saw the passenger liner pulling away, that he had only to continue to contribute to the greater world of the Third Reich to live an untroubled life. His attempted deceit was marked down in the Gestapo's dossier and an eye would be kept on him. He was at liberty, but on no account would the Gestapo ignore any future attempt to leave the country, or any effort by him to communicate to foreigners anything that "bears adversely on the interests of the state." Wife and son, of course, were "foreigners."

The early wars came quickly and were quickly and decisively fought to victory, but the war against the Soviet Union—it was plain in early 1942—would not be so quickly concluded. Axel was not formally in the military, he was in commerce. And in the world of commerce, Albert Speer was king.

Axel Reinhard knew that his boss, Franz Heidl, had been a friend of Albert Speer, more exactly a sometime collaborator. That was back in 1930, before Speer became a full-time appendage of the rising political star of Adolf Hitler. *The Fuehrer's house architect,* Herr Heidl had jocularly dubbed him, early on. Heidl would not use such language any longer, because although it intended only a slightly derisive reference to Speer, it was inextricably linked only to Speer's sponsor. The Fuehrer's title—the Leader—had been formally adopted by Hitler after the death of Hindenburg in 1934. Some wags thought it funny to go about referring constantly to "The Leader," funnier still to salute one another, going and coming, with "*Heil Hitler.*" But those voices quickly ebbed. There were no jokes anymore with the words *Der Fuehrer* in them.

As of now, February 8, 1942, Albert Speer was the Armaments Minister for the Third Reich. That made him the economic czar of Germany. In a nation at war, the line blurs between commerce and the military. Speer's responsibility was to keep arms flowing to maintain 155 German divisions pressing the war on Russia, and, in western Europe, to supply the forty divisions needed to oversee Nazi occupations in Norway, Denmark, Belgium, Holland, and France. And now, added to Speer's burden, was the provisioning of the indomitable army of General Erwin Rommel, still driving in North Africa toward Cairo.

Seated in his office, sharing a pot of scarce coffee with Axel, Herr Heidl spoke of the demands on his own firm. He acknowledged that among other privileges of the Armaments Minister—"my sometime associate"—was to set priorities that "will involve—us."

Axel interrupted. "Franz, there is *no way* the Armaments Minister of the Third Reich can use up any more of *my* time than he's using right now."

Heidl didn't need to be reminded. "I know what you're doing for them. I'll look at your complete docket tonight. In general, how is it going with Camp Joni?"

"I've done the basic construction designs. But Governor Frank in Warsaw—of all people!—is telling *me* he is short of construction labor. That's what he tells me in his morning calls. In his afternoon calls he tells me how urgent his Joni deadline is. But, let's face it, the workers will somehow materialize. Governor Frank has great resources when it comes to producing laborers."

Axel wasn't indirect when with Franz Heidl. They spoke the same language. Poland was long ago, two and a half years back, western Europe, eighteen months ago. Today there were 257 German divisions under arms. The Third Reich was militarily triumphant, but the strain was increasing. It hadn't surprised Axel when the edict went out that, henceforward, sixteen-year-olds would be required to report for military training. *That would have meant Sebastian, if he had stayed on in Hamburg,* Axel reflected. Forced labor, used covertly after the invasion of Poland, was now openly "recruited" from the conquered countries. Axel Reinhard didn't doubt that, in violation of accepted procedure, prisoners of war from the eastern front would be put to work; though he allowed himself to wonder—Doing what? Eighteen-year-olds trained to fire guns aren't trained as plumbers or electricians or carpenters. Lodz, the Polish city south of Warsaw from which he worked, was not an industrial center. It was excluded, even, from the main east-west rail line.

Camp Joni shall be structured to contain three thousand military prisoners. Those were the words heading up the commission by the War Ministry to the Heidl engineering firm. Beginning late in December 1942, the concrete foundations would be laid. Axel Reinhard, in charge, sketched out for review by his partners in Hamburg an electrical generating plant, military towers, the prisoner barracks, the command post, and the recreation yard.

But on the afternoon of Axel's departure for Hamburg, the importunate Hans Frank had circumvented him, sending a telegram directly to Heidl & Sons imposing an unconventional priority on what was to be done at Joni. After arriving in Hamburg, Axel telephoned Governor Frank, who reaffirmed that what was needed—immediately—was construction of those elements of the camp that had to do with security. "What we need first, Herr Reinhard, is staff personnel enclosures. Get them set up first. String up the barbed wire and the searchlights and the towers. The amenities will have to take their turn." Axel objected. There would have to be human shelter for the prisoners, the temperature in the Lodz area in winter descended to near zero. What he had got back from Governor Frank was unambiguous: "Adopt the Fuehrer's priorities, not those of Heidl & Sons."

The two partners were discussing the implications of the alteration in construction plans. "That schedule means, to me, Franz," said Axel, "that my round trips, Hamburg to Lodz, can't go on. I am going to have to live at Joni until the camp is pretty well completed."

"Wars do such things to us, Axel," Heidl said, not disguising the weariness he felt with the cliché he had used so often, and heard used so often. "But remember this. While it's Governor Frank who sets priorities, you are a partner of Heidl & Sons. And whatever we construct, even prisoner of war camps, our work will continue to conform to the highest standards of civil engineering."

Axel drove his Skoda to 38 Hempelstrasse, parked it, and soon pressed the elevator button for the ninth floor. The city street was no longer well tended. Sidewalk cracks had proliferated, grass obtruding at both sides. The hallway of the apartment building was without the trademark flower pot. Entering his apartment, after the six-week absence in Poland, he was reminded of the genteel deterioration of bachelor life. Pretty much everything was as Annabelle had left it. He didn't need to open the closet door to confirm that there were boy's clothes there as well as the odd piece of clothing of Annabelle's, ostentatiously left behind to give the impression that she would be coming back. The bookcases were full, mostly with books he or Annabelle had read what seemed decades ago. The furniture was undisturbed, only superficially dusted by the landlord's fourteen-year-old granddaughter. The framed family pictures were prominent on the circular table between the two armchairs. As he looked, almost dutifully, at the picture of his parents, the doctor and his nurse/wife, he could not feel sorry that they had died young, his father pre-Hitler, his mother after Hitler came to power but before the militarization.

Axel removed a paper sack from his briefcase and withdrew from it a ham sandwich and bottle of beer, setting them down on the coffee table. He lowered himself into the armchair, turning on the reading light by the bookcase and tilting it over his shoulder. Wearily, he pulled the newspaper from his pocket, laid it on his lap, and bit off a corner of the sandwich. He put it down and reached in the drawer for the bottle opener. The beer opened, he set it on the table, then paused, staring out the window into the winter blackness.

He removed the sandwich from his lap, placing it back on the table, and slowly reached over for the framed photograph of Annabelle and Sebastian, taken that afternoon in the summer of 1939 at the Hamburg Fair. After a moment he altered the light to shine without creating a reflecting glare. Axel studied the face of his wife, renewing his silent pledge that one heavenly day ahead he would be reunited with her and, more prosaically, that one day ahead he might devise a safe way to get word to her.

Word of what?—he interrupted his desultory thought. Not

much more than word that he was alive. What more could be said, could be risked?

He stared down again at the full face and full head of hair, the hint of a smile of surprise at the camera that was pointed at her, the bright brown eyes with their searching look.

Was there anything at all in that face that was discernible as—Jewish?

After she and Sebastian sailed, Axel had looked through an old scrapbook with the pictures of the Leddihn family, proud Austrian grandfather and grandmother; the blond young man, her twenty-year-old brother, standing stiffly at their side, Henrietta's hand over his shoulder. There was nothing in that scrapbook about Henrietta's life after she married and left Munich.

Well, if Annabelle couldn't be said to look Jewish, what about their son? Did *Sebastian* look Jewish? Look, more exactly, *one-quarter* Jewish?

He remembered the words of the Gestapo's Captain Gradler as clearly as when they were spoken at the Rialto Hotel, informing Axel that he could not be permitted to sail with wife and son:

"Alois William Steiner was a Jew," Captain Gradler had said. *"He was the father of your Annabelle, who is therefore also a Jew. And of course, Sebastian is her—your—Jewish son."*

Why, oh why did Henrietta have to write and tell Axel about her first marriage—to the Jew by whom she became pregnant. The Jewish father of his wife. The true father of Annabelle Linda Chapin Reinhard.

Henrietta had had to tell him because, he shuddered in disgust, there were actually people all over the Third Reich who walked about with magnifying glasses attempting to trace, or to establish, evidence of Jewishness. Henrietta had written that letter to him in 1938. It had been addressed to his office, to escape detection from her own daughter. She had written to warn Axel about the danger of staying on in Germany. To warn Axel meant to divulge Henrietta's family secret. Henrietta had left home to marry a Jew, conceive by him a daughter who, in 1938, was living in Hamburg, ignorant that her biological father had been Jewish. Living in Germany with her son, within easy reach of the dreaded *Einsatzgruppe*.

If he could manage to get a letter to Annabelle now, from Germany, athwart the ban against any communication with anybody in any country with which Germany was at war, would he reveal to her, tell Annabelle, what her own mother hadn't told her?

Why? The Leddihns were dead. Who else now knew about Sebastian's forebears?

Other, of course, than the Gestapo.

CHAPTER FOURTEEN

Lodz, February 1942

Lodz, only eighty miles southwest of Warsaw, lay in resolutely unglamorous potato farm country. Axel Reinhard spent his days and nights at the Staski Hotel. He had no trouble requisitioning additional rooms to serve as offices. There he kept the blueprints and construction memoranda and met with the foremen and, often, with the adjutant of Governor Frank.

He had devised means of dealing with Frank, his fellow German, telling him what he had to know, and talking around what he didn't want Frank to know, let alone dwell upon. It was less easy to manipulate Frank's adjutant, the Polish Captain Stefan Plekhov, whose knowledge of German was fluent. The adjutant's eyes were wide open, recording fastidiously everything going on at the construction site twenty miles south.

The orders had been to proceed to construct the security personnel placements and Axel had undertaken to do so, but he reminded Captain Plekhov that he could not construct efficient searchlight towers without first building a generating plant. This was now accomplished, using Polish forced labor. The workers included carpenters, engineers, and electricians. They were all periodically egged on to work fourteen-hour days. Exhortations and injunctions and threats were relayed to the workers by the construction chief. They came across to the workers in a Germanized Polish through the hoarse loudspeakers that surrounded the forty-acre compound. What the workers heard boiled down to: *Do more, or expect to hear your name called out to meet with the military court.* That court convened every Wednesday to review the performance of individual miscreants. They did not need to be told of the consequences of poor or insufficient work. Twice the adjutant Plekhov had taken the microphone to speak in his native Polish tongue, inveighing against delinquents, resisters, or shirkers. Captain Plekhov at one point asked Axel himself to deliver, as chief engineer, an intimidating message to the workers. Axel avoided the commission by pleading an insufficient knowledge of Polish.

As soon as he had completed his generating plant, Axel, negotiating through a German-speaking Polish foreman, directed carpenters and plumbers to take odd bits of time from the construction of the watchtowers in order to get on with the command post. Once the initial part was built, he could live at Joni, eliminating the tedious, and sometimes arduous, daily drive to the hotel in his Kubelwagen, so often done in freezing weather.

By February, he had his own quarters at Camp Joni, close to what would be the main entrance to the camp. He had a bedroom, a rudimentary kitchen, and a large separate room that served as the central office of the Joni operation. There he had his drafting tables and clipboards with construction schedules and, for necessary visitors, wooden chairs and coat hooks.

The eastern end of the suite was a plain, temporary wooden wall. When time came to complete the building, it would extend to additional offices for camp personnel and as headquarters for the *Totenkopfverbande*, the professional camp guards. Opposite, on the western end, Axel's architect had provided that the office of the construction superintendent should have two windows. From these Axel could see out to where the barracks would rise, and see also the large clearing that would serve for whatever congregations the camp commander, operating from his own headquarters outside the gate, ordained. The Kommandant would need only to go through the gate to his microphone to address the prisoners directly.

It was through one of those windows that Axel would get his first view of the tenants of Camp Joni when they arrived. Ignoring the palpably preposterous orders from Warsaw—that no provisions were to be made for the inmates until all else had been attended to—Axel contrived to get a detachment of laborers and carpenters to work on the first of the planned stretch of four-story barracks. He had persuaded Captain Plekhov, in personal exchanges, of the need for *something* in which to house the scheduled prisoners.

It seemed odd to need to inform him on a matter so rudimentary. Perhaps the problem was Plekhov's inexperience in construction scheduling. Before the Nazi invasion, Plekhov had been a librarian at the University of Cracow, highly literate to be sure, but librarians, Axel reminded himself, lead thoroughly indoor lives. Axel simply explained to him that it would not be possible to contain 100 Russian soldiers, *let alone three thousand Russian soldiers,* without providing them with basic elements of survival: food, sanitary facilities, and shelter. The adjutant was now standing in his overcoat, immediately outside the door of Axel's new headquarters. "They cannot sleep in the open, Captain Plekhov. Until late spring, they would simply perish from the cold."

"They will perish from something, Herr Reinhard."

"Goddamit, Plekhov. We have been commissioned to build a camp for prisoners of war. I came here to supervise the construction of exactly that, a camp for captured soldiers. I was not entirely surprised that you were depending—that we were depending—" Axel forced himself to remember that, although he was living and working in Poland, he was doing work for Germany, work for his native country—"that because of the exigencies of war we would need to depend on—forced labor. And of course the prisoners will not be coming to Joni of their own free will. They are men defeated at war and don't expect tender treatment. But it is hardly the intention of Governor Frank to bring them to Joni exclusively for the purpose of letting them freeze to death at night or die of malnutrition."

It was late in the afternoon and it had got dark in that hard winter country, the open fields cold and friendless. Stefan Plekhov turned to Axel. "Herr Reinhard, let us go in and sit down for a minute. Is there any point in discussing these problems outdoors in my overcoat, while standing?"

"Of course not." Axel opened the door and nodded toward a wooden chair, taking for himself the revolving stool by the workboard.

"And something else, Herr Reinhard. I am an older man. In fact, I do not mind telling you that today—February 22nd, 1942—is my seventieth birthday! Would you mind very much giving me a glass of vodka?" Captain Plekhov chuckled. "There is more vodka produced in the area of Lodz than in any equivalent area anywhere in the civilized world, except of course that no part of the world is truly civilized that doesn't produce vodka!"

Axel experienced a wave of relief in the informality of the language. He found himself, after hearing only a few words, in the company of someone in the huge, omnivorous, demanding Nazi Lodz machine with whom human conversation seemed conceivable, even plausible. What he had just now heard from the governor's adjutant was something other than the utilitarian conversations he had become used to since arriving in Lodz. Mostly these conversations were had over the telephone, burdened by the conceptual difficulties of conflicting priorities, generals talking to engineers, political deputies to architects. Now he was face-to-face with someone who talked as a human being about human subjects.

"Yes, Captain Plekhov. I have some vodka. And yes, I congratulate you on your feast day."

"*Feast* day? We don't celebrate feast days anymore."

"Birthday." Reinhard raised his glass.

CHAPTER FIFTEEN

Lodz, May 1942

It was May now and the twelve blockhouses were if not quite complete, habitable; prisoner-habitable. The camp's hospital unit was done and the camp administration office, the Kommandant's office, the SS guardhouse, and the kitchen. Camp Joni would be open for the POWs late in the month. An exact date had not been set. Captain Plekhov called from Warsaw.

"I will need to meet with you."

Plekhov was always welcome at Joni even when he brought, as he almost always did, a new demand from Governor Frank or from the Berlin military command. Two weeks ago it had been an order to increase the capacity of Camp Joni to contain not three but no less than five thousand prisoners. This did not completely surprise Axel. He listened to the news from the BBC night after night on the shortwave. Its use was proscribed by the military command in Warsaw but Axel had quietly reasoned that that order could not reasonably apply to him inasmuch as he was a civilian engineer from Hamburg, Germany, residing in Joni, Poland, only in order to do business for the army, which he was hardly a member of. The news from London was that both Russian and German casualties were heavy.

So, then, he knew something of military tidings. He had been appalled, the week before, to hear that the British had been able to send one thousand bombers over German skies, devastating Cologne. Would one of those bombs have fallen on the great Cologne cathedral? Once again he was face-to-face with his most carefully guarded secret, that his sentiments were not unequivocally on the side of his native country. He had had the same problem for two years and kept banishing it to the back of his mind; but an event such as the bombing of Cologne yanked it to the front of his mind, crying out for a commitment. It seemed starker, somehow, than the military casualties, which were the staples of wars.

He couldn't help but feel pride in the Nazi military accomplishments in western Europe and to marvel at the generalship of Adolf Hitler. But he needed psychological satisfaction from his own work. He was a truly accomplished engineer and had superintended the creation of a prisoner of war camp under seriously handicapped circumstances and done so on schedule. He would need eventually to give consideration to the end for which his work was being put, transient quarters for bloodied Russian soldiers. He didn't care who won the war, he decided, provided he could then be reunited with Annabelle and Sebastian.

On the matter of the incoming flood of prisoners of war, what more was there to be said other than that, in wars, there are prisoners? And when the news came in on the BBC about the Soviet spring counterattack on the Kharkov front, he knew that the volume of prisoners on both sides had to increase—Russian prisoners held by Germans, German prisoners held by Russians. When informed by Plekhov that quarters were needed for yet more prisoners, he pondered the alternatives. They were to build six more blockhouses, which could not be done in less than sixty days, or increase the density of prisoners in those already constructed. He had designed each of the buildings to house four hundred prisoners in three stories.

Plekhov made the decision for him: Headquarters could not wait for two new blockhouses? Double up.

The friendship having taken hold, Plekhov used a playful cipher in arranging his visits to Joni. On the telephone he would schedule a "day" visit, or an "evening" visit. The day visits bore directly on problems at hand, usually having to do with personnel: Who, e.g., was especially needed to complete one or another of the camp's requirements? Evening visits meant there was business to be transacted but that the adjutant, arriving some time after six, would expect companionship.

He'd sit and bring out from his traveling case his own contribution to their little feast—some cheese, sausage, or ham. Axel was especially grateful for the occasional jar of honey. Axel would contribute the vodka, which he had a weekly supply of, by special bargaining with one of the Polish foremen, whose uncle worked in a distillery.

"You don't have to tell me where you *get it* from, Axel," Plekhov said, bowing his head in a courtly manner before emptying his glass. If so, Axel rejoindered, that was the only aspect of the Camp Joni enterprise he had ever found Stefan Plekhov incurious about. Vodka glass in hand, Axel drew the shade on one of the two windows (it was light outside now, in early May). They chatted.

Plekhov asked for more vodka. He accepted the glass, then set it down.

"Herr Reinhard," he addressed Axel with unconventional formality, "the orders have come down from General Glucks of the SS. The requisitions for Camp Joni have been altered."

Axel felt a searing ache in his stomach. *Could it be . . .*

"—Camp Joni will now serve as a concentration camp."

Axel drew breath. "A concentration camp to serve what purpose?"

"To serve the great purpose of a final solution to the Jewish question."

The words Axel went on to hear might have been taken, verbatim, from a General Directive from Berlin. And Plekhov spoke then without any of the ironic nuance Axel had come to expect from the university librarian-turned-adjutant to the Nazi governor of Poland.

"The added facilities will need to be built. These are—extensive productions. They require decontamination quarters, gas chambers, and then crematoria."

Plekhov paused. He looked over at his glass of vodka, untouched. "It transpires that the means of eliminating the corpses were until quite recently primitive and undesirable. The bodies of the . . . enemy simply . . . accumulated outside and were consumed by kerosine fire. Our scientists have developed crematoria that take care of this problem . . . nicely. You will need first to inspect elsewhere such facilities as are needed to be constructed here. At Camp Birkenau there are such, which dispose of over three thousand undesirables per day. That is far larger than the quota SS Obergruppenfuehrer Glucks has assigned to Camp Joni. But the point of it is we must—you must—familiarize yourself with working facilities. Which is why I have here an itinerary, with the required authorizations, for your travel to Camp Birkenau. I would expect that you could arrange to make that trip within—shall we say, one week? Is that reasonable?"

Axel Reinhard could not put off a formal reaction indefinitely. So he sought to frame it with some knowledge of Plekhov's character and sensibilities. He adopted the formal address that Plekhov had used.

"Captain Plekhov, I'm afraid you have got the wrong man. I

work for the firm of Heidl & Sons and we have undertaken, in recognition of our obligations as faithful citizens, to construct your prisoner of war camp. But the—other—what you speak of—would not be an enterprise in which we would," he sought a formulation as unprovocative as he could come up with, "deem ourselves competent to engage in."

Now Captain Plekhov did bring the vodka to his mouth, swallowing it down at once. "You just finished saying that Heidl & Sons undertook to construct a prisoner of war facility because it acknowledges, how did you put it? your 'obligations.' Well, the extermination camps are a part of government policy, and in time of war, government policy must prevail, eliminating such flexibility as, in less stressful times, the government might indulge a firm of civil engineers."

Axel was baffled. What if he were to say, quite simply, that he could not engage in an activity that Christian tenets prohibited. Would he not hear back, simply, that the Third Reich dealt with state, not church, matters?

He did not want to ask questions about what was in prospect for Joni that would require Captain Plekhov to plead the—rightness? justification?—of the Reichpolicy. He would not elicit from him the fearful language of Hitler and Himmler and Goebbels and Streicher explaining the need for a "final solution" to the Jewish question.

He'd need, simply, to say—no.

"You will have to get another engineer."

"Ah but Axel, that is not so easy to contrive, given the terrible wartime scarcities. Besides which there is no living human being as familiar as you with the work that has already gone into the construction of our camp."

Axel would simply need to say it again. He struggled to keep his voice down. "Captain Plekhov, the answer is no."

"We had to consider that contingency."

He stood up and looked out the window, turning his back on Axel.

"I have in my briefcase a letter from General Glucks confirming your commission to proceed with the construction I have outlined."

Axel waited to be told what the alternative was.

Plekhov was silent. But finally he turned.

"If you decline, you will be arrested for sedition. You will be tried, and hanged."

Plekhov turned to the door and opened it to the darkening light. He turned his head back. "You should reflect, Axel, that others have had to come to terms with life as it is lived. In greater Germany. In the year of Our Lord, 1942."

He closed the door.

CHAPTER SIXTEEN

August 1945

Second Lieutenant Sebastian Reinhard showered gratefully in the bachelor officers' quarters at Camp Gordon. He wondered idly whether he would ever again leave the state of Georgia. He had had basic training at Camp Wheeler in Macon, then Officers' Candidate School in Columbus, and now another camp in Georgia, Camp Gordon in Augusta. An important difference: He was now a trainer, not a trainee; an officer, not an enlisted man. A better life.

But that hardly shielded him, he reminded himself in the hot shower, from hour after hour of hot grimy work overseeing the recruits' essential training as infantry soldiers. On this point Sebastian had been instructed thoroughly, at basic and infantry school. He had mastered, as well as could be done without combat experience, the infantry soldier's discipline. Lieutenant Sebastian Reinhard, Army of the United States, just over one year earlier inducted in Phoenix and sent across the continent to begin military life.

Why does the army *do such things*? Pick you up in Arizona—which is next door to plenty of infantry training centers in Colorado, in neighboring California, and in Texas—and send you on an endless trip, cramped sardine-style aboard a troop train to Georgia, at the other end of the country? Well, he supposed, some ledger somewhere must have informed G-2 (the logistics division of the army) that Camp Wheeler's inventory of trainees was less crowded than others'. It wasn't worth it, as a rule, to try to figure out why this or that happened in the army. At least they won the fucking war, he said to himself, turning off the shower, applying his towel, slipping it around his hips, and setting out down the hall to his room—"Hi, Felton"—he passed by a fellow officer. "Yeah, water's plenty hot. Everything's hot at Camp Gordon." Lieutenant Felton Horchak, a towel around his own waist, nodded. "And the twenty-miler is next week."

Maybe the weather will cool off, Sebastian thought. On the other hand it hadn't cooled off in Georgia in August of last year. Georgia just went from very hot before September to very cold after October. The twenty-mile hike wearing full field equipment was the last ordeal of the eighteen-week basic infantry training cycle. It meant eight hours of marching (ten minutes' rest the first hour, five minutes' rest each of the succeeding seven hours). As platoon leader he would not be lugging the sixty-pound field pack the trainees were burdened with, nor the sixteen-pound M-1 rifle; and he'd wear a thin plastic helmet liner instead of the heavy steel combat model and he would carry the slimmer backpack without all the components of a pup tent. The carbine strapped over his shoulder weighed only ten pounds.

But otherwise the long march was identical to what he had endured last year at Camp Wheeler, before his selection for officers' training had dispatched him to Fort Benning.

Dressed—khaki pants, khaki shirt, name tag (no tie), gold lieutenant's bar on his lapel, shoes shined—he walked down the stairs to the officers' common room. The Georgia sun was not quite through with its victims, at 1730, and it was hot in the common room, too, though removed from the sun. He walked to the bar and nodded at Jenkins, the orderly.

"Usual Coke, Lieutenant?"

Sebastian nodded and pulled a five-cent piece from his pocket. He had quite a few nickels, he thought contentedly, earning now $150 every month—augmented by the monthly $25 check from his grandmother in Phoenix. That plus a second $25, the money order from his mother in London. The monthly check had begun when, as an enlisted man, he was receiving only $50 in monthly pay. He had tried, when commissioned, to stop it.

"Dear Mama, don't send me any more money. Use it for—let me see, what can you hope to buy in London, 1945? The answer to that in U.S. military language would be—dead Nazis." He crossed out the two words, then scratched over them, in an attempt to make them illegible. "You can buy things at the PX, of course. So can I. Cigarettes are 10¢ and the *Reader's Digest* is 15¢. Mama, would you like me to send you—never mind. I can't send you anything you can't get yourself. So I'll just send you lots of love. I won't tell you anything more about infantry life because there isn't anything more to tell you about infantry life different from what I've been telling you now for... fourteen months, ever since I was drafted! Fourteen months plus ten months since you left Oma and me that sad day. I know you can't tell me what you have been working on, but *I can*—but I love you too much to tell you about my fascinating long hikes in Georgia sands and snaking under barbed wire when live tracer ammunition is firing over you, and doing a forced march at five the next morning, oh, *aren't you jealous*, dear Mama? And just think of it, they didn't need me in Japan to close down that theater, all they needed was an atomic bomb. In Oma's last letter she didn't say anything on the subject of dropping an atom bomb on a civilian population. Guess she gave up protesting, though when they did bomb Munich, that letter was *blistering*! Dumb question, do you have any idea when you'll be back? Dumb question #2, do I have any idea when *I'll* be out and free to go back to school? I'll show you mine if you'll show me yours. That's a play on a dirty joke. Ask the chief of intelligence about it. XXX Sebby."

He hadn't dwelled on the question he had pondered, the killing of one hundred thousand Japanese civilians with a single bomb. Well, we did that to the Germans, too. He wondered about what he had read in *Time* magazine about critics who said that the bombing of Dresden had no military justification. Personally, he had to admit, he was very glad that the bomb had been dropped at Hiroshima. It lessened dramatically the likelihood that he would have to practice firing bullets not at targets, but at human beings. He admitted there was a moral question out there, as the writer in *Time* had maintained—the whole question of war crimes. But he wasn't a theologian, he comforted himself.

He sat with his Coke at the card table and talked with Felton and shuffled the cards for their customary presupper game of Russian Bank. Jack Yardley, coming into the room from the hall, spotted him. "Seb, there's an envelope for you on the board at the CC's. I'd have pulled it off, but I wasn't sure you'd be here."

"Thanks, Jack. Hmm, where else, except here, would I be? Is there an opening tonight at Radio City Music Hall?"

"No. But the movie they're showing at our place is *Captain Eddie*, and I'm going. Terrific dogfights and stunt shots, I've heard. You guys want to go? After chow?"

"Count me in," Felton said.

"I'll probably go, too," Sebastian said. "But first I've got to check the bulletin board. I haven't been there. It might be I've pulled Duty Officer tonight. Hope not. Midnight's not my favorite hour to do duty."

The envelope was there, a message from the battalion commander. Sebastian was instructed to report to regimental headquarters at 0900 the following day. "We have made arrangements with Captain Hand to get a substitute platoon leader to meet your platoon," the order said.

He thought to show his message to Felton, but decided not to. He told Felton only that an appointment had been scheduled for him. He stopped. He thought suddenly—could it be personal news that was to be given him? If his mother had died in London, how would they pass the word along to her army son? By telegram? Annabelle Reinhard, after all, was in government service, however secret. Would this call for special personal treatment, if that was the unbelievable news? Would somebody in the army be delegated to break the news to him personally? *Mama dead?*

He would try to put in a long distance call to his grandmother, just in case she had had word.

"Sorry," Sebastian said to his friends sitting about the lounge. "I can't go to the flicks with you. I have to put in a call to Phoenix. God knows how long I'll be standing in line. I figure two, three hours." They walked off together to the mess hall.

He was there as ordered. The long flat building east of the parade ground had been constructed before the First World War and suppurated with age—paint peeling on the entrance door, windows stuck open. The right quarter of the building had fresh unpainted wood, patchwork wartime maintenance.

He was early, and scrutinized the information board on which, twice a day, world news bulletins were posted. His eyes turned searchingly for news with military implications that bore on him. General Douglas MacArthur had made a statement in Tokyo. He reported smooth progress in arranging for the military occupation of Japan, announcing that "a drastic cut" in the number of troops originally thought to be required in the Pacific Theater could now safely be predicted. Within six months—Sebastian read on, eagerly—the number of U.S. troops required would be "not more than two hundred thousand." Sebastian had celebrated, with a dozen other platoon leaders, the recent night of V-J Day. A great national victory, but celebrated also as meaning that they probably would not have to risk their lives fighting their way to Tokyo, island by island.

On the other hand.... He looked up from the bulletin board reflectively. Since he'd be stuck *God knew how long* in the army in Georgia—Macon, Columbus, Augusta—he might actually welcome duty in Japan. Another news bulletin on the board was especially heartening: Undersecretary of the Army Robert Patterson testified before a Senate committee that the army was demobilizing at the rate of ten thousand soldiers per day and expected to have discharged six million by the first of July 1946. But, Secretary Patterson had said, he saw no prospect of the elimination of the draft.

Sebastian did some quick arithmetic. As of the day he was drafted, August 10, 1944, how many men were there in the armed forces? He frowned. Certainly more than six million. That meant it would be only *after* July 1946, at the rate of ten thousand per day, that he could hope to be released. He didn't have enough seniority to be included with the first six million men qualifying to go home.

There was a second bulletin from Tokyo. Imperial Prince Higashikuni Naruhiko—Sebastian pitied the reporter responsible for writing down that name and bearing the responsibility for correct spelling—said at his very first press conference in Tokyo that the Japanese war and navy ministries would be abolished and democratic processes broadened. *Without giving details*, he read, *the Prime Minister said the Japanese themselves already have started to punish war criminals. He denies that the Emperor is a war criminal, saying he was led into the war by the Cabinet.*

Everybody will say that kind of thing, Sebastian thought.

He looked at his watch and then walked through the doorway to the duty officer sitting behind the long counter. He spoke to a master sergeant.

"I'm Lieutenant Reinhard." He handed the sergeant, a large man with a benign face, perhaps fifty years old, the order.

"Yes sir. Down the hall to Room 27. You're expected."

His heart began to beat faster as he walked down the corridor. He knocked on the door.

It was opened by an officer. "Lieutenant Reinhard?"

"Yes sir."

"That is Mr. Heinrich over there. I'm Major Stuyvesant."

Sebastian shook hands. He was asked to sit down.

CHAPTER SEVENTEEN

Camp Gordon, 1945

The major spoke without preamble. "Reinhard, you are being considered for a role as an interpreter at the war crimes tribunal assembling in Nuremberg. Are you aware of the International Military Tribunal?"

"Yes sir. I read about it in last week's issue of *Time* magazine."

"We will need to hear you out on a number of points. But let us begin at the beginning." The lean, prematurely gray major wore a single decoration below his combat infantry badge, the small yet imposing Silver Star, awarded for conspicuous gallantry in action. He leaned over a clipboard and made notes as he spoke.

"Your files show that you were born in Germany, is that correct?"

"Yes sir, Hamburg."

"And your father was?" The major's mustache tilted up, in an interrogatory mode.

"A civil engineer. A graduate of MIT."

"When?"

"The class of 1924."

"You were born, I see, in January 1926. The records do not

show when you left Germany to live in America. We have only that you have a high school diploma from Phoenix Central High School, class of 1944. The dossier lists your father as deceased. We need to know where he died."

"We don't know. I don't know."

"Was he a military casualty?"

"I don't know."

Major Stuyvesant put down his clipboard. "What do you mean, you don't know?"

"We received notice in July 1943 that he was deceased."

"Received notice from whom?"

"Headquarters, German War Ministry, Berlin."

Major Stuyvesant said nothing, but made another note. "Can you give me the text of the death notice?"

"All it said was that the Command regretted informing—my mother—of my father's death in the service of the Fatherland, and that when victory came, his services would be honored."

"What *were* those services?"

"Sir, we don't know. We had not heard from him since 1941 and that letter revealed nothing."

"Is it reasonable to suppose that he was doing military or paramilitary work?"

"I think that's reasonable to assume about everybody in Germany over the age of sixteen. Sir."

Major Stuyvesant continued his jotting and looked over at Heinrich, a civilian, wearing shirt and tie notwithstanding 100-degree heat only slightly alleviated by the electric fan. "There is no point in pursuing any question at this end without first establishing the most basic question, which has to do with your knowledge of the language. We can assume that you are fluent in German?"

"Yes sir."

The voice of Mr. Heinrich came in. He spoke now in German with what seemed deliberate speed, designed to test the subject's language capacity. It was a voice and language that betrayed a hint of hierarchical impatience, of the kind exhibited by schoolmasters and master sergeants and emperors. The interrogation was hardly in the style of Major Stuyvesant's. Mr. Heinrich said: "Answer me in full. What was your father's opinion of the Fuehrer?"

Sebastian was taken aback. He had expected a query that would permit him to demonstrate, simply, his command of the language. Instead he had been given a question that required of him a conclusory account of the great unsettled questions he had lived with ever since, at age thirteen, it dawned on him that mother and son could not wish father success, back in Germany, in the enterprise in which he was undoubtedly involved. But that conclusion had come in bits and pieces, consolidating only some time after the implications of those post–Pearl Harbor days were absorbed. His father's Germany was at war with his mother's native America, the country in which Sebastian was now living, had been schooled in, and had been prepared to fight for.

He had no trouble with the German words. His trouble was with the arrangement of his thoughts.

"Herr Heinrich, that question asks me to put in order all the questions I and my mother have lived with since the separation from my father. All I can say is, I am committed to the service of my country, and I have no—" he stumbled for the word, "no knowledge of—and, no *need* to learn about—my father's last years."

Heinrich began to speak his next question, but Sebastian interrupted him. "I should say this, that I loved and admired my father."

Heinrich nodded. And then, "Are you familiar with German

military nomenclature, which of course would be required in the proposed assignment?"

"As a matter of fact, sir, I am."

"What is an *Oberschutze*?"

"That is the equivalent of a Private First Class."

"Would you know what its equivalent would be in the SS?"

"That would be a *Stummann*."

"And an *Oberst*?"

"Would be a Colonel. In the SS—" Sebastian paused and smiled shyly. Was he maybe—showing off? "—more exactly, *Standartenfuehrer*."

Heinrich nodded, with a hint of appreciation. "If asked to render into German from the English, how would you handle: 'Did you at any time record your objection to that command, and if so, is there any written record of your doing so?'"

Sebastian spoke out the lines, with a few pauses, regrouping German syntax to accommodate English structure. But he was dissatisfied with his handling of the last phrase, "...of your doing so." He corrected himself: "*Das sie es so semacht haben*."

He turned then to Major Stuyvesant, as if needing to account for his competence. "You see, Major, at home in Phoenix we always spoke in German because my Austrian grandmother always preferred German. So I didn't stop speaking in German, except at school and at work, until I was drafted."

The major nodded. He looked over at Heinrich. Heinrich pointed to the door and opened the five fingers of his other hand.

The major understood. "Lieutenant Reinhard, kindly step outside. I will call you back in a few minutes."

Sebastian saluted and went out.

He paced in the direction of the entrance a few steps and paused over the neatly posted issue of the *New York Times*. The six-column headline announced the surrender of the Japanese.

He began to read the week-old story. "*President Truman announced at 7:00 P.M. that Japan has surrendered unconditionally. Commmanders in the field have issued cease-fire orders and the president announced that August 15 and 16 will be holidays with pay for federal employees. The president's announcement is expected to launch a worldwide celebration. . . .*" He read through the long story.

He heard the voice of Major Stuyvesant beckoning to him. He walked back into the room. The major did not ask him to sit down. He said merely, "We have the information we wish and will recommend your inclusion in the program. We are very pressed for time in the matter of the prosecution of the criminals. We will file our report with the regimental commander, recommending a reasonable leave of a few days before your departure from New York for Hamburg and on to Nuremberg, where the prosecution is laying the foundations for its case. You will receive orders, possibly within a few days. Meanwhile, you are to continue your duties with the infantry training program."

The major nodded his head slightly in dismissal, and returned Sebastian's salute.

Heinrich addressed him in German: "You are a quite exceptional young man, Herr Oberleutnant."

Sebastian returned the civility. "*Danke sehr,*" bowing his head slightly.

CHAPTER EIGHTEEN

August 1945

When on the hot afternoon of August 27 Sebastian actually saw his travel orders, he stopped breathing from excitement. Second Lieutenant Sebastian Reinhard was instructed to use public conveyance, Augusta, Georgia, to New York, New York, and report to the Transportation Officer, Third Army, on August 31, at Pier 42 in New York City, where he would embark for Hamburg, Germany, aboard the SS *Europa.*

He ran across the parade ground at full speed and bounded up the stairs of the bachelor officers' quarters. He pounded on the door of Felton Horchak.

"What is it? Come in."

In his excitement Sebastian said nothing. He thrust his mimeographed order under the eyes of Horchak, who was seated at his desk, pen in hand. "Just read it," was all Sebastian could manage.

Horchak tilted his shoulder to light up the text. He nodded his long head as he read. ". . . so you need to get your ass to New York City in two days. That shouldn't kill you, Sebby, old boy. At the rate we go at it at Gordon, you could walk there—forced march speed—in two days."

"Felton! Listen! *That's the same boat my mother and I came over on!* And guess what—sailing *on the same day!* August 31st! August 31st, 1939, was when we took off! The next day was when Hitler moved into Poland. So it'll be—exactly—" he mumbled his way through the addition—"39-40-41-42-43-44-45—exactly six years! Gosh. Six fucking years and I get to go to the same port I left from on the same boat. I mean, that's something else. Only this time the boat is U.S. military property!"

"Yup. There was a world war in between."

Sebastian Reinhard was brought to earth.

"Yes. And we won it. That means the *Europa* belongs to us. And this time around, Uncle Sam pays my fare across the Atlantic."

A company jeep was at hand, as arranged by the duty officer. Earlier in the day Sebastian had a brief good-bye with Captain Hand, the diminutive, tough company commander. He was in charge of the four platoons, each with four twelve-man squads, commanded by four second lieutenant platoon leaders, and of the company staff of one staff sergeant, six corporals, and four orderlies. If Captain Hand had been told by battalion headquarters what the reason was for detaching one of his four platoon leaders after only fourteen weeks of the eighteen-week training cycle, he gave no indication of it to the departing lieutenant. Sebastian wondered why. Surely it wasn't an assignment shrouded by security? He hadn't hesitated to tell his fellow officers what it was he was being assigned to do. But Captain Hand was a man of few words. His departing amenity would be confined to the ritual, "Good luck." Sebastian was pleased and surprised to hear his company commander add, "You did a good job with your platoon."

Three hours later his erstwhile platoon, led by a company corporal, pending the arrival of a replacement officer, returned from afternoon drill. The trainees were sweaty and silent after a hot sand-besotted afternoon's work on bayonet combat. Sebastian shook the hands of the forty-eight men individually. By the time he was done, Horchak, from Platoon C, was there. He grabbed the barracks bag from Sebastian, carried it to the jeep waiting in front of Company headquarters, and plunked it down in the back compartment. He and Lieutenant Jack Ponsonby from Platoon A climbed into the two back seats. They would see their buddy off.

The corporal at the wheel, they traveled the sixteen sandy miles on roads paved and unpaved. Approaching the city, they came upon the asphalt road that, bisecting the town, led to the railroad station. Augusta had golf courses and a steeplechase training park, but otherwise it was simply another Southern town burned down by General Sherman eighty-one years earlier.

They were at the depot in time to have coffee. Sebastian did not say very much. Jack talked about *Anchors Aweigh*, the movie that would play that night, and about his determination to see it "even though that means leaving off cards early with Horchak." Felton spoke of his loneliness for the cool of northern Wisconsin, where he grew up in Two Rivers, "right on the lake. You find this hot, Sebby, you should feel the *cold* of that water!"

They waited for the train to come by. "Let me know where you end up," Horchak said. "I have your Phoenix address, and I'll send you a postcard from Tokyo." Sebastian mounted the train steps and, from the railroad car's vestibule, exchanged a playful salute with his fellow platoon leaders, not without feeling.

In the Pullman car, sitting opposite a middle-aged woman engrossed in her book, he waited for the porter who would convert the space into an over-and-under sleeper. He applied himself to his paper pad, writing to his mother.

"Saying good-bye in the military is pretty sad. I've done it three times now, leaving Wheeler, leaving Benning, and now leaving Gordon. You get really attached, Mama, to some of the guys. But you get used to it pretty soon, I mean, the fact is, in the army somebody else is in charge and you just do what you have to do—so you HAVE *to get used to it. I wish you could meet Felton. I think you'd really like him. I'm thinking maybe of mailing this letter to you from Hamburg, probably quicker than putting it in the U.S. mail. How do you like* THAT *idea, a letter from me to you mailed in Hamburg six years after we left? At least there won't be any submarines around to sink the letter in transit.... I'll have just one day in New York City. I've got a guide brochure they give you at the railroad station. I'll certainly try to get in to Radio City. Remember—we didn't get a chance to go there when we got off the* Europa*? You weren't all that happy, I remember, that Oma had us booked to Phoenix so we had only those couple of hours. On the other hand nothing mattered back then except that Papa wasn't with us. You'll be getting this letter after, or maybe about the same time as, the letter I mailed you when I got the orders a week ago. Maybe I'll send you a postcard from Hamburg! Maybe I'll take a picture of 38 Hempelstrasse—hope it isn't damaged* TOO *much. Mama, of course the first thing I'll do is try to get some details about the... end of the line for Papa. The Germans, I know and have been told, keep very good records. So don't give up."* He lifted his head from the pad and said a silent prayer that he would find out what had happened to Axel Reinhard. He found himself hoping that he was a victim of an Allied bombing raid. He shrank from imagining other ends for the father whose absence he had mourned so intensively. *"Much love, Mama, can't wait for the day I see you. If you write her first, give my love also to Oma."*

The porter was there. Sebastian went to the men's room and came back in his trousers and a T-shirt. He nodded good night to the woman passenger who stood by and climbed up the ladder to his bunk, flicked on the reading light, closed the curtains at his side, and went back to his book, sent by Henrietta. It was *The Economic Consequences of the Peace,* written over twenty years earlier by John Maynard Keynes. The sleeping car rocked lazily but purposefully through the South Carolina forests and he consoled himself that he was not plodding through that distance carrying a field pack and carbine, step by step, hour after hour, day after day as, over this land of pine and clay, indistinguishable from the Georgia he felt he had come to know square inch by square inch, the armies had trod, north and south, fighting the great Civil War. He knew that Great-Grandfather Chapin had fought but when he did, it was late in the war, and Oma hadn't told Sebastian whether he was in South Carolina in 1865 when the war ended.

How fine when wars end, he thought, leaning his head over to read on in the book that had prophesied the terrible consequences of an unjust peace.

It wasn't until the midmorning of September 7 that he came upon First Lieutenant Harry Albright. September 7 was seven days after the noisy departure at Pier 42 in New York, and Sebastian, drawing deep and joyful breath for an entire week without infantry drills and joint morning exercises and long hot marches, spent his time walking on the one boat deck cleared for that purpose, sitting on whatever seat he could find, reading, and observing, with pity and gratitude for his apparent immunity, the seasickness around him.

Arrived now in Hamburg, he lugged his barracks bag to the designated Station 32. He could see, looking out from the starboard side, the long battered pier where six years ago friends and family stood and waved at departing passengers, as the band played on. Sebastian had nobody to wave to at the dock and, in fact, nobody to take poignant leave of aboard. It was oddly easy for any single passenger, traveling in the company of 3,500 others on a 936-foot liner, to cross the Atlantic Ocean without especially noticing, let alone befriending other than on a transient basis, any other passenger.

Deck stations 1 through 31 were rallying points for men and officers disembarking and bound for army divisions in Germany and France. Most were recruits who would relieve veterans qualified to return home. Some were re-enlistees. At Station 32, waiting out instructions over the loudspeakers for their turn to disembark, were two dozen army officers headed for myriad destinations. Leaning against the sturdy wooden boat rail, awaiting his call to proceed to the gangway, Sebastian looked over at the officer next to him. The nameplate read LT. ALBRIGHT. The slow movements of the long files of troops going down the gangway suggested it would be a while before they got around to Station 32. The troops making their slow, tedious way down the gangplanks would take—how long? In the army, time doesn't matter very much. An hour. Conceivably, two hours. Sebastian addressed the lieutenant at his side casually.

"Where you headed?" And added, "I never thought about it before—now that the war's over, can you ask a fellow officer a question like that? Where are you going?"

Lieutenant Albright lit a cigarette. The pause suggested to Sebastian that perhaps he had indeed been indiscreet. Albright, short, stocky, crew-cutted, dark-haired, gave off the air of someone seasoned in life, whether by the army or by other hardship Sebastian could not know. He wore air force insignia. Perhaps he should interject his own information, Sebastian thought. He wouldn't give up, pursuing his question with, "You know, Lieutenant— "

"Harry."

"You know something, Harry. Hamburg was where I lived for thirteen years. Last time I saw it was August 1939."

Albright's face lit up. Instantly he swung into German. "So you grew up in Krautland?"

"Yes. You obviously did, too. Were you—born here?"

"Yes. Nuremberg." He drew deeply from the cigarette. "The last time I saw Nuremberg was from five thousand feet. We managed to drop twenty tons on it. I'm talking about just *my* B-29. And there were six hundred of us, six hundred aircraft. I hope one of the bombs fell on Herr Hermenjat. He was my schoolteacher. After him, I was never surprised by accounts of Nazi sadism."

Sebastian smiled.

"Where are *you* headed?" Harry asked.

"Nuremberg."

"So am I. Got to put some of those buggers away, right? Stretch a little rope around their necks."

"I guess that's the idea," Sebastian said. "Would you show me around in Nuremberg? I'll do Hamburg."

CHAPTER NINETEEN

September 1945

At dockside, a WAC sergeant sat behind a long desk sheltered from the rain by a khaki-colored awning. It was attached to either end of what the dockside building had been, converted now into a huge warehouse with tight-packed provisions for a conquering army. The sergeant with the schedules on her clipboard for the larger army units was calling out information into a microphone. A cork bulletin board displayed schedules with troop departure times. The names of soldiers with urgent personal messages waiting were written in chalk on a blackboard. A dozen officers waited for special scheduling information as yet unposted. In the army, juniors instinctively yielded to seniors. Harry Albright was a first lieutenant. Second Lieutenant Reinhard edged casually back.

"We're going to Nuremberg," Albright told the WAC. "What do we do?"

The sergeant, wearing spectacles, leafed briskly through her clipboard. "There's a troop train going to Munich at 2020. You can connect north to Nuremberg from there, only, we can't be sure what time you'll get into Munich."

"What about commercial carriers?"

"There's a train at— " She looked at her watch. "Yes, you could make it, you've got just over an hour. It leaves at 1915, gets into Nuremberg at 0715."

"Reservations?"

The sergeant looked up and managed a smile. "Reservations? There's been a war, Lieutenant."

"Yes. I heard."

"No, no reservations, and there are no dining provisions. Though probably somebody will be selling something to eat. You'll certainly get some beer."

"How about getting to the railroad station?"

Sebastian interjected. "We can get there by subway."

"From here?"

"Yes."

"Then . . . we're off."

Sebastian leaned down to pick up his heavy bag. They were just outside the shed when an older man, unshaved and wearing a cap, approached them. "You want help bags?"

Albright replied in German. "Yes." He told him they were bound for the subway station. "Are the subway trains operating regularly?"

"Not regularly," the old man said. "But not irregularly. You are going to Hauptbahnhof? I have a friend who has a jeep. A *very good* jeep."

"How much?"

"Four dollars."

"Two dollars."

"Three dollars."

"Harry, listen," Sebastian interrupted. "Hempelstrasse isn't that much out of the way, going to the station." He turned to the old man. "We want to go by way of the park, by Hempelstrasse."

The man shrugged his shoulders. "Three dollars."

"I'll spring for it," Sebastian said in English to Albright.

At the dispatcher's signal, a big woman drove up in what had once been a conventional jeep, now enlarged to serve as truck or lorry. They drove off, Sebastian, in his native city, giving directions.

Through his shock at the desolation, he made out the block numbers. At midblock he told the woman at the wheel to stop. Looking about, he reconstructed the targeted area. He could make out the borders of the little playground. What had served as the iron fence to keep the children from spilling out was still discernible. The two tall apartment buildings were a jangle of wayward beams and joists and window glass.

"Do you want a picture?" Albright asked.

"I don't have a camera."

"I do." He zipped open his big bag and brought out a Brownie. "Here, you take it. But be fast about it. We've only got thirty-five minutes."

Sebastian raised the camera to his eye and snapped the picture. He returned the camera swiftly to Albright, and turned his face away. Albright understood, said nothing, and signaled to the woman to get on to the railroad station.

At the entrance off the broad street, flaunting surviving oak trees lush with summer leaves, a half-dozen boys and two or three girls clamored for patronage. The biggest boy, maybe twelve, shouted out to call attention to his baggage trolley. Two small wheels, probably appropriated from a baby carriage, had been affixed to the end of a wooden platform, and a serviceable cart was made.

The negotiation was done rapidly and the bags loaded on. They were off to track G7. On the way, the boy quarreled with his companion, and finally agreed to let him wheel the trolley the last half of the walk, across the station's huge waiting room choked with scaffolding, building materials, and luggage and boxes, soldiers coming and going.

"Hold it!" Albright motioned to the two boys. "Where can we buy—"

Sebastian spotted the makeshift kiosk and pointed over to it. Albright motioned the boys to follow.

Arriving, the taller boy asked, "Can you buy something for me and my brother to eat, Herr Oberleutnant?"

Albright didn't reply. At the kiosk he bought bread and ham and cheese and two bottles of German wine. He handed the brother whose hands were free a loaf of bread and a half kilo of cheese.

They walked past the imposing engine toward the railroad cars. That engine showed no traces of war strife. It wheezed its strength and eagerness for work and began its whistle screech as the two lieutenants climbed up the steps of a passenger car, grabbing the bags from "Mickey"—as the boy porter introduced himself, after accepting gleefully the twenty-five pfennigs and the package of food—and taking two empty seats halfway up the length of the car.

"I forgot to ask," Albright said. "Were you ever in Nuremberg? Back then?"

Sebastian shook his head. "Did I miss anything?"

"Only one of the most beautiful cities in the world."

"You took care of that, didn't you, Harry?"

"Did my best, Sebastian. As you can see, our bombers didn't neglect Hamburg. We didn't spare any German city just because it was beautiful and historic. Only Prague and Paris had immunity."

They opened a bottle of wine, removing the aluminum drinking cups from their gear.

CHAPTER TWENTY

Nuremberg, September 1945

Army orders had both officers reporting for duty to the Palace of Justice. The Palace was pretty much the only show in town, a huge compound which, along with the adjacent Grand Hotel, all but uniquely survived the devastation of Nuremberg. The ancient city with its hard-bitten military defenders finally yielded to the American Third and Forty-fifth Infantry Divisions of the Seventh Army, but surrender came only after bloody door-to-door fighting over a period of five days.

"Maybe they figured that since Nuremberg was the holy center of the National Socialist Party it ought to be the last to surrender," Sebastian commented, in awe. He leaned over in his seat in the jeep to view the rising sun's illumination of the redstone castle rock and the profile of what appeared to have been a medieval castle wall. Seated in front, alongside the MP at the wheel, Albright answered in German, "It'll be the last city our Nazi bigwigs will *ever* see, I'd guess."

Replying in German, Sebastian asked, "Why are you using the mother tongue all of a sudden?"

"Because what's ahead is supposed to be a trial. Not summary executions. I don't want to give our eighteen-year-old driver here any bad ideas about American justice. He might write his mother. Or the *New York Times.*"

He laughed and then, back in English, said, "We're on the Konigstrasse. That's the main street. Or was. Still is, I guess. See over there?" He pointed. "That was the dominant structure of the city, the Kaiserburg, the imperial palace. Just to one side is the house where Albrecht Durer lived and painted. He died in 1528. How do I know that? I went to school two blocks from there and Herr Hermenjat would have beaten me even harder if I had ever forgotten *Durer's* dates. Besides, my father worshiped him."

"Well that's not so unusual, is it? Sort of like worshiping, oh, Michelangelo."

"My father was an artist, by the way. A mosaicist. But, most important in this day and age, he was a Jew. Obviously I'm not going to be able to show you any of his surviving work, because probably there is none. He did a lot of restorations.... He would have had plenty to restore in Nuremberg, 1945. Like the whole city. He could begin here these days by learning to lay bricks. Never mind mosaics."

The Palace of Justice loomed ahead, east of the other surviving edifice, the Grand Hotel, eerily intact. The surrounding rubble and remnants of walls distorted with holes where windows had been, the concentrated desolation on all sides, gave the sense of a huge fortress that had survived a long and bloody war finally outlasting a besieging army.

The proportions of the Palace were astonishingly large. Stone building after stone building, some standing four stories high. The gabled roofs were marked with insets of small windows, themselves with gables, unburnished now. They would find, once inside, impressive, complex, endless corridors and high ceilings and hundreds of rooms of every size. It wasn't surprising that U.S.

Justice Robert Jackson's advance scouts had recommended the Palace of Justice as the central facility for the great trial.

Meanwhile, everyone checking in faced a thorough security examination, as if the guards, having trouble reorienting themselves as victors, were intuitively guarding against infiltration by members of the besieging army.

The old enemy were indeed outside, half-starved, spread out around the walls of the Palace in greater Nuremberg; but then some of them—their leaders—were within the Palace, in cells, monitored twenty-four hours a day by jailers looking through slits in the cell doors, a naked overhead light on, day and night. There, in individual cubicles, were the twenty-four most prominent Nazis the conquerors could lay their hands on. Hitler and Goebbels and Himmler were dead, unhappily at their own hands. The surviving leadership cadre were preparing, and being prepared, to face the first International Military Tribunal in history.

The driver unloaded his large file box, packed for the journey, on Sebastian's left, the box he had been dispatched to the railroad station to fetch, picking up his human cargo, the two lieutenants, as fellow soldiers of opportunity. "We can leave your gear in the back, Lieutenant," he said. "Do you know where you're billeted? Probably the Grand."

Neither of them did know where they would be quartered. Carrying only the canvas satchels that served them as briefcases, they followed the MP to the main entrance. East of the administrative building with its hundreds of offices, away in a sealed-off building, was the gray-stoned prisoner compound. In the months to come, Sebastian and Harry Albright would become experts on the site, experts also on the targeted officials, and on the ambitions of the judicial and moral imaginations that had come together, after the war, determined to affirm a need to write into the empty spaces of international law a fresh covenant: that war crimes were definable. And punishable as criminal behavior.

There was considerable bureaucratic routine for those checking in for duty at the Palace. The new arrivals needed to be processed for their security passes, photographs taken, rosters checked. By noon they had their passes and fresh orders. Sebastian would report to the prosecutor's office in the south wing, Albright to G-3 at the central courthouse. For housing, like most of the military personnel not accommodated in the Palace itself, they were assigned rooms in the Grand Hotel. They went out to the patient MP driver, contentedly smoking a cigarette and listening to the jeep's radio tuned to the armed services station. The driver was told to deposit the bags, securely identified, at the Grand Hotel checkroom. They walked back through the main entrance, showed their passes, and set out in search of their separate departments in the separate wings. They resolved to meet in the hotel lobby at 1830.

"The Grand used to be a pretty fancy place, Sebastian. Hitler had a private suite there. *Viel Gluck! Auf Wiedersehen.*"

CHAPTER TWENTY-ONE

Nuremberg, September 1945

Following faithfully after the long-gaited WAC sergeant, Sebastian arrived at the Palace's main hall. Passing by the large atrium, one end of which was now a reception area, Sebastian thought back on childhood visits, hand in hand with his mother, ogling exalted structures in the great buildings and museums around Hamburg. Here at the Palace, in the main hall, were extravagant touches of opulent public design. Burnished wood, myriad carvings and paintings, marble arches working their decorative way around large oval windows. The great Palace of Justice had miraculously escaped the bombs. Could this have been the protective design of the bomber dispatch center in London? *Ridiculous thought!* But fun to think it: the Palace made to survive the war in order to facilitate the trial of the warmakers! . . . No, the Palace's survival was plain luck.

Before the war, he learned, the Palace of Justice had served as the regional German appellate court. The glitter of other days shone through the distracting shabbiness of its current appearance and the disorder of internal arrangements. Boxes of olive green file cabinets piled high against one wall; clerks, military and civilian, clustered about improvised work surfaces, some of them great, massive wood desks, others, mere card tables joined together; a dozen typewriters clacking away metallically. The identical sound, he thought, he'd have heard if what was being typed out were names of passengers to be boarded onto the next death train.

On down through the long hall they walked, emptying into a narrower corridor with enclosed offices on the right. Deposited by the sergeant at a waiting room, Sebastian was motioned to sit on the plain wood banquette that made its L-shaped way around what had most recently been a picnic lunch. There was plenty on the table left over.

Sebastian awaited a summons from a Captain Carver, who was to be his boss. He hadn't eaten since the coffee and roll at the railroad station, what seemed many hours ago. Seated, his instinct from his year in the infantry moved him: *Take every opportunity you have.* To sleep, to eat, to piss. He plunked two slabs of cheese on a slice of bread and slapped a second slice over it. A mouthful of sandwich was in his mouth when he heard the voice to one side.

"You Reinhard?"

Sebastian turned to the tall figure, the collar of his shirt open, but the double silver bars of an army captain plainly visible.

"Yes sir," he managed to say.

"Finish your sandwich."

The captain, a man in his thirties with angular features and traces of blond in his hair, sat down on the banquette at the other end, leaned back against the wall, and raised his long legs, stretching them almost to where Sebastian was sitting.

"It's been a long day. Every day is a long day. You'll find out. I've looked at your dossier. Your German is red-hot, it says. That's good. We'll be relying on that when we visit our targets"—he motioned to the east, the prisoner wing. "You want to know anything about me?"

Sebastian smiled. "Sure, Captain."

"I graduated from the law school at the University of Wisconsin in 1935, was nicely settled, practicing in Sheboygan when a world war broke out. My wife and two kids are still there. I was drafted, commissioned, and sent to practice law in the J.D. I was an army prosecutor in London and then in France in 1944. You'll hear about it from somebody else if I don't tell you myself, so I may as well do it: I was the prosecutor at the trial of Private Slovik. The only U.S. soldier ever executed for cowardice. Now I'm here to help string up some people on the other side. You married?"

"No sir."

"You been briefed on the do's and no-can-do's here?"

"I got a mimeographed sheet when I checked in. I haven't had a chance to read it very carefully"—he pointed to his satchel where he had stuffed the folder.

"Well, let me see, where to begin? . . . There's no fraternizing permitted. There should be another word for what you can't do. We can use a little French—do not *cherchez la femme*. I don't speak three words of German. But you get the idea?"

Sebastian nodded.

"And don't get caught up in the black market. They'd kill for dollars out there," he waved his finger in a circle to denote the city outside. "And probably would, if they could get away with it, now that they've had to stop shooting at us from trenches. Go ahead with the cheese." Captain Carver liked Sebastian's smile—boyish—why not? What would one expect in a nineteen-year-old? But he thought he saw some cunning there. Captain Carver was himself cunning. Was Sebastian wondering how he'd ever get time enough away from prosecutorial duties to give chase to other quarry? "You finished eating? Come on into my office."

It was small. The large table was covered with folders marked in green ink. Sebastian sat on the proffered chair and looked over at the wall.

"Looking for my law library? Well, let me tell you something. There *is no library* for what we're up to. I mean, the IMT—that's the International Military Tribunal—is something *brand new*. This is September 8th? Exactly *one* month ago, in London, the Four Power people signed what's called the London Agreement. It included a charter for an International Military Tribunal and an agreement on general procedures. Our people and the Brits, once we got around the suggestion—Churchill was for it—that we just line up the bastards on a convenient wall and shoot them—insisted it should be a trial. A trial as in common law. Indictments, witnesses, defense counsel, et cetera, et cetera. The French wanted to use the Napoleonic approach—they're guilty and then you hear them out. The Russians, they wanted a show trial—you know, a Soviet specialty." He interrupted himself. "Come to think of it, maybe you don't know. Why *should* you know? Do you know *anything* about Soviet history? Soviet practices? Not that you have to know about these things, actually, in connection with what you have to do—"

"My grandmother—she was Austrian—was—is—very anti-Communist. My mother and I got quite an orientation from her. She—she defended the early Hitler on that account."

"What account?"

"Going after the Communists."

"Yes, well. Our Fuehrer persecuted the Communists, then made love to them in August 1939, just in time to give him eastern cover so he could invade Poland. And proceed to give half of it to the Communists. Then he decided in June '41 that the Wehrmacht needed a little more exercise. They hadn't conquered a new country for one whole year. So he celebrates the victory over France by invading Russia." George Carver paused reflectively. "That was a heap big mistake for Hitler."

Sebastian smiled at the understatement. Carver returned to his own half smile through clenched teeth. "Amazing thing, these dictators, how *dumb* they can be. So in June 1941 Hitler invades Russia. *Four years later he shoots himself.* In between there are maybe... forty million people killed. About six million of them by direct—no, indirect—that point will have to be probed in our proceedings—*indirect* orders from Hitler."

"You mean, they're doubting Hitler gave the marching orders?"

"No, no, hardly any doubt on that point. *Only* Hitler gave marching orders, marching orders to the army. What we don't know for sure is whether he gave the holocaust orders, as they're calling them, directly.

"But anyway, back to my minibriefing. So the London Agreement set up what we're engaged in right now. The Russians wanted to get maximum juice out of the war criminal business. They actually suggested trying the Nazis *individually!*" The lawyer from Sheboygan, Wisconsin, laughed. "Robert Jackson—Supreme Court Justice Robert Jackson—he's our boss, chief prosecutor—had to use baby talk (I got this from a J. D. Simon, who was actually taking notes) to explain to the Russian general that there is *no way* you can have individual trials of ten thousand people, or whatever the number is going to turn out to be. So they got together and decided on twenty-four big-name defendants. And you, Lieutenant, you'll get to know at least one of them *very well.* So will I. So, eventually, will the four judges."

There was pounding on the door.

"Come in."

The door opened. "Captain Carver! *Ley is dead.*"

"*Robert Ley dead?*" Carver shot upright, lurched forward, and grabbed the corporal by the shoulders. "Dead? Whaddaya mean dead?"

The corporal stepped back. "He hanged himself. Just behind the toilet. Just out of view of the guard. Sir, Colonel Andrus is going crazy. He's got armed guards going into each cell, searching every..."

"Cavity?"

"Yes sir. There's gonna be new, tough regulations going into effect—I heard Lieutenant Warfel say—effective tomorrow. Maybe even effective tonight. I knew you had a special interest in that prisoner—"

"Yes, I did, Corporal. Thanks."

The corporal left. There was silence. Carver walked to a shelf at one end of the room and pointed to folders stretching a quarter of the way across the wall. "And I hadn't actually *finished* with him. But I probably got to know more about that sonofabitch than—he was the head of the Deutsche Arbeiter Front—that's the German Labor Front..." Carver stopped and turned his head to the folders. "Herr Ley had thirty million workers doing what he told them to do, including killing each other." He stared vacantly at the files.

He resumed in quieter tones. "I was saying, I guess I know more about him than any ten other people combined. The one hundred first Airborne picked him up less than a week after the Nazis surrendered. He was hiding in a log cabin—guess where? Like three miles from the sacrosanct Berchtesgaden. The Fuehrer's sacred mountain hideout."

"When did he become one of the most-wanted twenty-four?"

"In London. He was on everybody's list of top twenty Nazis, number four on the British list. Oh shit. I was looking forward to that one, really looking forward to taking him on. You figure—I know you're thinking this—what the hell, you figure he's dead anyway? *That's not the point of this exercise.* We want to make a *legal* case for *hanging* them. They'd probably all gladly shoot themselves if we passed out revolvers. The point is *we* should shoot them. There's a difference between suicide and an *execution.*

And another *critical difference,* the difference between shooting them and *hanging* them. Shooting is what you do to, well, bank robbers."

He paused again. "Now there are twenty-three . . . this is going to mean altering schedules a whole lot." He sat down, then bolted up from his chair at the thought of what immediately needed doing. He adjusted his shirt collar, stuffed the folder marked SCHEDULE into his briefcase, and turned abruptly to Sebastian.

"Oh yes." He put down the briefcase and grabbed two bulky folders from the shelf. "Here. Take these to wherever you're billeted—Grand?"

"Yes sir."

"We'll have a desk for you here tomorrow. Go make yourself real familiar with this guy." He slapped the back of his hand on the folder. "I'll check with Justice Jackson on what will be the new schedule. I'd guess we'll begin interviewing our man maybe as soon as Friday. He is a tall assignment, this one."

"Who's that, Captain?"

"*That* is Brigadefuehrer Kurt Waldemar Amadeus. See you tomorrow."

CHAPTER TWENTY-TWO

September 1945

Sebastian waited for Harry Albright in the Grand Hotel's grand lobby. It greatly needed restoration, suffering as it had from heavy use in the war years. Only those repairs absolutely required to maintain the hotel's essential appearance had been undertaken.

But the luxurious appointments were all basically there, some of them hidden under drop cloths. There were plentiful sofas and armchairs, coffee tables and heavy glass cocktail tables supported on ornate wrought iron, once brass, now an oxidized green. The upholstery was heavy, the twenty-foot-long curtains, held aside by gilt tiebacks, sagging from their own undusted weight. Columns stood on both sides, eight sets of them on the window side, their appointments in marble. The Grand Hotel's lobby was designed to please the eyes of guests who, in the old days, elected to make their entrances by walking down the sweeping staircase, though of course the grand salon also pleased those who emerged from the solid mahogany elevators. The staff was mostly Bavarian, though it was Colonel Andrus of the Palace of Justice, very much an American, who made the critical decisions.

Colonel Andrus, Sebastian reflected, was in charge of just about everything in town. Burton Andrus gave no quarter. He had begun his army career in the First World War and stayed on in the regular army, so that now he had completed his second world war. Andrus had commanded the detention center at Fort Oglethorpe, where soldiers guilty of grave crimes were housed. He wore, always, a green helmet liner, styled after General Patton's, whom Andrus idolized. When he was asked to take on the IMT assignment, Andrus told Army Command that he would absolutely need to exercise supervision over the Grand Hotel, which he regarded as an auxiliary to the Palace. He had surveyed the scene and made his demands.

To coordinate the entire compound he needed control of essential auxiliary facilities. He would have to maintain efficiently the war criminals, which meant exercising and feeding them; provide working quarters and food services for the prosecution staff and their witnesses, many of these also under lock and key; allocate rooms for file storage; arrange for the intricate forthcoming simultaneous translations; revise the great courtroom of the Palace so that, when the trial started, it could efficiently accommodate defendants, prosecutors, judges, press, and spectators. "I cannot do all that," he had said, in his direct fashion, to the Berlin High Command, "without command authority at every vital quarter. At the Grand Hotel we are after all talking about 200 rooms." He was given the master key to this property, a spoil of war, for as long as it was useful to the conquering armies.

Harry, his hair still wet, greeted Sebastian. "You got your own shower?" Sebastian asked.

Yes, Albright assured him. Indeed he had found the assigned room entirely adequate. "Maybe it was used for Hitler's valet when he stayed here. Maybe they kept a little Jew in a cage there to keep him happy. You got to take care of the help."

Sebastian was a little startled by the language. He made no comment. He said simply, "Your room must be the same as mine.

Let's have a drink. I'm going to order sherry. I'm not sure I ever had sherry."

"You'll like it," Harry said.

"Henrietta—my grandmother—liked it, but I didn't drink yet, when I was living at home. The lieutenant who first met us at the desk this morning was just going off duty when I was taking off for the hotel. We walked over together. He told me our guys discovered almost an arsenal of sherries in the Nazi HQ, just off the Furtherstrasse. They brought it all to the hotel. Join me?"

Albright nodded; he'd go along.

Old-world manners of bourgeois German hotel life hadn't been bombed out of extinction. The elderly waiter was dressed in a courtly dark blue jacket with brass buttons that stretched up to his matching blue bow tie. He spoke an urbane English. "Dry, sir? Or semi-sweet?"

What the hell, Sebastian thought, he wouldn't pretend. "Which would you recommend?"

The waiter nodded. "I will bring you something nice."

"Not too expensive," Albright broke in.

"Not too expensive," the waiter affirmed, bowed, and left.

"Well, Harry, that was some interruption today, the Robert Ley business," Sebastian began.

"I had a personal interest there," Harry said. "My Papa was tipped off after the Nuremberg Declarations—that was 1935—that things were looking pretty black for him—and me. Here he was, a Jew, living in—Nuremberg. My mother, too. That made me 100 percent *Juden*. So, age fourteen, I find myself on a train to Genoa, off to enroll in a young artist's school—that was the story. My father didn't even tell *me* I was going to end up in America. I was looked after, from arrival in Genoa to arrival in New York, by the ship's bursar, Antonio Sedino. The ship was the *Conte di Savoia*. Sedino was, is, maybe—that was only ten years ago—my father's brother-in-law. My father told me he had hidden some things in the bottom of my suitcase, which was about as big as me, and heavier. When Signore Sedino met my train and took me to the boat he told me to leave the trunk with him after I took my clothes out. He said it would be safer that way—I was sharing my cabin with three Italian artists, mosaicists going to New York to do a big ceiling for a cathedral. St. John the Divine, I think it was. When we got to New York, Sedino drove me to a jeweler. We went into the back room together and with great big scissors he cut open the back of the trunk. There was a ton of gold coins there. My father's life savings, I guess."

"And your mum?—hey, this sherry's good stuff."

"She died in childbirth. A nice old drunken Irish lady in Brooklyn was paid to put me up and send me to school, PS 142. The next round trip of the *Conte di Savoia*—the circuit took sixteen days—Chief Sedino came by, see how I was making out. He told me my dad was scheduled for a labor camp by the Deutsche Arbeiter Front. Robert Ley must have needed a mosaicist at Dachau. But he took poison instead."

The hotel, pending restorations and personnel changes, served only a buffet. To get into the dining room at all you needed not only proof that you were a guest of the hotel, but also supplementary proof that, as a member of the military or of the International Tribunal team, you were authorized to draw on the U.S. rations the Grand Hotel had access to. There was little commercial traffic coming to Nuremberg. The few who came and went were directed to a separate dining room. There they could order the kind of food available to postwar German civilians, scant and starchy.

The fare at the Grand was heavily tilted to whatever could be cooked using grain or flour: spaghetti, breads, pastries. Fruit was scarce, but tonight the Grand served grapes, prised up from Italy. From the buffet, Albright brought back sausage and sauerkraut, Sebastian a meat stew of sorts. They drank beer.

"So what are you going to do to justify all the trouble the United States has taken to bring you here?" Sebastian asked. "Nothing to do with bombers, I'd guess. Or are you a witness of some kind?"

Albright puffed on his cigarette, then spoke through the smoke. "My B-29 was badly winged in March. The crew was held together for a while, waiting for a new plane, or repairs. But we were getting overstaffed, the bombing outfits. The krauts had no fighters left to shoot us down with and their antiaircraft units were slowly being wiped out. So our detachment was sent off to Bassingbourne for reassignment. Somebody poked into my dossier and found out what I was doing before dropping bombs."

"Which was what?"

"We Albrights—my father's name was Alkunstler—go in for oddball vocations."

"A mosaicist and—what?"

"I graduated from high school in Brooklyn—I did physics and learned from the physics teacher something about electricity. At seventeen I got a job with Hammerstein Radio Services, Inc. One of their jobs was to equip Radio City Music Hall with first-rate amplification. They did the installation, with me tagging along. Then one day I found myself in charge of maintenance. I had to be there, on duty, the whole time the theater was using the screen or the stage. I must have seen *Snow White* and her fucking dwarfs 300 times, always making sure the sound was just right. I had maybe eighty goes with the *Fantasia* movie when I was drafted, sent to the army air force. I was always on radio there, right through the bombing raids. I learned a *lot* about radios."

"And now?"

"I'm supposed to see that everybody over at the courthouse who is supposed to hear something hears it. And, oh yes, in the language he wants to hear it in. English, French, German, or Russian. Luckily, there's a kraut over here who used to work for Berlin radio, a sound technician. He now works for me. He speaks not one word of any of the languages we've got to send out except German. This is a pretty tough assignment. Colonel Andrus—he'd have made a good concentration camp commander—told me I'd have to have the simultaneous translation wiring set up by October 3rd."

"You can do that?"

"No. No way. But after fifteen minutes, I discovered you don't say no to Colonel Andrus. Fifteen minutes after we started talking was also when he got the news about Robert Ley. I'm only surprised Andrus didn't put a noose around his own neck when he heard about the suicide. His #1 responsibility is to keep the German prisoners alive until he kills them."

They agreed to walk over to work together the next morning at 0800 and went to their rooms.

Minutes later, seated in his chair, wearing khakis and a T-shirt, the lamp adjusted, Sebastian Reinhard opened the file on Brigadefuehrer Kurt Waldemar Amadeus.

CHAPTER TWENTY-THREE

September 1945

It was 0820 when Sebastian reached the Prosecutor's Central Office, reporting, as instructed, to Chief Landers. The warrant officer was at his desk and had begun to study his copy of the daily Palace bulletin when his telephone console rang. He leaned down to answer it but as he began to talk, the door of the office directly behind him banged open and a voice called out, "Landers? *Landers!*" Chief Landers put down the telephone and turned his head toward the open door.

"You want me, Justice?"

"No," the voice was clearly heard. "I want Major Gripsholm but he doesn't answer his phone. Track him down for me."

"Yes sir." He asked first the caller on the phone, then Sebastian, to wait, and dialed two numbers, unprofitably. He lifted a bulky folder and leafed through mimeographed pages. He dialed again. "Sergeant, this is Chief Landers at Justice Jackson's office. The Justice is looking for Major Gripsholm. He doesn't answer his phone or his room number at the Grand. I wondered if he might be with Colonel Andrus? . . . Yes, well. Yes, I know Colonel Andrus doesn't like to be interrupted, but you'll have to get word to Major Gripsholm that the Chief Prosecutor—"

The bell rang again. "Hang on a minute." The phone transfer was done. "...Yes sir? I think I've located him, Justice. Get right back to you...Sergeant? Get word to Major Gripsholm somehow. Yes, I see what you mean. Look, all *I* have to worry about is"—he cupped the receiver with his left hand but Sebastian had no difficulty in hearing his words—"looking after the Chief Prosecutor, who a while ago was a Justice of the Supreme Court and a while before that Attorney General of the United States. He feels he... *I understand.* Precedence. Yes, yes. Well, get to Major Gripsholm as soon as you can."

The chief warrant officer looked up at Sebastian. "Sorry about that, Lieutenant Reinhard." He looked down at the assignment sheet Sebastian had handed him when the Chief Prosecutor's summons had interrupted. "You're just here, just got here yesterday... I know, I have to find you an office to work in. I hope you have calm nerves. I do. I was a clerk in the New York Stock Exchange when I was drafted and I thought I'd never be rattled anywhere, not compared to back there. But this is something else. Thank god there are separate desks for non-U.S. judges and their aides. All *I* have to worry about is the Chief Prosecutor, a dozen assistant prosecutors, a hundred interrogators, and liaison with a million French, British, and Russian prosecutors' desks. That's all."

Chief Landers was enjoying the mute, smiling company of the tall, brown-eyed young lieutenant with the deep Georgia tan and indulged himself further. "It would be a lot different if I could smoke, but Justice Jackson doesn't like cigarette smoke. You smoke?"

Sebastian shook his head.

Chief Landers looked up from the office's floor layout. "Let's try B-242 for you. There's a stenographer has a desk there, one of the pool WACs—Sergeant Cyrilla Hempstone is one valuable lady, an old hand. Across the hall are two other stenographers.

I'm talking about German/English. Thank god all the defendants are German. It's not my job to quarter the German/Russian or German/French stenos. That's—again—Colonel Andrus. That's his worry. You got any special equipment you're going to need?"

"A typewriter. And a *Duden German-English Dictionary.* And, you know, paper, a few file boxes."

Landers took notes. "There's plenty of room. These offices were used for German prosecutors and staff right up through to when the bombing began. The German appellate court had fewer and fewer people to prosecute. The Nazis had a way of clearing up backlogs. They didn't need all that much room for preparing criminal cases against double-parkers. And—am I taking up too much of your time, Lieutenant?"

Sebastian shook his head vigorously. "No, no, Chief. I appreciate it, I really do." Sebastian gave his broad smile. "Maybe I'll come to you when I hit really bumpy problems in interpreting."

Landers liked that. "I've picked up just a little German, in the last year. I'd know how to order five shares of AT&T in German—" The phone rang. "Yes, Major Gripsholm. I'll put you right through."

Sebastian nodded his thanks and left in the direction Landers's forefinger pointed to. He needed to climb the stairs to another floor, but then soon came across Room B-242. He knocked, then opened the door. The little office was empty, the walls bare except for notices and floor plans Scotch-taped on one side. The nearer desk seemed occupied, a folder or two strewn about. He went to the desk at the other end, opened his satchel, and removed the file on Kurt Amadeus.

CHAPTER TWENTY-FOUR

Nuremberg, September 1945

His phone rang. Sebastian froze. Since the day he was commissioned a second lieutenant he had never before answered the telephone while on duty. What was he supposed to say? "Lieutenant Reinhard?" "Reinhard?" "This is Lieutenant Reinhard?" He had to say something. He managed, "Hello."

"Reinhard? This is Captain Carver. How you doing on that material?"

"I've got three days of reading behind me, Captain. There's a *ton* of footnotes marked but nothing in the accompanying material. And a lot of it is in German. Do you read German, sir?"

"No. It's up to you to mark passages you think I ought to have. Then translate them for me. Reinhard, if I had given you all the accompanying material, you'd have needed a truck to get to the hotel. You'll have access to all that stuff, obviously, as needed. There may be some trick terminology there you'll need help on. Oh. Before I forget, tell General Amadeus *like five seconds after we begin questioning him*, tell him that when he uses acronyms he is to say out the letters *one at a time*, like if he says 'DAF'—Deutsche Arbeiter Front—he must say Dee . . . Aay . . . Eff. There's going to be a lot of that kind of stuff."

"Who do I get help from on the technical terms, Captain?"

"Herr Professor Bruno Waldstein. He's a military historian. A cripple, one-legged—First World War. The Nazis left him alone. He taught at the university here. He's on full-time call, over the phone, or we can bring him in if you need to explore written material with him.

"Let's see, it's just about time to eat. You know where the officers' mess hall is? Well, Landers will tell you—he'll tell you anything you want to know and a lot you don't want to know. You just might ask him whether Brigadefuehrer Amadeus is guilty; if so, like how guilty? I mean, guilty meriting what? Hanging? Life? Twenty years?—save us a lot of trouble if he just told us... Okay, I'll cut the bullshit. Come to my office after chow and we'll dig in."

Captain Carver began the conference by taking his telephone off the hook. Sebastian sat down opposite, clipboard and legal pad in hand. He was ready to take notes.

Carver began. "Of course, just to begin with, he's guilty as sin."

Sebastian nodded.

"On the other hand, we've got to make our case. At several levels. The case against him, but also a case supporting our propositions on war crimes—that there is such a thing as a war crime. The principal argument at that level will be made by Justice Jackson. You know anything about him? Jackson?"

"Just a little."

"Well add to that little this: Robert Jackson is a hell of an eloquent guy. He has a terrific advantage over lawyers—like me. He didn't go to law school, so they never had a chance to teach him how not to write. He writes plain English. Great English. English English. Anyway, he'll be the opening gun.

"As of yesterday Jackson hadn't absolutely decided who to start in on, but almost certainly it will be Hermann Goering. As far as the public is concerned, never mind the internal feuding, he was Nazi #2. We'll go after him on all four counts."

Sebastian looked up.

"You're not familiar with the war crime counts?"

"They weren't in my folder. But I'm sure I can find them."

"It's surprising they aren't etched in stone outside the Palace."

Carver liked to stretch out his legs and brace his hands behind his full, blond-flecked hair. "We can move quickly past Counts One and Two—there'll be time to study up on them when we get around to interrogating Hans Frank and Albert Speer—I didn't draw any of the preliminary work on Goering. That's Major Guinzburg who's handling that. Nice touch—Guinzburg's an observant Jew." Carver changed his voice, rendering his idea of a New York accent. '*No questioning today, Reichsfuehrer. It's Saturday.*' Anyway, we'll have Goering up on *all four counts.* Count One is *conspiracy to wage wars of aggression*, Count Two is *crimes against peace.* What Count Two really amounts to is the activation of Count One. You *plan* Count One, you *do* Count Two. That's the simplest way to put it, get it?"

Sebastian nodded his head and made a note.

"But let's get on to Amadeus. What a name! Maybe he's a descendant of Mozart. Music's gotten worse ever since Mozart, maybe there's a biological reason for that. Yes, then there's the other two counts."

Captain Carver let down his legs and picked a sheet of paper from a folder. "They're only one sentence each. 'Count Three: *War Crimes; particularly those crimes involving the maltreatment of prisoners of war in breach of international agreements.*' No problem there, where Amadeus is concerned. Did the material you went over give the number of Russian POWs gassed at Joni?"

"No. But the résumés I read seemed to agree on two hundred fifty thousand."

"That's smelly. Has the sound of convenience. Too round a number."

"Yes sir. But there are a couple of affidavits here that say that General Amadeus worked hard to meet his quota—to kill the people who were sent in—but that he gave orders to his staff not to exaggerate his—Camp Joni's—record in the reports sent in to Himmler."

Carver snarled. "There's a strain of real integrity there. '*I won't report killing two hundred fifty-five thousand people when I've only really killed two hundred fifty thousand.*' But how many of the victims were prisoners of war?"

"On that point there's confusion. We have records of shipments from the eastern front in 1943 and 1944. I'd think forty thousand Russian prisoners going through Joni would be right, according to what I've read. Most of the POWs were sidetracked to Auschwitz. What we don't know is how many of those forty thousand actually arrived at Joni. A lot died en route. But one Russian interrogator got to one of the SS guards in charge of the gas section who said his records showed over twenty-two thousand POWs. No way to verify that, on the other hand. The Russians hanged that guy."

"Okay. Give me a memo using the round number. Write, 'in excess of twenty thousand.' We'll see how Amadeus reacts to that."

"The memos I prepare for you—are they supposed to be clipped onto the affidavits?"

"Put them in a marked, separate folder. You want a Coke?" Without waiting for an answer, Carver rang his corporal to bring two Coca-Colas.

"So we've got Count Three in our sights, we move on to Count Four.

"'Count Four: *Crimes Against Humanity; such as murder, extermination, enslavement, deportation, and other inhumane acts against civilian populations.'* There certainly is no problem there, right?"

Sebastian nodded but didn't look up from his note-taking.

Carver went on. "'Murder,' yes. Though we may run into problems of definition here. Stick somebody into a gas oven, are you murdering him, exactly? Or just exterminating him? We don't want Amadeus wasting a lot of time with that kind of thing. So much for murder. Enslavement. I'll have to decide whether to recommend to Colonel Amen that we also go for enslavement. You've got the names of survivors?"

"Some. According to the wrap-up account by the Russian captain, I guess those who were able to walk left as the camp was burning down. Most were too sick. They waited a few hours, and then the Russians arrived."

"What is the longest time any of the survivors actually spent at Joni?"

"Three of them had been there when it opened. That means from April 1943 to liberation day, February 1945: twenty-two months."

"How come they were still alive?"

"Doesn't say."

"I'll think about that. We can certainly call that enslavement, twenty-two months. But *extermination* is our big deal. How do you say extermination in German?"

"*Vernichtungslager.*"

"Is there a euphemism for extermination?"

"No. They use *vernichtung*. *Vernichtungslager* is an extermination camp."

"He's not going to try to fiddle with the word, I'd guess. The defense they'll be using.... There are two defenses. Amadeus won't use the first. The first is what we call the *tu quoque* defense. You know about that?"

Sebastian shook his head. "I know the Latin words, but not what they mean as a defense argument."

"The Latin comes in literally as, '*And you, too.*' We translate it, around the shop, as '*So's your old man.*' They'll be using that defense a lot, and that was anticipated at London. You know how they handled that problem?" He leaned his head back and grinned mischievously. "Well, they simply laid out the ruling that the court *would not admit tu quoque,* either as disqualifying, or mitigating. The Nazis will say: Sure, we *and* the British, *and* the French shot some prisoners! Well, *so did the Russians.*

"We didn't always rescue survivors from sub attacks? *The Americans didn't rescue survivors from sub attacks.*

"We engaged in imperialism? *You people invented imperialism.*

"We singled out the Jews? *Americans singled out the Indians.*

"The court, as I said, by its charter is instructed not to acknowledge that category of arguments, though that doesn't mean they're useless. The press will play them up. And the legal gang will, too, the people who say we are making ex post facto laws. Between you and me, I think that's formally correct. But from another perspective, we are enlarging the compass of the law."

"We do have the problem of having a Soviet judge on the tribunal, right, Captain?"

Carver looked hard at Sebastian. "I asked you a couple of days ago, on the Communist business—leave it alone. You sounded pretty well informed on Soviet practices."

"Captain, it wasn't just my grandmother who told me about the Communists. I've read *Time* magazine since 1940, and that was during the Hitler-Stalin pact. Everybody knows about Stalin and about his concentration camps and how they handle prisoners."

Carver wheeled his chair around. "Look. The only way we can get through this is just to eliminate from our minds the psychological problem of a Soviet judge participating in the tribunal. *Just don't think about it.* All we need to think about—and to explicate—to the judges—and to the world—is what the defendants and their emissaries *did.* That's *it.* Everything. Fuck *tu quoque.*

"The big defense Amadeus and some of the others are going to use is: 'We were only following orders.' That is the tough one because there isn't much precedent working for us. Our counter line is: *Doing what you did was illegal.* Germany was a partner to some treaties on the conduct of war. And some acts were forbidden—"

His voice trailed off. "Anyway, at a purely documentary level, I'm going to be asking Amadeus to *prove* that he was instructed to do some of the things he did."

"Even though we know he *was* instructed to do them?"

"Yes. I know. They weren't capitalist entrepreneurs, these people. But a lot of them got into the spirit of the idea and went substantially on their own, acted on their own. You have accounts in your file, they're in English—I remember from scanning the file—of executions, that kind of thing. Amadeus isn't going to come up with orders from Himmler that instructed him to execute individual prisoners."

"I understand. Captain, how does the routine go, I mean, the interrogation?" He grinned. "Or do you want me to save that question for Chief Landers?"

Carver laughed.

"We'll go to a room—which room, Landers *will* tell us—in the prisoner wing on Friday. Amadeus will be seated, his handcuffs removed. There'll be two armed GIs, guards. I'll be here"—he pointed opposite to his desk. "You'll be there"—he moved his finger to the right. "A stenographer—when we want one—will be there." He moved his finger to the left. "Then I ask a question. You put my question into German.

"Amadeus answers in German.

"You put that into English.

"I ask the next question... Reinhard, have you ever taken part in a court martial?"

Sebastian cocked his head slightly. "No, sir."

"I've done millions of them. But never before conducted any in a foreign language. I'm not looking forward to that."

He drew in breath deeply, and got up from his chair. Sebastian followed suit. Carver looked him in the eyes. Carver seemed burdened by the load of work and the tight schedule. Sebastian saw a hint of helplessness in his eyes.

"I'll try to help out, Captain."

George Carver stiffened up. His self-confidence was back.

"I'll be counting on you. Get back to the file. *International Military Tribunal vs. Kurt Waldemar Amadeus.* See you around, Sebastian."

CHAPTER TWENTY-FIVE

Nuremberg, September 1945

Sebastian and Harry met in the hotel lounge as they did every night. After a week or ten days they found themselves inched by the steward, who had taken on the responsibility of inducting Sebastian into the world of sherry, nearer and nearer to the bar. They were soon being treated like old patrons. And today they were seated right up by the bar, among the specially chosen.

Harry Albright said he had had a hell of a day. "Hans Waldheim, the German specialist I told you about, is a terrific sound expert, but he wants to do things according to his own priorities. But Colonel Andrus has *his* priorities, and what *Der Kommandant* said to me was a) Albright, fix it so the judges—that's eight people, Sebby, the four judges and four alternates—can hear the prosecutor in their own language, b) fix it so the defendants can hear in German what the prosecutor is saying. Then, c) fix it so there will be ten four-language earphones for the press, and forty three-language earphones for spectators. Odd figure, forty-three. But the colonel doesn't explain things like that.

"So my guy Hans has the diagrams made up and we go to work but—of course—there's a shortage. This particular shortage is of language-switch units, and who do you think Hans gives priority to on the units we have on hand? The judges?"

"No. Let me guess. The press?"

"Not even that. The *spectators.* Well, so, I mean, it'll all get done, even though the colonel has moved one target date forward, as you people know, to October 15th. There's *no way* we can be ready by then. Thank god other enterprises are also behind, like even the carpentry for the trial room—hell, you people are behind, too, aren't you?" Harry asked.

"On my particular guy we haven't even started, though I've done all the preparation. Tomorrow's the big day."

"You get to lay eyes on Wolfgang Amadeus?"

Sebastian pursed his lips. "Yes, he's supposed to show up. I've seen four photographs of him, at different ages. His eyes are the same in all of them, sort of suspicious. He has a long face, long Aryan nose. Good-looking guy. You know—I think I told you—he's only thirty-six years old."

"Fourteen years older than me," Harry said.

"He got off to an earlier start."

"Speaking of earlier starts, Sebby, what do you say we get out of this place? Seven straight dinners at the Grand Hotel is a lot of dinners at the Grand Hotel."

"You got any ideas?"

"I've done a little asking around. I made only one stipulation: It had to be out of bounds and against regulations. Otherwise we'd find ourselves in a mini-Grand Hotel, and *the* grand Grand is better than a mini-Grand."

"Okay. Let's go. But I got to watch it. Big deal tomorrow."

They walked out of the hotel. It was the last day in summer, September 21. They strolled in the direction of the setting sun.

"A year ago in London, eight months before V-E Day, they ended the official blackout," Albright reminisced. "That was a big big day. Ending *five years* of blackouts." He pointed down the darkening street. "When the twilight goes, it'll look like a blackout here, electricity's that rare."

Light still seeped through what seemed large peepholes in the devastated structures. A while ago, Sebastian reminded himself, this was an avenue of lights slowly being turned on as daylight diminished. But he had gotten used to the scarecrow profiles of the city. He had to think back on how things looked in cities that had escaped bombing. He thought with awe on the light galaxy in Manhattan the night before he sailed out.

Albright stopped. "I got an idea. A place, Marta's, near the Frauenkirche. I've been there. There's a hole-in-the-wall there, a little food and canned music, then, later on, a live lady. Maybe not completely dressed. What I'm thinking is, Marta's is over there on Konigstrasse and to get there we'd be walking up past the Palace entrance and around the wall in the direction of the prison compound. I got an itch to see the lights of— "

"The big guys?"

"Yep. I've spent a lot of time with the wiring in what's going to be the courtroom—you haven't even seen it. They're constructing a secure walkway from the defendant wing to the courtroom, so nobody can shoot at them while they're moving the prisoners that—what?—fifty yards? I'm just curious to look at the toughest security building in history. Just want to see what lights, if any, make their way from inside the cells area out to the street."

They walked past the billets of the Palace guards and followed the walled perimeter of the old prison. They rounded the north end and found the twilight now gone. "We've got to walk all the way around to get to where *they* are. So? It will give us a little appetite."

Following the prison wall they could see the rubble-shattered road. They moved toward the bright streetlight at the southeastern point, at Bernstrasse.

Albright stopped. His gaze turned slightly to the right. A dim light illuminated the easternmost point of the dark, two-story building.

"Look over there. But you can't make out the wire fence on the prisoner balcony—that's hidden. I haven't seen it but I've studied the electrical diagram. When they come out of their cells to go to their exercise walk or to their mess hall, the wire fence prevents them from committing suicide. Outside the actual cells there's spotlights shining in on every one of them and one guard each peering in. Since Ley's suicide they're not even allowed to keep their hands under the sheets. So much for their love life."

"Those are luxury quarters compared to Joni."

"I guess these guys have one thing in common with the people dragged into Joni. They both wish somebody would fire a gun through the cell doors and just kill them."

"I wouldn't guess it's going to be all that clear-cut with all twenty-three of them," Sebastian said. "Some of them think they'll be acquitted. Wonder which end of the building is housing *my* killer? Never mind, I'll be seeing him soon enough. Harry, let's get out of here. Let's go to your Marta's place."

Albright nodded and pointed the way north.

Marta's was one capacious room in a building the top half of which had been destroyed. The windows in the bottom floor were blacked out. At the entrance, Marta's father was stationed. Harry, having been to Marta's once before, served now as guide. "You can't mistake him," Harry said, as, walking briskly, they approached the bar. "He's bald, benevolent, and always has a beer in his hand."

His assignment, Harry explained, was to send out a signal if

MPs came to the door. "There's a bell at his fingertips. When he pushes it, a little alarm goes off at the bar. The stripper, if she's on stage, takes shelter; the lights brighten and the volume of the music is turned down."

Twice, in the eight weeks since the bar opened, the MPs had come in, Marta told Harry. Their examination of the premises had been perfunctory. None of the military patrons (there were about twenty) were questioned.

Standing at the bar with his beer and a big bowl of chips, Sebastian was himself now listening to Marta's account of her good relations with the MPs. Sebastian recalled his Latin teacher and the distinction she taught her students between *malum in se* and *malum prohibitum.* Descending on Marta's, the MPs coming in would sniff around for *malum in se*—a bar sheltering black markets or prostitutes peddling their venereal diseases. Not discerning any, they would conclude that what was going on at Marta's was just a little bit of *malum prohibitum*—soldiers off-limits, but what the hell, go ahead and enjoy yourselves, just don't create a civil disturbance.

Sebastian and Harry sat at a small table they had to share with two Germans of middle age, already seated. The younger of the two addressed, in German, his beefy companion. He said jocularly, "I guess we're going to be sharing the table with a couple of U.S. hangmen."

Sebastian looked over, mock-amiably, and said in German: "Ah, *mein freund,* would you rather we let them out, and you people can just do the Third Reich thing all over again?"

Startled, the German hesitated, then smiled, then introduced himself and his companion. They were veterans. The first one said that the day the Nazis surrendered, his wife had a baby boy, and they named him Eiche.

"You get that, comrade? *Eiche?* In English, that's *Ike.* We named him after General Eisenhower. That's how we feel about the Americans."

He raised his beer glass, and his companion raised his.

There was a moment before Sebastian and Albright raised theirs. But the tension passed, and the four of them drank to the good health of Ike, and then of Eiche.

BOOK THREE

CHAPTER TWENTY-SIX

Nuremberg, September 1945

He was seated in a two-armed wooden chair, the seat and back lined with leather turned shiny over the years. The defendant wore his metallic-gray SS jacket, shorn from Day One at Nuremberg of any identifying features indicating rank or military order. The pants matched his jacket and he wore boots that rose to a few inches from his knee. An MP guard stood at either side, in the parade-rest position. When the door opened, he rose and the guards snapped to attention.

He looked first at Sebastian, who walked at the head of the little procession to his seat opposite. Sebastian was followed by Captain Carver and Sergeant Hempstone. Carver nodded curtly and sat down. He waited for the portly Sergeant Hempstone to set up her stenotype machine. She moved her chair and her stand deftly and turned an experienced glance at Captain Carver: She was ready.

Carver cleared his throat and read out for the record: *We will proceed with the interrogation of defendant Kurt Waldemar Amadeus.*

"*General* Amadeus," the defendant corrected, revealing at

least enough familiarity with English to recognize that his rank had not been acknowledged.

"We do not use rank," Carver said offhandedly, looking down at his notes. Then, "That you attained the rank of brigadier general will be revealed in the interrogatory."

Sebastian interpreted, his rendition only once requiring the telltale pause of the alien phrase going from one language to another.

Amadeus turned his eyes to Sebastian, a hint of curiosity on his face at the young man's fluency.

"You are charged..."

Captain Carver read out Counts Three and Four from the London Agreement, and then launched into the step-by-step interrogatory. This was tedious because he already had the answers to the preliminary material. Such, he sighed inwardly, would always figure in encounters with the law. He knew that from experience. Time wasted, but perhaps necessarily.

"You were born in Essen, Germany, in 1909." The questions were rapidly interpreted and answered.

"You attended the Technical Institute of Berlin where you studied civil engineering and architecture. You graduated in 1929 and did work for defendant Albert Speer while he was at the Institute. You returned to the Institute in 1933, where you served as instructor. In 1937 you left to join the SS. Why?"

Amadeus looked up, his pale face without expression, his body erect. "The SS needed younger men with experience. Herr Speer urged me to take the assignment."

"After you joined the SS and received training you were sent to a camp called Dachau to supervise the completion of a new wing. Which part of the Dachau camp were you engaged in building?"

"The new barracks, and attendant buildings."

"Were there prisoners resident in Dachau when you were doing this?"

"Yes. But in a different part of the camp."

"Were you aware what these prisoners were in Dachau for?"

"They were there, I was told, for miscellaneous misconduct against the state."

"Did you receive help in the construction of your new buildings from the Dachau prisoners?"

"Yes."

"Did any of these prisoners die, while at work for your division?"

"You mean die at work? Die while working?"

"Yes."

"No."

Captain Carver leaned over to Sebastian. He lowered his voice. "There's no affidavit on this point that I can remember, is there?"

"None, sir."

Back to Amadeus. "After you did your work at Dachau, you were assigned to an SS unit in the Leibstandarte SS Adolf Hitler?"

"Yes."

"And participated in the war against France."

Amadeus paused. "I participated in the action against the Lowlands and France."

"We call that a war."

"Herr Captain, that was a defensive military action. France had been at war with us since September 1939."

Sebastian wondered if Carver would let that go. He guessed rightly; he would; it didn't matter. And it was true that France and England had already declared war on Germany.

"What was the nature of your duties in France?"

"I was head of the SS intelligence unit for the Leibstandarte."

"And what were the activities you engaged in as intelligence officer?"

Amadeus smiled. "May I smoke, Herr Captain?"

Colonel Andrus had said yes, defendants could smoke during interrogation, unless the interrogating officer found the smoke offensive. Carver motioned an okay.

Amadeus nodded, withdrew a package of cigarettes, and lit one. "What did I do? What all intelligence officers do, Herr Captain."

"I do not know what 'all intelligence officers do.' My questions are directed to you to answer. You are not to assume my knowledge of the answers to the questions I direct to you. Now: Did you engage in apprehending any non-German citizens and shipping them to Germany or Poland?"

"A few Jews."

Carver looked up. Sebastian scratched a hard exclamation point on his steno pad. The stenotypist paused, waiting for more.

Captain Carver fiddled with his briefing papers. Then, "You say 'a few Jews.' What do you mean by 'a few'?"

Amadeus blew smoke from his mouth and furrowed his brow. "Maybe eight or ten thousand."

"And why Jews?"

Amadeus seemed surprised. "They were enemies of the state."

Carver thought to depart from the script. "Who decided that?"

"The Fuehrer."

"You therefore considered it a legal act?"

"Everything the Fuehrer did was legal."

Suggested procedure, Colonel John Harlan Amen, in charge of coordinating interrogations, had said in his memo, was a five-minute break at the end of every hour of questioning. The guards would lead the prisoner out of the hearing room into the washroom. The interrogation staff would wait outside.

Sebastian stretched his limbs, awaiting access to the lavatory. From one of the twin urinals, Carver leaned over to Sebastian. “He’s not going to give us any problem on the Jewish question. He’s a cool, unrepentant cat.”

“Speer certainly thought he was a competent executive when he gave him that last assignment. But hold on, Captain. Amadeus never said he *agreed* with Hitler’s orders. He just said Hitler’s orders made what he did legal.”

“Right. That’s worth pursuing.”

They reassembled.

CHAPTER TWENTY-SEVEN

October 1945

On October 10, Justice Jackson called together the English-speaking prosecutorial staff. To Colonel Andrus, who would make the arrangements for the meeting, he had cautioned, "Burt, I just couldn't stand it if the Russians, with all their complaints at our administrative meeting, were to protract our problems. But just so they can't get mad at us if they find out we conducted a meeting on policy without them, I'll also exclude the French—we'll just say it was an all-English-language meeting, and the translating machine wasn't up to the job, et cetera, et cetera."

"I don't know about that, Justice."

Colonel Andrus would rather have been boiled in oil than use the familiar when addressing a superior. Never mind that Justice Jackson wasn't exactly his superior. In the chain of command, Andrus was in charge of the Palace of Justice; Colonel Amen was in charge of interrogation; Justice Jackson headed up the prosecution. Never mind the question of first names, Colonel Andrus was uneasy about excluding the Russians and pressed the point.

Jackson's patience diminished. "Burt, just get over it."

"Then who do you want there?"

"Just the prosecutorial team—"

"That's four. Three if you exclude the Russians. Two if you exclude the French."

"Plus the interrogators—"

"That would be, depending how you count it, eighteen."

"Plus the lawyers. What's that, a thousand?"

Colonel Andrus attempted a snicker. "Not quite. And anyway, some of them are out of town. Say twenty-five."

"Then that's who I want there. And Burt, this will be a top-security Anglo discussion. *Nobody* gets in except those people."

Robert Jackson—well-regarded, urbane, handsome—enjoyed addressing an assembly. On moving from Attorney General to the Supreme Court in 1941, he had forfeited his live audiences. That loneliness of a Supreme Court Justice's life had been a five-year trial of sorts. Jackson always took pride, understandably, in his delivery. His arguments were carefully arranged. His spoken language reflected his renown as a judicial stylist.

"I don't need to tell you," he began, when the meeting was called to order, "how sweaty these preparations have been. We began interrogations on August 27th, six weeks ago. You know what we've been through. A trying period. Ley's suicide. Diplomatic problems always hit us with something or other, requiring us to go to Berlin, or to London, or to Washington. The sheer immensity of the material amassed by the Nazis—I hardly need to tell you—is, most of it, now in our hands, in the hands of the Allies. And again I don't need to tell you, that's saddled us with a huge problem of bibliographic research, beginning of course with the basic requirement—a knowledge of German."

Jackson touched on the evolving questions of criminal law and the scrutiny being given to the whole question of newfound international war crimes and the apparent conflicts of Nuremberg procedures with common-law codes. He then did a quick survey of the four prosecution counts and gave his opinion that the interrogations he had surveyed had compiled abundant grounds to proceed before the international tribunal. They needed, he said, to get on with a trial.

"Now, I'll do this in a schoolmasterly way. I want to know, after I tick off each name, that the prosecutor in charge of preparing that case has written out the charges to be presented to the defendants—the 'criminal defendants,' as they will formally be designated the minute these indictments are served. I'll give their names in the order of the indictment schedule. Just say, 'Okay' after your defendant's name."

There was silence in the meeting room.

"Hermann Goering."

Sitting in the front row, Colonel John Harlan Amen said, "Okay."

"Rudolf Hess." There was an okay from the back of the room.

. . . And on:

"Joachim von Ribbentrop.

"Wilhelm Keitel.

"Ernst Kaltenbrunner.

"Alfred Rosenberg.

"Hans Frank.

"Wilhelm Frick.

"Julius Streicher.

"Walther Funk.

"Hjalmar Schacht.

"Karl Doenitz.

"Erich Raeder.

"Baldur von Schirach.

"Fritz Sauckel.

"Alfred Jodl.

"Martin Bormann.

"Franz von Papen.

"Arthur Seyss-Inquart.

"Kurt Amadeus.

"Albert Speer.

"Konstantin von Neurath.

"Hans Fritzsche."

Having gotten the confirmations he wanted to hear, Jackson went on.

"What we have here, in rough categories, is five groups, which I'll label: 1) top Nazis; 2) top criminals; 3) bank presidents; and 4) admirals and generals. Plus, 5) some in their own categories."

A hand was raised. "In which of those categories is Speer?"

"He's certainly unique, one of the unclassified ones. Now we've got an uphill challenge here, dealing with Speer and a few others. As every one of you who attended law school knows"—there was an appreciative titter—"we're making a lot of new law as we go. The toughest cases will also be the most combative, legally and factually. Their lawyers will raise every objection they can possibly raise. Thank the good Lord they don't get to sound off during the prosecution's case—"

"We'll hear from Goering, you can count on it," said Colonel Amen.

"Yes. Goering will find some way to interrupt, but Judge Lawrence—has anybody here had any experience with Sir Geoffrey? I know he looks like a good old boy. But take it from me, he can handle a gavel, he'll keep order.

"Now golden, from our point of view, are the defendants who accept the prosecution's factual allegations. And worth double gold is anybody who flat-out *repents*. That's not going to achieve, for anybody who does repent—as far as I'm concerned—any commutation of sentence. But it will ease up the whole judicial picture."

A beckoned aide turned over a page on the large paper pad display resting on the easel. Jackson picked up his pointer.

"Now here's how we've broken down the groups by degree of projected difficulty. We have Category One, the toughest nuts to crack. And first in that group is Hermann Goering. Thanks to the fine facilities of our bugging system, about which," he cautioned, "we do not speak to the press—here is what Goering had to say on one of the exercise walks a week ago. He was talking to Walther Funk and giving him advice. Quote: 'Our defense should be, *lick our ass.*'"

Someone in the crowd whistled plaintively. Carver, sitting in the front row, observed, "Licking *his* ass would certainly take a lot of time." There was a ripple of amusement...and the lull of resignation.

"At the opposite end—the compliant end—is Albert Speer. What he has been saying is a fine example of pleading in the alternative. Number One: *I'm not 100 percent sure it happened.* Number Two: *I didn't know it happened.* Number Three: *If it happened, I didn't order it to happen.* And Number Four: *I'm truly sorry that it did happen.*

"During the interrogation, Speer pretty well abandoned the first point—cultivated skepticism. He now acknowledges that it all *happened.* What we need to do is try real hard to move as many of the defendants as we can from the Goering camp to the Speer camp."

"What can we offer them?" John Amen asked.

"That's a problem. Maybe a firing squad. Those of them expecting execution—that's what they all want, a soldier's death. Some of them—I wouldn't want to name names here—might persuade the judges that their involvement in the whole business was, ah, in some critical way, indirect—that special pressures had been put on them—that there was a confusion of orders.... Who knows? But I'm going to ask the four special prosecutors to read over the interrogations as closely as you can, probing just the one question: *Is this guy somebody we can bring around?* Bring around to the Speer camp? And we can keep working on that point, urging them on in the direction of a) admitting that it happened, and b) saying, I'm sorry it did happen. Hammer away at it right through the prosecution's case up until they're on the stand, defending themselves. *Keep working on them.* Go back again and again if you see any possibilities. We've already had thirty-five sessions with Goering."

Another whistle. From the ranks somebody said, skeptically, "Thirty-five *interrogations*?"

"Thirty-five. Ask John Amen. And I was there for some of them. And I heard some of the others on tape. And I've talked with Gilbert. He's one industrious psychologist, considering that, as an army officer, he's not being paid by the hour. He's spending hours and hours with Goering. Keeps us well advised. But let's deal with any questions you have. I'm shooting for Monday, October 15th to start courtroom proceedings."

There were questions, and the excitement was felt. Many of the men there had fought in the war, some as infantrymen, others in other military branches. The combatant's spirit was there and for the lawyers among them, this was the showdown: the War Crimes Trial at the Palace of Justice. They would do the preliminary work, confront the enemy, plead their case, and hope to win a victory one day down the line, at the gallows.

Back at the work unit, Carver walked to Sebastian's office. The evidence of work done was clear, cabinets full, one or two spilled over. Sergeant Hempstone wasn't there so Carver pulled up her chair and sat down. He felt the raw curiosity of Sebastian, who knew that a critical meeting had taken place, but nothing else about it.

"I can't give you any details, but I can say this much: October 15th is a big day. From that day on in our dealings with Amadeus he will have become a formally indicted defendant."

"I think he's thought that's what he was all along."

"Probably. Besides, as we've discussed, I don't think Amadeus is inclined to lie about what he did."

"Or about what Camp Joni was like."

"We'll test the waters on that tomorrow."

"Yes sir."

"And Sebastian . . . when nobody else is around, call me George."

"Yes sir. George."

CHAPTER TWENTY-EIGHT

Nuremberg, October 1945

In the interrogation room it was as before except that the stenographer, Sergeant Hempstone, was not there. Along with the other defendants, General Amadeus had been formally indicted by the war crimes tribunal. He had the right, he had been advised by Captain Carver, to refuse further interrogations. Amadeus quickly declined to exercise that right. Carver knew that he was following the advice of Albert Speer, with whom almost every day in the exercise yard Amadeus exchanged words. The bugged conversations were transcribed and given to Robert Jackson, who passed them down, as useful, to individual prosecutors. Some of the other defendants were following the lead of Hermann Goering, who conversed chattily with one and all both in the yard and, as opportunities came up, in the cellblock hallway. He advised his cadre to decline further interrogation, though he did not himself heed that counsel.

The civilities that Amadeus had in the early weeks exchanged with fellow-defendant Goering had ended. Goering cherished his preeminence under the Fuehrer and, derivatively, in the eyes of the tribunal. He had sensed Albert Speer's conciliatory tone and had begun to draw away not only from Speer but from his protégé, Amadeus.

Goering and Speer had become silent antagonists in the late stages of the war, outspokenly at odds toward the end of the war. Goering had served as the Third Reich's vice chancellor, but no one knew more reliably than Speer that in the end, Adolf Hitler was backing away from Goering. And no one was a more authoritative witness to the final repudiation of his vice chancellor than Speer. Hitler had blurted out to him, in the last days of the war, that he would not appoint Goering as his successor. "He's not up to it," the Fuehrer had said. And then, a few weeks later, the final estrangement: The Fuehrer, persuaded that Goering was plotting to surrender to the Allies, signed an order to have Goering shot on sight at his villa in Obersalzberg.

But Hitler's misgivings about Goering leading, finally, to his decision to execute him, came in the last days of the Third Reich. It came during the "bunker-time," as Captain Carver referred to the period, January–April 1945, when Hitler lived in and ruled from his underground compound. Even those defendants who had been totally in thrall to Hitler, accepting his word as law, overpowered by his magnetism, hesitated now to affirm their faith in the Fuehrer.

They could understand judicial opportunism, so no one was surprised by the prison-yard gravitation of Amadeus to Speer. Some knew of the old association, Speer-Amadeus, which was one reason for the affinity of the two defendants. Those who hadn't known of it were quickly informed by prison gossip: Speer had figured in the early architectural career of the brigadier general, and had got him into the SS. Amadeus became a part of the Speer faction.

Lieutenant Harry Albright was pointedly helpful in recording the private exchanges between the two, using his ubiquitous listening devices. Albright's orders had been to pay special attention to Goering, which meant that the invisible directional microphone was focused on the Reichsfuehrer whenever he conversed with his fellow prisoners. Goering loved these exchanges. Back in his cell he had no one to talk to except his interrogators and, on his frequent visits, the psychiatrist, Captain G. M. Gilbert. With Gilbert, Goering quickly became expressive and voluble. The official psychiatrist spent great stretches of time with him, diligently writing down Goering's monologues immediately after returning to his study from the cell. Goering did not disguise from Gilbert, or indeed from the interrogators, that he was counseling defiance among his colleagues, stressing what he kept insisting were the legal disqualifications of the tribunal judges. He would say it again and again: The Soviet judge—of course—but also the others, were unqualified, and the court's indictments invalid as *ex post facto*. In one exchange with former Governor of Poland Hans Frank, whose defiance Goering encouraged, he had said, "The Americans? These are people who invaded Texas and California with ethnic savagery. What do they have against us?"

Today's was the fourth session conducted with Amadeus by Captain Carver, who focused now on two points: the exact nature of the defendant's activities as head of Camp Joni and the missing records. Carver was under special pressure from the Soviet delegation to extract from Amadeus some clue as to where such records might be hidden. They would yield the names of Russian prisoners of war gassed or executed.

"Herr Amadeus," Captain Carver persisted in the interrogation, "who was it who actually maintained the records of the victims—of the men and women—who went into the gas chamber?"

"We had record keepers. The formal responsibility was that of the Rottenfuehrer. A corporal. I was given only the gross figures, which I then relayed to Gruppenfuehrer Richard Glucks, who reported to Reichsfuehrer Himmler."

"Did the victims ever pass through your office?"

Amadeus hesitated. "If you are saying, were there people who, as you say, passed through my office and subsequently—died?" (*Yet again, Sebastian noted, General Amadeus had worked his way around the word "killed."*) "Yes."

"What was it that prevented such people, who subsequently died, from being taken directly from the train to the execution chamber? Why were they detained? And how many were there?"

"I assume you are talking about going from the train to that part of the compound that provided living quarters? Well, that would mean many people."

"Why 'many'?"

"Joni required a considerable workforce to maintain it."

"The people"—Carver tired of using the word *victims*; it was the correct word, but he was now bent on inducing a measure of relaxation in the defendant's formalistic answers. To go on using the words *victims* and *kill*, let alone *torture*, emphasized the antagonistic character of the interrogation, which would be unprofitable. Carver was seeking two things, one was factual information, the other the cultivation of whatever humane sensibility lay dormant in the man across the table. Whether or not such sensibility was there, Carver assumed that the prosecution would recommend—with Carver's entire approval—hanging. But repentance on the stand, at the trial, was always a second objective. "The people who were taken from the train to do labor work, they were what percentage of the arriving prisoners?"

"That would depend on the needs of the camp on any particular day."

"What percentage of the incoming prisoners might that be?"

"As low as ten percent, as high as thirty percent."

There was a knock on the door.

"Yes?" Carver called out.

One of the Amadeus guards walked over to the door and opened it to a sergeant. "Captain Carver, I need to pass on a personal message to you, sir."

Carver stood up and walked to the door. He caught the sergeant's signal, stepped into the corridor, and closed the door behind him. He quickly reappeared and addressed Sebastian. "I have to go . . . upstairs. Translate the following: 'Herr Amadeus, I am called to headquarters. Are you willing to talk with Lieutenant Reinhard while I am gone?' "

"Yes," Amadeus answered. "It will be a relief to speak in German, to do without the need of an interpreter."

Carver paused for a moment, then said, "Reinhard, why not go ahead? Yes. Go ahead with the line of questioning I was taking. If the son of a bitch doesn't cooperate, well—he doesn't cooperate. You know what we're after, you can fill me in later. Right now Colonel Amen needs to see me, and my guess is that his problem will use up a bit of time." He turned to the stenographer. "You can stop making a record unless Lieutenant Reinhard asks you to resume." He turned back to Sebastian. "Okay?"

"Yes sir."

The door closed.

Army of the United States Second Lieutenant Sebastian Reinhard was in the room with the Nazi Brigadefuehrer Kurt Waldemar Amadeus, former commander of an extermination camp, along with a stenographer and two MP guards who spoke not a word of German.

Sebastian thought it prudent to strike an informal note. So he started by saying, "I lived in Hamburg, where I was born. I was there until 1939, when my mother took me to America."

Amadeus looked sharply at Sebastian. Then said: "I know Hamburg. There is not much left of it, I understand."

"No, not much. I came through it on the way here. It is like

Nuremberg. . . . Well, the captain wishes me to continue the inquiry."

"Go ahead," Amadeus said. "I will say the same thing to you that I would to your captain."

"If an arrival was not sent immediately to the death chambers, how long did he continue in the workforce?"

"That depended. Some workers were especially qualified. For instance, a good electrician, an experienced carpenter."

"Did that mean if they continued to work in Camp Joni, they could hope to escape the . . . oven?" The German word was less burdened than *gas chamber.*

"No. I never told them that. On the other hand, I cannot answer for the practices of my subordinates. I thought it wrong to arouse false hopes."

"Why false?"

"Because there was a reason for such people to have arrived in the first place at an elimination camp. Some of them were Jews."

Sebastian made a note on his pad. "How did you know they were Jews?"

Amadeus seemed surprised by the question. "They arrived in a shipload of Jews. And most wore markings, identifying marks. Besides, I have had much experience. I can tell by just looking. For instance, you are part Jewish."

Sebastian looked up, intrigued.

"All that you have proved by saying that, Herr Amadeus, is that in fact you *cannot* discern Jewishness."

Amadeus shrugged, and gave out a tight little smile. "You were saying that when the trains arrived at Joni, there were people in the cars who were not Jewish? Yes, that's true, there were such people. But they were all in the cars for a reason. They were being *deported* for a reason. If they were Russians, for instance, they were either prisoners of war or Soviet sympathizers. And there were many who were suspected."

"Suspected of what?"

"Of cooperating with the Soviets. My job, Lieutenant Reinhard, was not to try them, but to eliminate them."

"Did you have the authority to suspend a sentence indefinitely, or to remit it?"

"No."

"Did you inquire directly from those who—who passed through your office—into the nature of their offense?"

"Their offense, most of them, was to be Jewish."

"Did you consider it a part of your duty to inquire why being Jewish meant being an enemy of the Third Reich?"

Amadeus began a smile, then stopped it abruptly. His tone was earnest. "You speak, Lieutenant Reinhard, as if the case against Jews was only a—what shall I say?—a peculiarity of the Fuehrer. Of course that is not the case. It was simply that the Fuehrer had the courage to act on the anti-Semitism of most Europeans."

Maybe, Sebastian thought, as substitute interrogator he was moving in a direction Captain Carver would not have taken. Still, here was Brigadefuehrer Kurt Amadeus, the stenographer Sergeant Hempstone, and two MP guards. Who would object? Carver was not present, and Carver had told him to pursue the interrogation.

So Sebastian decided to go ahead and try something different. Something that would be very difficult to do, perhaps impossible for a non-German-speaking interrogator. He said, "Would you consent to tell me in your own words what it was that brought you to believe the... strictures of Hitler—of the Fuehrer—on the matter of the Jews?"

Amadeus searched in his pocket and extracted a cigarette. "I was just beginning my career as an architect—" He stopped suddenly, reached back into his pocket, and brought out the package again. He extended it to Sebastian. "I should have offered you one. Would you care for a cigarette?"

"I don't smoke." A pause. "Thank you."

"*Bitte, bitte.* I was saying that I did some drafting with Herr Speer after graduating. He then got me a job—it was practically a starvation-level salary, but it was something—as assistant instructor at the Berlin Institute. At Christmas I sent him a card. He telephoned me and said he had become closely associated with the Fuehrer. That was when he advised me to enroll with the SS. To continue teaching was not an alternative—I was a junior and would be dropped at the end of the spring. Employment in architectural commerce was unlikely. You are aware of the unemployment figures in 1933, Lieutenant Reinhard?"

Sebastian nodded. "In 1933, my own father was a civil engineer in Hamburg and—" Sebastian blurted it out, immediately regretting that he had done so—"he voted for Hitler in 1933."

Amadeus puffed deeply from his cigarette, then stamped it out. Again he stared hard at Sebastian. "I became an officer in the SS. The discipline I accepted was to do as the Fuehrer's subordinates instructed me to do. But I accepted another obligation, a derivative obligation. Do you understand my language? You are manifestly too young to have been in college."

"Yes. I follow you all right."

"—which was to do what the Fuehrer said *and to try to think what he thought.* One is a better soldier for doing so. So I was a soldier of the Fuehrer. His orders became my orders, and his thinking, my thinking. And do you know, Lieutenant Reinhard, it wasn't only people named Amadeus, and Goering, and Frank, and Kaltenbrunner who believed in Aryan supremacy. Others, with... more familiar names, also followed his orders."

The door swung open. Captain Carver returned to his seat. He addressed Sebastian. "You getting anywhere?"

"He began talking. But we ended on the usual line, him saying the usual thing—Hitler gave the orders, he followed them."

"Did you get into where the records might be?"

"Actually, no."

"Well," Carver sighed, "let's try one more time. The Soviets are really hot on this and they're convinced the records weren't destroyed. Here we go—" He turned to the defendant.

"Herr Amadeus, when you were relieved of command, did you take any records from Camp Joni with you?"

"No," Brigadefuehrer Amadeus said, the tone of his voice returning to the laconic humdrum of the three previous sessions.

A half hour later they were overdue for the break. "Tell him we're cutting out. He'll be told when we want another session with him."

Sebastian relayed the message. Captain Carver stood up and motioned to the guards.

CHAPTER TWENTY-NINE

Nuremberg, November 20, 1945

The big day came. Deadline after deadline had come and gone, aborted. The hope that the trial could begin on October 15 proved illusory. Only the indictments had got done by then.

Now, on November 20, what seemed the entire press of the world was in the huge courtroom of the Palace of Justice. The room had been redone before the event, designed as the final act of the Nazi warlords. They would not be standing arms raised to Hitler, or commanding army divisions or submarine squadrons or radio and news outlets. They'd be sitting silent in two rows, earphones on, wearing the drab clothes issued by the victors and blinking, from time to time, for relief from the piercing lights designed for newsreel photographers. The press was lodged to the right of the defendants; behind the press were the spectators. Immediately in front, the defense attorneys, beyond them the august tribunal, eight judges, two from each of the Allied powers.

The Russian detachment had recommended at preparatory sessions in London and, later, in Berlin, that the judges appear at the bench wearing military uniforms. The Russians wanted the finery of military conquerors, presiding over the fate of the dastardly conquered.

But that was exactly *not* the theatrical vision of the principal actors at the London Conference. Great Britain's Sir Geoffrey Lawrence argued the point strenuously: This was to be a trial, not a court martial. He was joined in that opinion by United States Judge Francis Biddle. They had a problem with the prideful French, who a mere twelve months earlier had still not succeeded in ejecting the last Nazi occupier from the republic—they were not opposed to displaying uniforms even though they had not distinguished themselves on the battlefield. Donnedieu de Vabres argued briefly in favor of the Russians' suggested procedure. In Napoleonic tradition, he reminded his colleagues, legal procedures were not thought to require judicial robing. But he ended up voting with his western colleagues, leaving only the Russians' I. T. Nikitchenko and his Russian alternate dissenting. Faced with the majority vote against, Nikitchenko announced, simply, that the Russians would appear in military uniforms... never mind what the other judges wore; and now they did so, entering the courtroom, succeeding their brother judges who filed in silently, wearing judicial robes. Only the sound of whirring movie cameras reached the ear. The procession brought the assembled to their feet—defendants, prosecutors, interpreters, reporters, VIP spectators. The judges' countenances were grave as they took their seats behind the long wooden bench. Lord Lawrence left no doubt, by his expression and manner, that he had the sense of it, that he was superintending a historic proceeding.

He began, as required, with formalities especially touching on the defendants. He expressed satisfaction that the Chief of Prosecution had accommodated, as required by basic law, the defense attorneys. In fact, the defense had used profligately the resources of the prosecution in collecting material and summoning witnesses, complaining right until the trial started that they needed more time.

The twenty-three German attorneys sat at their desks, wearing robes of black, purple, and red, according to the tradition of the schools of law from which they had graduated. To one side of the dock, in glass booths, the interpreters were intense and active. Cable lines snaked from these booths across the silver-gray carpet to the defendants' dock and to the defendants' lawyers and, in another direction, to the 250 journalists and newspapermen greedily relying on facilities for interpreting and for intercommunicating. Those facilities were extensive, as ordered by Colonel Andrus a mere eight weeks ago, greatly exceeding the forty-three terminals he had thought would be sufficient. But it was too late for anyone left behind to complain, and the horde of journalists would diminish as trial tedium set in.

Judge Lawrence directed that the indictments should be read out, word for word. One reporter unearthed the undisclosed reason for the decision to go through this laborious exercise. The Russian judge, Nikitchenko, had been absent from Nuremberg. Arriving in town only the day before, he said simply to the presiding judge that he wasn't prepared. What to do? Judge Lawrence declined to postpone the entire proceeding. How to delay the trial? One way to diddle away time permitting Nikitchenko to do his homework was, precisely, to read out all the indictments. This was done, at tedious length.

It was after that that the court composed itself to listen to the inevitable, predictable pleas. Twenty-three defense lawyers, one after another, pleaded the illegitimacy of the court. The court had no authority, they said, one after another, using, for the most part, identical arguments and sometimes identical language.

The defense plea was to the effect that neither the Kellogg-Briand Pact nor any binding international covenant had established the alleged criminality of "starting an unjust war." The pleading went further, asserting an inherent disqualification in the presiding judges on the grounds that they represented victorious powers and could therefore not reasonably be expected to administer justice when weighing the conduct of leaders in the enemy camp.

Those arguments had been anticipated at the London Conference. Judge Lawrence summarily dismissed the appeal, making—with no evident embarrassment—the circular point that such pleadings conflicted with Article 3 of the Charter promulgated by the International Military Tribunal, which provided that neither the Tribunal nor its membership nor its decrees could be challenged by either the prosecution or the defense. "Thus, the appeal was without substance... because we have ruled that it is without substance."

The moment arrived, though not until the following day, to hear the defendants' individual pleas. Did they plead guilty?

Or not guilty? "Herr Goering"—titles and honorifics were conspicuously gone—"how do you plead?"

The defendant began what threatened to be a statement—"*Before I answer the question of the Tribunal whether or not I am guilty*—" but was stopped dead. Judge Lawrence told Goering that he must plead simply *guilty* or *not guilty.*

Reichsmarschall Goering, his face contorted in sulk, capitulated. "In the sense of the indictment, not guilty."

Lawrence called the next name. Rudolf Hess said into the microphone: "*Nein.*"

From the bench: "That will be entered as a plea of not guilty."

The court heard the same plea—not guilty—from all twenty-three defendants.

Now was the time to hear from the prosecution. Justice Jackson did not disappoint.

He tackled head on the business about victors prosecuting the defeated. It didn't matter who was victorious, who vanquished. What was happening in Nuremberg was a trial. There were heavy responsibilities to international law, and to history, to uphold the rights of defendants *to make their case.* But the Articles formulated by the International Military Tribunal were overarchingly applicable. Individual Germans were being held responsible for laws that transcended victor/vanquished.

Suppose, Jackson went on, that no trial whatever had been organized? That the Allies had undertaken no initiative at all to redress the wrongs of the past six years? "That four great nations, flushed with victory and stung with injury, [should] stay the hand of vengeance and voluntarily submit their captive enemies to the judgment of the law?—this is one of the most significant tributes that power has ever paid to reason." Justice Jackson was telling the defendants that if it had been, as now they charged it was, simply a matter of victors' justice, then the defendants would not be sitting in Nuremberg with twenty-three lawyers. They'd have been shot after V-E Day.

Those opening sentences by Robert Jackson sought to convey the august character of the trial and to generate excitement about the historic idea of international war crimes. Here, for the first time in history, were representatives of the countries that had won a great world war face-to-face with representatives of the defeated nation, summoned not merely to hand over their swords, but to answer for their conduct: for waging wars of aggression, for violating the rules of warfare, and for engaging in practices which in years to come would be routinely perceived as genocidal. His words evoked the sublime purposes of an avenging noose, and it dangled in the imagination of everyone crowded into the room. It was all but palpable over the two tiers of benches on which the defendants sat. They were bedraggled and seemed fatalistic, their days of glory so inescapably gone, their forlorn demeanor enhancing the gravity of Justice Jackson's words, so carefully chosen, artfully arranged, suggesting that these were vermin of the earth who should be reduced to dust.

Jackson took outspoken pride in the trial's procedures, which would permit the defense lawyers to make their cases and to summon their witnesses. To do otherwise would be "to pass these defendants a poisoned chalice, putting it to our lips as well."

The renowned Jackson rhetoric went on in near voluptuous judicial waves. "We must summon such detachment and intellectual integrity to our task that this trial will commend itself to posterity as fulfilling humanity's aspirations to do justice." Press and spectators—and defendants—were warned that much time would need to be spent. "The catalog of crimes will omit nothing that could be conceived by a pathological prince, engaged in cruelty, and lusting for power." And the defendants were advised that there would be no diffidence in the case the Allies would make against them. "Against their opponents, the Nazis directed such a campaign of arrogance, brutality, and annihilation as the world has not witnessed since the pre-Christian era. At length, bestiality and bad faith reached such excess that they aroused the sleeping strength of imperiled civilization. Its united efforts have ground the Nazi war machine to fragments. But the struggle has left Europe a liberated yet prostrate land where a demoralized society struggles to survive. These are the fruits of the sinister forces that sit with these defendants in the prisoners' dock."

"Hell of a speech," Harry Albright commented that evening at the bar of the Grand when he linked up with Sebastian. "I picked up some reactions. Those two guys over there"—he pointed to the far end of the bar—"one UPI, one Reuters. We walked here together from the Palace. Were they *impressed*. . . . Did you—by the way—know that the defendants lunched in the same room with their defense attorneys today?"

Sebastian said he hadn't known that. He assumed the conversations had been . . . overheard. Albright nodded.

"So much for the poisoned chalice. Are you going to report to Captain Carver what Amadeus avowed to the defense lawyers?"

"Oh shit, Reinhard. You know we've been eavesdropping from the beginning. I won't ask myself whether Justice Robert Jackson knows it all, and whether he'd think of that as poisoning the chalice of justice. And anyway—does it really matter? Is there any defense those murderers can come up with, anything that would make any difference?"

"You're saying they're all going to hang?"

Albright retreated. "Let me put it this way: None of the stuff we've bugged and given to the prosecution, as far as I can figure it out, is going to change much."

"Why, in that case, am I spending so much time with Amadeus?"

"I guess to make him show contrition. Someone should. Maybe the hangman will take pity. Refuse to spring the trapdoor."

Sebastian did not smile.

"But I repeat, Sebby. Jackson made a hell of a speech. He made me feel this whole thing is worth it. But, oh god, it is going to take forever, isn't it?"

"Sounds like it," Sebastian agreed. "Let's hope it leads to—well, to fewer war crimes."

CHAPTER THIRTY

Nuremberg, November 1945

The defendants were of course entitled to individual counsel. One or two dragged their feet in the matter, writing to wives or sons or former associates for advice on whom to retain; and then there was the problem of persuading the lawyer of choice to take on the job.

Working against their taking on these clients was the reluctance of many German attorneys, some of them prominent, to associate themselves in so public a theater with the defense of egregious Nazi figures. Working in favor of the defendants was the dormant legal industry in the months after surrender. Everyone had complaints, major and minor. Whom to sue because your husband had been killed at the front? Or, for that matter, in a concentration camp? Would the United States Army Air Force appear at the dock to answer for the destruction of a dozen German cities, and pay retribution? What about your neighbor? Sue him? For what? Insufficient heat for your apartment? An uneven supply of electrical power? What would be the expression on the grocer's face if served a complaint for failing to provide regular rations of milk and butter and cheese?

Yet there were lawyers hungry for work, and the war crimes tribunal paid a defense attorney 4,000 marks in advance, and then 2,500 marks per month of service.

Amadeus was one of the defendants who dragged his feet. Finally, only one week before the trial began and defense attorneys needed to be at their stations, Amadeus advised Captain Carver, who passed the word on to Colonel Amen, that he wished as defense counsel his brother.

"Who in the hell is he?" Colonel John Harlan Amen, interrogations chief and renowned New York lawyer before the war, asked Carver.

"All I got was this handwritten memo from Amadeus. From our Amadeus. Here's what it says: '*George Friedrich Amadeus, born 1918—I think.*' Got that? '*I think,*' says big brother. He's not even sure when his brother was born. Then he wrote, '*Address, 20 Nottingerstrasse. Heidelberg. Graduated, Juristische Fakultat der Universitat Heidelberg 1939. Tuberculosis. Exempt from military duty. Self-employed, lawyer.*'"

"That's all?"

"That's everything he wrote down."

"Well." Colonel Amen grunted out his displeasure. "This guy—twenty-seven years old! He'll certainly bowl over our learned judges." Amen fiddled with his unlit pipe. "Obviously he has had zero experience in international law. On the other hand, I don't think we have the authority to refuse him. Hell. *Of course* we don't have that authority." He gave it more thought. "Whatever high points in international law are going to be made by the defendants, assuming any *are* going to be made, will be made by the flossy German lawyers the other defendants have working for them. It's just a question, in this case, whether a resourceful lawyer could come up with a defense that could mitigate Amadeus's sentence. Tell you what. Hand Amadeus—*our* Amadeus—a memo, in the form of questions. Just a few questions. Like," Colonel Amen looked up and closed his eyes, as if a stenographer were standing by.

"'Does Herr George Friedrich Amadeus have experience in international law? . . . Do you deem him competent to assert your rights under German law? . . . Has he had experience arguing the law before, uh, before judges'—"

"Come on, Colonel. I can't ask him that. It would suggest that if brother George Friedrich *hadn't* had experience arguing in court he wouldn't qualify to act before *this* court."

"You're right," Amen conceded. "As far as we're concerned, this could be his very first trial case as a lawyer—if he's the defense counsel the defendant nominates. . . . Well, just the same, shoot a couple of those questions at him. In writing. And get Amadeus, *in writing*, to affirm that his brother is the man he wants."

George Friedrich Amadeus arrived two days later and presented himself at the desk. The WAC sergeant looked down at her schedule sheet. "Yes, we are expecting you, Herr Amadeus. Please sit. I'll notify Colonel Andrus's office."

There was much briefing to be done of defense attorneys. This included a general introduction to the judicial scene and to protocols of the court by Major Esterhazy. The briefings were of course in German.

Now the conversation became specific. "I have here also a copy of the indictment." Amadeus was handed a fat folder, which included copies of the war crimes charter. "And I have arranged for a room in which Captain Carver, who has been in charge of the interrogation of Kurt Amadeus, can brief you more particularly in the matter of your client's case. You can of course question him."

"*Spricht er Deutsch?*"

"No. But there will be an interpreter. After that you will be taken to your brother, your client."

"I've got to admit, Captain, I'm *really* eager to see this guy, twenty-seven years old!"

"How old is *our* Amadeus? The killer Amadeus? I forget."

"Kurt Amadeus is thirty-six," Sebastian said.

"I wonder how he got on with his kid brother? Were you able to dig out anything else about his career?"

"All I did was check the military and civil records for the Heidelberg area. His name didn't appear in any roster of Nazis or account of Nazi activities."

"I don't suppose it would make any difference if it had. We've got a total of forty-eight defense attorneys and eighteen of them were Nazis. As long as they're not war criminals, that's okay by our rules." There was a knock. "Sebby, go open the door, will you?"

A sergeant was there with the visitor. "Lieutenant, this is Herr George Friedrich Amadeus." He motioned to the tall young man. His shirt collar was loose around his neck. He wore a dark blue tie, a small gold object at tie-clasp level, a black corduroy jacket and pants that brought the blondness of his hair and white-pinkness of his cheeks into broad relief. In one hand he carried a hat of the kind that closes tight over your ears and a threadbare coat; in the other, a briefcase.

Carver rose from his chair and extended his hand. "I am Captain Carver, an official on the interrogation team. Please sit down." Sebastian rendered the words in German. He was not himself introduced. Interpreters were not introduced. They were intentionally treated as mechanical accessories.

Sebastian wondered whether there would be any small talk. Carver said only, "I hope you will be comfortable in your quarters." Carver didn't know and didn't care what quarters Colonel Andrus's staff had secured for the German lawyer and also didn't care that Amadeus should know he didn't know or care. Amadeus simply nodded.

"You are familiar with the indictment?"

"No. I have it here but I have not read it."

"You are familiar with the war crimes charter, promulgated in London?"

"No. I know that it exists, but I have not read it."

"We have spent many hours with your brother. And you are entitled, as you know, to be familiar with our case, though not of course with the exact shape of our arguments as the trial unfolds."

"When is my brother on the dock?"

"He is the seventeenth, in the order made up."

"I shall object to that."

"On what grounds?"

"It will be prejudicial to hear the case against the other prisoners before my client is at the dock."

Carver spoke now to Sebastian. "Tell him the decision was made back in London to go with a multiple-defendant trial. We can't prevent him from filing an objection, but you can tell him that objections of that nature are foreclosed by the charter."

Sebastian relayed the information.

George Friedrich Amadeus opened his briefcase, extracted a folder, and began reading the language of the indictment.

Carver waited.

After a minute or two he said, "Is there a question you wish to ask me concerning the indictment?"

"How can I tell? I have not finished reading it."

The muscles clenched in Carver's face. He spoke to Sebastian. "Maybe he wants us to sit here while he reads up on the Hague Convention." And then, addressing the young lawyer, "Herr Amadeus, if there are questions that arise after your readings, you can inform the office of Colonel Amen that you wish to get through to me."

"I don't believe I will have anything further to discuss with you. Kindly take me to my brother."

Captain Carver got up, his patience at an end. He said nothing to Amadeus. To Sebastian, "Tell him to keep his seat. You go over to Chief Landers, set up a cubicle, and have them fetch the prisoner. Explain to this character that he'll be conferring through a glass grate with a slot for document exchanges."

Walking to the door, Carver paused. "Tell you what, Sebby. It'll be a while before they can set all that up, and he's just sitting here. Why don't you come back in after seeing Landers, and sit in the room with him. Maybe you can fill him in on the world war."

"I'll do that, Captain. I'd kind of like to know more about him. About the Amadeus clan."

"If he wants to talk to you, that's his business."

Sebastian told Herr Amadeus he would return after making arrangements for the visit with his brother.

CHAPTER THIRTY-ONE

Nuremberg, December 1945

The prosecution had spent ten vigorous days arguing not the guilt of individual defendants but rather the corporate guilt of entire organizations. The objective was nakedly there: to lay convenient groundwork for *prima facie* guilt-by-association.

The prosecution was asking the tribunal to affirm that participation by Germans in any of several Nazi activities should, *eo ipso*, justify a finding of guilt of war criminal activity, such guilt to be punishable by whatever the court, reviewing the evidence against individual defendants, thought appropriate, including a death sentence. A defendant shall be held guilty, the prosecution pleaded, if he had been 1) part of the Nazi Party "leadership," 2) a member of the Reich Cabinet, 3) a member of the SS, Gestapo, SD, or SA, or 4) if he had been an officer in the German High Command.

This was big-time judicial activism. If the Nuremberg tribunal, in the matter of the twenty-three individual defendants seated opposite in the courtroom, concurred in these pleadings of the prosecution, future courts—of which there would be many, dealing with lesser figures—would need only to establish that a defendant had been any-of-the-above in order immediately to be judged guilty, under the law, of criminal conduct.

Sitting alongside Albright, Sebastian, for an hour or two, took in the arguments being made by U.S., British, and Soviet prosecutors, after which he repaired to his little office with its typewriter and mimeograph machine and dictionary and, by now, twenty file cabinets. There he would resume his work on German-language affidavits, records, and archives.

The interrogation of Amadeus had been suspended for an interval. Sebastian was instructed by Captain Carver on what especially to look for, and after a while he needed no day-to-day guidance. Carver, meticulous but dogmatically antibureaucratic, came to trust the young man who learned his job so quickly and accepted his workload without complaint. When Sebastian came upon long stretches of reports or memoranda or affidavits that he judged routine, he would not go to the pains of translating them word for word. Instead, he'd write a few paragraphs of paraphrase and attach them to a folder. To it he sometimes appended a three-by-five card with a personal note, which Captain Carver would be expected to discard after reading. *This character*—Sebastian was describing one *Obersturmfuehrer* (First Lieutenant) named Heinrich Lichtman—*did extra, unreported work at Joni and beat up his prisoners before sending them up to the gas chamber. I hope you can keep him alive for a while. I'd like to go to college, then law school, then come back and prosecute this one myself. —Again, seat of the pants, boss, I think Humbolt here is telling the truth. The mathematics don't work. The camp couldn't have handled the claimed volume. Must have been terribly disappointing.*

Sometimes Captain Carver would ask for more detail. Sebastian had begun his mission with an almost exclusive concern for the life and work of Kurt Amadeus, especially at Camp Joni, but the focus on Joni implicated another Nuremberg defendant, Governor General Frank, who exercised civil authority over the region. Hans Frank reigned from nearby Cracow, where Amadeus, among other duties, had personally supervised the forced-labor construction of Frank's personal bunker. Sebastian nurtured a great yearning to travel, some day, to the area. A twelve-hour train trip from Berlin to Cracow and then the forty miles to Lodz and then to the site, to view Camp Joni and see with his own eyes where it all took place. He wondered how many years would go by before such a trip, through 500 miles of Soviet-occupied territory, would be possible.

He wasn't clear how much of Joni still existed today, December of 1945, ten months after the last Jew there had been killed. In March and April, the final two months of the war, and on into the summer until approximately the same time the war crimes trial began, reports from the Russians were to the effect that Joni was being used as a prisoner of war camp for German soldiers. But then, in October, Sebastian saw the report that Joni was "being destroyed." It was confusing.

There were almost daily communications, at headquarters in the Palace, coming in from one or another Soviet desk, whether in Moscow, Berlin, or (most frequently) the Soviet command at the Palace itself. One of those bulletins contradicted the earlier bulletin: Camp Joni would continue in use (until further notice) as a POW facility. Sebastian thought more about it, and brought it up with Albright one day. Might he at some point during the trial find himself free to travel the 500 miles? Not inconceivably, he might wangle some kind of a commission from Captain Carver to travel to Cracow and Lodz to do research. Harry threw cold water on the idea. "The Soviets permit a U.S. officer to just amble into Soviet Poland and look around? Moonshine, Reinhard."

Sebastian didn't know what Camp Joni looked like, as of December 1945, but he could have drawn a fairly detailed diagram of how it looked a year ago, when Amadeus was still its commander. After reading a thousand intracamp memoranda he could compose a detailed picture of Camp Joni in his mind. He knew the camp's layout almost by feel.

Tuesday morning, while U.S. Assistant Prosecutor Thomas Dodd was addressing the tribunal on the subject of the organizational guilt of the SS, Sebastian closed his eyes. He conjured up the neatly designed row of ten barracks; the kitchen, the SS quarters, the hospital, the railroad terminal building. Then, at the southwestern end, the gas chamber and crematorium, housed in gray concrete, the large smokestack jutting up from one end, which gave up into the Polish air traces of the ashen remains of the wretched men, women, and children whose final portal this had been.

Bizarre that the room in which the victims were made to disrobe lay in the center of that building. From that room Amadeus's charges walked, or were made to walk—or crawl—into the gas chamber at one end. When the heavy, airtight door closed and the gas-slaughter proceeded, twenty-one minutes were counted: Everyone would be safely dead then. But now—Sebastian forced himself to focus on the building's odd design—the bodies would have to be physically removed. That was the work of the *Sonderkommandos*—conscripted Jews—who came in and opened the iron door on the stench. Their job was to transport the corpses (800 of them at a time fitted into Joni's gas chamber) back across the same room in which, a half hour earlier, they had disrobed—on into the crematorium, where four corpses, one after another, fitted onto each of the four steel belts that conveyed them into the molten heat, producing ashes which in due course were emptied into the Vistula, which wound its sleepy way by the camp, a half kilometer away.

The arguments in the courtroom carried on. Two weeks went by. A certain restlessness crept into the Palace of Justice.

It was appeased by the Christmas break, awaited with breathless eagerness by the entire cadre at the Palace. Sebastian had plotted his ten-day leave step by step. He would take a train to Frankfurt, another to Paris. He would spend the night and board the Eurostar train to Calais, and then take the ferry to Dover. Two more hours by train and then the Underground (his mother, Annabelle, had sent him a tiny route map). He would go from Charing Cross to Baker Street Station. He'd be at 22 Heath Street some time early in the afternoon. "I don't care what time, Sebby," his mother had said excitedly in their phone call. "I'll be waiting for you on Sunday, December 23rd. Oh my darling Sebby, it's been more than two years! Twenty-nine months—" Sebastian had leaned into the telephone to permit him to lower his voice when speaking out his affection for his mother. The bank of six telephone units in the Palace lobby was crowded. Two enlisted men were close behind him, waiting their turn.

Departing Nuremberg, he felt a strong stirring of impatience with the entire judicial process. The day before he set out for London, the *Stars and Stripes* reported that two Japanese had been convicted by an Australian military court at Wewak, New Guinea. Lieutenant Takehiko Tazaki was charged with eating flesh from the body of an Australian soldier. A second military court at Morotai found Captain Tokio Iwasa guilty of bayoneting an Australian airman. It all appeared endless.

He needed to assault himself over and over again with the same question most of his colleagues were asking: *What was the alternative?* Sebastian Reinhard knew in great detail what Kurt Amadeus had presided over at Camp Joni, and a great deal, in recent weeks, about the awful rule of Hans Frank. And then, up an echelon or two in the hierarchical ranks, there were Goering and SS #2 chief Ernst Kaltenbrunner. And over there in another division of the hierarchy, the generals and admirals and diplomats and munitions makers. The whole despicable lot. But did he, frustrated by the judicial process, feel that, if left alone and given the authority, he'd be willing to take a pistol from his pocket and fire it at the head of Amadeus? It vexed him that he could not imagine making himself do this, he explained to his mother in her tiny, cozy flat off Portland Place.

"There's something creepy-crawly inside most of us that says you can't shoot somebody unless you're in combat or—unless some... body... some *official* has condemned him to death." Perhaps it was that reservation that reassured him that he could never have accepted service in the SS. Perhaps he had his bloodlines to thank for this.

His mother had listened to her son for the better part of an afternoon and now, after serving him the best she had managed to put together from what she could buy at the PX, plus the Virginia ham Henrietta had sent her for Christmas, she listened again, and heard the descriptions of Camp Joni and the prisoner, Kurt Waldemar Amadeus, and reflected gratefully on the relative aridity, after the death of her husband Axel, of her own experience, decoding transmission after transmission of directives from sundry command posts in the Reich to sundry officials in Germany, and in the conquered territories.

"Funny, Mama, that we'd both be spending our time translating German documents into English. Only you have an extra step to travel. You have to go code to German, then German to English."

She smiled her broad smile and poured another glass of wine. "It's not like translating Goethe. One folder I spent maybe two weeks on was abruptly declassified. So I sent it to Oma. Dear mother. She wrote back wondering why I was spending that kind of time decoding and translating a long official document on revising laundry procedures in military camps."

Sebastian brightened at the mention of his grandmother. "I had a letter from her a couple of weeks ago—"

"Did she mention Munich?"

"*Exactly!* She said I should maneuver to convict anyone—*Alle!*—who had been involved in the bombing of Munich. 'And it doesn't matter whether they're Germans or Americans. They should all be hanged.'"

Sebastian stopped and, looking up, said, "I guess everybody has somebody he'd like to hang. I've got my Amadeus."

"Amadeus," Annabelle repeated the word. "What a name for such a man. *Amadeus:* God-love. Love-God."

"*Amo, amas, amat—*" Sebastian put on the look of a dutiful schoolchild giving his lines. Annabelle chimed in. Together they completed the conjugation of the basic Latin verb, to love: "*Amamus, amatis, amant.*"

They giggled, and Annabelle leaned over and kissed her son on his curly brown hair.

CHAPTER THIRTY-TWO

Nuremberg, January 1946

Two days later, the phone rang in his office. It didn't ring often but whenever it did, Sebastian was glad for the interruption. Whoever was calling, on whatever subject, it got him relief from the tedium of translation. When it was Albright on the line, the call promised to yield five minutes or more of courthouse gossip. When it was Captain Carver, it meant fresh instructions or comments on previously done work.

Sometimes when the trial was going on Harry would ring from his listening aerie. He did so now. "Tom Dodd says he's going to show a documentary on the death camps tomorrow. Otto Stahmer is objecting. So would I, if I was Goering's attorney. Those films aren't going to be much fun to look at, but I think you ought to see them when they're shown. I'll tell you tonight what the ruling is, though it's pretty much predictable. How's your protégé doing with his kid-attorney? Hey listen, Sebby, I've got an idea. I won't tell you about it now. Maybe tonight. Maybe not till tomorrow night."

"Sounds mysterious."

"*Pluck the mystery from my heart*—you think you're the only war-crimes regular who reads books all the time? That's *Hamlet,* Sebastian."

"I thought it was Dick Tracy. Hang on, someone's at the door . . . Well I'll be damned. That was a guy from Carver's office, says Carver's been trying to reach me on the phone but it's busy. I get about one call a day and—never mind. I'm going to hang up."

He dialed the assistant prosecutor.

"Sebastian? Listen. Get here in a hurry. Young Amadeus is on his way. He says he has a message from—the prisoner. He's coming to tell me about it. Then he made a sort of oddball request. He wants *you* there to serve as interpreter. Which is fine, but there are one or two other interpreters around, like maybe fifty. I said okay, I'd get you. So come on up here."

"Yes sir."

George Friedrich Amadeus arrived, as directed, at Room B-442 and was led in by the pool secretary who did duty for Captain Carver and two other prosecutors. Amadeus was dressed exactly as on the first day. He took a seat and turned his head not to Carver, but to Sebastian. Sebastian attempted diplomatically to compensate for this by tilting his head to one side, sufficiently to make it imaginable that the new defense counsel was addressing not him, but the prosecutor.

"My client has authorized me to communicate something to you *on the absolute promise of secrecy from the other prisoners.*"

"Yes," Carver said, anxiously.

"My client has decided, subject to several considerations, to give thought to changing his plea."

George Carver stared at Amadeus. To Sebastian he said, "Tell him to say that again."

The interpretation was the same.

"Ask him what 'changing his plea' means, exactly, in German."

Amadeus replied that, in German, changing a plea of *not guilty* meant entering a plea of *guilty*.

To Sebastian, without revealing in facial expression his excitement, Carver said, "Sebby, this is like the end of the world!" Then, to Amadeus: "What are these considerations your client is referring to?"

"He wishes unlimited time, before his turn comes on the dock, to consult with Lieutenant Reinhard."

"Ahh. Yes. And what else?"

"If he decides to change his plea, he wishes to be called to the dock *after* Herr Speer has been heard, not before."

"Yes. And what else?"

"If he decides to alter his plea, he must be protected against any further physical contact with the other defendants."

"Yes. And then . . ."

"If he decides to alter his plea and is condemned to death, he wishes to be shot rather than hanged." Herr Amadeus's facial expression was unchanged.

Carver paused. "Is that the list?"

"That is the list."

"I will of course need to consult my superior. Do you wish to ask anything further?"

"No. I have my office here at the Palace." He reached into the pocket of his black pants and pulled out a key to remind himself of the number. "I am at C-482."

"We will find you, Herr Amadeus. But I cannot tell you how long it will take to rule—to decide upon—your requests. Good day."

Amadeus nodded and rose. His head erect, he stood up in his ill-fitting suit and walked to the door.

Justice Jackson stared at Carver in disbelief. "There's no possibility there was a misunderstanding, a mistranslation?"

"None. I had him say it three times."

"Jesus Christ. This could change the whole scene, getting Amadeus as a cooperative witness! But there are lots of problems. We're both lawyers—hell, everybody under this roof is a lawyer—could this court now *permit* a revised plea of guilty?"

"I know you can in a military court, Judge."

"Well, you can't on a capital charge in conventional criminal proceedings. That's correct, isn't it, George?"

"That's what they told us at law school—"

"But I'm not sure they addressed that point in London. I'll find out from Biddle." He wrote a note. "Oh my god, imagine sharing this information with the Soviets. There are a ton of things here we'll have to consider. Let me see where he's now scheduled in the defense roster." He brought a folder from a desk drawer. "He's slotted at number seventeen. Speer is in the number eighteen slot. If we went for it, if the whole thing flushes out, we'd move Speer to number seventeen and Amadeus to number eighteen. By the way, what the hell's the meaning of *that* request?"

"Amadeus was a protégé of Speer."

"Yeah, I remember. It still isn't obvious to me why he wants to go *after* Speer. Hmm. . . . What the hell, this is topsy-turvy stuff, but it could be a great development. Lordy, lordy. If we could persuade him to be the *first* defense guy! . . . No, that wouldn't work, that would take too much unraveling of things. Carver, listen. There's one of his requests that makes no difference to us, the one involving his interpreter, the lieutenant. Reinhard. Let him go in to Amadeus beginning right away. As often as he wants. That costs us nothing."

"What reason do we give to Chief Landers for authorizing those visits?"

Jackson furrowed his brow. "Yeah. It would be easier bureaucratically if Reinhard was a priest."

"Or a psychologist."

"Right. Captain Gilbert goes wherever he wants, whenever he wants. We're going to have to get an okay from Andrus on this. What should we tell him? Eventually, we'll have to let him in on the big picture."

Jackson paused. "I've got it."

"What'll it be, sir?"

"It will be this. *Justice Robert Jackson, United States Chief Prosecutor, desires it.* Make me up a memo addressed to Landers. *The U.S. Prosecutor orders that Lieutenant*—what's his first name?—"

"Sebastian."

"*Lieutenant Sebastian Reinhard be admitted into the cell of prisoner Kurt Amadeus whenever the prisoner wishes and*"—Jackson broke out into a large smile, interrupting the draft directive—"we mustn't sound too sycophantic!—*whenever the prisoner wishes and Lieutenant Reinhard is available.*"

Carver returned to his office. Once again that morning, Sebastian's telephone rang. But this call, from Chief Landers, brought dismaying news—had Sebastian not got his notice? No. Notice to what effect? Beginning on January 22, crowding at the Grand Hotel required doubling up by all bachelors. "I hear you, Chief," was all that Sebastian could say.

He dialed Harry. "I got the same notice. Shit."

They would discuss the ultimatum that afternoon when they met before dinner.

CHAPTER THIRTY-THREE

January 1946

Teresa Cadonau walked quickly from her job at the Nuremberg-Furth Enclave laundry in order to arrive at the bakery before the line grew too long, which it always did, late in the afternoon. So that she would be permitted to leave work early, she took to arriving at work at 0730 instead of 0800. The warrant officer in charge of the considerable enterprise thought this reasonable enough—trade a late half hour for an early half hour. There were twenty-two laundresses engaged in doing Third Division camp laundry, some of it by hand because of the shortage of electrical washing machines. The machine factory had been bombed, and reconstruction was taking longer than anticipated.

Laundering by hand was a job given to junior employees, and Teresa had now risen to washing-machine seniority. But she wasn't as satisfied as she thought she would be, merely moving up from the laundry's hand-washing section. The reason for it was frustration with the preset cycle speed of the Miele model machine. It required fourteen minutes to do a ration of washing. After two days of experimentation, she approached the chief and asked if she might be given an additional machine. She explained that she would then fill one machine and, five minutes later, the second, so that they could alternately disgorge their laundered loads, giving her time to press one lot while a stock of fresh laundering was being done.

"What you are saying, Teresa," the chief commented, "is that you are eager to undertake exactly twice the load that you would otherwise undertake."

Teresa, strong, blue-eyed, full-bodied, her corn-colored hair held back by the hair net, acknowledged the point. "*Ja.* But I was not asking for double pay."

"And you wouldn't get it, no matter how much you accomplished."

"I was thinking perhaps fifty percent more? Fifteen marks a day? Herr Chief, I have been here almost six weeks, and I have climbed from number eighteen to number ten. That means that you have hired eight people in eight weeks. That's, then, one every week. If I do double work, and you pay me only two marks more, you have saved two marks."

"And if your work isn't up to standard?"

Teresa smiled urbanely. "You *know* that would never be the case."

"I'll think about it. Of course, I would need to clear it with Clara." Clara was the head laundress.

"Thank you, Herr Chief."

Teresa got the extra two marks and for the first week was frazzled by the workload. That Friday, at the desk in her mother's old room, she scratched out a note and enclosed the money order for thirty marks.

"The living room, Mama," she wrote, "is being worked on. I pay the carpenter, who works when off duty from his American army job, by letting him and his Fraulein use it—the big holes are gone, so the couple are protected from the rain. I hope he completes it before he is gone. He told me on Wednesday that in one week, perhaps two, he will be eligible for discharge. He is thinking of marrying the girl and taking her home with him. But there is the problem that he is breaking regulations by being with her in the first place! He speaks some French, which is how we talk. I was hoping after he was finished with that room that he'd do some fixing in the cellar, so that I could move there and have *two* rooms to rent out. Food is very dear and the Stadtverwaltung has informed me that I must pay taxes! Taxes on 301 Musikerstrasse! I will protest, et cetera, et cetera. What are they going to do? Send another bomber to punish me? Perhaps the pilot who dropped the bomb in the March raid has been punished for failing to completely destroy your old house. There are none left standing in the block which are in any better condition than... ours."

She licked the envelope shut and wondered idly who, in the religious asylum for the blind in Wiesbaden, would read the letter to her mother. Somebody. One of the faithful sisters. But the faithful sisters also demanded from the blind lady's daughter the monthly contribution to expenses.

The American carpenter was now at work, and repairs to the ceiling and side wall of what he had been using as a bedroom were completed. He was now replacing what had been the window, boarded up until now to guard against the cold.

"You know," he said in schoolboy French, "your window very broken and must now have glass. At my base they have glass, but it is very difficult to get out a section."

Teresa sat on the workbench and sighed. "Could you not perhaps take glass from one of the bombed buildings?"

Red Wolford thought about it.

"Yeah. That's an idea. I'll take Erika with me after work tomorrow and she'll help me carry it back."

"That is very fine of you, Herr Red."

Sergeant Wolford beamed. "You are a nice lady. I will be sorry to say good-bye." He took her hand and, as in the movie with Charles Boyer at the base on Sunday, raised it to his lips.

Two weeks later Sergeant Wolford and his Fraulein were gone, after a tearful good-bye at which Red Wolford gave Teresa a bottle of sherry he had purchased at the PX and two packages of cigarettes, highly prized on the street. "I wanted to get for you something more—" he struggled with the French—"more... memorable. But with the expenses of Erika coming to America..."

"I understand, Sergeant Red."

"What did you used to do—before the war?"

Teresa, her hair let down, her lips marked with a trace of lipstick, answered, "Before the war, Sergeant Red, I was a girl."

"*Mais naturellement.* But were you married to Herr Cadonau—I mean, Lieutenant Cadonau—right after school?"

Teresa knew what he was asking—had she always been a laundress? "We married in 1943. I worked as an assistant to the mother superior at Our Lady of Sorrows convent here. It was destroyed in the bombing. That was where I went to school. The nuns spoke to us in French. I wish they had taught me English instead. My mother then went to live there, in Wiesbaden, after the splinters destroyed her eyes. The nuns looked after her. She was—is—blind. And where did *you* learn such *excellent* French?"

"I'm from New Orleans, ma'am. *Tout le monde* down there speaks—a mountain of French."

"A mountain of French." She smiled at him, and at the pretty, chubby Erika, and emptied her little glass of sherry. She was glad they hadn't asked for a second glass. She could save it now. For a special occasion.

What special occasion? She wondered about the life she was living. A day when the soldiers at Camp Wilson stopped dirtying their socks, underwear, shirts, and pants? That would be a special occasion, but then she would not receive her daily wages, and that would be a very special occasion, without food, and without the pittance pledged to the nuns to look after her mother.

But her immediate task was to rent out the room. The room in the cellar now had a mattress and an electrical connection. If she moved herself there, she would have two rooms to rent, but the tenants would have to let her use the bathroom. The next day she would bring Clara to see it.

Clara was the senior laundress, a Nuremberg native, about fifty. She showed abundantly the managerial talent expected of her by the U.S. Army, but also a concern, however detached her manner of expressing it, for the women at work. Last week it was the problem of Karen, whose pregnancy was becoming obvious. After work on Monday, Clara left the laundry with Karen in tow. The next day, Karen wasn't there. Others chipped in to take on her load. But the following day she was back, unsmiling, at work. The pregnancy was gone.

Clara and Teresa walked down Speizstrasse, past the rubble they had become so accustomed to. "So you want to rent out a room. Maybe two, is that right, Teresa?"

"Yes, I need the income."

"You are already earning 150 percent at work."

"I am so grateful to you, Clara, and of course to the Chief, for permitting that."

"You do good work," Clara acknowledged, then pointed to what had been a large building in the block ahead.

"Do you know what that was?"

"Yes. That was the boys' military school, the Hindenburg Academy."

"I worked there. I was the matron! I would inspect the little boys before bedtime. See that their teeth had been brushed and that they were properly scrubbed. Every now and then," she smiled, making her way around a pile of stones on the sidewalk, "I would spank a boy—right there in the bathroom—if I found he had been dirty two times or more in a row. Just pull down his little shorts, put him over my knee, and slap him hard till he cried. That told the boys the matron meant business."

Teresa withheld comment, but only for a moment. "Clara, my Gustav, my husband, was a student there."

"You don't say, Teresa? When would that have been?"

"Gustav left Hindenburg when he was fourteen. He went to the Prussian military academy outside Munich. They accelerated the program, of course, and he finished in three years—1942. We married in 1943, when he was nineteen. So I guess he was being spanked by you before then!" She giggled. "He must have been in the class of 1939."

"Eastern front?"

"Yes. We had one month together."

Clara went up the four stone steps. Teresa opened the door for her, eager for her reaction.

Clara inspected the bedroom on the left, where Teresa now slept but was prepared to abandon. Then, walking through the bathroom, she went into the room on the right, freshly repaired by Sergeant Wolford. She sat on the chair in the corner and shook her head.

Teresa had brought in a glass of sherry.

"Teresa, dear Teresa. You would have to find people truly desperate to rent these two rooms, large though they are. And they would not be able to pay you anything."

Teresa was crestfallen.

"You need—decoration! Life! Each room has a bed and a table and a chair, yes. But they compare unfavorably with the prisoners' cells at the Palace. You saw the picture of Goering in his cell?"

Teresa stiffened. "I do not remember that the Reichsmarschall's cell was . . . decorated."

"No. But the walls were painted. The table and the bed were . . . Were what?" She stopped. "Who do you think would rent this?"

"American military, Clara."

She was a worldly woman. "The only person you could get was someone who wished to keep a woman."

Teresa's response was less than immediate. Then: "I would not forbid that."

"You ask for my opinion. It is that you will need curtains, painting or wallpaper, some pictures on the walls, an upholstered cushion or two."

"What would you guess it would take, to furnish—decorate—the rooms?"

"You can get everything except food very cheap these days. I would guess perhaps 550 marks."

"That would be six weeks' pay."

Clara finished her sherry and rose. "I trust your arithmetic, dear Teresa."

CHAPTER THIRTY-FOUR

January 1946

Marta's was especially crowded on Saturday night and the music seemed ever louder, though the customers didn't complain, accepting contentedly the background jazz from recordings of Benny Goodman and Artie Shaw and Stan Kenton. Those who wanted to hear the music had to resign themselves to competing human voices, which rose in volume as the room filled. Patrons, fueled by high spirits and by the intoxicants that served their purpose, struggled to be heard. Harry Albright, having made a friend of the owner, sat with her at the far end of the bar, chatting. The veterans called it Marta's Corner.

"Where's your buddy Sebastian?" she wanted to know.

Albright told her that he had begged off. "He's finishing a book he's reading. It's called *U.S. Foreign Policy*, and it's by Walter Lippmann. Did you like that book when you read it, Marta?" he teased.

"Fuck you, Harry." They both laughed and Marta turned to welcome the girl she had just glimpsed coming in.

Marta hadn't seen her before. A shapely blond who was wearing a dark blue suit, obviously prewar—but then practically all good clothing was prewar—and fake diamond earrings. Marta could see through jewelry as if it had a price tag printed on it. Marta liked it when attractive, unescorted single women came in. Good for business. "Hi ya, honey. Welcome to Marta's. Guess what, I'm Marta."

Teresa smiled. The smile was warm, but there was a trepidation in the eyes that Marta resolved instantly to dissipate. "How's about a glass of beer, the first one is on the house—"

Teresa leaned forward to hear.

"I said, *on the house.*" Marta had to fight, like everybody else, to be heard. The bartender, heeding the summons, placed the large glass on the counter and Teresa reached over for it.

"What's your name, honey?"

"Teresa."

"Teresa, this is Harry. Harry's a first lieutenant, and he's so bright and talented they're going to make him a general. Like when, Harry?"

He grinned and turned to Teresa. "Would you like to be a general's aide?"

She smiled back. "You are American. But you speak like a German."

Harry had heard the same thing ever since coming back to what had been his homeland. Might just as well get it said, he thought: "I was born in Nuremberg, and lived here until I was fourteen." This time Teresa's smile really lit up and for a half hour their conversation was animated by cross-queries: Did you ever know... Herr Schmidt, Frau Heinrich, anyone who went to school at Hindenburg? Our Lady of Sorrows? Finally Harry said, "Next thing you're going to ask is: Did I ever know Adolf Hitler? Let's sit down." Marta kept RESERVED notices on two tables for two, and three tables for four. She caught Harry's request and motioned them to a table for two, whisking away the RESERVED sign.

They drank beer and Harry ordered the sausage and sauerkraut. The stripper performed for twenty minutes and after that the little stage was cleared for dancing. Harry found Teresa wonderfully light of step, and though not trained in the jitterbug, responsive to his lead. After dancing, they returned to the table for more beer and talk. She knew that he worked at the Palace and had something to do with translation devices, exactly what, he didn't say. And he knew that she was a war widow in straitened circumstances.

An hour later they saw the stripper perform again. Then more dancing. Then more beer. Harry was in high spirits and at two in the morning he complained in a quiet tone of voice of the army regulations and their proctorial hold over life and manners at the Grand Hotel. He took a deep breath and said, looking straight into her astonishingly blue eyes, "I would like to take you to my room, but there'd be an antifraternization MP there in the lobby..."

"I have a room. Two rooms. But they are very simple."

It was done! Harry celebrated.

He scarcely took notice of decorations. He kissed her as soon as the door closed behind them. "You are the best thing that's happened to me since I was—the best thing *ever.*"

He ran his fingers down to her breasts. They kissed again and Teresa panted, and between kisses said, "I've never done this since my husband—"

Harry said, "It's time to make peace."

She led him into Sergeant Red's room and went into the bathroom, closing the door. Harry's excitement brought a craving to mind and body. He took off his shirt and pants, and lay down on the bed. He looked up at the bed lamp. He'd get a dimmer for that. She came to him in a coarse bathrobe. He eased her out of it, tenderly but firmly, put her down on the bed, and kissed her under him, avidly, hungrily, and soon reached down to make his pleasure whole, delirious, endless, it seemed.

CHAPTER THIRTY-FIVE

January 1946

Albright didn't show up at the Grand Hotel's bar on Sunday. Sebastian waited a half hour, went alone into the dining room, and sat at a corner table with his book, nodding back at two or three officers and officials who greeted him as they passed by. He thought to check the message desk on the way back to his room. There was a note from Harry. "I checked in at HQ this afternoon before going to my room to get some fresh clothes. —Sebby, I have found a lady who will do my laundry!!! Won't be with you tonight but IMPORTANT, late Saturday the tribunal overruled the defense objection, so Justice Jackson's movie—documentary—whatever you call it—will be shown at 1000 sharp Monday. Be there, kid. Will reserve your usual throne. Harry."

From his own room, Sebastian called Carver's number.

"It's Sebastian, Captain. I'm told they're going to show the war movies—"

"The concentration camp movies?"

"Yes. Monday, 1000. And I got word just when I left this afternoon that Amadeus wanted to see me. This'll be the first time since Justice Jackson's clearance for us to meet. I've got two questions. Is it a good idea to go see him at 0800, before the... documentary?"

Carver deliberated. Then, "I think maybe not. But you might find him in a state of shock *after* he's seen the documentary. If there is such a thing as a state of shock for Kurt Amadeus. That wouldn't suit our purposes."

"Okay. Then the other thing is: If, when I do see him, he starts asking how his other requests are being treated—the business about coming in after Speer—am I supposed to know anything about those requests?"

"No. You're not even supposed to have any knowledge that he's made them. Maybe the kid brother will leak that to you. But theoretically you haven't heard. All you've heard is that Justice Jackson has permitted you to visit with him to 'get the whole story.' That's all. The afternoon session in the courtroom should be over at 1600. After that, you can go to Amadeus in his cell."

"Am I supposed to stay in there till he's tired of talking?"

Again Carver paused. "Yes. I think so. He'll be called to supper at 1830, if he hasn't called off your session with him before then. I kind of like the idea of letting him blow on and on. By the way, careful about taking notes every second when he's talking. Better to put it all down when you're back at your desk."

Sebastian wondered whether the prosecution intended furtively to bug his meeting. Carver hadn't said this would be done, but Sebastian knew him well enough: If the eavesdropping was intended, Carver would not necessarily tip Sebastian off. Sebastian rather hoped there would be no bug. But it would be easy enough to find out. Harry would know... *Harry!* What the hell was going on with Harry and his need for clothes from his room? Sebastian was eager to talk with him about the Grand Hotel room-doubling order. That was important. Maybe tomorrow, during boring stretches of the courthouse session. During... boring moments in the documentary? Hardly possible.

Sebastian waited outside the audio booth. In his briefcase were two folders he'd reread the night before, in anticipation of his meeting with Amadeus.

Albright didn't show up until 0925. He greeted Sebastian cheerily and accosted the combination lock outside the booth. "Come on in. But don't talk to me until I do my checklist."

Facing them was a long switchboard with plugs and toggle switches and sockets. Albright put on his earphones and tested the connections, one after another. He got on the intercom with the lighting engineer in the booth next door. "You set for the session coming up, Jim?" Sebastian saw him nod at the reply. "Okay. I've got my hands on the screen's sound amplifier. The narrative is in English and we'll play the sound good and loud. The interpreters' stations all check out."

He put down the headphones. It was 0945. Through the glass overview window they had a clear view of the courtroom. On the far left was the door the judges would file through. Immediately in front of the judges were the secretaries' tables. Their job was to come up with whatever documents were requested by the bench. Behind them sat the bank of stenographers accommodating three languages. To their right, the lectern from which the master of ceremonies would officiate. Behind the lectern, in a longitudinal row, the prosecutors' tables, French, Soviet, American, and, closest to the judges' row, British. Behind the prosecutors was the press row, which ran from wall to wall. The VIP spectator gallery began behind the press, and at the far end of it, on the judges' end, the elevated platform for the movie projector. The projection would be on a screen at the end of the courtroom, opposite, above the witness stand. The defendants would be looking left to view it, the judges, looking right.

The view of the courtroom from the sound cockpit was not complete. Albright had to imagine the rightmost six rows of spectator seats. But, looking down, he could see the two tables at which the defense counsel sat. Sebastian had a clear view of the defendants themselves.

"Harry, you got any binoculars here? I'd like to train them on Amadeus."

"Yup." He reached into a drawer. "Now listen, Sebastian. We've got a few minutes. And the judges are always late, anyway. The prisoners will be seated on time. Everybody else will be a little late. And the judges, I *guarantee you,* won't come on in till 1010."

He leaned forward. "I've been thinking about the Grand Hotel problem and I have an idea. I've found two rooms. Actually, three rooms, counting the cellar. Kind of messy, they need a little fine tuning."

"Is there a third party?"

"Well, yes. And she is the love of my life. She'll be the love of your life, too, if you go along. If we quit the Grand, we get the GI housing allowance, which is fifty-five bucks per month, each. My lady will let us have the two rooms for fifty bucks. That's for *both* rooms. We clear sixty bucks! And we can plow a part of that into making the rooms, well—more comfortable. Fancier. Now when you see them—"

But the defendants were now filing in. Amadeus occupied his regular seat, third from the far right, first row. Directly on his right, Ribbentrop. On Ribbentrop's right, Goering. On Amadeus's left, Hans Frank. To Frank's left, Albert Speer.

Albright donned his earphones and leaned over to the microphone. He flicked a toggle switch and spoke to a fellow technician. "Judges lined up ready to go? . . . We're going to be on time today? Well, not quite." He motioned to Sebastian to put on his earphones. He reached over and flicked a switch: Now Sebastian was hearing what everyone in the courtroom heard. The silence was immediate when the marshal banged down his gavel and called out, *"Rise for the honorable judges."*

After the judges had sat down, attention focused on Navy Commander James Donovan, standing at the lectern.

"May it please the tribunal," he began, "I refer to document number 2430 PS. It is a motion picture. It is labeled 'Nazi Concentration Camps.' It was compiled from motion pictures taken by Allied military photographers as the armies in the west liberated areas in which these camps were located."

Commander Donovan informed the court that the documentary had been assembled at the direction of General Eisenhower, and that the production of the film had been done by George Stevens. "He is, gentlemen, a leading director in Hollywood. When the film was made, he was serving as a lieutenant colonel in the army."

Donovan was ready. He pointed a finger up to the lighting booth adjacent to Albright, and then to the projection room.

All the lights dimmed except for those that shone down on the defendants. Colonel Andrus had vetoed turning these off. "Security," was all he had to say.

The projector's beam shone across the room and lit up the screen. And then, for over sixty-five minutes, they saw it all. GIs, wearing gas masks to protect themselves from the stench, maneuvering around bodies stacked like cordwood. An American navy lieutenant, identified as having been captured on an OSS mission behind the lines, described the Mauthausen extermination camp being shown on screen. There were shots of prisoners lugging huge stones out of a quarry on their backs. "Many of these died from exhaustion," Prosecutor Dodd recounted as he provided the live voice-over. He explained that SS guards would sometimes divert themselves by seizing a prisoner and pushing him back to the bottom of the quarry. He would struggle to climb out again, but often failed, and was there the next day, if not dead, in agony. There were bulldozers shoving moon-white corpses into mass graves. On and on: butchery, torture, starvation, studied dehumanization.

And the screen went black.

Sebastian trained the binoculars on the face of Amadeus. His face was without expression, but his mouth was partly open, as if in wonder. Goering, on his right, appeared bored, and put his hand over his forehead, as if to help him pierce the darkness in front and on his right. The interval was only a few seconds. Commander Donovan then showed snatches of film taken from files hidden by the Nazis but unearthed by an OSS team. At a camp near Leipzig, 200 prisoners were seen being herded into a barn. SS men doused the building with gasoline and set it afire. A few prisoners who had worked their way out of the building were mowed down by machine guns.

Almost two hours had gone by. The marshal banged down the gavel, calling an end to the morning session.

There were no sounds from the defendants, who filed their way out of the room silently. There were no sounds from press or spectators for a period of almost a minute. Then Sebastian could hear the general murmur of horror, and a ululation from someone in the spectators' gallery. He turned his binoculars to the right and spotted the woman, shoulders shaking, a handkerchief held to her mouth.

CHAPTER THIRTY-SIX

January 1946

Sebastian was led down the cell corridor. He had never before set foot in the prison compound. He and the Master Sergeant walked by four cells, in which Kaltenbrunner, Keitel, Jodl, and Seyss-Inquart could be seen through the broad slits in the doors. Having returned from the afternoon sessions, they were seen leaning over their prim desks, two of them, stubby pencils in hand (pens were not permitted—they could be instruments of suicide), two of them reading. Sebastian hadn't taken in the afternoon session but he had got a grisly briefing about it over the phone from Albright. Harry reported that there had been a legal argument, yet again, over the documentary films shown in the morning. Goering's defense counsel, Otto Stahmer, argued that having now seen the films, he could say with authority what in his pleadings on Friday he had only been able to surmise, namely that the scenes portrayed had *no bearing* on the allegations being made against his client. They were designed merely—"I'm quoting his words here, I jotted them down—'merely to stimulate appetites of undifferentiated revenge.'" Albright went on, "Then Stahmer said that if the victorious powers were to bring into court those individuals shown that morning engaging in such barbaric activity, quote, 'Who would raise a hand in protest against prosecuting them?' Nice try, the son of a bitch. All that slaughter and filth, but the Reichsmarschall had nothing to do with it, no responsibility for it— "

"Was Amadeus Junior one of the defense attorneys who spoke up?"

"Yes, actually. His maiden appearance. He began reading what he identified as a monograph by Immanuel Kant—that's Immanuel K-a-n-t—on the nature of guilt. After about three minutes of Lord Lawrence gaveling him down, the marshal actually approached him on the stand and whispered to him to shut up."

"Did he say anything about Amadeus directly?"

"No. Just the obligatory opening lines about whom he represented."

"Did you catch the expression on the face of... Amadeus Senior, when Junior was speaking?"

"Actually I did look down at him, thinking you'd ask. He seemed to be pleased, kind of puffed up. Probably just biological pride—twenty-seven-year-old kid brother with eight movie cameras on him, plus four luminary judges, plus the entire surviving first rank of the Third Reich. You know something, Sebastian? *I* wouldn't mind giving a speech in that theater."

"Oh? What would you say?"

Harry's voice came over now in a different pitch. "I think I'd talk about my father's mosaic studio. How he'd stare down at twenty-seven different colors of blue until he found the one he thought was just right."

"What does that have to do with sticking 200 prisoners in a barn and setting it on fire?"

"It has to do with different approaches to life. Do I really have to explain that to you? Jerk."

"No, Harry. You don't. But I'm not sure it's something I'm

going to be able to bring up at 1600 in my audience of just one defendant."

"And one non-German-speaking guard."

"And two guards, actually. I'm told one guard will enter the cell with me, and the regular outside guard will be at his post, looking in through the cell door."

"Well, good luck, Sebby. I'll meet you at the Grand, 1800, and we'll walk over to 301 Musikerstrasse and you can see what great new quarters you'll have after the Grand kicks us out."

"How far is it?"

"A few blocks."

"A few how many blocks?"

"Figure ten, twelve."

"Give us a little exercise."

"Good for you, exercise. Those poor, poor . . . cocksuckers in the prison get only two up-and-downs in their courtyard, once a day."

"That's really terrible, Harry. Isn't it."

"Poor darlings."

"Poor darlings." Sebastian spat into the wastebasket.

The master sergeant opened the cell door. An accompanying soldier brought in an upright wooden chair. Prison rules allowed only a single chair for defendants, withdrawn at night—chairs, after all, could be dismembered to create weapons. Amadeus moved his own chair back, placing it directly by the pillow of his bed. Sebastian's chair was placed opposite, next to the recessed toilet and sink.

The sergeant turned to Sebastian. "Whenever you want, sir, just nod to the guard outside and we'll open up for you." To the guard remaining in the cell he said simply: "You can lean back against the wall there, Bradford." He pointed to the opposite windowless wall.

Sebastian sat down and withdrew his steno pad from his briefcase, though remembering Carver's counsel to go easy on note-taking.

"Why do you need a pad of paper to write on?"

"I don't, Herr Amadeus—"

"Lieutenant, would it derange you to call me *General* Amadeus? No one else here," he pointed to one, then the other guard, "knows any German, so they would not notice your breach of prison protocol."

Sebastian's mouth opened slightly. What to do? Violate the prison rules because no one would notice? Would he be rejecting the operative principles of Colonel Andrus and the prison commission if he used the prisoner's title? If he did so, would that suggest that he was privately out of sympathy with standing formalities? The rules were, after all, appropriate to the treatment of war criminals. On the other hand—isn't it enough just to hang the guy?

"—the reason for the pad, General Amadeus, is that you may be bringing up something which I'd want to relay accurately to my superior—"

"Ah, your superior. I understand such language. I was taught to acknowledge my superiors the day I entered service with the SS. I went to the SS—but you will recall this from our interrogatory sessions—after a dispirited year teaching architecture—"

Sebastian thought to act other than merely as a human recording device. "Why *dispirited*, General?"

Amadeus brightened at the prospect of a colloquy, instead of one more interrogation. "Because in 1932 all of Germany was dispirited. My father died from wounds in the war our Kaiser gave up on, which the victorious powers at Versailles transformed into a deep territorial humiliation. How would you feel if after a war you were required to give up the whole of the western United States?"

Amadeus actually waited for an answer.

"Not good, General."

"I had used up my mother's pension paying for architecture school and even there, in the work of our teachers and our most esteemed architects, I could see that demoralization. They tried to make up for it by a massiveness of architectural design. I saw that, and didn't approve of it aesthetically, but at the same time I was attracted by the idea of a massive national recovery. So when Herr Speer suggested I give up architecture and go to the SS, I found the idea appealing, and then the experience itself, bracing. Spiritually bracing. Are you a Christian?"

"Yes. My father was a Lutheran, and I studied the Lutheran catechism."

"Ah! Martin Luther had some pretty good ideas. About the Jews."

"They didn't teach us Luther's position on Jews."

"No, they wouldn't. The Jews would not like that, not permit that."

"General, in America, Jews do not dictate Christian dogma."

"The Jews never appear to be dictating anything, except interest terms on their usurious loans."

"General, is that what you wanted to talk to me about? Jewish influence?"

Amadeus looked over at the young, brown-haired lieutenant with the quick tongue and an informal manner he had never seen in a German of that age. "No. But my wish is to engage in a general conversation, so that I can decide whether to alter my plea of not guilty."

"And you feel you need to talk about so-called Jewish influence in order to do that?"

"Clearly. There had to be a reason for the Fuehrer to single out the Jews."

Sebastian made no comment.

"You do realize, do you not, Lieutenant Reinhard—a fine name that, Reinhard. A good German name. I have known Reinhards—that what this exercise is all about is Jewish revenge? As Reichsmarschall Goering said in the interview published in July, just before we all got here, all the other lines of legal argument are barren. All of them. Aggressive war? Every country engages in it. Have you ever been in the Southwest of your own country?"

"Yes. I went from Hamburg to Arizona. That is my home."

"And how did America inherit Arizona? But then, the whole business of adherence to conventions on warfare—I wonder whether George Friedrich will succeed in calling as witnesses some of your submarine commanders who let the crews of stricken Japanese merchant ships drown or be eaten by sharks? No. But all of that is the high price of modern warfare. The most eloquent witness to your idea of legitimate warfare would be a survivor of Hiroshima, except I don't think there is such a person."

"General, I'm not a lawyer. But I don't have to be a lawyer to see the difference between a Hiroshima bomb and an elimination camp. Like Joni."

"Well, of course, I see your perspective. But perhaps you will see my perspective—"

Sebastian bit his lip. "We saw your perspective," he said, "in the films shown this morning."

"Yes. They were quite terrible, quite bad. There are unruly people in the world, including many among the ranks of soldiers. Would you expect any of the defendants to excuse what was shown today?"

"I can't see that it would matter—to many of them. Herr Goering—"

"Reichsmarschall Goering—"

"No. I will do it for *you*, but I see no need to do it for anybody else." Sebastian was emboldened to go further. "I would not refer to Hitler as Fuehrer."

Amadeus winced. Then, "You are refusing to give concentrated attention to my point, which is that the so-called war crimes trial is a Jewish extravaganza designed to exact revenge. What is your comment about that?"

"Well, General, I guess my comment would be: If that's so, why not? The Jews have a lot to avenge."

"But then why all these legal formalities? Here I am, trying to decide whether to change my plea. You should know this, Lieutenant, that my innocent little brother is—a Christian. That small ornament on his tie is a cross. It was he who told me to consider changing my plea. To tell you the truth, I had not considered doing anything of the sort. But in conversations with my brother, I suddenly found myself thinking: Well, just as I had a perspective, the perspective that led me to follow gladly and devotedly the perspectives of my Fuehrer, perhaps I ought to try to understand *other* perspectives, like yours, and my brother's, and the abominable Justice Jackson—is he by any chance Jewish? I am good at discerning Jewish appearances. Perhaps he is only a half-breed."

"What is a half-breed?"

Amadeus seemed surprised. "You have not seen the minutes of the Wannsee Conference?"

"No."

"That is strange." He leaned his well-shaped head back, raised his eyebrows, and adopted a didactic tone of voice. "My brother was given a copy, though I have not heard it discussed yet in the proceedings. That is the conference of German officials at which the final solution to the Jewish problem was resolved upon. It was held in January—sometime in January—1942. Some definitions were set down. A Jew who is married to a non-Jew and has a child creates a half-breed. That is, a Half-Breed First Degree. A Half-Breed Second Degree is the ensuing generation. What, by a different nomenclature, might be called a 'Quarter-Jew.'"

"Did you handle half-breeds in Joni?"

"Half-Breeds First Degree? Oh yes, under our laws they are fully Jewish. To be exterminated."

"And half-breeds of the second degree?"

"By our code they are reunited with the Aryan race, but with two qualifications. The first is that if the descendant is of a bastard marriage, he is to be treated as a Jew. A second qualifier—that would be Clause B, under Section Two—if the subject's outer appearance makes him *look* Jewish, then the final solution called for his elimination."

Amadeus paused. "I wish they would let us have a cigarette here in the cell.... I was talking about other peoples' perspectives, and the challenge of my brother to try to look through such a person's eyes. I do not mind telling you—I suppose it does not matter, if you wish to report this to your superior—that I am greatly deterred by what would surely be interpreted as a capitulation by me to the assumptions and formalities of a tribunal which is so blind as not to understand that it is engaged quite simply in racial vengeance."

The loudspeaker blared out the dinner signal. Amadeus looked to the cell door, visibly annoyed. The trays would be brought in within minutes.

Amadeus turned to Sebastian. "I said before that I thought you looked part Jewish. I was being provocative."

The guard outside called in. "Time, Lieutenant."

Amadeus said, "I will be seeing you again. You agree to see me again?"

"Those are my orders, General."

Shake hands with him? Sebastian wondered.

Amadeus did not initiate a handshake.

Sebastian was relieved. He nodded and walked out of the opened door. He didn't know whether he'd have extended his hand, if that terrible man had extended his.

CHAPTER THIRTY-SEVEN

January 1946

Sebastian knew he'd have to give serious thought to the idea of moving to Musikerstrasse—he wouldn't welcome doubling up at the hotel. The two officers hailed what advertised itself as a bus and was heading, Harry declared, in the right direction. What had stopped, at their signal, was a converted army truck. The entrepreneur had provided boarding steps and even a handrail to permit passengers to make their way to the benches on either side. Twenty passengers could sit, and a few extra stand, holding on to the painted pipe that ran overhead. The cost of the ride was five pfennigs. The driver-entrepreneur gave off exuberance, written or verbal, wherever, whenever possible, at intersections, stop signs, passenger stops. Hand-painted signs on both sides of the bus, red on yellow, were in German and in English.

WELCOME TO THE NEW GERMANY!

TELL YOUR FRIENDS ABOUT HERMANN'S LIMOUSINE BUS SERVICE! *Empfehlen Sie ihren Freunden Bus-und-Limousinen—Dienst von Hermann.*

The happy entrepreneur wore dark glasses, even though the light was now very dim. He reached out to shake hands with every passenger who boarded. He was perhaps sixteen years old.

Two hours later, using the same conveyance, they were back at the Grand, seated at their usual table by the bar. Sebastian started in, confirming his awe. "I think Teresa is a really attractive lady."

"She likes you, too. I could tell."

Sebastian thought to get back to the Nuremberg agenda. "Let's think a bit about the goddam trial. If we knew it was going to be over at the end of March or even April, I guess we could double up at the Grand without too much pain. Hell, six months ago I was sharing quarters with thirty candidates at officers' school, a couple of months before that, with sixty privates doing basic training."

"Yep. We both know what we've been through. But I've liked private quarters since back when I started flying missions. And we've both got desk work to do at night, work that takes thinking. And anyway, Sebby, we both know the trial *isn't* going to end in April—more like January 1947. No, that's bad-news horseshit. But it is going to go... a long time."

The waiter asked if they wanted another beer. The answer was yes.

"Have you made any calculations?" Sebastian pressed. "Today is January 11th, 1946, and we've only just finished the prosecution's case against Nazi *organizations*, plus viewed the documentary. We're ready to go only just now with the indictments of *individual* defendants—"

"How long do you figure for that?"

"Say, one day each? We've been going at the rate of six days of trial work per week. That would take us to mid-February. *Then* the defense begins.... Harry, would you mind blowing your smoke just a little away from my face?"

"How long do you calculate for the defense?"

"Everything depends on the bench, what they permit, what they don't permit. The last thing they want to do is encourage the idea that this is an assembly-line trial."

"Does your ongoing business with Amadeus have a bearing on all this?"

"I think it probably does. Carver hasn't laid it out in just so many words. But I figure: If Amadeus decided to change to a guilty plea, word of that might have an effect on the piss-on-all-of-you Goering phalanx. If that happened, and the defense just wilted, that could save us some time."

"Yep. But you can't expect these people to go to the gallows without whatever braking action motions they can come up with."

"No. And of course after the defense we get the actual trial. I don't see any way to get out before midsummer.... Let's listen a minute." The piano player was doing imitations of Fats Waller. There was a smattering of applause. "Fats Waller deserves that," Harry agreed.

Sebastian hadn't thought to ask the question before: "Harry, how are you on the discharge point system?"

"You need sixty of those precious things to go to the top of the line, as of last week. I'm up to forty-one. Year and a half training, year and a half combat duty, plus four months here. I figure if I were doing regular duty, I'd qualify for a discharge maybe in June. How about you?"

"I'm low on points. All I've had is basic training, officer candidate school, infantry training—till we started here. But they did tell me, when I was recruited in Camp Gordon, that when the trial was over, I'd qualify for discharge." He brought the beer glass to his lips and, before drinking, laughed with affected hysteria. "I guess my option would be to spend the rest of my life interviewing General Amadeus."

"So you get out more or less contractually—but only when the trial is over." Albright thought about it. "They're giving you some priority they're not giving me—and *I* had combat duty. I could qualify to get out *before* the trial is over, with my points adding up every month, but they might find some special-need reason to keep me in."

"Is your work something other people with less training could handle?"

"Up to a point. My little kraut, Hans, knows it all, the whole sound scene, and he has some English by now. They'd need me for special problems. There's a lot going on in that courtroom, but I get bored after a while."

"Harry, it sounds like you could take a few days off."

"Hey, remember when you went flitting off to London on leave, and us technicians had to stay here? But nowadays I wouldn't want to be anywhere Teresa wasn't."

"I'd like a few extra days myself. Down the line, at some point. I want to go to Munich. I've heard a lot about Munich—and Innsbruck—from my grandmother. I'd poke around a bit, hear the Munich Symphony, maybe see if I can find my great-uncle. Leddihn—that's my grandparents' family."

"Okay. But meanwhile, we've got to decide on Teresa's apartment. That's where *I'm* headed. I'm going to move my gear before the Friday deadline. It would be nice if you rented her other room. And with the savings on the housing allowance, we could fix up the place a bit."

Sebastian began to focus on the sunnier side of it all, off-hours at Musikerstrasse. "Yes. Get a few more books in there, some couches, headlamps, a record player . . . I think, Harry, we'd have to become pretty regular patrons of Hermann's Limousine Bus Service."

"So? If the bus is there when we set out, we climb on board. Otherwise, we walk."

"And there are always jeeps running around."

Sebastian hesitated for a moment. Harry Albright looked at him eagerly, hoping for the nod. "Tell you what, Harry, let's go with Musikerstrasse. We'll pay Teresa the fifty bucks rent and commit the sixty bucks left over for a Musikerstrasse renovation fund. Make up a little bit for the bomb you dropped there. High time you thought of compensating for what you've done. What are you planning to do for Hamburg?"

First Lieutenant Albright raised his beer glass in enthusiastic endorsement of the idea.

"Be nice to break the glass against the fireplace," Sebastian said, "in the old feudal tradition. But Colonel Andrus would put us in a prison cell."

"Shall we drink to Colonel Andrus?"

"No. But let's drink to the United States Secretary of the Army. And his pledge to return four hundred thousand GIs from the Pacific in four months. Eventually he'll get around to—Yes! Let's drink to us."

CHAPTER THIRTY-EIGHT

Winter 1946

Present at the hastily called meeting in Justice Jackson's chambers were three men. The two preeminent colonels—John Harlan Amen, in charge of prosecutorial arrangements, Burton Andrus, in charge of the Palace—and the security chief, Major Allard Fitzgerald.

Justice Jackson could be easygoing and affable—his personal secretary very nearly took his affability to the altar—but he could be direct when on single-minded duty. Today's problem had nothing to do with the prosecution of war criminals. Somebody, some criminal on the loose, or, in any event, someone criminally minded, had shot a pistol into the front seat of the Soviet prosecutor's limousine, on which two men sat. The gun discharged, the assailant had run off unhampered, his features seen, perhaps, but unremarked. The bullet didn't hurt the prosecutor, but killed the driver alongside.

"You will not be surprised, gentlemen, that *Pravda* this morning alleges that the assassination was done by an American."

"Do we know that it *wasn't*?" Fitzgerald asked.

Jackson turned on him sharply. "Whatever there is to know,

it's your business to know it, Fitzgerald. You've spoken, of course, with the Nuremberg police. What have they got?"

"They've got nothing, Justice. Zero."

"Has anybody come up with a motive for shooting Rudenko's driver?"

"No. We figure he wasn't the intended victim."

"Who was?"

"Colonel Likhatchev."

"Why him? He's the chief examining magistrate, right, Colonel Amen?"

"Yes."

Jackson thought about it. "Well, if we're looking for a motive, Likhatchev would qualify. He's hardly popular with the prisoners he's torn to pieces here—"

"Or with those he examined at Lubyanka before he got here—if there are any left alive."

"Yes. The defendants do have friends, and one or more of them may be fanatical and are perhaps roaming around Nuremberg with loaded pistols. But why, Fitz? What we have is a dead driver on our hands."

"Rudenko—he's your Soviet counterpart, Mr. Justice—"

"I know that. I confer with him ten times every week."

"—Rudenko rides around a lot in a fancy limousine. His favorite limo—this particular one—was liberated from Hitler's private car pool. He almost always carried Likhatchev with him, riding in the front seat next to the driver. Only this time Likhatchev had stepped out of the car when the bullet homed in—hitting the driver."

Jackson sighed. "So I can report to the State Department that no one has any reason to suppose involvement by an American in the assassination. Correct?"

Fitzgerald said, "Yes sir." Jackson looked across the table; no one demurred.

"Okay, so much for the killing of the driver. Now here's what I don't know. Rudenko—I like Rudenko. You like him, Colonel Amen?"

"He's a good prosecutor."

"Well, just two weeks ago he called me. This was before you came aboard, Fitzgerald. I dealt with your predecessor..."

"Major Lowenstein."

"Yes. Rudenko called and asked me to get him permission to fly a Russian body out of here—out of the American zone—to Russia. We're talking about the late assistant prosecutor Zorya.

"Rudenko said that his assistant had a fatal accident. That was assistant prosecutor Major-General Nikolai Dmitriyevich Zorya. I took down the interpreter's phrase. Zorya 'perished owing to the incautious usage of a firearm.' We got him the permission to fly out to Moscow, of course. After which I clammed up. I mean I really *did* clam up. What I did was write just one note to Ike, because he knew Zorya. I told him I thought it very unusual that a major-general should kill himself while cleaning a gun. I said it was especially peculiar that he should clean it while loaded, with the muzzle against his forehead.

"Now I'm bringing this up, and calling your attention to it, because what's going on is—Soviet politics. You saw yesterday, Comrade Stalin declaring that war didn't resolve the struggle between socialism and capitalism? We know that. We also knew that when Stalin got into bed with Hitler in 1939—"

He stopped. Bob Jackson wouldn't deny his colleagues this historical gossip. "Speaking of the Soviet scene, here's something from the Nazi scene. Bill Shirer sent me a draft chapter of the book he's working on, a history of the Third Reich. Shirer's dug up a mountain of Hitler's papers. Some really spooky stuff. Shirer reports that after Stalin signed the Nazi-Soviet pact—August 1939—Ribbentrop flew back from Moscow with the signed treaty and brought with him a photograph of Stalin signing it. Ribbentrop, of course, signed it on behalf of Germany. Ribbentrop wanted an okay to send the photo on to the press. But Hitler looked at it real hard—because, he said to Ribbentrop, he wanted to make sure he didn't spot any Jewishness in Stalin's face! If Stalin was part Jewish, Hitler didn't want his photograph reproduced!"

Jackson leaned back in laughter. "And then, Shirer told me, the photograph of Stalin signing the pact showed a lit cigarette in his mouth. Hitler instructed Ribbentrop to have the cigarette air-brushed out before sending it on to the papers."

"That story makes me want to smoke," Fitzgerald said. "Any objection?"

Jackson waved him to go ahead. And then got back to business.

"Whatever *Pravda* is up to—saying it was an American who fired the shot—we just *stay out of it.* We *are not* going to get into the whole Communist business here. We faced the basic question before the London Conference, which was that sure, the Soviets are guilty of just about everything we are gathered here to condemn legally. But these aren't points that are going to be raised, if we can prevent that from happening. Certainly not by us. The judges in the tribunal—our people—are fully indoctrinated on that point and they'll gavel down defense attorneys who bring up Soviet atrocities. *No tu quoque, dear,* they'll tell learned counsel."

Amen said, "Obviously the Soviets aren't going to bring up Soviet atrocities, and I assume the Brits are wired in—they'd have to be. But are you so sure the *French* will clam up on the subject? General de Gaulle isn't in power right now, but he knows how to raise his voice, all the way from Colombey-les-Deux-Églises to Nuremberg, Bavaria."

"Put it this way, John. We're not expecting any French fire on that subject. As far as we're concerned, I know none of you is about to give a speech picking a fight with Stalin—or with

Pravda, same thing. But when we get things like the Zorya quote unquote suicide, and the shooting into the Soviet limo, we say only two things: a) Too bad about the shooting accident, and b) No American had anything to do with the killing of the driver. Any comment?"

Fitzgerald spoke. "Sir, in my press briefing, what do I say if a reporter asks me to comment on the *Pravda* charge that it was a U.S. serviceman who shot the driver?"

"Say you know nothing about anything that might have given grounds for any such suspicion, et cetera, et cetera. God, this place is really crawling with press people. But that's our fault. Right, gentlemen?"

He got up.

When that happened, they all knew the meeting was ended.

CHAPTER THIRTY-NINE

February 1946

A wintry month had gone by and the prosecution rolled on with its indictments. Amadeus had three times summoned Sebastian. He bantered mostly about his early years of service to the National Socialist Party and spoke of the pride he had felt seeing Adolf Hitler riding up the Champs-Élysées in his car.

"Has he decided on the changing of his plea?" Harry asked.

"No. The next time around, I'm going to press him a little harder on that. A strange man. He can speak like a normal, even attentive, human being. If he came by in hospital garb and I was in a sickbed, I'd take him, after a minute or two, as a caring young doctor."

Harry didn't comment.

They had thrown themselves with gusto into the enterprise of reconstructing 301 Musikerstrasse. Teresa undertook to do all the repainting. She liked to sing *lieder* when she worked, her voice a slight bel canto. Sebastian, applying the sandpaper, recalled his experiences as a teenager on summer nights with fellow staff at the Grand Canyon. They would avail themselves, after the professional maintenance workers were done for the day, of the woodworking shop and undertake to repair assorted broken objects they acquired, occasionally creating wooden oddments (he made Henrietta a handsome crucifix). He remembered the worn canoe he had refinished.

By the end of January they had assembled and stored in the hallway outside the cellar room the basic tools they needed—hammer, saw, sawhorse, file, paint, varnish. The windows were now nicely painted and, as required, rebuilt, both in Albright's outer room where Sergeant Red had worked and in the room Teresa had surrendered to Sebastian when she moved herself down to the cellar room.

Assembling the material necessary for making curtains and shelves proved remarkably easy and cheap. A block-long thieves' market of sorts lay just off the market square, exhibiting the fruit of hours and days of foraging Germans of all ages. Beginning only weeks after the bomb smoke had lifted, they had combed the rubble and pulled away doorknobs and carpets and toilet seats and curtain rods and kitchenware. "Gee," Harry said after their first tour of the market, "you could furnish a whole house for a hundred bucks."

The radio, fabricated in 1938 by Heinze Electronics, was plugged in, and it was grand and cozy to get news and music right there in the ample-sized living room/dining room/bedroom. Harry thought of getting a record player for Teresa's birthday, which fell on the same day as George Washington's, but the problem would then be to get a supply of records to play. There were not many of these at the market. Shellac 78 rpm records burned in the fires after the bombings. But there was the beginning of a library taking shape at the Palace. Clerks and lawyers and army officials borrowed on a lending basis from the growing supply, playing popular and classical music in barracks and apartments and hotel rooms.

"It'll be a while, getting our own record player," Harry said resignedly, snuffing out his cigarette. "Teresa, how about stealing me some fresh undershorts from your laundry? I spilled paint on mine."

"Why don't you try painting without shorts?" Sebastian said, grinning.

"I'll have to try that. When I do, Sebastian, don't look."

The language spoken at Musikerstrasse was German when Teresa was present. When she was gone, off to work, or doing something outside the house on whatever mission, they spoke to one another in English. Sometimes, when she was elsewhere in the house, seated in the living room in anticipation of the increasingly resourceful suppers brought up by Teresa, they would shift away from German to English. The day before, when she had left the room with the dirty dishes, Sebastian asked, "Did you ever find out what unit her husband fought in?"

"No. I've never asked her. The picture of them at their wedding was in her room, framed, but she took it down after I started keeping her regular company. It's in a drawer in her bureau. I studied it. Handsome guy, looked about eighteen years old—he was only nineteen, as a matter of fact. From the collar bars I could see he was a lieutenant, but I couldn't make out the insignia."

Teresa returned with the precious coffee, slim blue ribbons attached to her braided hair. "One day I will learn how to speak English," she said, pouring the coffee. "But now there is no time. Perhaps after we are finished creating our palace."

Sebastian went early to his room and picked up *The Thurber Carnival.* He had brought the book from the library at the Palace, and it brought laughter. The same library stored an estimated two hundred thousand files documenting the murderous reign of Adolf Hitler and records of what he had made men do in his name. It was wonderful that Thurber was also there.

On Monday, just after Teresa left, Harry complained to Sebastian that he was having pains in his back. The Saturday before, they had gone by bus with Teresa to the Alpenpark with a picnic basket. It was a fairly steep hill they had taken on, with its slick rock surface, but Sebastian hadn't remembered any complaint from Harry when at one point he slipped and fell. He had picked himself up with agility.

"Maybe you need to get an x-ray. Something might have gone out when we were climbing."

"Maybe it's that fucking chair I sit in hour after hour at the control booth. It's straight-backed, did you notice?"

"You'd better check with the infirmary."

On Wednesday, in midafternoon, the telephone rang in Sebastian's office. "I got to see you." Harry's voice was off pitch.

"Come on down."

"Can't." He spoke hurriedly. "Keitel's record is being read out, and there's an interpretation going on from Russian. Just don't leave without me. I'll be there as soon as I can."

At 1600 Sebastian was curious. Normally, sessions ended by 1530. He rang Chief Landers, who had a private wire to the courtroom. "Chief, tell me, is the trial still going on?"

Landers said yes.

"Any idea for how much longer?"

Landers pulled out one telephone jack, inserted another, spoke a few words, and got back with self-satisfied dispatch to Sebastian. "Lieutenant, Judge Lawrence has just led the honorable judges out."

"Thanks, Chief."

Ten minutes later Harry opened the door. He was disappointed to see the stenographer there, but then saw that Cyrilla Hempstone was packing up. She bade the lieutenants good night.

Harry Albright sat down wearily on the extra chair.

"Sebby, I've got syphilis. They're going to have to do a spinal tap and give me sulfa shots." He pointed in the direction of his groin. "I'm poisoned down there. For maybe six weeks, the doc said."

"Harry... Teresa?"

"I couldn't believe that. It must have been that fucking hooker at Marta's back in September."

In other circumstances, Sebastian would have commented on the expletive. He said instead, simply, "What are you going to do?"

"A sergeant in our detachment is going on furlough for two weeks beginning tomorrow. I can have his space in a joint apartment he lives in. But I can't go home. Couldn't possibly talk to Teresa. For tonight, I'll be sleeping on the couch in the sergeant's pad, then I get his room for a couple of weeks. Oh shit. What should I tell her?"

"Well, Harry, I can tell her you've been arrested for war crimes."

That brought a pained smile. "Come with me, I need a drink."

Much later, after the dinner hour, Sebastian set out in the cold for Musikerstrasse, hoping the bus would come by. It didn't. It was very cold. When he arrived, he was ready with the official story.

The translation device in Stuttgart had gone screwy, he told her. Lieutenant Albright was sent to take care of the situation.... Wasn't certain how long it would take... Might have to spend a few days... Sebastian would pack a bag and the army would deliver it to Harry the next day.

Teresa sighed. She said warily that it would be lonely without

Harry there. But soon her face brightened. "We can try to make up for his being away."

Sebastian nodded and sat down at the dining room table for some cold meat and potatoes. Later, they played a game of dominoes and drank a beer.

Poor Harry.

Poor Teresa? Sebastian wondered. If she hadn't infected Harry, had Harry infected her?

CHAPTER FORTY

February 1946

The formal greetings were, as ever, spare. General Amadeus began by asking whether Sebastian had listened to the arguments made by his brother in the courtroom the afternoon before. George Friedrich Amadeus had raised his hand to question the testimony of Auschwitz commander Rudolf Hess, not to be confused with Nuremberg defendant Rudolph Hoess, who had been brought to the war crimes courtroom from his own jail cell in Landsberg to testify.

He had not heard the other Amadeus, Sebastian said. "I did hear the Hoess testimony. I would have stayed on if I had known your brother would be arguing."

"He said very interesting things, George Friedrich, but profoundly wrong, I thought. He was taking the usual line: We defendants are to be excused because of the rigidity of the command structure under the Fuehrer."

"Nobody questions that command structure, General."

"I do. It is the ideologist's mystique. Book-people, lawyers especially, assume that the man in command of the whole is in command of all of its parts. Let me tell you that Rudolph Hoess was absolutely correct—I *know*—when he testified that at

Auschwitz a great deal went on that he personally disapproved of, but that it is simply impossible to impress the commander's will on everyone who, theoretically, works for him."

"Are you saying that it was that way at Camp Joni? That things were done there that you didn't approve of? Other things, I mean, than just trying to wipe out a whole race of people?"

"Yes, I am saying exactly that. I have never expressed admiration for Rudolph Hoess, except as a genocidal technician with over one million gassings to his credit. But I am prepared to believe that he did not order killed everyone who *was* killed at Auschwitz."

"General, how is it possible to load one thousand people into a gas chamber without knowledge of it by the camp's Kommandant?"

"*I am not talking about that.* Obviously Hoess had knowledge of that part of his camp's operations, even as I did of mine. I am speaking of what one might call *incidental* brutality, which is different from *correlative* brutality. Rudolph Hoess recounted my own experience when he testified that even the duty officers appointed by him did not always carry out his orders. And subordinates of the duty officers often acted in their own way. It is incorrect, Herr Lieutenant, to make judgments that do not reflect reality—which is that subordinates can exercise their own wills, giving in to their own impulses. And here is where I think my brother was wrong—"

"General, it is known—and there has been testimony on this, though it was not brought up on Monday—that when the new commander replaced Hoess in 1943, he did, in fact, impose reforms."

"What do you call reforms, Herr Lieutenant?"

Sebastian raised his voice a little. "Well, for one thing, General, the beatings stopped. There was testimony on *that* subject. Some Kapos resisted the order to stop beating the prisoners and they were punished by being shoved back into the ranks. That's a reform, isn't it?"

"Yes, it is—"

"What did you do to a subordinate who disobeyed your orders?"

"I would discipline him."

"Would you execute him?"

"Only if his conduct was seditious. I am endeavoring to make a different point, and not one to which I think you will automatically object, dear Lieutenant. My point has to do with the self-serving insistence by . . . many of my codefendants that—that—well, what the argument implies is that only Adolf Hitler was responsible for what you call the atrocities."

Sebastian reflected on this. *Atrocities!* Was Amadeus here distinguishing between in-camp brutality—inexcusable—and the extermination of six million Jews—understandable? Was he suggesting that in-camp brutalities were to be dismissed as impulsive acts of subordinates? "You are aware of Auschwitz's '*Stehbunker*'?"

"I do not know what that is."

Sebastian was so surprised by this that he found himself wondering whether Amadeus was now lying. But he had never caught Amadeus up in a falsehood. Kurt Amadeus was without guile. Hideously so.

"Well, what the *Stehbunker* in Auschwitz was, General, was an enclosure. A punishment cell. It was about three feet square. Two hundred and fifty square centimeters. As many as five—*five*—prisoners condemned to punishment were squeezed into the *Stehbunker.* They were given nothing to eat, nothing to drink. The ceiling was bricked down so that only just enough air got in to permit them to breathe, barely. They were left there until they died. That took three days, sometimes four. Is this the work of Adolf Hitler? Or the work of Rudolph Hoess?"

"It is, actually, the work of neither. It is the work of the Auschwitz guards who shoved them into the cell and bricked them in."

"But the law we're looking into here doesn't hold the guards guiltless, but it does assume, which is reasonable, that the guards were instruments of the Kommandant."

"There is a distinction between the camp commander who ordered death by what you call a *Stehbunker*, and a commander who merely authorized the punishment of a prisoner."

Sebastian had spent much time the week before surveying the records of Auschwitz in order to brief Captain Carver, who, in building the war crimes case against Kaltenbrunner, would conduct the testimony of Auschwitz commander Hoess. "General, Auschwitz had an execution wall. It is recorded that more than twenty thousand prisoners were shot there."

"That would be a regular execution."

Sebastian rose to his feet. The guard turned to him anxiously. Sebastian backed up until he was resting against the cell wall. He caught his breath. "*So executions like that are all right?*"

"I am trying, Herr Lieutenant, to parse questions that explore both legal and moral issues. I presided over—that means that I was Kommandant while the operations took place—the gassing of two hundred and fifty-five thousand prisoners, mostly Jewish. I did not myself shove them into the gas chamber. That was done by others, many of them themselves Jews, the *Sonderkommandos*, in the brief intervals before their own executions. There are different levels of responsibility that crystallize in a moral ledger. For the sake of convenience, let us stipulate three levels: *one*, Hitler; *two*, me; *three*, the guards. You can string that out as you please. Hitler—Himmler—Glucks—me—duty officer—Kapo—*Sonderkommandos*—the guard who released the gas pellets into the chamber—"

"I know what you are saying, the whole chain of command business. But how are you now disagreeing with your brother?"

"He holds everyone under the level of Hitler to be blameless because they are merely executing his orders. In the first place, the chain of command is vulnerable to variations down the line. And then—most interesting here, I think—my own view is that the closer you get to the gas chamber itself, the more blameworthy the agent. You see, Herr Lieutenant, Hitler was a conceptualist. He envisioned a better world without Jews in it. That is a theory—you disapprove of it, of course—and on the stand yesterday, Rudolph Hoess said that, on reflection, he, too, thought it was wrong to gas the Jews. But he did exactly that, gas the Jews, and in doing so he was more guilty than Hitler, because Hitler was an ideologist, Hoess a mechanic. Stalin is more guilty than Marx because it has been Stalin, not Marx, who sends millions to die, millions who are dying as we speak. Dying pursuant to a concept of Marx. And the commanders of Stalin's concentration camps are more guilty than Stalin, because they do the work; it is they who fit the noose around the neck of the victim."

Sebastian, back in his chair, stared down at his stenographic pad, his unused pen in hand. "Does it then follow that you reject your brother's defense, that only Hitler was guilty? But in rejecting that argument, you'd need to acknowledge personal responsibility. Does that mean that you will be willing to change your plea to guilty?"

"Not necessarily. That is a tactical decision. What it does mean is that I consider *myself* guiltier of what you call war crimes than Hitler. And—I hope you can follow me now—my underlings, guiltier than me."

Sebastian thought to press his own plea more directly. "Wouldn't it be consistent with your reasoning that you should plead guilty?"

"Yes, it would. And I may end up doing just that. I continue to be hampered by my reluctance to associate myself with the whole Jewish performance in which we—you—are engaged."

Both men were silent. After a moment, Sebastian rose. "I think I will go now."

"Good day, Herr Lieutenant."

Yet again Amadeus had the good taste not to proffer his hand.

CHAPTER FORTY-ONE

Late February 1946

As the days went by, Teresa all but stopped talking about the absent Harry. She had detected that Sebastian had packed up much more for him in clothes and accessories than would be needed for only the two or three days he spoke of. On the evening of the third day, Sebastian informed her that Harry was running into difficulties at Stuttgart. Teresa gave him a skeptical glance. He changed the subject and that night again they listened to music on the radio and played cards. Teresa, looking down at her hand, said that she had to give some thought to her future. But she added nothing more, resuming play.

When Sebastian was shuffling the deck for the second round, Teresa got back on the theme. "I do not intend to be a laundress forever, but with my extra salary, and the rental of my apartment, I'm—just—all right for now. Tell me, Sebastian, how—how could I go about getting a better paying job? Doing more interesting work?"

"Teresa. Everybody in Germany is looking for work that pays in dollars, never mind interesting work."

"... is it true that the army has forbidden army personnel to bring their American wives to Germany?"

"It is. General Eisenhower set the example last May. When the war ended he did not bring Mrs. Eisenhower to Paris. And Justice Biddle is without his wife."

"But hardly lonely." She smiled.

What could Sebastian say? Everyone knew about the justice's living arrangements.

"If there are no women in residence with the married officers, then women are needed, no? To do the work that would otherwise be done by wives?"

Sebastian turned his head. He let himself smile. "You mean like wash their husbands' clothes?"

She smiled. "And other things."

"Teresa, we have a weekly newspaper of sorts that goes out to the Palace personnel. It has a little—we call them 'Personals.' Like, 'I want to buy a record player.' Or, 'I am willing to give German lessons.' That kind of thing. I could place an ad in your name, if you wish."

"But what would I say in the ad? Especially since no fraternizing is permitted."

"You could say that you would be willing to give lessons in German to GIs who wanted to study."

"How much money would I ask for? In dollars? Per hour?"

"I'd have to ask around, see what people are paying to private tutors."

"Not much, I'd guess." She leaned over and kissed him. "You will do that for Teresa?"

"Of course."

The next morning, Sebastian picked up his phone. It was Harry. "They're going to start with Doenitz in fifteen, twenty minutes. I bet *he's* sorry he surrendered last May."

"They want to string him up?"

"Yep. But that kind of thing is harder to do—wouldn't you guess?—to military officers? Take Keitel. He is like Doenitz—a professional military man. He was commissioned in the German field artillery before the first war. . . . But I'm not calling you about Keitel. At 0800 I had a session with the doctor. I'm in the third stage, which means I got infected way back in England. I'm infectious myself, and have to be . . . extra cautious on the social front for six weeks minimum. Till I test negative."

"Harry. What about Teresa? Does *she* need a blood test?"

"I was pretty specific with the doctor on that point. But he was reassuring when I told him that I always used rubbers with her. Not a hard decision. Teresa didn't want any pregnancy."

"So what do I tell her now?"

"I can't . . . move back there, just can't, Sebby. Not any time in the foreseeable future."

"I understand."

"I got another five days here before Sergeant Chatterley repossesses his apartment. I'll have to look around. Look around for sure-enough bachelor's quarters. On what to tell Teresa? Tell her I got emergency leave. My mother in Wisconsin is sick, I wangled my way onto one of the army transports going home. They got an apprentice to do my work. He and the German are looking after the courtroom audio."

"Okay."

"Sebby?"

"I'm listening, Harry."

"I'm sad and lonely. Will you have dinner with me and go to the movie? It's Orson Welles, *Tomorrow Is Forever.* We haven't been to a movie since your twentieth birthday."

"Sure I will. Meet at the Grand? Like old times?"

"The Grand, 1800."

It was late when the movie ended and then—as expected—the couple of beers. After that, on the street, no bus was running. Sebastian set out on foot, hugging his overcoat to him, hoping to see an army car drift by. It was close to midnight.

He turned the lock in the door at Musikerstrasse and hung up his coat. The door to the cellar apartment was open slightly. He saw no light in the door crack. He walked quietly up the staircase and brushed his teeth in the bathroom. Undressed, he walked into his room and turned on the reading lamp, but even Thurber was not for tonight. He closed the book, turned off the light, and fell quickly to sleep. He was awakened by her kiss, and the movement of her bare breasts on his chest. She told him it was always he she truly loved, and made him believe it.

CHAPTER FORTY-TWO

March 1946

At the end of the prosecution case there would be a week's leave for most of the Palace personnel, before the defense began to hold sway. That was predicted for early in March, and indeed the prosecution rested on March 6.

Sebastian had been kept busy translating, alongside another linguist—a German civilian—a fresh trove of documents unearthed by the Russians in Breslau, Poland, near the Czech frontier. There they found five years of dispatches "by everyone to everyone," as Sebastian described them to Teresa. Carver was interested primarily in the evidence yielded against Hans Frank, though if Adolf Eichmann or Heinrich Himmler had been sitting in court, those dispatches, Carver remarked, "would have clinched the noose ever tighter around their necks." Sebastian, awash with the evidence, permitted himself, over coffee in the officers' mess, to ask Captain Carver, "What do you people *need* on Frank that you haven't already got?"

"I see your point. We have a ton of stuff. But if anything's sitting there, we want to know about it. And Frank's defense attorney has put it to us to get everything about his client we have in hand or is accessible. I can't believe there's exonerative stuff lying around, though everybody has what one might call good days. Hans Frank almost surely did. He apostatized from the Catholic Church—you must have come across that—when he joined Hitler. Now he's rejoining the Church, I'm told. That will challenge Saint Peter."

"Am I supposed to translate for the benefit of Frank's defense counsel?"

Carver laughed. "No. Alfred Seidl can read German all by himself. But anything he gets to read, I want to know about. So, Sebby, you have two alternatives. Translate that dunghill, or teach me German so I can read it myself."

"Okay, sir. But that's not going to prevent me from taking the March leave.... just reassure me on that. Okay?"

"Going somewhere?"

"Yes, to Munich and to Innsbruck. I'm looking for remote relatives. And I'd like to hear the Munich Symphony."

"Where are they going to play after our bombing? In the park?"

"The Risenztheater is functioning again, I found out. The concertmaster at the theater was my great-grandfather."

"Not Jewish, I hope."

"No. From a couple of things I heard from my grandmother, I'd guess he was a little anti-Semitic himself."

"That would have been useful when Herr Hitler moved down."

"There were Jews in the Munich Symphony, and my grandmother said he would have protected them to his death."

"That's about what it would have taken, to save those Bavarian Jews."

"His wife was dead. But he was nearly eighty when the Nazis moved in."

"So who're you going to try to track down?"

"My great-uncle. But he's not in Munich anymore. The family's from Innsbruck. My Oma—that's grandmother in German—"

"Thanks. Now I know six words of German."

"—she got word her brother has gone back to Innsbruck. I've got an address."

"What does he do?"

"He's a musician. A conductor."

"What does he conduct in Innsbruck?"

"I don't know. But I promise to tell you when I find out. I just wanted to be sure I'd be . . . free to go next week."

"Okay. But take some work with you. You can translate on the train, can't you?"

"Yeah. Thanks. Say, Captain. One day I want to know why you executed Private Slovik."

Carver smiled. He liked the young lieutenant. "We'll have dinner after you get back. I'll tell you about it."

It had been almost exactly one year since the venerable Risenz-theater suffered the bomb that had smashed the rear end of the theater. They were making do with a temporary structure, but one which served to keep out the cold, and to shelter musicians who, since December, had resumed regular performances.

Flush with a few American dollars, Sebastian set out on his planned tour of the city, relying on a prewar guidebook picked up in the thieves' market. He walked to the old clock tower, still standing, and tried to imagine what the grand avenue must have looked like before the bombs came. And over there was the beer hall, intact, where Adolf Hitler, age thirty-four, had initiated the famous putsch that landed him in jail. Jail where? He turned the page in the guidebook. The jail, a monument of sorts in the prewar guide, was actually outside Munich, in the small town of Landsberg. It was in the Landsberg prison that Hitler had written *Mein Kampf.* The hoary old question pressed on his mind: *How many people would now be alive if Hitler had been kept in jail?*—instead of being released after nine months.

Sebastian made his way back to the busy Bergahof Hotel. It was half full, mostly with bustling Germans, one or two of whom he overheard discussing reconstruction projects. There was an American there, seated at a table, cigarette in hand, a glass of wine to one side and a folder of papers in front of him. He sported, oddly enough—such facial decoration had gone out of style—a Hitler mustache. Sebastian sat down at the next table. The man with the folder noticed his curiosity and introduced himself. He was the director of an American television team of three in New York. They were in Germany doing a documentary based on Hitler's early life. "We'll spend a lot of time in Vienna," he told Sebastian, who asked if the team planned to go to Nuremberg.

"Haven't decided. There's been *so much* footage on Nuremberg in the last six months. People in America are getting kind of bored with the war crimes scene. Nothing ever seems to happen."

"I see what you mean," Sebastian said.

He went by himself to the Risenztheater and heard a symphony by Mozart, then the violin concerto of Mendelssohn, and, after the intermission, some Mahler. He walked after the performance to a café next door and saw, hanging on the wall, photographs of artists. Beer in hand, he surveyed them in descending chronological order, beginning with the conductor he had just heard perform. He was excited at the prospect of looking into the face of the Munich Symphony conductor at the turn of the century, whom his great-grandfather would have served as concertmaster. He didn't know the name but did notice the picture of the conductor who had performed on the millennial eve, one Alois Steiner. He would mention that name when next he wrote to Oma.

The next day he was on the train to Innsbruck. It was snowing lightly. He wondered whether it had snowed in February of 1938 when Hitler traveled down this route in his special train to Vienna to celebrate the annexation of Austria.

It had occurred to him in Nuremberg, when he got his grandmother's letter, that it might be prudent if he simply appeared cautiously on the Innsbruck scene, rather than write ahead to his great-uncle. Possibly, if Sebastian's arrival was heralded in a letter, Walther Leddihn would make extravagant efforts to entertain him. Another possibility was that Uncle Walther was infirm, or indigent, in which case Sebastian would adjust his visit appropriately. Better to tread cautiously.

So when Sebastian arrived at the hotel he inspected the telephone directory in his room, after satisfying himself that it was current. He found the name he was looking for and two telephone numbers. The first number was presumably his great-uncle's home telephone. The second appeared under *Orchester.* He dialed it. A hotel operator answered. "Herr Leddihn is rehearsing with the orchestra now."

It was midafternoon. Should he leave a message?

Better just to appear. "Will he be there—at four o'clock?"

The operator, with just a hint of impatience, told Sebastian she did not know how long the rehearsal today would last, but that Herr Leddihn usually went to his office after rehearsals. "The orchestra begins performing at five, for tea."

"His office is in the hotel?"

"Yes, *mein Herr.*"

"Thanks very much."

"*Bitte.*"

The cab took him to the door of the large, gabled, Tyrolean-style hotel, blessedly unscarred by the war. A terrace on the second floor looked over the driveway and the two ornate slate columns at the entrance. Sebastian paid the taxi driver and went to the concierge, who wore a Tyrolean jacket. "Where can I find Herr Leddihn?"

The elderly man with the white mustache looked up. "The rehearsal is finished. You would find him at the office, ground floor, #14." He pointed out the direction. Sebastian, his heart now beating a little faster, walked across the lobby.

He had been greeted with astonishment and joy.

He was instructed to sit in the huge parlor for tea while Herr Leddihn led the predinner music. Then they would dine together, here at the hotel. After dinner, Herr Leddihn would play again, from 2000 until 2315. "Then we will drive to your hotel and pick up your bags. Henrietta would not forgive me if she learned you were in Innsbruck and staying at a hotel! *Then* we will go to my house—I live alone—and you have the spare bedroom. And we can have a *real* visit! Maybe—does Henrietta have a telephone?—we can telephone her. Probably not," he mused. "Long distance lines from here go through Munich, ever since—the amalgamation. Never mind." He stood back and looked at Sebastian. "I was just twenty when your grandmother left us! Your age, approximately. But all of that later."

In the parlor, thirty or forty guests, some of them transients, others, Sebastian suspected, seasonal patrons of the hotel, sipped tea and ate pastry. Herr Leddihn led twelve musicians in light music, heavy on waltzes, but also with some music from America. Sebastian recognized "Alexander's Ragtime Band" and "I Get a Kick Out of You." The conductor and the young American officer ate well. Before the tart and ice cream were finished, Leddihn excused himself to go off and change into white tie and tails.

In his corner of the dining room Sebastian read on in his paperback while the band played and a dozen couples danced, their spirits visibly quickened by the lift of the music. Herr Walther Leddihn, a smile on his face whenever his head was turned to the diners, picked up a violin and, moving closer to the microphone, played "Liebestraum" tearfully and then changed tempo and orchestration to do a polka with the same theme.

His house was trim, far enough from town to permit the owner a generous lawn. He took Sebastian's bag to his room, and conducted him into the living room, lit a fire, and brought out a bottle of sparkling white wine.

It was after midnight when he told his story. "Even Henrietta doesn't know the details. I just gave her the outlines. When the Nazis came down, Papa was no longer first violinist. He had retired, Mama was dead, but he was still the president of the orchestra union. We always opened— "

"You were playing with the orchestra, Uncle Walther?"

"Yes. In 1938 I had been playing violin under my father's leadership almost ten years. We always opened the Saturday concert with the Austrian national anthem. Ironically, the music—by Haydn, of course—was also the music for the German national anthem, the 'Deutschlandlied,' though of course the words were different. In May, our conductor, Herr Schell, told us—I remember that it was on a Thursday, we were rehearsing Bruckner's *Fifth Symphony*—that we would not be playing the anthem on Saturday. There was a stir of protest. 'That's the way it will have to be,' the Musikdirektor said.

"I reported the news to my father when I got home. He made about six telephone calls. He heard back what he wanted to hear and then called Herr Schell. He said that unless the anthem was played, the orchestra would strike."

"The players were unanimous on the point?"

"My father called the principal personnel, who were unanimous except for a dissenting Jewish cellist. We could understand that. He could not afford to bring notice to himself in any movement to defy authorities doing the bidding of the Nazis. There was a true explosion when word of the players' ultimatum got out on Friday. On Saturday, everyone—press, security, officials, patrons—was tense, waiting to see what would happen. The concertmaster, the musical coordinator, waited to hear from my father, and my father was waiting to hear from Herr Schell."

"And Herr Schell was waiting to hear from the Gestapo?"

"Exactly."

"What did happen?"

"They played the Austrian national anthem and the audience sang out the Austrian words.

"That night, the Gestapo came. They began by throwing me out of the house. I waited outside, hoping I could see through the window what was happening."

"Did you?"

"Yes, the Gestapo began by beating my father, smashing him on the head, and then kicking him while he was on the floor. I went to the locked door and banged on it.

"The agent in charge opened it and asked if I would prefer to spend the night in Gestapo headquarters. My father called out and begged me to go away. I ran as fast as I could to our neighbor and called the newspaper. Then I called Herr Schell. The newspaper reporter didn't want to hear about it, changed the subject, then hung up. Schell said, 'What am I supposed to do, Walther?' I waited outside and finally the Gestapo went off in their car. They were carrying a bag. I went back to my father. He was in terrible pain and his eyes were bruised. He told me they had carried away everything on his desk and also the large book of clippings and Mama's journal, which she had kept for fifty years.

"The next day the conductor called my father. Papa said Herr Schell was crying over the telephone when he spoke to him. A special meeting of the orchestra union had been called and Papa was no longer president. The following Saturday we did not play the national anthem. On Monday, when I was away from the house, teaching, the Gestapo came back and spent the whole morning with Papa. I don't know what they said. They brought the papers back. Papa never fully recovered."

Sebastian saw that the fire was dying. Walther Leddihn caught his eye. "We must go to bed. A long day. I will make breakfast for you in the morning."

The next morning Leddihn called a friend, a retired musician who had a motorcar. "Stefan will pick you up at ten and take you to lunch and show you Greater Innsbruck. I would not inflict my hotel music on you again, but I will arrange for a substitute to fill in for me for the after-dinner music, and we will have dinner at my favorite restaurant. In the afternoon, Stefan will bring you back here after you have finished with the tour. You are to make yourself at home. You will want to look at the scrapbooks and at your Oma's journals."

He embraced his great-nephew and went, contentedly, out the door with his music case.

Stefan took fine care of Sebastian, showing him the period churches and old estates tucked around the hill town, and the gallery and the museum. But by four in the afternoon, Sebastian was ready to get back to the house. He would do some translating for Captain Carver.

Sitting on a couch, his papers spread out on the coffee table, he scanned a dozen documents and made notes doggedly with his little Hermes typewriter, digesting any material he thought conceivably germane, including the documentation of Hans Frank's sending the household cook to a forced labor camp after a prolonged complaint from his wife about the food. An hour later he rose to stretch his limbs and looked over at the bookcase Uncle Walther had pointed to. He opened the scrapbooks and pulled out the one likeliest to have pictures of his grandmother.

There were page after page of clippings and photographs and explanatory notes written by hand. He turned a page that showed a picture of Alois Steiner, guest conductor for the millennial celebration. He recalled the same picture at the restaurant in Munich. Here now was a favorable critical review of the millennial concerts, praising the "young American Jewish conductor." A few pages on, a society notice: *Herr Alois William Steiner has become betrothed to young Henrietta Leddihn, daughter of the Symphony's concertmaster.*

Sebastian had known about Oma's first marriage but never remembered hearing his name. He had known about the death from pneumonia, so soon after the wedding, of the musician Oma had married. He hadn't known that her first husband was Jewish.

He turned more pages in the sturdy big book and came upon the telegram—Oma in Rochester to her mother in Munich. The telegram from Henrietta Steiner disclosed that she was pregnant. It was pasted on the page and under it the jubilant words of his great-grandmother. "*So Eine Freude! —What great joy! A grandchild is coming!*" The telegram was dated April 10, 1901.

A few pages later, he stopped to read the clipping in the Rochester paper about the pneumonia plague. It was dated August 22, 1901. One passage in it had been underlined, in his great-grandmother's characteristic red ink. "*Another death from the pneumonia outbreak, recorded yesterday, was that of the conductor of the Rochester Symphony, the promising Alois Steiner.*"

Three pages later he read the telegram from Henrietta to her mother dated January 6, 1902. A BEAUTIFUL LITTLE GIRL. I WILL CALL HER ANNABELLE.

And a few pages after that, the social note from the Rochester paper recording the marriage in March of "the widow Henrietta Steiner to the prominent American businessman, Roderick Chapin."

He put the book down.

Roderick Chapin was not his grandfather.

Alois Steiner was his grandfather. Never mind that he was dead when his mother was born.

Alois Steiner was Jewish. That meant that he, Walter Sebastian Reinhard, was—Jewish.

One-quarter Jewish.

Under the German code, he was: Half-Breed Second Degree.

His mind swirled in wonder, speculation, projection, bitterness, indignation. Mostly wonder. As a Half-Breed Second Degree in Hitler's Germany he would have been exposed to the same treatment handed out to other... Jews. The treatment Amadeus handed out to—two hundred and fifty-five thousand Jews. Mostly Jews.

Amadeus!

So Amadeus was right. So he, Sebastian, *was* part Jewish. He "*looked* part Jewish." *What does "part Jewish" look like?*... On the other hand, why *shouldn't* he look part Jewish? Alois Steiner, *Jew*, was his grandfather.

He put away the scrapbook carefully; sat on the sofa, and stared down at the carpet, letting the wild tumblers in his mind go round and round.

CHAPTER FORTY-THREE

March 1946

The moment had arrived. The challenge was electrically there: to argue persuasively the postulates of the war crimes trial against the challenges of the defense. It had to be more than an autarchic recital of its self-constituted authority. A critical legal and moral world was tuned in. It would not do simply to adduce the Charter of the London Agreement to justify the trial. The Charter was in fact the governing instrument, but the prosecutors had to accept the burden of persuading the moral community of the rightness of the proceedings.

The defense attorney for Karl Doenitz was in place. Admiral Doenitz had served as chief of naval operations for Germany, devotedly following orders received from the Fuehrer. These directives had specified the conduct of naval operations, and called for sinking at sea survivors of German submarine operations.

Herr Kranzbuhler bore himself with assurance. He was manifestly pleased with the suspense he created when he solemnly advised the court that he wished to introduce an affidavit filed by Doenitz's U.S. counterpart, Admiral Chester Nimitz.

The objection from prosecutor Jackson was instantaneous. "Mr. President, *nothing* that Admiral Nimitz has to say could have any bearing on the guilt or nonguilt of the defendant Doenitz."

Lord Lawrence spotted the danger. He advised the defendant's counsel to stand by while he conferred with his colleagues.

The judges, interpreters at hand, huddled together and spoke in whispers.

"They're going for *tu quoque*, obviously," Lord Lawrence said, pursing his lips.

The Russian Nikitchenko agreed heartily. He had the clearest reason for objecting to the direction the defense was taking. "We cannot let that kind of thing begin. Otherwise, we will be here for many years."

But Judge Biddle resisted. He argued that the language with which the defense attorney pleaded, whatever it was he proposed to display from Admiral Nimitz, could itself affect the court's ruling on admissibility.

Lawrence and Nikitchenko, whispering their dissent, clung to their objections. They appealed to the French judge. He said he was not committed on one side or the other on the admissibility of an affidavit by an American military official.

But Francis Biddle felt strongly enough to plead personal privilege. If any one member of the tribunal did so, on a procedural point at issue, the other judges had agreed to defer to him.

Lord Lawrence sat back on his chair, upright, and brought down the gavel.

"The defense counsel may proceed in the matter."

Kranzbuhler was proud of his hold, however rudimentary, on English and waved aside the proffered help of an English-speaking aide. He read out in heavily accented tones the affidavit from Chester Nimitz, Admiral of the United States Pacific Fleet, hero of the historic engagement at Midway in 1942.

"On general principles, the U.S. submarines [under my command] did not rescue enemy survivors if undue additional hazard to the submarine resulted, or [if by any delays entailed] the submarine would be prevented from accomplishing its further mission."

Herr Kranzbuhler declaimed at some length that the affidavit, by the mere force of what it said, transcended formalistic rules of the London Charter disallowing *tu quoque* argumentation.

After the close of the afternoon session, junior prosecutors met in a corner of the officers' mess hall. After recesses, that corner had become a tea or coffee bar for eight or ten of the legal staff. Captain Carver, through the billow of cigarette smoke he disconsolately contended with, declared his disappointment with Judge Biddle's plea.

"So what has been planted in front of judges, defense, press, and spectators? Our chief admiral, *our* great Chet Nimitz, testifies by affidavit"—he picked up the memorandum sheet distributed to prosecutors and press by courtroom clerks minutes after exhibits were filed, and read Nimitz's words out again.

"So of course Kranzbuhler is running with it. The position he's urging is that anything that proves necessary to modern warfare, like abandoning survivors at sea, has got to be accepted as—nothing more than a part of modern warfare. Therefore? Therefore what by older historical perspectives was ruled a violation of Geneva standards, doesn't apply anymore. So drop Counts three and four against Doenitz."

"Right." A French prosecutor, M. Duharnais, spoke up. He had learned his English as a student at Harrow, where Churchill liked to say he himself had truly learned the language. "And it's plain to see where the whole defense team will now go. And, God bless them, the buggers will use their arguments in such a way as to appear to be defending primarily *Allied action.* Instead of saying, which the rule against *tu quoque* won't let them do—'Well, you people bombed Dresden and Hiroshima'—they will be saying, '*We understand* why the Allies felt it necessary to stretch the old Geneva rules enough to—'"

Carver took the rest of the sentence away from him: "—enough to bomb Dresden and Hiroshima. It's a lucky thing we've got Doenitz on other counts."

"Like what?" the deliberate English lawyer came in. "I'm not up on Doenitz."

"Like what? Like applauding the execution of all Communists in a camp in Austria two weeks before the war ended. In his interrogation he said he had thought the people being executed were spies. Utter, provable baloney. Yes, sure, by the rules, you can execute prisoners if they're spies. Not if they're mere POWs. But we can prove that the difference was made plain to him."

Conversation turned to the impending courtroom session on Monday. Chief U.S. prosecutor Robert Jackson versus Reichsmarschall Hermann Goering, the brightest guy in the dock. "I tried to get a press pass for a guy from New York doing a documentary on Hitler," Carver told Duharnais. "No way. Everybody in the world wants to be there for that one."

Back in his office, Carver rang for Sebastian. After a few rings he heard a woman's voice. "Sergeant Hempstone here."

"Hemp, this is Captain Carver. Where is Reinhard?"

"He has gone to a meeting with Amadeus."

"Tell him to call me when he gets back."

"I might not still be here, sir."

"Leave a note. I'll be in the office until . . . 1830."

At 1815, Sebastian returned the call.

"How did it go?" Carver asked.

"Interesting. He's *always* interesting. I'll type up a memo for you, you'll have it tomorrow. I got some especially interesting stuff about Governor General Frank and Amadeus's dealings with him. He had a way of manipulating Frank—and even Himmler. If they wanted to send him more prisoners than he thought he could handle in his own way, he'd find means to maneuver around them."

"Something we ought to know when his defense comes up?"

"Not really. How he did it, mostly, was by effecting delays, pleading this and that and the other. Management, bureaucratic stuff. Nothing there that his lawyer could plausibly suggest was Amadeus's formula for killing fewer people."

"What I called about is Goering. Did you bring his name up with Amadeus? He's coming up to the dock next Monday."

"Yes. Amadeus said that in the exercise yard two days ago Goering looked at him suspiciously, then asked whether he knew that Speer was 'consorting with the enemy'—his words. Amadeus said he is confident that the negotiations we're up to regarding a plea change haven't leaked. 'Otherwise Goering wouldn't be civil to me,' he said."

"Any hint on Goering's behavior when he takes the stand?"

"Amadeus just said that a lot of people are counting on him—and"—Sebastian laughed at this—"and Amadeus said that although Goering was a hidden homosexual, he always 'acted like a man.' Amadeus told me he had been given a copy, when he was on bunker duty, of Hitler's order to execute Goering. Amadeus said that was probably the biggest thing Goering has going for him in his defense—that, at the end, Hitler got mad at him."

"Okay. And nothing new on changing Amadeus's plea?"

"Captain, I don't *ever* forget to bring that up. And he always says the same thing—he's thinking about it. He asked me to tell him what date, approximately, his turn at the dock would come."

"If you have an answer to that, I wish you'd tell *me*, Sebby."

"I don't, of course. I said I thought it too hard to project based on the few defendants we've had so far, Doenitz and Kesselring. But then, by agreement with you people, Amadeus is scheduled to come up at Number Eighteen, *after* Speer, not before him. But that's got to be two months down the line, don't you figure, Captain?"

"Yeah. But here's a nice dream sequence for you on the ides of March. Next time you see Amadeus, one, you try to persuade him to change his plea; two, he agrees; three, he broadcasts his upcoming plea of guilty; four, all remaining defendants throw in the towel! If one defendant agrees that what he did was a war crime, you've got a chief Nazi accepting the premises of the prosecution—and what do you know?—the judges hand down their rulings by—the end of April!"

"Okay. But if I may, George, you're getting carried away."

"Of course I am. It makes life tolerable at Nuremberg."

"But seriously, Captain Carver, sir, can I tell him we'll shoot him as he wants, instead of hanging him?"

Carver was silent. He would not confide to the young lieutenant the top-secret decision that had been arrived at on that point. He himself knew it only because he, George Carver, was the keeper of defendant Kurt Amadeus. Only three other persons were party to it: Jackson, Lawrence, and Amen.

"No, you can't tell him that. The guys upstairs haven't ruled. They might put that question to one side until they see what he says on the stand when he changes his plea. See you later, Sebby."

"Captain, you want to know something about me you don't know?"

"Are you a Communist?"

Sebastian laughed. "No. But I *am* a Half-Breed, Second Degree."

Carver paused. And then focused on the odd nomenclature from Wannsee. "That says you're a quarter Jewish? So what?"

"I just found out. I'm not going to tell Amadeus. But way back in October—you remember?—he said I looked part Jewish."

"Yeah, I remember."

"Funny, that. Do you think I look part Jewish?"

"I hadn't noticed. I'll look hard next time I see you. What about Hitler? Did he look part Jewish?"

"That business of Hitler's mother—grandmother?—has never been proved, has it?"

"Jackson says Shirer believes it's true, that Hitler's grandmother was Jewish."

"That will sell more copies of his book if it's true."

"Good night. Remember, tomorrow's the Sabbath."

Sebastian felt better, in the Nuremberg scene, passing the word out that he, a young American—German-American—interpreter was, in a way, one of them, one of the millions they were all there to avenge.

How would his German father have reacted to the news? That he had married an American woman who was *half Jewish. Would* it have been news to him? Had Annabelle ever told him that she was the daughter of Alois Steiner?

Sebastian could speak lightly of the whole matter in conversation with Captain Carver. He could not think lightly of it in reflections of his own.

Every night, in Teresa's arms, he wondered whether to take her into his confidence. It wasn't that his Jewishness was of objective importance. But he needed to talk about the subject, the mystery, the contingencies of the past, his mysteriously dead father—and he relished most the prospect of talking about thoughts recessed in his mind with the beautiful and engrossing woman he lived with.

CHAPTER FORTY-FOUR

March 1946

Before leaving for Innsbruck, Sebastian had written to his mother. He couldn't hold it back any longer.

He told her that he had met the woman he wanted to spend the rest of his life with. He spoke of her beauty and of her care for him, told of her short, unhappy life, her young husband "one more of Hitler's victims." He would be inquiring in the weeks ahead to see what provisions were made for American servicemen returning to their country with German wives. "Teresa is a war widow, Mama, but how could anyone blame a twenty-three-year-old German woman because she had a husband in the Nazi military, a man who then died on the war front? You will love her, I know, and needless to say, you will enjoy speaking with her in German. She doesn't yet know much English."

Five days later, after the Innsbruck revelation, he had begun an entirely different letter to his mother. It started out angrily. Briefly into it, he had had a premonition. *Could it be that she didn't know?* He'd ponder again about it.

He did; and the next day his thinking moved in an entirely different direction.

As she dusted the growing book collection, Teresa could see that he was preoccupied. She decided against a game of hearts but did suggest, with a slight tilt of her head, her lips parted to expose her pearl teeth, "*eine baldiges rendezvous* in our love-bed." Sebastian walked over and gave her a lingering kiss. But then he returned to his writing pad. Teresa interrupted him again. She mentioned for the first time in weeks his—predecessor. "Have you heard from Harry?"

"No. I'm sure he'll send me a telegram if his mother dies."

"Are soldiers allowed to stay away permanently if a parent is sick?"

"Not permanently. But if the surviving parent is a dependent, and the soldier is the only child, sometimes the army tries to accommodate."

"How?"

"They might transfer him to a camp near his hometown."

"What is Harry's hometown?"

Sebastian's mind raced. *Had a hometown been mentioned?* "—it's somewhere in Wisconsin. I don't remember exactly where, though I know he was flying to New York."

"Everybody flies to New York."

"Yes, Teresa. Now I must get back to my letter to my mother."

"Is your mother sick? Will you be going to see *her*?"

"Teresa. My mother is forty-four years old."

"Some people get sick before forty."

He lost his patience. "Yes, and some people get killed before they're forty."

"Like my Gustav."

"Yes. Like your Gustav, and whoever he killed before he was killed himself, who was less than forty."

Teresa went into the kitchen, carrying the radio, stretching out the long electrical cord. Then she called out: "Will it distract you if I turn on the radio?"

"No," Sebastian said, and then stared down at the opening line he had written. "*Dear Mama, Why did you not confide—*" Again his hand stopped. Could it be—was it conceivable?—that Annabelle Linda Chapin herself thought that she was Roderick Chapin's child?

He redid the mathematics on his notepad... Fourteen months from Henrietta's departure from Munich to the telegram announcing a pregnancy... Four months to the death notice... Seven months to the remarriage. Count forward nine months from the first telegram....

He envisioned Roderick Chapin at the Episcopal church, looking down on the baby Annabelle, a few months old, as she was being baptized Annabelle Linda (Henrietta, wanting some trace of her family name, had anglicized "Leddihn") Chapin.

Was it possible his mother never knew she was sired by Alois Steiner? Not only possible, he now concluded, but probable; and entirely believable.

He tore up the sheet he had started on and addressed instead a letter to Henrietta. "Dear Oma. I was in Innsbruck. I stayed with Uncle Walther. We thought of telephoning you, but you can't just put in a long distance call to America from Innsbruck yet. When Walther was out of the house—you were right, he plays with an orchestra—I looked at your mother's scrapbook. It's all there, like A. B. C. What I want to know is: Did you ever tell Mama? Please write to me. Love, Sebastian."

He looked over at Teresa, sitting on the chair in the kitchen, her hair braided about her young face, the radio on, tuned low, the Nuremberg newspaper on her lap. She looked up at him and turned up the music.

"*Liebe* Sebastian, are you coming to keep me company now?"

He wondered if his grin was concupiscent as he rose ardently from his chair.

PHOTO BY THE AUTHOR

BOOK FOUR

CHAPTER FORTY-FIVE

Spring 1943

Axel Reinhard—SS Captain Axel Reinhard—was back from Auschwitz. He had studied the designs of the latest crematorium at Auschwitz's subcamp, Birkenau. In Joni, using mostly Polish forced labor, he applied himself to the construction of a unit, appropriately modified. Sometimes, when critical supplies hadn't come, work was suspended or retarded. On such days he worked only eight or ten hours. He preferred it when he was working sixteen hours. When idle, he had the time, that awful time, to allow his mind to focus on what he was doing. He sought refuge in vodka.

Stefan Plekhov, adjutant for Governor Frank, had been all but detached from other duties in Cracow. His orders were to devote himself fully to rounding up the labor forces required for the Joni enterprise, the completion of which Reichsfuehrer Himmler was so insistently demanding. "I have to have plumbers," Axel said when, at midday, Plekhov appeared in his office. "And not, Stefan, so-called plumbers who came to the profession the day before yesterday in order to qualify for survival. I need the kind of plumbers who can create pipes through which your poison gas can pass without danger of leakage."

"*My* poison gas?" Plekhov raised his hand and his eyebrows. "*You're* German, Axel. *I'm* Polish."

"And we're both working for *him*. Doing *his* work..." He knew to check this flow of conversation. "I was talking about the need for plumbers."

"That will not be easy, Axel."

"Shall we just report that we will abandon the construction of the crematorium because it will not be easy?"

Captain Plekhov had dealt with fractiousness from Axel Reinhard ever since the crematorium business had come up and Axel had accepted the commission to get on with Joni. Once again Plekhov advised him to swallow such sentiments, or at the very least, to confine the expression of them to Plekhov—"I am used to them, but I know"—he lowered his own voice—"that such reservations as we have about this business simply have to be overcome. That is *die Natur de Ware*, the nature of the situation. We have talked about that. It would not do, not do at all, for someone to overhear you when you give voice to such sentiments and carry the word to General Amadeus."

"Fuck General Amadeus."

Plekhov seized the slide rule on the desk and banged it down on Reinhard's knees. "*Do you want to become a forced laborer yourself?*"

"Let's get to work." Axel went back to calculating the lengths of pipe needed.

Captain Plekhov faced a problem of his own only days later. He learned that one Lieutenant Sigmund Soddeberg of the SS had undertaken to segregate, in the library of the University of Cracow, those library books he deemed corrupting. The Governor General called a staff meeting to review Soddeberg's recommendations. Frank told Plekhov to be present whatever the demands on him at Joni. "You were a university librarian. Obviously you should be present at a meeting at which we discuss library books and the recommendations of Lieutenant Soddeberg."

At Cracow headquarters, staff meetings were held in what was once the audience chamber of the royal palace of the Wawel dynasty. From both ends of the governor's large desk, tables stretched out. As many as twenty-four officials could be seated, but at routine staff meetings there was only the cadre of nine. In the high-ceilinged room, with the lighthearted frescoes and decorative gilt, Governor Frank gaveled the meeting to order.

"Admit Lieutenant Soddeberg." He motioned to an aide.

The huge wooden door framed in brass opened and the young, blond lieutenant with the clipped hair strode in with his briefcase. He was bidden to go to a chair at the far end of the table. He raised his arm and declaimed "Heil Hitler!" Plekhov discerned a militant reverence in the young man's voice.

Lieutenant Soddeberg removed a sheaf of papers from the briefcase and started in. In what seemed a practiced voice, he said that the great movement of the National Socialist Party was best illuminated by the Fuehrer's reference to a thousand-year Reich. "What this means," said the young officer, "is that the great work being undertaken by the Wehrmacht on the eastern front, and in the oceans of the west by the navy, and by the liberating Nazi forces in North Africa, and by the important progress in eliminating from Europe the contaminating presence of the Jews— "

"Soddeberg, do not consume the morning describing what is being done by the Third Reich at military, political, and social levels. Get to the point."

Soddeberg snapped to attention. "As you say, Herr Governor General. I was seeking merely to give the background for the intellectual challenge before us, which is to inform the class of university young people who will one day bear the responsibility for directing the Fuehrer's thought into congenial intellectual, social, and academic channels for the thousand years we speak of—"

"What books do you want to eliminate?" Hans Frank interrupted again.

"I have here a list of fifty books that are especially subversive. We begin, of course, with the Bible," he said dramatically.

Governor Frank, a graduate of Catholic schools, winced. "Go on."

"I will not abuse the humbling experience of appearing before you and your distinguished staff by reading out a list of *all* the titles I propose be burned in Cracow's great public square—"

"It is the largest square of any city in Europe," Governor Frank paused to record.

"Yes, Herr Governor General. All the more fitting that they should be burned here."

Why doesn't that young fart just gas the books! Plekhov internalized his exasperation, which was now more like fury.

"Who came up with the titles you wish disposed of?" Frank pressed him.

"May I say, Herr Governor General, with great humility, that I had a bit of a hand in putting the list together. Some of the books—the works of Marx, for instance, and any number by other Jewish authors, for instance, Freud and Spengler—"

Plekhov spoke up. "Spengler was not Jewish."

Soddeberg seemed surprised. Then said, "He might as well be Jewish!" and laughed heartily. Others contrived a modest chuckle.

"But as I say, I would hardly presume to read aloud the entire list. Suffice to say that I deem it an urgent, path-setting event, designed to further the holy aims of the Fuehrer."

"What do you say, Plekhov?" As an aside to Soddeberg, Frank explained, "Captain Plekhov worked as a librarian at the university library before—before joining our staff as adjutant."

Plekhov had the floor. He proceeded cautiously. "May I ask, Herr Lieutenant, what your own background is?"

"I was commissioned a lieutenant after a year's military work in Hanover, which included the military maneuvers once praised by General Jodl."

"I mean, where did you do your academic work?"

"Academic work was offered at the Bismarck High School."

"You did not, Herr Lieutenant, have any academic training after you graduated from gymnasium?"

"I went happily into military service."

"How old were you when commissioned?"

"I was eighteen."

"How old are you now?"

Soddeberg tilted back his head. "I am twenty-one, Herr Captain."

No, thought Plekhov. He wouldn't ask him if he had read any of the condemned books. Presumably, he had read the Bible. He turned instead to Governor Frank. "Perhaps, Herr Governor, the books should be locked away in a reserve area, inaccessible to students except by special arrangement."

"*No, no!*" Soddeberg broke in. "By simply sequestering them, Herr Governor, you would deprive yourself of a great dramatic possibility and of a symbolic opportunity which would surely commend itself in the . . . higher reaches of Berlin. On this theme, I am moved, Herr Governor, by words spoken by the Fuehrer. I keep them pasted to my writing board." He reached into his briefcase and began to read:

"'The heroic strivings of the German people are exercised not only through victorious feats on military fronts, in athletics, in art, in music, in literature. They are exercised by the inspired search for the Aryan purity which comes from stamping out decadent thought in our intellectual life. We must weed out those corrupting sources of misleading and evil thought propagated through the years by alien elements of the academy.'"

Soddeberg looked up, his eyes partly closed by the sheer poetry of the language.

Governor Frank looked about him. "Are there any questions?"

Nobody raised a voice.

"You, Herr Librarian?" He looked at Plekhov on his left.

"No, Herr Governor."

"Very well, Soddeberg. You will hear from me."

Lieutenant Soddeberg picked up his briefcase, gave the Nazi salute, and walked out.

CHAPTER FORTY-SIX

May 1943

Axel Reinhard was surprised by the query over the telephone. It came from a Gestapo official in Governor Frank's office. In all the months he had worked on the construction of Camp Joni, in his dealings with Cracow he had worked only through Captain Plekhov and, occasionally, Governor Frank.

The Gestapo officer asked, "Does Captain Plekhov have quarters in your building at Camp Joni?"

"Well, yes. Sometimes he spends the night. He uses a room in this building."

"Does the room contain anything other than the captain's clothing?"

"I don't know. How *would* I know, without going into the room and inspecting it?"

"We are just asking questions, Herr Kapitan. Has Captain Plekhov ever discussed with you the question of subversive books in the Cracow University library?"

"No."

"When he arrives at Camp Joni in the quarter-ton, does his vehicle arrive within view of the office in which you work?"

"Yes. It parks directly outside. I can see it through my window."

"Have you, in the past week, noticed Captain Plekhov bringing from the vehicle any packages—or bags—of substantial size?"

In fact Reinhard had noticed, on Monday, Plekhov carrying a bag, obviously heavy, to his quarters, and then going back to the car for a second bag. "I have no memory of any such thing."

"Very well. You are under instructions, Herr Kapitan, to permit no one access to Captain Plekhov's quarters until my deputy arrives at Camp Joni."

"Captain Plekhov enters his quarters from a door outside, using his own key."

"I will arrange with the Postenkommandant to put a guard outside that entrance. But since there is also access to his room in the wing from your own office, you say, you have the responsibility of preventing anyone from approaching his room through your own quarters."

Axel put down the telephone, locked the outside door, and walked down the hallway to the room at the other end of the building. He found the door to Plekhov's room locked. Axel had a passkey.

He opened the door. At the far end stood the two closets that Axel had designed to accommodate officers' coats and miscellaneous gear. He opened the first one. He found clothes and, on the shelf, a case of precious vodka.

The Gestapo could not be raising this kind of alarm over a missing case of vodka.

He moved to the second closet. A large trench coat hung there, and at one side, a shotgun and two rifles, one of them a hunting rifle Plekhov had once brought in to show Axel when the two men were drinking vodka together—it had been his father's. On the higher shelf, wrapped in newspapers, were two rows of objects which he supposed were books. He put a pencil through the paper at one end and tore open a hole large enough to see through. It was a large antique edition of a Bible. He went to the other end and made a second exploration. It was a book by Santayana.

He thought hard and quickly on the questions he had been asked. *These must be stolen books.* But why?

What mattered was to get word to Plekhov. Axel's mind raced. The telephone number he regularly used when calling Plekhov in Cracow was surely bugged. One possibility was physically to remove the books, which were what the Gestapo was presumably looking for, so that they would not be found. But if the Gestapo was on its way, contacted by radio, there would be no time to transport them to a hiding place, intimately though he knew every corner of the buildings he had constructed.

Where *was* Plekhov? In his military car traveling to Joni?

Axel walked quickly back to his office.

Plekhov was sitting there, in the chair he so frequently occupied.

"Hope you didn't mind my using my passkey, Herr Axel." Plekhov grinned.

The door flung open. Two Gestapo agents walked in.

Plekhov was billeted now in Block 11, with 110 other prisoners. Four days later, Axel saw the order: Plekhov, that afternoon, in the presence of the workers returned from their labor at the chemical factory, was to be hanged for seditious insubordination.

Axel concentrated his mind, and made it up.

He walked outside. As Superintendent of Construction, he was free to use any of the vehicles in the pool, and his badge permitted him access everywhere. He walked to a lorry with the heavy canvas awning used to protect men and materiel from sun and rain.

He turned on the engine and drove the truck directly outside the door of Block 11. He kept the engine running and walked into the barracks. A dozen men, too infirm or weakened to report for work, lay on their mattresses, or loitered aimlessly on the first floor of the building. He searched their faces and then raced up the steps to the second floor. In the complement there he spotted Plekhov, face swollen, one eye shut from the beating. He whispered to him and led him down the stairs and into the back of the lorry, placing him under the awning.

He drove to the gate.

But a train blocked the way out to the road. He could see a detachment of men unloading cement.

Axel got out from the driver's seat and walked past a familiar guard at the gate. He addressed the officer supervising the cement removal. "I am Captain Reinhard, in charge of construction here. I need to move out with my lorry. Stand aside."

"You will need to give instructions to the engineer, Herr Kapitan."

The engine was three cars up.

He walked briskly and called up to the engineer. "Move forward immediately. I am in charge here. We need to get through the gate."

The engineer saluted. The engine steam began to pump from the narrow smokestack.

Axel walked quickly back to the gate, past the guard, and into the driver's seat of the lorry.

The train was inching forward, but the guard now stood directly in front of his lorry, facing him.

Axel looked out at the man who approached from his left.

"What's your hurry, Captain Reinhard?" Kommandant Amadeus asked.

CHAPTER FORTY-SEVEN

Spring 1946

Prosecutor Robert Jackson's resolve not to permit Soviet crimes to distract from the prosecutors' focus kept coming up against distracting problems. Justice Parker, the American alternate judge, even gave thought, however fleeting, to resigning from the tribunal. That would have been a devastating development, after so many months of hearings.

When tapped for Nuremberg, John J. Parker, universally acclaimed as a distinguished jurist, was serving in Virginia as chief judge of the Court of Appeals. Judge Parker accepted as a matter of duty that while serving as judge at Nuremberg, he would need to attend incidental social gatherings hosted by major figures. It had never occurred to him that that might include exposure to Andrei Vishinsky.

Months before the Vishinsky episode, Parker had attended the compulsory annual Russian celebration of their October revolution. The Russians were quartered closely together in the Erlenstegehn sector on the eastern edge of Nuremberg. At their lively October celebration, the Russians and their guests had had to dither for an hour, waiting for U.S. potentate Robert Jackson to show up. When, by 2045, he still hadn't arrived, a driver was dispatched to Jackson's home address. He returned twenty minutes later to report that Justice Jackson had appeared at the door of his apartment in shirtsleeves, and responded that he had never even *received* an invitation to the party. A clerical error, obviously, but he submitted his compliments to the Soviet hosts, along with word that unfortunately he could not, on such short notice, abandon the pressing project he had undertaken earlier in the evening.

The driver passed the message to Captain Guernsey, U.S. diplomatic coordinator. Guernsey was distressed. Everybody in the room was industriously drinking the proffered liquors and liqueurs, and the volume of the social hubbub was at high pitch. For all the effort Captain Guernsey always made at social integration at such affairs, an hour or so after the party began, the Russians were reamalgamated, speaking to each other in their native language. One or two French diplomats circulated among the anglophones; and Judge Parker, of retiring disposition, chatted with a subordinate in the corner of the room.

Captain Guernsey made his way to Judge Parker and whispered an urgent request: Would he, at toastmaking time, now an hour overdue, please substitute for Justice Jackson? That would mean there'd be the required two U.S. toasts, Chief U.S. Judge Francis Biddle assuming the senior burden. Judge Parker told Captain Guernsey that the idea of toasting the Soviet revolution ran against the grain—

"Sir, just say something nice about the Russian people, that's all."

All right. There was no alternative.

Other toastmakers worked their way around the problem of making a direct toast to the revolution of Vladimir Ilyich Lenin. The British prosecutor, Maxwell Fyfe, spoke about the great deeds of the Red Army. Judge Biddle did a hymn to the Russian people, but left room for Judge Parker's ensuing reference to the Russian civilians who had faced such arduous years.

The wit and grace of deputy French prosecutor Dubost itself became a toast. He ended his speech by saying: "*La France est connue comme le pays de la revolution. Nous pouvons l'avouer sans rougir.*" Interpreters were busy explaining the pun to the Russians. Monsieur Dubost had said that the French were historically the country of revolution and therefore could hail the Russian revolution without any need to blush—*rougir* (turn "Red"). Judge Parker was glad to get home. He marveled at the Russian host at his own table who, in the course of the evening, consummated a total of twenty-five toasts.

But a month later it wasn't a ritual national feast day, it was a special visit to Nuremberg by the Soviet Deputy Foreign Minister and delegate to the United Nations, the sinister Andrei Vishinsky. This terrible man had presided over Stalin's show trials before the war, a close study of which had generated the report of the commission headed by U.S. philosopher John Dewey, exposing the Soviet trials as bloody frauds. Judge Parker's adult life had been devoted to the integrity of the judiciary, and it had especially offended him, in 1939, that what amounted to political executions had been presented to the public as judicial exercises.

Parker knew that Jackson was committed to acting out the resolutions of the London Conference by the simple expedient of ignoring Soviet crimes against humanity. But, riding in the car on their way to the party, he now confided to his senior colleague, Francis Biddle, that he thought it quite unnecessary that a reception for the infamous Vishinsky should be hosted by the American prosecutor.

"Oh well," Biddle said, "these things happen. Nothing of notice will get said."

But something of notice most definitely *had* been said, as it turned out. The antecedent toasts at this Nuremberg party had been what had become routine—glasses lifted to the ideals of justice for war criminals, on which objective the guests could routinely agree. But the toast by Vishinsky turned out to be much more. "I propose a toast to the defendants," he said, and waited as, glasses in hand, the guests also waited: *"May their paths lead straight from the courthouse to the grave."*

Judge Parker put down his glass and stared hard at Biddle. This was judicial infamy.

That night he wrote to his wife in North Carolina and told her about the evening. "I hope to heaven Vishinsky's toast is not reported to the press. The indifference to it—by Biddle, by Jackson, by just about everybody—dramatizes the relativist overlay of Nuremberg. I think we are doing, here, the right thing, but we find ourselves accessories to a great imposture—the Soviets as qualified judges of the behavior of other countries' war crimes! I'm not sure I'm glad I accepted this assignment."

But the next day, having thought about the whole picture, Parker was dutifully at his station, sitting alongside the four principal judges and the three other alternate judges as the prosecutor recounted the history of Camp Joni.

Listening to the evidence, Judge Parker renewed his private conviction that such as Amadeus *should* go straight from the courthouse to the grave. Though he must of course be willing, as a matter of judicial rectitude, to *listen* to the defense of Amadeus, undertaken—in this case—by his brother. The young Amadeus struggled to do his duty, and indeed, to serve as his brother's keeper.

CHAPTER FORTY-EIGHT

March 1946

Sebastian didn't need to be prompted by Harry Albright. He was there at the sound control booth promptly on the morning of March 8. Hermann Goering versus Robert Jackson. Nazi Germany versus the Allied Powers.

Jackson came in high on the wings of his soaring declamation at the outset of the prosecution's case: "*The wrongs which we seek to condemn and punish have been so calculated, so malignant, and so devastating, that civilization cannot tolerate their being ignored, because it cannot survive their being repeated.*" His antagonist, Hermann Goering, had matter-of-factly assumed the role of Nazi successor; the primary living representative of the Third Reich.

And of course Goering, at the outset of the trial, had pleaded not guilty. Goering, by his own accounting, was therefore:

—Not guilty of plotting with others to wage wars of aggression;

—Not guilty of initiating and waging wars of aggression;

—Not guilty of war crimes involving the maltreatment of prisoners of war;

—Not guilty of crimes against humanity;

—Not guilty or responsible for murder, extermination, enslavement, deportation.

"Of course," Sebastian ventured to Albright as he was conducting his sound checks, "we've had witnesses and documentaries for four months that establish *all* of those things about Goering."

"Yes," Albright said, "*—no, you got full volume on right now, Giovanni.*" He reached over and slightly rotated a dial at the far end of the control panel. "*That any better?*" he asked the operative by the interpreters' stand. "*Gut.* Sure those documents are there and have been displayed, and everybody knows what's in them, and if you work backward, Sebby, you have six million dead Jews—somebody had to kill them, and that seems to me a Count-Four crime, pure and simple. And you had aggressive wars—Poland and Norway didn't invade Germany—Count Two. To initiate an aggressive war you obviously have to *conspire* to wage it, because paratroopers do not materialize from overhanging clouds the minute the chief of state decides to invade a country, so there you have Count One. What did I forget?"

"Count Three. Go twiddle your dials, Harry. You're forgetting important things. Count Three is war crimes—"

"—yeah. Hold on." He leaned into the microphone. "*I got you. They're all miked in now.*" To Harry he said the judges were on their way. Almost immediately, Sebastian saw them filing in.

A minute later, Goering was on the stand. Sallow, after the loss of fifty pounds, his neck loose in his shirt collar, his prison uniform droopy, he was nevertheless, in manner, always imperious. Robert Jackson, middle-sized, middle-weight, his hair still a youthful brown, his eyeglasses tilting just slightly down on his nose, looked determined, his eyes focused sharply on his prey.

Jackson's opening question was the subject of a hundred conversations that night at the Palace, in the Grand Hotel, and in pressrooms at Nuremberg, Chicago, and Sydney.

"You are perhaps aware that you are the only man living who can expound to us the true purposes of the Nazi Party and the inner workings of its leadership?"

Goering ate that up. "I am perfectly aware of that."

A wrong psychological note had been struck. After four months' increasingly fulsome display of materials reviewed and testimony heard, the chief prosecutor seemed to be saying that only a confirmation of the case against the Nazis by Hermann Goering would suffice to establish the criminal nature of the Nazi enterprise.

It got worse. Within what seemed like mere minutes, Goering's dialectical prowess had apparently unsettled Jackson. He found himself asking Goering about practices in the early days of the concentration camps when Goering exercised direct authority over them. Jackson's question baffled everybody:

"Was it also necessary in operating this [concentration camp] system, that you must not have persons entitled to public trials in independent courts? And you immediately issued an order that your political police would not be subject to court review or to court orders, did you not?" As Goering attempted to decipher the question, Jackson cut him off, demanding a simple yes or no.

Assistant prosecutor Telford Taylor would later remark that the question obviously could not be answered yes or no, requiring as it did an explication of several issues. Were all arrestees barred from public trials? Were all camp inmates so barred? If so, was it "necessary" that they should be? What orders did Goering actually issue, and for what reasons?

But the most humiliating point came when, discussing prewar events on the Nazi calendar, Jackson asked whether the German remilitarization of the Rhineland on March 7, 1936, had been planned long in advance.

Goering replied, "At most, two to three weeks."

Whereupon Jackson triumphantly produced the record of a meeting of the Reich Defense Council on June 26, 1935, a full ten months before the Rhineland question, which called for "preparation for the liberation of the Rhine."

Goering commented languidly that the wording Jackson had used, "the liberation of the Rhine," was odd, inasmuch as the German words spoke of the "*clearing* of the *Rhine*." The document, Goering explained with mock patience, said nothing at all about *militarizing* the *Rhineland*. And "the Rhine"—he spoke as though to a schoolboy—is the river running through the Rhineland and yes, at that conference the need to keep the river clear was discussed. Basic directions had been given for military mobilization *in the event that war should break out at some point in the future*; rudimentary strategic safeguards.

Jackson attempted recovery. "The preparations you speak of were of a character which had to be kept entirely secret from foreign powers—"

"Yes," Goering said. "I do not think I can recall reading beforehand the publication of mobilization preparations of the United States."

Jackson called on the court to rebuke Goering's words as irrelevant and tendentious and evasive. Lord Lawrence agreed that Goering's reference to American mobilization plans was "irrelevant," and that his answer ought not to have been made. But he quietly rejected Jackson's appeal to forbid Goering from answering questions put to him in such language as Goering elected to use.

Jackson would not give up ground. He suggested that the tribunal's latitudinarian rulings had the effect of permitting the defense to run away with the trial. He went so far as to say that the court should be aware that "outside of this courtroom is a great social question of the revival of Nazism, and that one of the purposes of the defendant Goering—I think he would be the first to admit—is to revive and perpetuate it by propaganda from this trial now in process."

Goering's defense counsel rose to his feet in surprise and indignation.

Sophisticated observers were flabbergasted at the very suggestion that the revival of Nazism could be thought an objective of Hermann Goering, at trial in a clearly hopeless attempt to prove himself not guilty of myriad acts in which he had been shown complicit. "Even physically," commented one experienced reporter, "Jackson cut a poor figure. He unbuttoned his coat, whisked it back over his hips, and, with his hands in his back pockets, spraddled and teetered like a country lawyer. It was sad."

Suddenly Harry poked Sebastian in the arm. *"Hey, guess what! Birkett just whispered to Lawrence for God's sake to close this session down!"*

And indeed Lord Lawrence did just that. He announced simply, "Perhaps we had better adjourn now at this stage." Rising, he gave no time for comment from prosecution or defense.

The other judges rose with him as the marshal banged down his gavel, adjourning the session. The eyes of everyone trained on Hermann Goering. His self-satisfaction radiated in flushed cheeks and the defiant composure of his famous face.

Sebastian stared at him. Goering was now removing his headphones. He brought them from his head and, holding them between thumb and forefinger, stretched his arm out to the right. Without turning to see whether anybody was there to take them, Goering dropped them, as he might have dropped a used napkin, and strode back to join his fellow defendants, the faces of most of them alight with pride and pleasure over the performance of their onetime Reichsmarschall.

Hermann Goering's case took up twelve days of court time. When it was done, on March 22, the court made an announcement.

The defendant Goering had been allowed to give his evidence "without any interruption whatever, and he has covered the whole history of the Nazi regime from its inception to the defeat of Germany. The tribunal does not propose to allow any of the other defendants to go over the same ground in their evidence except insofar as it is necessary for their own defense."

"Maybe we'll be home for Christmas," Harry, stopping by Sebastian's office, said. Sebastian was at work at his desk, numbly digesting and translating the seemingly endless supply of documents. "Send me a postcard when you get home. I can't imagine ever leaving Nuremberg. Fucking Nuremberg."

CHAPTER FORTY-NINE

March 1946

The telephone call was from Chief Landers. "Lieutenant, you've had a couple of pieces of mail down at the post office—one of 'em's been there a week, it came registered, the corporal there said." Teasingly, he asked, "Do you want him to mark it *Addressee Unknown* and send it back?"

"Sorry about that, Chief." Sebastian accepted the rebuke. Normally, Harry checked the post for both of them, but Harry had got out of the habit since his hospitalization. "I'll pick them up. I'll be leaving here in a few minutes."

Has to be Mama, he reflected. It was probably too soon to hear back from his grandmother in Arizona. Though perhaps the APO address the huge U.S. staff was using had been given postal priority.

En route to the hotel, he picked up the two letters from the clerk, and noticed right away that one letter was from Henrietta, her trademark green ink on the envelope. He would take the letters to the Grand and read them while waiting for Harry. The day was radiant, a hint of spring genuinely on its way, taking the light later into the evening. At 1830 he could even read the newspaper he brought along without having to edge up toward the wall lamp. He opened, first, the letter from his grandmother.

"My darling boy," it began, as ever in German. "Yes. It is all as recorded in my mother's scrapbook. I thought no purpose served in telling your mother she was not the child of the only man she ever knew as a father. Can you think of any reason why I'd have done differently?"

Walther Leddihn, that last night at Innsbruck, had confessed to Sebastian that there had been concern in the family over Henrietta's marrying a Jew. The thought passed through Sebastian's mind—had his Oma indeed acted on her own? Or had husband Roderick Chapin perhaps chafed at acknowledging the baby as a stepchild, moreover, a stepchild who was half Jewish?

He turned the page of the letter. "I did discuss with your grandfather—your step-grandfather—the possibility of telling your mother some day, perhaps after she graduated from Radcliffe, the whole story. But then she married your father and went off to live in Hamburg. I was relieved, when the Fuehrer came on the scene, that no one knew her real father was Jewish."

Harry walked into the bar and sat down beside Sebastian, signaling to the waiter.

"Hang on a second, Harry. I just want to finish this letter."

"Okay. Lend me your newspaper."

Sebastian handed it over and continued reading. "It was completely gone from my mind. But then in 1938, I got the letter from my Papa telling me the Gestapo had been to the house in Munich and had taken his papers and the scrapbooks. And then when they went back to see him, the Nazi official had said to him—I have my father's letter here, I keep it with my bankbook. This is what my Papa wrote:

"The Gestapo man said to me, 'Your daughter married an American Jew and had a child, who would be half Jewish. And that child later married a German, we know from the wedding invita-

tion in the book. One Axel Reinhard. There is a letter in the book—we have made a copy of it and other incriminating material—with a picture: Herr Reinhard and his half-Jewish wife, your daughter, and a small boy. And an address in Hamburg. We will be looking into that.'"

Harry was impatiently tapping on the table.

"Hang on, Harry," Sebastian said. "Yes, sure, I want to know about Rudenko and Goering."

"Goering had a great line."

"Shut up a second."

Harry returned to his newspaper, Sebastian to the last page of his grandmother's letter.

"That was in the late spring. I wrote to Annabelle and told her that the European scene was terrible, that she and Axel should bring you to America. She answered that Axel was busy with his work, and happy doing it, that you were doing well at school. Et cetera.

"I wrote a second time. She replied saying much the same thing.... Munich came, and then the invasion of Czechoslovakia and then the British-Poland defense pact. That's when I wrote again, but this time *to your father.* And to him I revealed it all, quoting my own father's letter, and begging him to leave the country. And the next thing I heard from your mother was that suddenly Axel had agreed to take the family to America. She never even suggested she knew why he had changed his mind. And—of course—he didn't come with you.

"You are a grown boy, darling Sebastian, and I know how important your work must be in Nuremberg. I cannot prevent you from telling your mother, but I pray you will not do so. Dear Alois. I can hardly remember what he looked like—his name never came up, except that one time, when I told your mother he had died. I told her he died a year before she was born.

"All love from your Oma.

"P.S. I have had a letter from Walther, after so very long. And he paid you many compliments, but asks why I didn't insist you have music lessons. I reminded him that my daughter was in charge of your education."

Harry, the newspaper spread out on the table, had turned his chair around and was discussing the afternoon's events with Captain Carver at the next table.

Sebastian put away his grandmother's letter. He was relieved he didn't immediately need to talk with Harry. He distracted himself by retrieving the newspaper and running his eyes over the headlines. The lead story was about Soviet delegate Gromyko, who had stormed out of the United Nations in New York protesting the Security Council's vote calling on Moscow to withdraw Soviet troops from Iran.

He thought back to that last day in August 1939, a thirteen-year-old visiting his schoolmates on the eve of his departure, and the especially melancholy visit with his playmate, Pauline. Sebastian had never confessed to his mother that he had confided to Pauline that he would not, in fact, be coming back to live in Hamburg, that his father was only pretending he would return in a few weeks. Pauline had been disconsolate. Back home that afternoon, she might even have confided her secret to her mother, and to her father, the Hauptsturmfuehrer, and her fear that she would never see Sebastian again.

He had put the second letter out of his mind. Undressing in his room at Musikerstrasse later in the evening, his hand came upon it. He tore it open and rushed to the lamplight.

Dear Sebastian. You are losing your mind. You may be involved in cosmic matters in Nuremberg but you are only just twenty years old. You need to go to college when you get done with the Nazis, and get a job and start a life. You will be ready to have a family in maybe seven or eight years. The girl—for God's sake take precautions.

It was signed, *The mother who loves you, Annabelle.*

Teresa's arms were around his neck.

"Is that from your mother?"

"Yes."

"I wish I could read English. Will you translate it for me?"

His voice husky, he said, "I don't know how to translate from English," managing a self-derisive smile. "It's just a letter about—her work."

"When I go to America with you I will work, too. At something."

He kissed her. And then he said he had had a very bad and stressful day. "Do you understand?"

"Yes. I understand. I will sleep in my own room tonight."

Again they kissed.

CHAPTER FIFTY

January 1945

The radio wire was terse. 8TH SOVIET DIVISION ESTIMATED WILL REACH WARSAW-LODZ-CRACOW LINE APPROX 14-16 JAN. DESTROY CAMP FACILITIES ESPECIALLY CREMATORIUM. TIMING IN YOUR HANDS. YOU TO REPORT TO BERLIN SS HEADQUARTERS. PLACE DEPUTY IN CHARGE. CAMP PERSONNEL WILL REPORT TO STAGING AREA 12-C--HIMMLER.

Amadeus reflected a moment and made a few notes. He called then for his duty officer and instructed him to assemble the guards and the Kapos at 1100 in the mess hall. Nowhere else at Camp Joni could 325 persons assemble in winter.

He brought in an orderly and signaled him to follow. They walked one site over to Building B2 to the Kommandant's small suite of rooms. They went directly into his bedroom. Amadeus pointed to a uniform and set of boots inside a chest of drawers and to a closet. He instructed the orderly to pack everything he designated into the two large army bags stored in the closet. "I will put other things I want in a third bag." The orderly nodded.

He walked past the quadrangle to the traffic officer's room, outside the gate. "I shall need a car and driver to take me to Breslau."

"When, Herr Oberstfuehrer?"

"Have him stand by from 1600."

The staff members were assembled at the mess hall. Everyone stood at attention when he entered the room. The Kommandant's voice would not carry from one end to the other, so he walked down the narrow passageway between the tables to the center of the room. He climbed up on a mess hall table and motioned with his hands that the company should sit down.

"I have instructions from headquarters. When I complete the exact schedule, we are rapidly to do the following:

"Set every building in Joni on fire with the exception of the barracks in which the prisoners are housed. Lay dynamite in the crematorium and destroy it. Burn all records in the records building.

"Effective on my departure, perhaps as soon as later today, Major Bruler becomes the Kommandant of Joni. He will allocate the duties I have enumerated among those responsible to carry them out. I expect that the dismantlement of the camp will begin some time after the workforce returns in the afternoon."

Two words reached up to him, spoken by someone at the table on which he was standing. "The prisoners?"

"Yes. The prisoners." He looked about over the heads of the guards at the surrounding tables, their faces clean shaven, as Amadeus had always required. Many wore overcoats against the penetrating cold. "Hellich, where are you?"

"Here, Herr Kommandant." Hellich was seated toward the end of the hall.

"How many are there, Lieutenant?"

"Two thousand, two hundred and ninety, Herr Kommandant."

"What is the breakdown?"

There was a delay while Hellich reached in his pocket.

"Two hundred and five prisoners of war. One hundred eighty Polish nationals. Forty-five criminals. One thousand, eight hundred and sixty Hungarian Jews."

The crematorium could handle only 800 occupants at a time, and could recycle only after the twelve hours needed to remove the bodies, hose down the chamber, and check the gas vents.

Amadeus reflected on the problem. The timing, Himmler had explicitly said, was up to him. If Amadeus kept the death facilities operating another thirty-six hours, he could liquidate his entire inventory. But that would also mean the elimination of the workforce. Every day, over one thousand prisoners reported to work, most of them going to the chemical plant four kilometers away. Amadeus didn't know what orders had been sent by Berlin to the general manager of the I. G. Farben factory, but presumably it too had been ordered destroyed. He could counsel with Governor Frank—but why should he do so? Unless he really wished to? Himmler had not told him to coordinate his activities with the civil authority.

What it came down to, he reassured himself, standing up on the table, brow furrowed, staff and personnel silent awaiting his intructions, was: Do whatever he thought best. *Do what he wished.*

Yes, in thirty-six hours, he could liquidate the prisoners by the usual procedures, and he could accelerate the liquidation by ordering a thousand or so prisoners shot; but there would be no time to unearth graves for them, and general orders had forbidden eliminations that resulted in the putridity of the years before the crematoriums had been devised.

Best to gas and cremate the POWs, at the very least. Any delay or dereliction on that question would mean the survival and reenlistment in the Soviet army of an entire battalion of Russian soldiers. The criminals could be fitted—easily—into the same gas chamber with the POWs. The criminals were, granted, the most skilled of the workers, but to arrange for their evacuation and integration into work units and for their transport safely west of the war front would strain facilities, slowing down the evacuation.

And the Jews? He rather wished that Himmler had decided this question for him, as he had done all others for so long. The objective was of course to eliminate the Jews, but that job was not going to be finished, never mind the Soviet advance about which Himmler had warned. It was hardly as if there weren't Jews outside the sphere of the Third Reich. The Wannsee document revealed that there were more than three hundred thousand Jews in England alone—untouched, untouchable, obviously.

He reflected, suddenly, that his delay, in front of his entire staff, gave the impression of indecisiveness.

"Captain Mahler, prepare the facilities for an instant round of activity. I will go over the tabulations with Lieutenant Hellich and give detailed instructions within an hour."

Exactly an hour later, Hellich and Mahler at his side, Amadeus went over the breakdown. Hellich apologized: He could not absolutely record the demographic pattern, but what he had was very close. Amadeus looked down, pencil in hand.

Barrack 11A—205 prisoners of war; 45 criminals
Barrack 11B—180 Poles; 150 Jews (male)
Barrack 11C—310 Jews (male)
Barrack 11D—300 Jews (male)
Barrack 11E—300 Jews (male)
Barrack 11F—300 Jews (male)
Barrack 12A—300 Jews (female)
Barrack 12B—180 Jews (children, both sexes)

Colonel Amadeus penciled some quick subtotals.

He affixed checks down the roster, one by one, counting subtotals as he went, mouthing the figures. He put a pencil check on barracks 11A, 11B, 11C, 11D, 11E, 11F.

"That makes just about 1,600."

He turned to Mahler. "Leave the women and children. And when you depart Joni, which I assume you can do in forty-eight hours, leave them with rations."

The orders went out.

By midafternoon, Amadeus was ready, his miscellaneous gear, including books and journals, filling the third bag. The quarter-ton vehicle drove up and the orderly put the baggage into the back.

"It is warming up, Herr Kommandant," Mahler said.

"I hadn't noticed." He shook the proferred hand and also that of the orderly.

"Heil Hitler."

"Heil Hitler."

He was fortunate at Cracow. He had directed the driver to the railroad station, where he would stand by for any train bound west. He did not have to wait long. Walking down the platform he carried his work case, the driver the two bags.

The train was crowded. He walked past the first two cars, hospital wagons with large red crosses painted on their sides and, he supposed, on their roofs. On the side of the fourth car down he could detect frayed letters that had one day appeared bright and golden. *Premiere Classe.* He walked up the three car steps and opened the door. The officers' car was crowded and dense with tobacco smoke. But he could move the junior officer with his leg in a splint in the third row over to one side, and make room in the seat next to him. He walked back and signaled to his driver to bring up the bags.

He did so, stuffing two of them, as Amadeus had instructed, into the baggage section. He saluted. Amadeus returned the salute. A half hour later the train started moving. It was dark but very warm in the officers' car. He could not bring out his flask of vodka without having to offer to share it with the wounded lieutenant, so he walked out to the passageway and, keeping his balance with one hand on the rail, brought the flask to his lips and drank deeply.

CHAPTER FIFTY-ONE

January 1945

After prolonged stopovers, the train arrived in midmorning in Berlin. Proceedings at Frankfurt had been slow, especially cumbersome because the chief railroad engineer refused to permit the train to linger at the station, a target of near-daily bombings. Having arrived in Berlin, Amadeus impressed a private into service, giving him two bags to carry. Amadeus made his way through the bomb-fractured railroad station, inaugurated in 1896 by Kaiser Wilhelm. He sneaked a look up at the gaping holes in its arched roof. He felt pain and embarrassment, any facial expression of which he refrained from revealing to his porter. They reached the taxi site in the light snow. Amadeus nodded thanks to the soldier who had helped with the bags and got into a car. The driver dodged around fresh rubble, caused by what must have been last night's bombing, and drove to SS headquarters.

Amadeus gave his name to the stiff-shirted lieutenant at the desk. He identified himself. "I was Kommandant at Camp Joni and am here on Reichsfuehrer Himmler's instructions. If he is ready for me, fine. If there is to be a delay, kindly advise me where I am billeted. I will need to clean up and deposit my gear."

The lieutenant made a telephone call. "You can have temporary quarters at—" he pulled out a Berlin map and with his pencil identified a building a few blocks away—"the Hotel Rougemont. They will give you a room. You will need help with your bags? Never mind, I will have a driver take you." He inserted a jack into the switchboard and gave instructions. He then turned his back to Amadeus, permitting the lieutenant to speak into the telephone out of earshot. In moments, he turned around. "Herr Colonel, Herr Himmler will see you at 1400. Do you have German money? . . . That often is a problem for officials returning from Poland." He opened a strongbox behind the desk and came back with an envelope. "Here are 1,000 marks. Kindly sign the receipt in the ledger." He handed it over. Amadeus signed it and went gratefully to the car in the underground garage.

In the hotel, now converted to utilitarian quarters for officers and government officials, he bathed and was shaving when a knock at the door came. His face still soaped, he admitted what seemed a sixteen-year-old soldier.

"Herr Colonel Amadeus?"

"Yes."

He was handed an envelope. The soldier waited.

It was a summons to the office of Armament Minister Albert Speer. "He is waiting for you, Herr Colonel. I will take you there." Amadeus nodded. He would be down in the lobby in a few minutes.

Ten minutes later, the boy behind the wheel of a prewar Fiat pulled it up before the massive building. Amadeus stepped out. A guard led him through the cordon of SS men to the dimly lit, sparsely decorated lobby with the regal oil painting of the Fuehrer hanging over the reception desk. Only the high, ornate ceilings suggested to the visitor that there had been grander days for the Ministry.

He was led to the office of the arms minister. The huge door with the inlaid gilt panels opened. Albert Speer, his head bent over his desk, was dressed in a green tweed suit. He rose and extended his hand.

"Ah, Kurt. It has been many days since we spent time together."

"Many years, Herr Arms Minister."

"You have not forgotten your manners, Herr Brigadefuehrer."

Amadeus shook his head. "I am a colonel, not a general."

"You are a general now."

Amadeus did not conceal his surprise or his pleasure. "This is for my... services at Joni?"

"I do not get involved in the matter of the camps. I take it from Himmler that your record was good, no scandal. Exemplary performance. Total stability in trying circumstances—that is what he reported. Yes, you were recommended on that account, but your elevation is owing to the trust we are placing in you on your next assignment."

"What is that, Herr Albert?"

"You will be placed in charge of security in the Fuehrer's bunker."

General Amadeus drew in his breath.

"You were carefully selected. You will be replacing Brigadefuehrer Helvetius Spahr. Spahr is a very experienced military division-commander. The Russian advance, which must of course be stopped—and will be stopped—needs the most experienced fighting men in critical positions. General Spahr will be sent to Zharkov Zone B, replacing General Ober, who fell victim last week to enemy fire. My advice in the matter of the protection of the bunker was solicited in part because of my closeness to the Fuehrer, in part because, as armaments minister, the security of critical positions in Berlin is my responsibility. And of course there is no site more critical than whatever site the Fuehrer is housed in."

"What, concretely, are my duties?"

"You have an orderly mind, Kurt. For that reason I have prepared a memorandum, which I will now read to you, giving us the opportunity to discuss individual points."

He drew it from a desk drawer. "One. The personal security of the Fuehrer. I had nothing to do with the layout, as most recently revised, but I can quickly describe it from its plans and past visits, especially as an architect speaking to someone who studied architecture."

He drew from an adjacent table a large sheet of heavy paper. He sketched a rough rectangle. "These are the borders of the emplacement. They are constructed with concrete pillars and barbed wire. A... large... tent-patterned cover—" he sketched with a facile pen "—is designed to deflect bomb fragments. Over here is the main entrance. We arrive at the top story." His fingers sketched out an area. "Here you are billeted. And 120 personnel. They attend to everything."

"How many of the 120 are guards?"

"The SS detachment is eighty men. The others are technicians, radio, telegraph, printing. And yes, cooks."

"The Fuehrer?"

He turned the sheet over and resumed sketching.

"Here is his bedroom. There, the suite of Fraulein Braun. There, his dressing suite... There, his private office... There, his cabinet room... There, the dining room... There, the theater. There, a substantial area for aides. They have their own dining quarters and bathrooms. Here are stairs. The Fuehrer can climb these, when the skies are clear, to a small garden, outside the view of anyone, though of course we are in the heart of Berlin. I shall resume in the order of my memorandum.

"Two. There will be visits—there are always visits to the Fuehrer. I myself go often. And then visiting dignitaries. You are to confer with General Spahr to learn details of the security arrangements he devised a month ago. If satisfactory, maintain them. If less than that, revise them."

Amadeus nodded.

"Three." He put down the sheaf of paper. "This is not written down. The Fuehrer, as is perfectly understandable given the pressures of the last months, is under very considerable strain. Accordingly, he receives medication. Sometimes this medication can—affect him."

"How am I to judge this? Am I to descend to the Fuehrer's quarters?"

"*Never.* Your domain is the top story and the surrounding area. The Fuehrer does not like to be reminded that there is a military detachment surrounding him to ensure security. Although he has very direct memories of the attempt on his life on July 20th, he is persuaded that 100 percent of the German people are supporting him and supporting the war effort against the Communists and their allies... and, of course, of course, against the Jews."

"Can he see my guards when he climbs up to his garden?"

"No. The area is entirely enclosed."

"So what is it I am to do in the matter of—the Fuehrer's health?"

"All of his cables come up to your floor to be transmitted. They go through your hands, that is to say. Kurt, when I proposed you for the rank of general, it was because I had personal knowledge of your background, of your—intelligence."

Kurt Amadeus divined the line of Speer's thought.

"If I have reason to suspect that... some medicine has affected... our Fuehrer's thinking, I am to—" Amadeus nodded his understanding.

"Exactly. In that case you are to call me. You will find that there is a direct line to me in your office in the bunker."

"As also to Reichsfuehrer Himmler?"

"There is an operator who will always put you through to him. In the unlikely event that you need to speak to him. Your visit with me, I should have informed you, replaces your scheduled visit with him."

Speer depressed one of the buttons on his desk.

"You will meet Corporal Danzig. He has a jeep and radio telephone. He is permanently assigned to you, day and night."

Albert Speer rose.

"We will be in touch, Herr General." He smiled. The color of his suit did nothing to give color to his wan cheeks.

CHAPTER FIFTY-TWO

June 1946

Robert Jackson presided at the informal meeting. Sitting at the table opposite were the acid-tongued British prosecutor Maxwell Fyfe, Captain George Carver, and interrogation chief Colonel John Amen.

"Well, we're done with Albert Speer, five interesting days. Nice try, trying to convince the judges that, toward the end, he was really working *against* Hitler. And then he pops the business about how defendant Kurt Amadeus will bear him out. How come we didn't get anything on that from the Amadeus interrogation?"

"We didn't have any leads in that direction," Carver said. "All we got from Amadeus was that Speer recommended him as bunker security chief."

"Well, we can't do much with it now. The defense has the ball. So, Carver, what does your informant, Lieutenant Reinhard, tell you? Will Amadeus change his plea tomorrow on the stand?"

"We've given him two-thirds of what he asked for, Mr. Jackson. He got the access he wanted to Lieutenant Reinhard— "

"Did he invoke that privilege?"

"Last time I counted, Reinhard had been in to see him eight times."

"And always pressed on the matter of the plea?"

Dumb question, Carver thought. On the other hand, he himself had asked Sebastian that same question after the fourth or fifth visit.

He nodded his head. "I was going to say, prosecution request number one—Amadeus got the visiting privilege; and request number two—we adjusted the entire prosecution schedule so that he would come in *after* Speer. Now we have some idea, after hearing Speer, why he wanted that."

Jackson reflected. "If he testifies that Speer told him to keep his eye on Hitler, and to prepare to pull the cord on him when Speer said go—is he likely to base his defense on that?"

"He might," Max Fyfe said. "Of course, if he pleads guilty, he wouldn't have anything relevant to say except later, in the matter of mitigation of sentence. Still...yes. That defense would be something along the lines of: 'I became so opposed to Hitler when I got to Berlin that I coconspired with Herr Speer and agreed to bump him off.'"

"Amadeus took over the bunker on January 10th. Hitler shot himself on April 30th. That's almost sixteen weeks—"

"Maybe Hitler shot himself because he was so afraid of Amadeus," Fyfe volunteered.

They appreciated the levity.

Carver continued. "And maybe he can explain to the court how he plans to bring a quarter of a million of his Camp Joni graduates back to life....Favor number three, you remember, was that, when found guilty, he was to be shot."

"Nobody much wants to be hanged, there isn't any doubt on that point," Jackson said. "And when the sentences are handed down, hanging sentences, we can imagine what the principal stink will be from the admirals and generals."

"To say nothing of Goering," Fyfe added.

"Well, we're the prosecutors, not the judges," said Colonel

Amen. There was a hint of rebuke in his voice. "All we can say to Amadeus, let's face it, is that we are not going to recommend capital punishment other than by hanging for *anybody.*"

"But we haven't told him even that, Colonel. We've strung him along—shit. I didn't mean that pun, sorry. I haven't even told Reinhard that it's nix on the firing squad."

"Well, here's the nub of it." Chief U.S. Prosecutor Robert Jackson had a way of asserting his authority whenever he thought the temptation to ramble was taking hold. "Tomorrow, the lawyer Amadeus will speak first; the defendant Amadeus, of course, on the stand. If there's to be a plea change, counsel can do it. Or he can just turn to the defendant and let the plea change come out of his own mouth.

"But here's the thing: If Amadeus sings—and it would be great if he did—it would substantially weaken the defense arguments of the whole pack. We'd have to reconsider the whole line of cross-examination. If, for instance, General Amadeus says that it was Governor Hans Frank who told him to gas the prisoners of war, we'll goose up the case against Frank and try for corroborating documents. But we can't do that while Amadeus is on the stand."

"So?" Colonel Amen asked.

"So if he goes for guilty, Carver, you proceed to cross-examine and get everything you can from him, but after you've done the vital work, move for an adjournment on the grounds that the cross-examination, given the revised plea, needs more time to prepare. Got it?"

Carver nodded.

Jackson got up. "Take heart, gentlemen. Only five more to go after Amadeus."

CHAPTER FIFTY-THREE

July 1946

The marshal called out. "The Court recognizes George Friedrich Amadeus, counsel for the defendant Kurt Waldemar Amadeus."

The younger Amadeus rose from the row of defense tables. Walking over to the left side of the courtroom, he stood by the lectern. Simultaneously, Kurt Amadeus filed by the four defendants on his right, making his way, finally, past Hermann Goering. He walked to the dock on the right. Both lecterns had chairs. Attorneys and defendants could not be expected to remain standing for what could be days at a time.

George Friedrich Amadeus wore his same corduroy suit, manifestly not made to order. His closed, white-starched collar crowded against his Adam's apple.

He cleared his throat. "Honorable judges. The objection I made at the time of the indictments was overruled. You will perhaps recall that I asserted that collective trials were a fundamental violation of individualized justice, which is the basis of individual rights—"

The gavel came down. Lord Lawrence's voice was quiet but

emphatic. "You are out of order, Counsel. There is no provision for appeal from a ruling of the tribunal."

"But Judge Lawrence, I wish that this final objection I am now making should appear on the record as a necessary adjunct to the testimony of my client."

"Strike that," Lawrence ordered the clerk. "Proceed, Herr Amadeus."

"Very well."

He turned to look opposite him to his brother at the dock. "Kurt Waldemar Amadeus. You have considered the possibility of altering your plea to guilty. How then do you plead?"

Several of the defendants leaned forward tensely. The gallery, which had not been full to hear through the defense of the last half-dozen witnesses, was crowded today. There had been the rumor that something out of the ordinary was up with the Amadeus prosecution. Only the encephalophonic whir of the cameras could be heard. Sebastian Reinhard sat stiffly in the control room, at the side of Harry Albright, looking down on the eerily still scene. Albright whispered. "*This is it.*"

Kurt Amadeus stood straight, his gray prison uniform suit well pressed. He looked over at his brother, then turned to face the judges.

"I reiterate my plea of not guilty."

The whole of the prosecution staff seemed to draw breath. There was a smile over clenched teeth and Goering turned to Hess on his left, and then over to Keitel. There was the hint of a nod.

"Very well," Counsel said.

Then, "On the matter of your role as Kommandant of the camp at Joni in Poland. It is alleged that while you were in charge, many thousands of people were gassed."

"Two hundred and fifty-one thousand were eliminated."

"It is alleged that among them were prisoners of war."

"That is correct."

"Were you aware, while Kommandant, of the regulations of the Geneva Convention respecting the treatment of prisoners of war?"

"I was."

"How then can you plead not guilty to Count Number Three?"

"Because, on mature reflection, I concluded that I am merely a cog in the machinery of this court, which is a charade whose primary purpose is to avenge Jewish sensibilities."

Everyone, it seemed, began talking. Hissing could be heard. Goering bit his lip and turned his eyes quizzically toward his own defense counsel, seated, his jaw clenched. Judge Lawrence brought down his gavel. "There will be silence."

"How does the . . . construction you presume to place on the proceedings and constitution of this court bear on the direct question? You ordered the execution of prisoners of war, in violation of an agreement to which Germany had been a part."

"I believed that the decisions of the Fuehrer were the supreme law, even as President Truman considered the use of the atomic bomb his supreme authority."

"What right did *you* have to consider Adolf Hitler's word as outweighing sovereign commitments made by predecessor governments?"

"I considered the National Socialist Party a revolutionary party, and therefore unbound, as the France of Napoleon and the Russia of Lenin declared themselves unbound by prerevolutionary conventions."

The stir now was general. The Russian judge, Nikitchenko, frowning, scribbled on a pad. Again Judge Lawrence had to insist on silence.

Counsel resumed. "There is the matter of the Poles who were executed at Camp Joni. Why were they executed?"

"Because Governor Frank gave me the orders to do so."

All eyes were now turned to Frank, seated in the higher of the two defendants' tiers, between Frick and Rosenberg. He twitched, then closed his eyes and bent his head forward.

"It is alleged that you authorized the . . . elimination of perhaps as many as two hundred thousand Jews."

"That figure is approximately correct."

"Why did you execute them?"

The writer Rebecca West, seated in the front row of the press section, opened her mouth in a rhetorical yawn. She knew what the answer to *that* question would be. Everybody knew what the answer to that question would be. Amadeus did not surprise them.

"Those were the orders of Herr Himmler, speaking for the Fuehrer."

"Again, why are you pleading not guilty?"

"The matter of guilt or nonguilt reflects the biases of this particular court, which are not universal."

"When you left Camp Joni, in January of last year, you were placed in charge of security for Hitler's bunker."

"Fuehrer Hitler's bunker, correct."

"Did that give you an opportunity to revise your opinions about the correctness of following Hitler's orders?"

"Yes."

There was silence. Sebastian grabbed Harry's shoulder. Harry adjusted his left earphone. "*He's going to say . . . Watch—*"

"Well, did you revise them?"

"No."

George Friedrich looked despairingly at his brother. He fiddled with papers on the lectern for a few seconds. Then looked up at the court. "I have no further questions for my client."

Again, a stir in the gallery.

"The court will hear the cross-examination by the prosecution."

Captain George Carver rose determinedly, but quickly bent his head, giving his attention to what was being said to him over the earphones. He listened and nodded his head acquiescently.

"*Jackson told him to ask for a recess,*" Harry tipped off his associate.

Captain Carver bowed to the judges. "Your honor, the defense took much less time than anticipated, the prosecution needs a short respite, and it has in any case been over an hour. May I petition the court for a recess of thirty minutes?"

The approval was gaveled by Lord Lawrence, and all rose to their feet.

CHAPTER FIFTY-FOUR

July 1946

In the U.S. prosecutors' lounge, Jackson was waiting for Carver. The U.K.'s Maxwell Fyfe joined them.

Carver sat down and lit a cigarette. "So much for four months' seduction of Kurt Waldemar Amadeus, boss."

"Yeah, yeah. It would have been nice. On the other hand, the stands he has taken aren't going to get any sympathy from the judges for any of the other people."

"Certainly not from Nikitchenko," said Fyfe. "The business about both Hitler and Lenin starting off from scratch! So if you want to prosecute Hitler, prosecute Lenin."

"*And Napoleon!*" Jackson grinned. "We can be grateful that Amadeus didn't go into the subject at any length, though he'd have been stopped by the faithful Lawrence."

"Yes. But *now*, Carver," Jackson said, "you *go after him.* After him *hard.* And clear up the Speer business. Let's find out why Amadeus thought it was so important to come up on the court calendar *after* Speer. I love it, Amadeus doesn't want to hang, just be shot. Yeah, we can get special favors for that guy."

"Hang on, Bob," Maxwell Fyfe was adding to the haze of tobacco by puffing on his pipe. "We refused to agree to shoot him. *We* didn't give him what *he* wanted, he didn't give us what *we* wanted."

The five-minute bell rang.

"Herr Amadeus, you show no contrition over what you did at Camp Joni. So you are agreeably acquiescent in the acts of Nazis depicted on this screen"—he pointed behind him—"as recently as a few months ago—"

"No."

Carver looked up. "What did you say just now?"

"I never engaged in atrocities."

Carver laughed scornfully. "You gassed victims by the tens of thousands but were not guilty of atrocities?"

"They were eliminated, as ordered. But at Camp Joni, they were never starved or beaten."

Carver eyed quickly his carefully prepared summary of activities traceable to Amadeus. "Well, that's very reassuring. So when you marched them into the gas chamber, you did not simultaneously beat them."

"There is a difference."

Carver waved his hand dismissively. "Perhaps an international treaty in the future will make that distinction. It is all right to eliminate prisoners of war and refugees and members of an ethnic group, so long as they are not tortured. They may think it torture when they lean back and begin to smell the poison issuing from the vents over their heads, but that torture is—what were your words? That it is *different*?"

Amadeus said nothing.

"Now let me ask you to expand just a little on the matter of the sovereignty of Adolf Hitler over the law. Suppose he had ordered you to murder—your brother, sitting over there."

"I wouldn't blame him," Harry muttered, without removing his headphones.

Amadeus did not answer immediately.

"You are thinking about that question?"

"I would not wish, Herr Carver, to say anything on the stand that would disrupt family relations."

Everyone laughed. Judge Lawrence had to repress his own reaction. He gaveled for order. Carver was unsmiling.

"No, you would not wish to do that. You are perhaps aware, Herr Amadeus, that there were brothers you gassed who had brothers—and mothers and fathers and children—alive somewhere? You were not concerned about their family feelings?"

"I did not permit myself to be distracted by emotions perfectly understandable in those who did not acknowledge the authority and foresight of the Fuehrer."

"*The foresight of the Fuehrer*, Herr Amadeus? There are four million Germans—I am not counting German Jews—add another one to four million—who would be living today but for your Fuehrer. German cities are in ruin. The German people are stricken with remorse over what your Fuehrer did. Do you call that foresight?"

Amadeus paused, then said: "I very much regret the consequences of the war."

"There is nothing to be done about the consequences of your gassing of its victims."

Amadeus did not reply.

"I turn to another subject. On January 10th, 1945, you were given command of security over Hitler's bunker."

Amadeus nodded.

"You met with the defendant Speer in his offices before going to the bunker?"

Again Amadeus nodded.

Judge Lawrence broke in. "The defendant will acknowledge verbally the questions of the prosecutor."

Amadeus nodded. Then, on second thought, said, "Yes."

"Now the defendant Speer has testified that in the conversation he had with you, he began by advising you of your promotion to the rank of Brigadefuehrer."

"That is correct."

"Did you interpret this as a move designed to enhance your dependence on the defendant Speer?"

"I considered it a promotion."

"A promotion initiated by Speer?"

"It crossed my mind that he played a role."

"Why?"

"We had been acquaintances, and he had sponsored me at other stages in my activity."

"He has testified that he communicated to you that you were to keep your eyes on the directives issued by the Fuehrer. Is that correct?"

"That is correct."

"What was the presumed purpose of your engaging in such supervision?"

"Herr Speer said that the Fuehrer was taking medication which sometimes affected his . . . faculties."

"Were you under the impression that the defendant Speer was suggesting the possibility that Hitler be deposed, and that you should be instrumental in that action?"

"Absolutely not."

"What was supposed to happen if you detected an order from the Fuehrer which you thought indicated that he was not in full possession of his faculties?"

"Herr Speer would have decided what action to take. Perhaps to consult with another doctor."

"Suppose that Herr Speer was actually *looking* for evidence of the Fuehrer's derangement, such as would justify removing him from power—"

"If he reached that conclusion, he would have needed to replace me with someone willing to betray the Fuehrer."

Goering looked up with evident satisfaction.

"You are saying that you would never have permitted yourself to use your own judgment on the question whether Hitler was—insane?"

Amadeus was angered. "I would never have stood in the way of the exercise of the authority of the Fuehrer."

Carver paused, and then decided that a pursuit of Amadeus's statement might be illuminating.

"Did your proximity to the Fuehrer enhance your respect for him?"

"Perhaps that is so. I was directly vested with his safekeeping."

"Did he, in exchanges with you during that period, persuade you yet again of his authority and foresight?"

"I never laid eyes on the Fuehrer."

Surprise registered on the faces of press and prosecutors.

"You—you say you did not lay eyes on Adolf Hitler in the—fifteen weeks during which you were bunker Kommandant?"

"That is correct."

"How did you receive instructions from him?"

"I never received instructions from him. Herr Speer had told me the Fuehrer did not wish to be reminded of the need for external security."

"Are you telling the court that you never saw Hitler?"

"Not face-to-face, until he was dead in the garden."

"Otherwise you never laid eyes on him?"

"I saw him in his car at the birthday parade. And at a rally in Salzburg. And in Paris. He was driving in his car up the Champs-

Élysées." Amadeus's eyes brightened at the memory. "And when he—when it all ended, I superintended the cremation, in the garden."

"So the confidence you placed in him wasn't based on your personal exposure to his—charisma?"

"I heard him speak many times on the radio."

Carver stopped. *Where else to go?* he wondered. He waited, in the event Jackson wanted anything further from him.

The earphones were silent. He turned to the court. "The cross-examiner rests."

Judge Lawrence turned to defense counsel. George Friedrich Amadeus walked up and took the lectern vacated by Carver.

He was still for a moment, and then looked up at his brother and said, "Kurt. Do you want to add anything?"

Amadeus shook his head. He remembered that the judge had ordered that responses should be voiced.

He said, "No."

CHAPTER FIFTY-FIVE

August 1946

Harry was seated in the control room with Sebastian, waiting for Robert Jackson's summation. After checking his sound contacts, he busied himself filling out college application forms. "Have you done yours?" he asked Sebastian.

"This is August. We've got Jackson's summary coming up, then final defense statements, then the tribunals' deliberations, then the verdicts—then the sentences carried out. I'm guessing it won't be over until almost the end of the year. So I figure I won't start college until the fall term, '47."

"The point system is looking up for me. They're demobilizing like mad at home. I'm counting on getting out maybe October or November. So I'm doing applications now."

"For where?"

"I'm thinking a technical college. Maybe MIT? Rensselaer? I'm putting my records together but there's something I can't find, the record of my job with Hammerstein. Remember? I told you about it. The company that got me working with sound for Radio City."

"You need *that*? After everything you've done here?"

"The MIT application form wants everything."

"Can't you write New York and get a copy?"

"Yeah, but that would take weeks. I brought one with me and the only thing I can think is I left it at Teresa's, that and a couple of letters and clips I kept from my bombing days in England. Do me a favor and look for it. Maybe tomorrow? After Teresa's gone to work?"

The following day she left home as usual at 0730. Sebastian had an hour at Musikerstrasse before setting out for the Palace. He went down to the basement room, which was showing signs of life from the paint and curtains and decorations, and opened the drawers of Teresa's desk. The bottom drawer had several folders. The first, he quickly identified as personal, relating to her schoolwork and her first marriage. He closed it. A second folder was marked "Harry." He spotted the documents Harry had asked for. He was drawn to a third folder, marked "Sebastian." He opened it to a letter, in German, in longhand. He was startled to see that it began, "Dear Sebby."

Dear Sebby?

He read on.

The German was clumsy. *Hast du den Verstandt Verloren?* The English words in the original stayed in his memory. His mother had written, "*You are losing your mind.*" He was reading someone's translation of his mother's letter.

His eyes traveled quickly to the letter's end. His mother had made abrupt reference to the girl Sebastian had written to say he wished to bring home and marry. He now read: *Um Himmel's Willen, schuetze Dich!* That translated to, *For heaven's sake, look out in bed.* His mother had written in English something a little different: "The girl—for God's sake take precautions."

When had Teresa pulled out his mother's letter? Sebastian had thought it safe simply to store it in his writing case with his army documents. The letter, after all, was in English.

In past weeks he had found Teresa progressively detached. One day, a week ago, she had declined to come up to bed with him. A few days later she had said she was going to spend the evening out with school friends.

He would say nothing to her tonight about the letter.

She came in after work and began listlessly to cook dinner. Sebastian, on the couch, read his book. He offered, as always—he had already prepared the salad—to help. She declined even to acknowledge the offer, so he read on. They ate in silence and after dinner went routinely to the card table.

She dealt out the cards and then said, abruptly, "You are not really going to marry me and take me to the United States, are you, Sebastian?"

Without waiting for an answer, her face had got red. "I was not so surprised when Harry stopped seeing me. Harry is *Jewish* and Jews are *that way*, they are not reliable, not loyal, not—"

Sebastian dropped his cards and stared at her.

In tears she stormed out of the room. He heard the outside door slam shut.

Sebastian brought out his two bags from the closet, surveyed the room in which he had spent so much time, pulled books from the bookcase, and then, from the next room, his clothes.

The summation by Robert Jackson, followed by summations from British, French, and Soviet prosecutors, lasted two full weeks. The calendar then called for final statements by the defendants. To the immense relief of the press, by now a visibly dwindled gathering of reporters, radio commentators, newsreel cameramen, and commentators, word passed that each defendant would be given only fifteen minutes. "After all, what more can they say?" Sebastian commented to Captain Carver in his office.

"That isn't so much the point in the law, Sebby. The point is that the defense has to be given the *final* say."

"Fifteen minutes, never mind that the prosecution took a whole week for each defendant?"

"You—never mind such things." Carver showed his impatience. "We are trying twenty-three people. Are you suggesting they *each* be given a week?"

"I give up."

"I wish they'd give up too."

"Well, my guy has all but given up."

"Your guy has been a pain in the ass."

Sebastian said nothing. It hadn't been a pain for *him* to spend the hours he had with Amadeus, listening, questioning, even arguing, though there was abundant reason to despair over Amadeus, an incorrigible man. Sebastian needed to remind himself that he was required, as a Christian, to acknowledge that he was dealing with a human being.

But there was a fine distraction. The nurture of the ardently planned visit to Berlin bore fruit. The visit by the two young officers would actually take place during the judges' deliberations, set to begin on the first day of September. As he signed Sebastian's three-day leave, Carver said not to worry, there was no way the judges would be done in less than three days. "Besides, Reinhard, you don't necessarily have to be here when the judgments are handed down."

Sebastian couldn't believe what he had heard. "I wouldn't miss that, Captain."

"I should hope not. If you did, I'd tell your grandchildren how indifferent you were to the most important moment in judicial history."

"There's going to be a lot of hanging, I expect."

"I hope so."

Sebastian feigned urbanity. "On the other hand, Captain, you're used to executing people."

Carver looked up sharply. Then his features relaxed. This was Reinhard's once-every-quarter taunt on the matter of the execution of Private Slovik for cowardice.

"I didn't much like doing that. But as a prosecutor you get so you can feel institutional imperatives. And in 1944 that imperative, from Ike on down to the company commander, was saying: *We can't let this happen.* An army private simply refusing to fight? Not with a full-scale war going on, not with that coward flaunting his defiance of basic army discipline."

"At least he wasn't hanged."

"He was a soldier."

"So are some of the people here, no?"

"Sebby, the point of this exercise—what, eleven months of it?—is that they're *not* simply soldiers. They're criminals."

"So we hang them."

"As I said, I hope so."

Both Harry and Sebastian had seen documentaries on the condition of postwar Berlin, many of them filmed almost immediately after its liberation and the formal surrender of Germany—in Berlin, on May 7 of the year before. There was not much left to shock them. They had seen destruction in Hamburg, and lived with it in Nuremberg.

Yet Berlin still had its special magic. The Brandenburg Gate had actually survived the bombs and, late that summer afternoon, projected its majestic shadows deep into the eastern sector of the city.

They stared, as so many did, at the remains of the bunker, that large swollen mound of earth under which thirty-six rooms had bustled with frantic activity in the final months, the heliocentric cause of it all wilting, day by day, but issuing fierce injunctions to fight to the last German. Hitler could do no less, having done his own best over five years to reduce hugely the number of Germans still alive and even the number of Germans who would live to hear about the final end of their Fuehrer's lieutenants in Nuremberg.

They arrived back at eight, caught a jeep at the railroad station, and headed to the Grand.

"Tell you what!" Harry suggested. "Let's shake the gloom of Berlin with a nightcap at Marta's before work begins again tomorrow."

They set out, retracing the route they had taken almost a year ago. Marta, who never forgot a name, greeted them with a solid kiss each and ordered a free beer to celebrate their return. They sat at that same little table they had first sat at, and the music roared out new melodies. The room was bustling with talk and laughter and toasts, the patrons enjoying each others' company, a view of the stage obstructed by tobacco haze. A woman dancer's purse fell down beside the table and Harry stooped to pick it up. Purse in hand, he raised his head and looked into the animated face of Teresa, one arm clenched tight around the waist of a portly British major. She had only time to grab the purse and glance at the American officer who had picked it up off the floor before her partner swirled her away, to keep time with "Stomping at the Savoy."

CHAPTER FIFTY-SIX

October 1, 1946

The judges' deliberations had lasted the entire month of September.

"What can be taking so *fucking* long?" Harry asked. He had a bottle of beer at his side as he scrutinized the electric stove that was bringing the water to boil under the spaghetti pot. It was his turn to cook in the two-room apartment he and Sebastian now occupied, conveniently vacated by two U.S. warrant officers dispatched to Berlin.

"I'd be surprised if they're stalled on the matter of guilt and innocence."

"What else would they be stalled on? What are the ground rules, Sebby?"

Sitting on the couch where he had been reading his novel, Sebastian said, "There are eight votes, the four judges and the four alternate judges. In order to hang a defendant, there have to be five hanging votes. Same thing, actually, all the way around: Five votes are needed to acquit. I'd guess the Russians almost certainly want to hang everybody, that being how they do things. And they'll want to hang Schacht because even though he went out of business in Germany in 1939, he did early financing for the

National Socialist Party. And they'll want to hang Keitel and Jodl because they fought and killed Russians, and of course they'll want to hang Frank and Amadeus because they killed POWs."

"Sebby, I had a telegram from my mother—"

"Your sick mother?"

He grinned. "Yes. She is, uh, much better. But the point is, she is a friend of the head of the draft board at home and she asked him to check out my point rating, gave him all the details about my combat hours, months here in Nuremberg—"

"Did she tell him how many medals you had won?"

"Oh, go screw, Reinhard. *Anyway,* she's going to wire me tomorrow if he tells her my points add up to what I need to get out, in the opinion of the board. Next thing, I'll be checking in with Chief Landers and asking him when's the next train for Milwaukee!"

"That's great, Harry. You got people in place to take over your work here?"

"Yep. There's Hans, of course, but also a warrant officer I've brought in. Nothing scheduled for the immediate future of the Palace is going to require more than the versatile infrastructure we've built up. It's all here for them. Everything's the same—except, everything changes. Maybe they'll come up with a defendant who speaks only Romansch. Odd thought. Speaking of odd thoughts, I hope Teresa isn't enjoying herself with that old prick she picked up."

"Maybe we ought to hang him, too."

But Sebastian wasn't in the mood for levity.

The whole city seemed seized by the suspense of the ultimate day ahead. The judges' cars, black and bulletproof, filed into the special parking lot, led by siren-blaring jeeps on which machine guns were mounted. The long deliberations had brought a flicker of hope to the defendant class, especially to wives and children, who had been permitted to visit in the prison cells up until the Saturday before. On Sunday, with the news that the judges had reached agreement, everyone wanted to be in the courtroom to hear what that agreement was. Not even Judge Biddle, the newspapers reported, had been able to wangle an extra pair of tickets in the spectators' gallery.

But the whole of the morning, and then the whole of the afternoon, was given over to the verbal recital of the judges' findings not on individual defendants, but on underlying matters of law, questions of evidence, and on the legal—and, indeed, philosophical—definition of their mandate at Nuremberg.

The judges were as sensitive of the drama as the defendants. But the judges' declamations did not dispose of elusive legal questions. U.S. Judge Biddle tackled the foremost of them: How do you define a "war of aggression"? His judgment: "To initiate a war of aggression is not *an* international crime, it is *the* supreme international crime, different only from other war crimes in that it contains within itself the accumulated evil of the whole."

"What that says," Sebastian in the control booth commented without expression, "is that very bad is worse than bad."

"*Quiet!*"

"To assert," Biddle explained, "that it is unjust to punish those who in defiance of treaties and assurances have attacked neighboring states without warning is obviously untrue, for in such circumstances the attacker must know that he is doing wrong, and so far from it being unjust to punish him, it would be unjust if his wrongs were allowed to go unpunished."

Sebastian thought to himself: *Amadeus didn't consider it wrong*. What matters is *whether* it was wrong.

It came the turn of John J. Parker to speak, and Sebastian recalled hearing of the southern judge's discomfort at the party celebrating the visit of Stalin's Vishinsky. He listened eagerly, hoping for interesting philosophical developments.

There was none. "The evidence relating to war crimes has been overwhelming," Judge Parker said. "War crimes were committed on a vast scale, never before seen in the history of war. They were perpetrated in all the countries occupied by Germany, and on the high seas, and were attended by every conceivable circumstance of cruelty and horror. There could be no doubt that the majority of the war crimes arose from the Nazi conception of 'total war.'"

Judge Parker stressed the mobilization in the Third Reich of all energies to the war-making enterprise. "Everything is made subordinate to the overmastering dictates of war. Rules, regulations, assurances, and treaties all alike are of no moment; freed as they are from the restraining influence of international law, the aggressive war was conducted by the Nazi leaders in the most barbaric way. War crimes were committed when and wherever the Fuehrer and his close associates thought them to be advantageous. They were for the most part the result of cold and criminal calculation."

"That just isn't so," Sebastian whispered to Harry, removing his headphones. "It's even *worse* than that with some defendants—with one, anyway. Amadeus didn't even give a thought to the notion that what he did was criminal."

The next judge rose to address the implications of Count One, *conspiring to wage aggressive war.* Everyone listened intently, but Judge Birkett's reasoning, eagerly anticipated by several lawyers who knew him and his work, did not prove to be anything anxious legal minds hoped for: a creative formulation that would persuasively distinguish what the Third Reich had criminally done from evolutionarily defensible uses of war-making. Birkett simply stressed the evidence (abundant) that the Nazis had prepared themselves to wage their wars and that the wars' designs were indisputably aggressive.

Suddenly it was over, except for disparate findings directed at individual defendants, due the next day.

That night at the Grand Hotel a young Jewish photojournalist whose father had been a croupier in Hamburg was spiritedly giving odds and taking bets. Five-to-one for conviction were the default odds, reduced for Rudolf Hess to three-to-one, and for the banker Schacht to two-to-one. Staff, journalists, visitors, and prosecutors discreetly placed bets. "What are you giving on Amadeus?" Harry asked the oddsmaker inquisitively.

"Default. Five-to-one." By betting one mark that Amadeus would be found not guilty, Harry would win five marks. If found guilty, lose one mark. "Not worth the gamble," he said to Sebastian. They stayed a while, observing the bettors, and remarking their sense of the odds on individual defendants.

Even Harry Albright had difficulty sleeping soundly on Monday night.

Lord Lawrence began promptly at 0930. The press had received a bulletin explaining that individual sentences would be read out by individual judges. The schedule gave the judges' names and the defendants they would address. Lawrence, the chief judge, would read the finding on Hermann Goering; de facto, the chief defendant.

To that finding, Judge Lawrence devoted only fifteen hundred words. He began by ruling that the Luftwaffe, of which Goering was in command, was exonerated in the matter of the bombings of Warsaw, Rotterdam, and Coventry, exonerated of the charge that these bombings were, by the definition of the tribunal, "war crimes."

Lawrence pronounced Goering himself guilty on all four counts. "By the decree of 31 July 1941, he directed Himmler and Heydrich to 'bring about a complete solution of the Jewish question in the German sphere of influence in Europe.' There is nothing to be said in mitigation. For Goering was often, indeed almost always, the moving force, second only to his leader. On some specific cases there may be a conflict of testimony, but, in terms of the broad outline, his own admissions are more than sufficiently wide to breed conclusions of his guilt. His guilt is unique in its enormity. The record discloses no excuses for this man."

Successive judges, in national sequence, and then in rotation, went down the list.

Judge Biddle read out the exoneration of Hjalmar Schacht as not directly involved in the war crimes that were central to the prosecution. His immediate release was ordered. Sebastian waited anxiously for #17.

The U.K.'s Norman Birkett read out the finding.

"The defendant Amadeus presided over the entire lifetime of the vicious Camp Joni, where by the evidence and his own admission, one-quarter million lives were taken in pursuit of the Third Reich's total war and its genocidal obsession. That Kurt Amadeus was following orders merely reiterates a defense repeatedly rejected by this tribunal as irrelevant and debasing."

The findings were completed before the lunch break.

The sentences were read out immediately after the afternoon session began.

For Fritzsche and von Papen—like Schacht—acquittal. For Funk, Hess, and Raeder, life in prison. For Speer and von Schirach, twenty years. For von Neurath, fifteen years. For Doenitz, ten years.

For the rest, hanging.

CHAPTER FIFTY-SEVEN

October 11, 1946

Chief Landers was on the telephone. "Amadeus wants to see you. If you want to see him, say yes. I don't see why we can't go with the usual arrangements."

"Chief, do you have any idea when the executions will be?"

"I don't. If I did I wouldn't tell you. If I did tell you, I'd take a blood oath that I didn't tell you."

"That means you don't know?"

"All I can tell you, Lieutenant, is that the talk is they're not going to delay it for very long."

Harry was able to do better than that, with his routine eavesdropping. "I can't give you a date, Sebby. But I can tell you that the hangman has been notified. They used him over at Landsberg. That's where the Fuehrer was locked up, 1923—the year I was born! Dachau, around the corner from Landsberg, was used for some pretty savage work during the war, and they tried and strung them up at Landsberg a few weeks after the war ended. Our boy should have plenty of practice."

"Harry, Amadeus has put in to see me, and the chief said go ahead, usual arrangements."

Albright whistled. "Your man slipped through the bureaucracy there. Even family visits have been prohibited. Everybody's on edge. Wonder what he wants to talk to you about? Changing his plea, ha-ha?"

"I'll let you know."

It was exactly as before, the first guard preceding Sebastian into the cell; the second guard, as ever, peering through the eye aperture in the cell door.

Amadeus rose and, as customary, did not extend his hand.

"Thank you for coming."

Sebastian by instinct almost found himself saying that he was very sorry about Amadeus's bad news, but caught himself in time with relief. He said only, "Well, it seems to be the end of the line."

At least in German "end of the line" was not a pun.

Amadeus nodded. "Yes, and I suppose that this will be our last meeting. The time to tell you my story is, therefore, not something I can put off."

"You mean, a story beyond what the interrogation—and our conversations—have given us?"

"Yes, Herr Lieutenant." Amadeus leaned back in his chair and, for an instant, closed his eyes.

He spoke in a near monotone. "When I gave orders to burn the records of Joni, I did not order the blueprints of the camp, which reposed elsewhere, destroyed. They were stored in the engineer's office, and as they had nothing whatever to do with the identities of the people who were killed, they were not records of the kind Herr Himmler wanted gone."

"I understand."

"The blueprints and construction papers had nothing to do with people who were eliminated, but a great deal to do with how to go about eliminating them."

records, which were shown to me. They revealed that Captain Reinhard had married a Jew."

"My mother."

"Yes, your mother."

"I knew that. Though not until a few months ago. I did not know it back when you told me in October that I looked part Jewish."

Amadeus's smile was astringent. "We war criminals enjoy our little ironies.... His marriage to your mother was not directly relevant to what then happened, but it certainly had a bearing on the three-man Gestapo court that tried him and sentenced him to hang for the offense of trying to help an enemy of the state to escape. He very much did not wish to go to the gallows, so early in the morning of his scheduled execution I had him shot, as though I had not accurately read the fine print decreeing hanging.

"I am asking you, Herr Lieutenant, to return the favor by contriving to pass me some poison."

Sebastian stood up. He stared at Amadeus, still seated. And walked over to the cell door and waited for the officer of the watch, standing by, to unlock the door and let him leave.

BOOK FIVE

CHAPTER FIFTY-EIGHT

October 12, 1946

Albright was finding it hard that night to get Sebastian's attention. He proposed going to the movie being shown in the rec hall of the Palace. "It's *Notorious.* Cary Grant and Ingrid Bergman *and* Alfred Hitchcock, which means it must be exciting and incredible. What do you say, Sebby?"

Sebastian said he, too, had college application forms to fill out. "Maybe a movie tomorrow."

"Where are you applying?"

"I'm thinking of law school eventually, so maybe Berkeley undergrad. I can probably start in as a sophomore. I think they'd give me a year's credit for all this stuff I've been doing. So three years' undergraduate work, then three years in law school. Then I can come back to Nuremberg and help hang whoever they have left over."

Harry didn't pursue that line.

"You've been edgy ever since your spell with Amadeus this afternoon. Anything I should know about?"

Sebastian turned to him, face flushed. He stopped then said, "Something you shouldn't know about. Harry," he turned deadly serious, "I really need you."

They set out together the next night, Friday, after work—Sebastian had been translating yet more documents, these relating to subordinate prisoners whose trials were coming up in November. They walked from the Palace to their apartment and changed clothes.

All traces of military habit were gone. Sebastian had on jeans and the same checkered red woolen jacket he had used when hiking in the mountains of Arizona. Harry had on the jumpsuit worn by crew members who might need to bail out of unlucky bombing runs over enemy territory. The Air Force insignia had been carefully removed.

"You got cash?" Harry asked.

"Plenty. I have over 200 simoleons."

"U.S.?"

"Yes. In twenties."

"I'm thinking maybe we should start right out offering him the whole 200."

"Your call, Harry."

"Your money, Sebastian."

There were buses running now, in October 1946, fanning the old city. Harry flagged the Gilderstrasse bus. It had been repainted and reupholstered. The driver drove it skillfully with his one arm.

"We'll have a good hike to get to the Kaiserburg area. I haven't been back. Didn't want to stare at the remains of what I did when my plane let the bombs go."

He paused as the bus went bumpily on. "Sebby, I'm just assuming the old man we're going to see is the same man who came up with the stuff for my Papa. Wolfgang Froude looked after everything we needed after Mama died. Papa never went to the doctor, not ever, just to Herr Froude."

They alighted from the bus and Harry pointed the way.

There were streetlights now, though not on every block. Harry carried a flashlight and looked up at the street signs, some of them showing evidence of restoration designed to illuminate the original lettering. Himmelstrasse was back to Kaiserstrasse.

"I'm beginning to get my bearings. Down there a few blocks on the left was my school. In the opposite direction, four blocks down, my father's atelier. Our apartment, if any of it exists, was behind it."

"And Froude?"

"Just three blocks up."

The little two-story building Harry looked for was still there, its roof recently patched. The sign in front was neatly drawn, yellow lettering over a dark blue background. It bore the sign, W. FROUDE, APOTHEKE. BERGRUNDET 1901.

A small light shone from inside.

"Let's just look at it a bit."

They walked by the pharmacy casually. Harry slowed up by the window. He whispered to Sebastian. "*That's him.* But there's a woman there also. Maybe his wife. I don't actually remember his wife."

"Well, Froude is old, isn't he?"

"It was... 1935 when I last saw him. That was only eleven years ago. He was too old to fight in the first war. He's maybe sixty, seventy."

"Let's walk by again, find out if any customers are dropping by. See if you can make out the pharmacy's closing hour on the door, it's pretty dark."

"I'll try. But if I remember, the old man kept the pharmacy open late."

"It's 2100. We can keep an eye on him and knock on his door just as he closes down."

"Yep.... It's getting cold."

"I'll stand watch. You go back to the coffeehouse we passed a block up," Sebastian said, "and wait there."

"That's no good. It's *me* who has to make the opening. You go. I'll go get you at the coffeehouse when he closes up."

After establishing that the closing hour was 2200, they settled for walking together around the block to keep warm. Harry was glad to spot the light turned on upstairs, Froude's wife no longer in view in the pharmacy.

They waited, this time just out of view of the entrance, for the light to turn off.

At exactly 2155 it did so. "You wait here."

Harry knocked on the door.

It opened a few inches, latched by a chain.

"We are closed," the elderly man said.

"Herr Froude. It is Heinrich Alkunstler."

Silence.

"You were my Papa's good friend."

The door opened wide. "Jungen Alkunstler! You are all grown up! It's cold, come in. I would not believe I would ever see you again! You'll have some tea? Upstairs? Your Papa liked to have tea with me."

"No, thank you, Herr Froude. Because I am on duty tonight, you see. I am on the midnight train to Berlin. I have been discharged from the American army, and I have work on the railroad, translating in English."

"So Berlin is your headquarters?"

"Yes, Herr Froude." He entered the pharmacy and exchanged a warm handshake.

"Come and tell me all about where you have been. I know your father—your poor father—sent you to America—"

"Herr Froude, I'll visit with you another day. But right now I need special, emergency help from you. I have . . . a lady in Berlin.

Next time I visit I will bring a picture. Her mother is dying a terrible death from cancer and implores relief. But the doctor will not give it to her."

"What kind of relief?"

"I promised her I'd ask for the same pill you gave to my father." He took the risk. "He wrote to me in America that he had got it from you, and would take it before ever consenting to go on one of the death trains."

Froude drew back, looked about him as if the conversation might be overheard. "*It is illegal*, Heinrich."

"I know, Herr Froude. But in this turmoil practically everything is illegal, and we cannot just stop life's—emergencies. My friend—Nona's mother—is quite well-to-do. Her brother, who went to the camps—as my father was fated to do, but did not, thanks to you, Herr Froude—her brother hid gold, and Nona's mother got dollars for it when the gold ban was declared."

Froude looked up, his attention keen. "Times are very hard, Heinrich."

"I know that. Nona gave me 200 U.S. dollars."

Froude's eyebrows raised. "That is a great deal of money."

"Her mother is suffering a great deal of pain."

"It takes time to prepare a cyanide pill."

"How much time?"

"At least one hour."

"Can I have it in one hour, Herr Froude? I would be so grateful to you, as my dear father was."

Froude looked up, the hint of a question on his face.

"Heinrich, is that 200 dollars in addition to the pharmaceutical cost of the cyanide?"

"How much is that, Herr Froude?"

He walked to the back of the counter and turned on a light. He looked at a catalogue.

"The replacement cost to me of the cyanide would be 200 marks. That would be . . . 28 dollars."

"I would add that drug-replacement money out of my own purse, Herr Froude. Nona, after all, is my special lady."

"Very well. Do you wish to wait here?"

He thought to say he'd go out and come back in an hour. But that might give grounds for suspicion.

"I will stay right here."

"Very well."

Froude called out to his wife. He would be late in coming up, he told her.

There had to be a reason for Harry's not having passed word to him. He didn't know what it was, but Sebastian was patient, if wretchedly cold. Through the window he could see the old man at work behind the chemical counter. There was nothing to do but wait. He walked away from the window and, in a lightless corner, did some gymnastic exercises to fight the cold.

At 2230 Harry came out and signaled to Sebastian. Wordlessly they set out at a brisk pace.

"God almighty, Reinhard. The things—the *thing*—you come up with. If anybody traces this expedition, they'll hang the lot of us."

"Thanks, Harry."

"Two hundred and twenty-eight bucks that cost us. That cost you."

"Thanks, Harry."

"Let's stop and have a drink."

CHAPTER FIFTY-NINE

October 13, 1946

He hadn't thought this problem through. Visits with Amadeus had been at the prisoner's initiative, but this time it was Sebastian who wanted to go to Amadeus.

He didn't want to risk going through Chief Landers, who was bureaucratically formal. He would risk direct contact with the warder at the prison, with whom he had exchanged civil greetings on previous visits.

He took a deep breath and rang the extension number.

"Sergeant Early, this is Lieutenant Reinhard. As requested by the prisoner Amadeus, 1500 is okay with me. I've checked the hour."

"Stand by, please, sir."

What would he say if challenged?

He was.

"Lieutenant, we have no record of that request."

"The prisoner told me that he would endeavor in forty-eight hours, after consulting with his attorney, to have the answers to the final questions Captain Carver wants. That makes it 1500 today. Perhaps he neglected to tell you."

"Very well, sir."

He opened his drawer and removed the top of his fountain pen. Froude's vial was not encased in a metal container. The one-and-a-half-inch pill lay in a crystal ampoule. "This is not," Froude had told Harry, "designed to be stored for any prolonged period—" Harry winced at the next words "—in the mouth or in the rectum. But of course, that does not matter, does it, Heinrich? Because your sick lady is not going to postpone ingesting the poison, from what you tell me."

Sebastian would have to relay that information to Amadeus, yet the appearances of their exchange would need to be circumspect, entirely like those that had gone before.

Suddenly he felt a spasm of doubt: *Do I really want to go through with this?*

He leaned back against the wall and summoned the picture of his father sitting in a cell at Joni, dreading the scheduled gallows. Yet his contemplated act of gratitude for what his father was spared was, for one thing, not exactly complementary. His father did not deserve to die, but was shot. Amadeus deserved to die, by whatever means. The risk in what Sebastian was doing was enormous. How, if detected, would he justify his conduct?

If only he could contrive to have his father's counsel. He recited a prayer, one of Henrietta's. "*Omnipotens sempiterne Deus, suscipe propitius orationem nostram.*" Eternal Lord, grant us our prayer. He looked down at his hands in awe and wondered at the power that rested in them.

The irresolution ended. He would not go to lunch in the mess hall. He buried himself in the file on the background of Oberstleutnant Shnayerson, charged with authorizing the execution of seven U.S. prisoners escaped from the Heilbronn POW camp. But the endless German affidavits and records and testimony blurred in his eyes. He went out into the hallway for a glass of water. Carver was walking by.

"Going to lunch, Sebby?"

"Actually, Captain, I— "

"Those records I gave you aren't so pressing you can't eat lunch."

The thought flashed through his mind. *I must behave normally.* "Well, that's a good idea, Captain. Can I tag along?"

"Why do you think I brought the subject up?"

On no account must Amadeus figure in the lunch conversation! But what excuse could Sebastian later have for failing to mention an impending visit?

The risk was too great. *Damn. I forgot to bring over the folder Albright asked for.* Saying nothing more he turned abruptly around. "See you in the mess hall, Captain."

"Okay."

He'd have to warn Harry! Tell him to say, if questioned later, that Sebastian had promised to bring him a folder before lunch. A folder on what? Shit. A folder on *anything*. —No. Better to be specific, if asked. A folder on application requirements at the University of California at Berkeley. He had these on his desk.

He must get down to the prison cell exactly on time. In his hands would be only the steno pad. His fountain pen was in its usual place, in the pocket of his shirt.

It would be all right, he thought, if he appeared a little bit excited. After all, he was on his way to interview for the last time a man who had been sentenced to hang and would be hanged, who knows, maybe by midweek. He didn't know the day exactly, but then neither would Sergeant Early know it.

At twelve minutes to three, he set out to walk the long corridors that led to the prison cell. He carried his identification and the seven-month-old order from chief prosecutor Robert Jackson authorizing special visits with the defendant Kurt Amadeus.

Outside the prison quarters he stopped by Early's desk. "This will be the last time, I guess, Sergeant."

"You've been here a lot, Lieutenant."

"Yes. I tried everything the prosecution asked me to do."

Sergeant Early nodded, signaled to the guard at the door, and they walked together to Amadeus's cell.

The big key turned. The guard stepped inside.

Amadeus, sitting in his chair behind the desk, looked up abruptly as Sebastian entered. The meaning of the unexpected visit, and its implications, instantly registered on him.

He stood, as he usually did. "Good afternoon, Herr Lieutenant."

The cell door closed. The guard stationed himself behind the visitor, his back to the wall.

Speaking a German more rapid than usual, Sebastian said to Amadeus in a routine tone of voice: "Talk to me. It does not matter what you say. But talk volubly, as though informing me of something. I will take notes."

"I understand."

Amadeus began, and continued, to talk. The words did matter. What he said was that if Sebastian had the opportunity, he should convey to his younger brother what he had neglected to tell him that morning, at the terminal meeting. Tell George Friedrich that he had deported himself very well in his first experience at the bar. He permitted himself a half smile. "You can add some version of the old joke about how the operation was very successful, though the patient died."

Sebastian let him go on, with only enough interruptions to feign an exchange.

Sebastian scribbled a few times on his pad, as he customarily did.

Just after 1520 he said in a humdrum voice, "Listen very carefully. You are not to stick it into your mouth or rectum. It is fragile. Do not use it until late in the evening. After the guard outside changes watch. I will now rise. You are, this time, to extend a hand. I will appear reluctant to take it. But I will, and when I do, you will have the vial. Avoid any unusual expressions on your face."

"I shall not even thank you, Herr Sebastian."

Herr Sebastian! The killer. Calls me Mr. Sebastian.

But when the killer executed my father, he was, in his own way, extending mercy.

Sebastian motioned to the guard, who signaled to the guard outside to summon the chief in to open the door.

Kurt Amadeus stood. The guard saw him extend his hand. Sebastian paused, then took it, and turned to the door, which opened a few seconds later.

Sebastian did not look back.

CHAPTER SIXTY

October 14, 1946

It was just after 0100 that the knock on the door woke him. The sound of it was loud enough to wake also Albright in the other bedroom, who appeared by the door in his shorts as Sebastian, wearing pajamas, let in the caller.

It was an MP. The sergeant said simply, "You are wanted at headquarters, Lieutenant."

"Me?" Sebastian asked. "Or Lieutenant Albright?"

"Just you, sir."

"What is it?" He turned to Harry. "Could it be . . . news of my mother?"

"They wouldn't wake you for that, not unless your mother killed the king."

The sergeant had not moved from the door. "You can sit in there," Sebastian pointed to their living room/dining room, "while I dress."

"Thank you, sir. I will wait here in the hallway."

Sebastian nodded. He closed the door, reached for shorts and trousers, and edged over to Harry. Donning his clothes he whispered, "It's happened, Harry."

"There is a record of a request for an interview with you by the prisoner on Friday, October 11th, and the logs show that that meeting took place. But there is no record of a petition by the prisoner to see you yesterday."

"He asked me, sir, at the Friday meeting, to come back in two days. He said he would have information for me after his final visit with his brother."

"What kind of information?"

"He did not say."

"Why didn't you consult with Captain Carver on the point?"

"I thought it routine, Colonel."

Sebastian looked over at Carver.

"I kept Captain Carver informed of my visits, but not always on a visit-by-visit basis unless I thought there was something that the defendant— "

"The criminal. Kurt Amadeus has been—had been—convicted."

"—that the criminal said that, I thought would be especially interesting to the captain."

"You are aware that someone passed a cyanide pill to Amadeus?"

"I was not aware of that, Colonel— "

"We have uncovered no container of the kind that would have kept the poison intact over a long period of time. Are you aware that the prisoners are searched bodily every other day?"

"I did not know that—no, sir."

"Which means that as of Sunday morning—yesterday morning—that vial of poison was not present in the prisoner's cell. That means that the poison was given him some time between the Sunday inspection and the prisoner's ingestion of it— "

"Colonel, I don't know what has happened. All I know was what a reporter in the entrance hall said—that there had been a suicide."

Andrus, Amen, Carver, and West all looked hard across the table at Sebastian.

Carver spoke. "Reinhard, Amadeus took poison, cyanide we assume it was. He was dragged off to the hospital. Sometime just before midnight, the guard spotted him collapsed over the toilet. The alarm went out. After he was taken away, Colonel Andrus's staff went over the logs and roused Sergeant Early. You were with the criminal at 1500. His brother was with him at 1130. What the colonel is saying is that we have to assume he got the poison from one of you, since it wasn't in the cell at inspection time earlier than that."

"Thanks for the explanation, Captain. I know nothing about the cyanide."

There was a knock on the door. "Come in," Andrus barked.

The MP opened the door. "Herr Amadeus is here, sir."

"Already? Shit." The colonel turned to Amen. "John, can you handle German?"

Colonel Amen shook his head.

"You, Carver?"

"No."

"It's almost three in the morning. We've got Amadeus outside. How the hell are we going to question him?"

"I'd be glad to help, if you want, Colonel," Sebastian said.

Andrus said nothing. He sat and he fumed and lit a cigarette. Finally, "What do you think, Amen?"

"I don't see why not. The only alternative is to wait for another interpreter, and that would mean hours of waiting."

"Bring him in," Andrus said.

George Friedrich Amadeus had heard nothing about his brother, he said after the initial question was put to him. He was dressed in the same suit he wore when he had arrived in Nuremberg last November. His tie, hastily put on, was askew, disordering his whole presence.

Colonel Amen spoke and Sebastian interpreted.

"Herr Amadeus. Your brother's suicide, as of just a few hours ago, was done by cyanide, we assume. We have rigorously examined the relevant material and conclude that he was given the cyanide pill some time yesterday. You are one of two people who visited him yesterday. You are charged with suspicion of an attempt to obstruct justice. I demand to know if you handed the . . . criminal a vial of cyanide when you saw him yesterday."

"I cannot answer that question."

Amen was disbelieving.

"Why?"

"Client-lawyer privilege."

To Sebastian. "Reinhard. Are you *certain* you have correctly translated Herr Amadeus's reply?"

"*Klient advokat privileg*. Client-lawyer privilege is what he said."

Colonel Andrus opened his mouth. He turned to Amen. "John, what in the *hell* is he talking about? Client-lawyer doesn't cover this situation! . . . Does it?"

"No. It covers only conversations with his client. You're not talking about conversations."

"Herr Amadeus, lawyer-client privilege has *nothing* to do with whether you passed contraband to your client permitting him to defy the sentence of the court."

"I am not an expert on criminal procedures, but my understanding of the law is that all transactions between lawyers and their clients are privileged."

Burt Andrus was mystified, then frustrated, then choleric.

He turned to Sebastian. "Tell him unless he cooperates he will be taken from this room directly to a holding cell."

Sebastian relayed the words, and gave Amadeus's answer to Andrus. "He says he wishes to consult an attorney."

Andrus was speechless.

The sergeant opened the door without knocking.

They all looked up at him.

"Sir, a report from the hospital. The doctor says that the prisoner has been revived and will live."

Colonel Andrus was dumbfounded. Recover from cyanide? Was the dose insufficient? Could it have been a different poison? He drew the deepest sigh of relief.

He turned to Amen, the features of his face sagging with exhaustion. "John. We're saved. By the bell. What do you say we call it quits. Attend to loose ends . . . later. It'll be dawn in a couple of hours."

Amen nodded his head.

"You agree, George?"

Carver nodded his head.

To Sebastian. "Don't think this investigation is over, though. Amadeus is obviously the primary suspect. Tell him to go home but *under no circumstances to leave town.*"

Sebastian relayed the message. Then to Andrus, "Okay to go, Colonel?"

"Yes."

Captain Carver addressed him. "Report tomorrow, as usual, Reinhard."

"Yes sir."

Sebastian left the room.

Reaching the apartment, he woke Harry.

Sebastian was pale. "It didn't work," he said.

"What didn't work? Your alibi?"

"No. The poison."

CHAPTER SIXTY-ONE

Nuremberg, October 15–16, 1946

It was bad enough that what happened next came during the climactic few hours at the Palace of Justice. But worse—incredibly—it happened while Andrus was engaged in what his aide called "the death tour."

No one was to know, the Colonel had ordered, until *after* the condemned were themselves told, when the hour of their death would be. The denial of the appeals on Monday by the Allied Control Council in Berlin was the very final judicial step. The execution of sentences could go forward.

Anxious journalists, standing by, were caught up in rumors that the executioners were actually setting up shop, as indeed they were. The supervisor of the executions, Lieutenant Stanley Tilles, had been drafted for routine military service in the early days of the war. After V-E Day, he found himself—placed by the Provost Marshal of the Third Army—in charge of executions in Landsberg of war criminals from nearby Dachau. The executioner proper, the official who would place the nooses around the necks of the condemned, was a practiced hangman, his occupation begun in his youth in Texas, where he apprenticed under the regular hangman.

At Nuremberg they would need three gallows. Colonel Andrus did not wish intervals between executions to take too long. An inordinate hiatus between the first and the twelfth hanging could result in leaks and demonstrations outside the Palace. Each of the condemned would use up twenty to twenty-five minutes. After the drop through the trap door, the not-yet-formally-deceased subject would hang on the rope, legs strapped together to prevent flailing, awaiting final asphyxiation following the broken neck. Sergeant John Woods, the accredited hangman who had executed 347 persons since the start of his career, would do his job on Gallows #1, pull the trap, and walk over to Gallows #2, to which the next criminal would have been led; then on to Gallows #3; then back to Gallows #1, at which point the deceased, shrouded behind the black curtain that enclosed the area under the gallows' platform, would have been removed, noose still around his neck, photographed, and laid out in the waiting coffin.

Tilles was pleased with the discretion of his caravan of three trucks that drove into Nuremberg carrying into the segregated gymnasium of the Palace the component parts of the gallows borrowed from the prison in Landsberg. Sergeant Woods had estimated that eleven hours would be required to completely assemble the gallows in the Palace's gymnasium, now converted into an execution chamber. The Tilles/Woods team of ten men had worked undisturbed, but one Palace guard, noting the long wooden beams being removed from trucks outside, drew conclusions which he related to his special friend at the PX who saved for him, every week, a carton of Kool cigarettes, his favorite. Nothing more was needed to fire the curiosity of the press, so eager for the terminal moment of the vast, seemingly endless, year-long enterprise.

Everything was ready to go, Colonel Andrus set out on his macabre walk down the corridors along the prisoners' cells. He began with the first cell at the far end of the top row. It was Frick's. He informed him that he would be escorted to the gallows before midnight; and proceeded, one by one, to give the same notice to others of the condemned.

It was while he was still on the top row of cells that the alarm went out. In the bottom row, the guard outside Goering's door had heard a convulsive sound and rung the alarm. In seconds, a doctor was there, followed quickly by the chaplain. A minute later Andrus was also in the cell, his orderly death march interrupted. His reaction was near hysterical. He ordered guards to link themselves by handcuffs to each of the eleven surviving gallows-bent prisoners. And he bellowed out to the staff that the executions would proceed *on schedule,* two hours later.

Hermann Goering's cyanide pill did not fail him. Because he was the central figure in the Nuremberg proceedings, the German people went wild, as did Colonel Andrus—in his case with utter rage that despite the extraordinary precautions of the prison house, Goering had pulled it off. Hours later, reports flooded in over the radio, notwithstanding the embargo Colonel Andrus sought to impose on the events of Nuremberg, reports of a Germany seemingly united in pride and glee. *The old man had outfoxed the whole lot of them!*—Americans, British, French, Russians. This was not a moment for Germans to reflect on what Goering had done to Germany. It was his final ingenuity that was the cause, in their drab lives, for exhilaration.

It was especially humiliating for Andrus. Not only because of the care he had taken to preserve order and avoid premature publicity, but also because Amadeus's brush with death had been successfully transformed, on Andrus's orders, into nothing more than a case of acute indigestion. The press, which had reported an attempt at suicide, could do nothing more with the story. Kurt Amadeus was, after all, alive and back in his cell, and the doctor in the hospital who had looked after him declined to answer any questions. Now Goering was indisputably dead, but by his own hand. If Colonel Andrus could have discovered who had handed him the pill, there'd have been an extra hanging.

At midnight, as agreed, Harry Albright came by Sebastian's office. "The whole place is dead. Nothing, nobody, anywhere."

"The press?"

"They're in the gym, waiting."

He pulled a flask from the overcoat he brought under his arm. He looked about and took down two glasses from the bookcase. He poured two jiggers of rum into each of them, handing one to Sebastian, who fingered it absentmindedly, then raised it to his lips.

Harry said nothing for a minute or two. Then, "Are we going to do it?"

"I guess," Sebastian said.

At 0100 they sat in Harry's control room.

Albright had done the instrumentation.

One microphone hung directly overhead at the landing from which the steps descended to the floor of the gymnasium. They heard a voice in German addressing "Your excellency."

"That's got to be Ribbentrop. They've restored his honorific. He'd be first, now that Goering is out of reach."

They heard a muffled response, and then a second voice, this one speaking in English. "Ready to go, Major." They did not hear the response, but a few seconds later they could make out the sound of steps. Then there was nothing, for what seemed a full minute. The microphone overhead, lowered for referees when basketball was played or boxing matches conducted, picked up the sound of voices on Gallows #1.

An American voice gave an order, unintelligible. "An assistant, must be," Harry said.

They heard then the sounds of the death party mounting the steps. A voice spoke in German. Did the condemned have a final word?

The voice of the foreign minister of the Third Reich was hesitant before he said his final words. Then, "God protect Germany. My last wish is that Germany's unity shall be preserved and that an understanding be reached between East and West." They could not hear the trapdoor sprung, but could make out the thump of the falling body arrested by the rope.

Harry miked in the press section. There was whispering...

Jodl carried himself with military bearing, they learned from soft exchanges overheard. Also Keitel...

Frank's manacled hand was gripped by the chaplain in a spiritual gesture...

Streicher made a scene at Gallows #3, spitting out his defiance....

"Which one is that coming down the steps?" a woman's voice was heard, asking a companion.

"That's Kurt Amadeus. The Camp Joni guy."

"He's headed for Gallows #1," Harry said, simply.

And in a few seconds: "Do you have any last words, Kurt Amadeus?"

"No," he said. "Not actually. No."

They heard the thump, and then Sebastian's weeping came, uncontrolled. He imagined at this moment not the scene at the gymnasium, but the scene after a springtime dawn at Camp Joni, his father led from his cell, relieved—the final marginalization of human reliefs!—to see a firing squad waiting for him, not a hangman, thinking no doubt in his final moments of his wife and of

Sebastian. And standing—in his mind's eye Sebastian knew exactly where, at Joni, the occasional execution took place—less than 100 yards from the terrible charnel house he had created—had been forced to create—where *one-quarter million Axels, Annabelles, and Sebastians* had choked to death on the gas dispatched from Joni's vents on orders of Kurt Waldemar Amadeus, the god-lovingly named Amadeus, detested surely by the God of justice, gone now to a fiery next world in which perhaps he would be sentenced to look in the face all the men, women, and children he had crammed into Sebastian's father's crematorium. Add the faces of those others, six million in the other slaughterhouses, eight million dead of enemy fire and allied bombs in the hell of the four terrible years, so modest an attempt at whose requital Sebastian heard now, in the thump that ended the life of the man competent to kill everybody except himself. Sebastian wept on, and all that Harry could think to do was just look away.